# THE PRIDE OF LITTLE FLOWER

# THE PRIDE OF LITTLE FLOWER

## LAURA NAPOLI

# CONTENTS

This book is dedicated in loving memory to my grandmother.
Thank you for encouraging my creativity and supporting my passions
in whatever forms they took.

The Pride of Little Flower

This is a work of fiction. All the characters and events portrayed in this book are fictional, and any resemblance to real people or incidents is purely coincidental.



Cover art by Jessie Marony
https://jessiemarony.com

Images used under license from Shutterstock.com.



First Printing, 2022

Paperback ISBN: 979-8-9871949-2-8
EBook ISBN:  979-8-9871949-3-5

Heating Cats Pawblishing, LLC
https://heatingcats.com

# CHAPTER 1

# Myra: Accusation

Myra yawned as she stared at yet another requisition form. The afternoon heat was starting to wear on her, and she was about ready to call it quits for the day, when Marsee knocked on her open door. The look on Marsee's face told her something was horribly wrong.

"Is there something wrong with Little Flower?" she asked, praying that her daughter hadn't had another flare up of her hunting instinct, and actually hurt the cub, or worse.

Her daughter nodded but rather than explaining, walked over and set a large sketchbook down in front of her.

Myra, remembering Little Flower's first drawing, cautiously opened the book, but was surprised when she just saw portraits of several bipeds. She looked back up at her daughter confused.

"Keep going," her daughter said in a tone that she'd never heard from her before. This wasn't just a suggestion, but had with it the weight of a command she did not want to give.

Ears flicked back in surprise, she did as her daughter ordered. As the drawings changed, it was all she could do to keep her healer's mask firmly in place, and not show the horror that she was really feeling.

When she'd finally made her way through the book, Marsee explained the conversation she'd had with Little Flower.

While Marsee was still too young to fully grasp what had happened, Myra understood immediately. She sent Marsee off to the family room, with instructions to leave Little Flower alone for now, and write up a full report of what had happened, along with exactly what Little Flower had signed, as closely as she could remember, not just what Marsee had thought she'd meant.

"Mama..." Marsee started.

"Report first, then we'll talk," she told her daughter.

Thankfully Marsee left without arguing. Myra closed her office door and leaned her head up against the ancient wood, eyes closed, for several long moments, before grabbing her tablet and pulling up the footage from Little Flower's fight on her monitor, or what they had all assumed was a fight. She started watching from where Healer Brice had marked the recordings, which was basically when she'd entered the room. The monitors embedded in Little Flower had notified Brice of a problem but she'd been with another patient and hadn't noticed right away. From there it clearly showed the male beating Little Flower with a broken toy. As her daughter had done, she scrolled back to the beginning of the visit and watched. Then she watched it again to be sure. The second viewing made her physically sick, and it was all she could do to keep from throwing up.

"Idiots!" she swore as she started to pace. She couldn't sit still with this knowledge. There was no doubt in her mind. Not the slightest bit. Not only had the poor thing been forced to mate against her will, *she* was the one that put her in that situation. How had they not realized what had happened or even considered it a possibility? Why hadn't she personally reviewed the footage before? She berated herself and swore for a good five minutes.

Not in over ten thousand years had someone been forced to mate, on any of the sentient worlds, not that she knew of anyway. It was one of the primary tenets of their society and a major requirement for being considered fully sentient and members of the Consortium. The healers of her world worked hard to ensure it didn't happen, but they'd been the ones to put Little Flower, and potentially others, in harm's way. But it was worse than that. If she was understanding Little Flower's drawings correctly, they'd actively encouraged it. Myra thought back to all the orders she'd given with regards to reintroduction and repopulation. She'd honestly hoped the bipeds would choose to mate, in order to start repopulating the species, had ordered that they be paired up to best make that a possibility, and had even ordered that the hormone blockers be stopped, so that if they wanted to mate, they could.

"Moons forsaken blithering idiots!" she swore again, and threw her tablet hard on the desk. *No wonder she wouldn't drink or eat for two days. This wasn't just isolation sickness or a failure to thrive due to some missing nutrient. She was actively trying to end her life.* Myra didn't blame her one bit. She probably would have felt the same in her situation, and frankly, she felt like doing the same right now, completely overwhelmed by the disgust she felt at herself for the role she'd played in making this happen. It was the antithesis of everything they believed in, everything *she* believed in. They weren't the heroes, valiantly trying to save the remains of a dying species, they were the villains holding them in captivity, and forcing them to mate, the very monsters Little Flower believed them to be.

When her emotions calmed enough that she could think again, she froze mid pace as a horrible thought crossed her mind. *The hormone blockers!* Had she inadvertently triggered a heat by stopping the hormone blockers? Clearly the male had been ready to mate. In Myra's species that wasn't possible unless they were around a female in heat, but Little Flower was still a small cub. She hadn't developed the large breasts the adult females had, and she was still significantly smaller than the others, although she did appear to have all the same parts as the adult females. She picked up her tablet again, relieved that she hadn't broken it in her violent outburst, and pulled up the medical records from that day, comparing them to the most recent scans. Then she pulled the records of the other females and compared those records as well. There were significant hormonal differences but they knew so little about the bipeds reproductive cycle that she wasn't sure if Little Flower had come into heat, and was now pregnant, or not. *We may not know for a while,* she thought. *We don't even know if she's even old enough to be fertile or how long their gestation period is. I'll need to run a full scan to be sure, but... Dark moons, she's just a cub! She's not even fully grown, how is she going to safely carry a cub to term? We had a hard enough time with the two mothers that were pregnant when we rescued them, and they were both significantly taller. Oh, Ancient Gods! Please don't let her be pregnant,* she prayed.

Myra started pacing again, her mind racing with the implications and the dangers facing Little Flower, when there was a hesitant knock at the door. She took a deep breath, then two more, struggling to bring her emotions under control, and back under the calm healer's mask she was trained to wear in difficult situations. "Come in."

"I finished my report and sent it to you," Marsee stated after opening the door, but she didn't enter.

"Thank you, Sweetheart, I'll read it immediately. You were right in coming to me, but you need to know things will probably get very complicated. You may even be questioned by the Council directly."

"I thought so," Marsee replied sadly, then asked with hesitation, "Mama is...is Little Flower pregnant?"

Myra sighed. "I don't know yet, Marsee. She might be. I'll need to do a full scan to be sure." *Not now,* she thought. *How do I explain this to her, when I've barely grasped it myself? Please don't ask any more questions,* she silently begged her daughter.

"She's so young and so very alone. Mama, do you think that...did that other biped...did he really force her to mate? Is that even possible?" Marsee asked.

*Oh, holy suns and all the moons in the universe!* Myra closed her eyes and prayed to the Ancient Gods again. Surely they knew what to do in this situation. She certainly didn't. "Yes. It's called rape, and it's not something we've seen for thousands of years. For our species it's not really possible anymore, since we have full control over when we come into heat. That may not be the same for her species." Myra hesitated. She really didn't want to go into the ways in which it could still occur. That was a closely guarded medical secret reserved to just master healers in order to protect the population. "It's pretty clear from her comments to you, and from her drawings, that she did not want to mate," she finally answered softly, deciding honesty was the best response. She hadn't even learned about rape until well after she'd earned her masters, and had been horrified at the concept, never expecting to have to deal with it in reality, much less talk to her daughter about it.

"Oh, Mama!" Marsee cried and ran to her mother. "Oh, the poor thing! To lose her world, her family, her hearing, and now this?" Myra scooped her daughter up into her arms, and hugged her with all she had. After a while, Myra sent her daughter off and told her to go spend some time in the garden. She would join her later after she'd had a chance to talk to her father. Marsee left without a word, tail dragging along the ground.

When she was out of sight, Myra picked up her tablet again and read Marsee's report and swallowed hard at what she read. *Marsee's Mother Choose.* The words Little Flower had signed ran over and over in her mind, hitting her hard with the weight of the accusation and the truth that she *had* chosen, *had* ordered the cub placed with that male, against Brice's recommendation, *had* ordered the stop of the hormone blockers, and *had* allowed them to be left in a room unsupervised. Taking a deep shuddering breath, Myra walked over to her medical bag and pulled out her scanner, and stared at it for a long time, before leaving her office to find Little Flower, and the answers she prayed she wouldn't find.

When she arrived at the tower, Little Flower was fast asleep in her nest. Myra's heart broke at the sight of the tiny cub, curled up protectively around the equally tiny stuffy, but secretly she was glad Little Flower was asleep. It saved her from trying to answer questions she honestly had no way of answering. Several minutes later she quietly left the room, and went to find her partner. The Council needed to be informed, immediately.

CHAPTER 2

# Jeran: Investigation

To say that Jeran was stunned was an understatement. He was thrilled with the progress his daughter had made with the little cub. Their ability to communicate with the pictionary and sign language in the face of Little Flower's hearing loss alone, would have warranted an update to the Council at the next scheduled meeting. Recognizing and being able to speak her own name was a clear indication of sentience. But the information his partner shared with him left him absolutely heart-sick and beyond terrified.

He was horrified by what had happened to Little Flower and he knew first-hand how dangerous pregnancy could be, but terrified didn't even come close to how he felt for Myra and her protege and the consequences he knew they would face. Their direct involvement in the events leading up to Little Flower's rape meant it was highly likely they would be found guilty of collusion, and suffer the same consequences as her rapist. But Little Flower hadn't just accused Myra and Brice, she'd accused their entire Council.

Seen from Little Flower's perspective, he believed Little Flower had every right to those accusations. They'd held her in isolation for months, voted to begin repopulation and reintroduction, and left them locked in a room, unsupervised, with the hopes that they would form an attachment and choose to mate on their own, and from what his partner had indicated, quite likely triggered a heat in a cub that was not fully grown. Even if she hadn't accused the healers and Council for being complicit in her rape, that information would have eventually been found during his investigation, even if he hadn't already been fully aware of what the Council had decided, and what his partner had intended with regards to repopulation.

It had never even dawned on him that something like this might happen. He hadn't bothered to review the footage from the Agency himself as there was little he could do until she was recognized as sentient and a member of the Consortium. And, as both had been injured in the fight, and according to Myra still suffering from isolation sickness, he'd had no reason to press charges against either of them. He'd ordered a replacement toy for the male and outside of requiring that he be watched during all future interactions, had considered the affair closed.

Further complicating the matter was the fact that Little Flower had been a ward of the Council at the time this had occurred, and they had put her care in the hands of the Agency. Even though the Agency was a joint effort supported by all five worlds, it resided in his district, which ultimately made him responsible for everything that occurred there. As both her legal guardian and representative, it was his sworn duty to investigate her claims, and pass judgment on those she accused, now that she'd accused someone from his species of a crime. Although in a case of this severity, his decision would have been reviewed by Senior Councilor Tabor before the verdict and sentencing occurred. That Little Flower had accused him meant that it would have to go to the Local Council, and a different councilor would be chosen to advocate for her. That she had also accused the entire Local Council, since the vote on reintroduction and repopulation had been unanimous, meant the case would be required to go all the way up to the Full Council, and any decisions there would be final, since there wasn't a higher court to appeal to.

He wasn't even sure if there had ever been a situation where an entire council had been accused, and the legal ramifications of a guilty verdict were staggering. At a minimum every member of his local council would lose their position, requiring reelections. Any councilor found guilty for any crime, no matter how big or small, automatically lost their position on the Council. How could you pass judgment on someone else if you couldn't be trusted to follow the law? There were however provisions in the Charter in the event of a natural disaster or plague that resulted in the death of everyone on the Council. In that situation, authority would pass to the four remaining Senior Councilors, until such time as new elections could be held, and that could take months. In light of an event like this however, it could mean that the Senior Council could severely sanction his planet, not only for reparations for the harm done to Little Flower and her people, but for the time and resources that would be taken from the other planets needed to oversee new elections and govern his world until that new council could be elected. There was also the very real concern that Little Flower's people would be denied sentience and membership into the Consortium in order to avoid those consequences. It was a mess.

Regardless of the legal consequences, he was far more worried about Myra's current mental state. He'd never seen his partner more distraught, and that included the loss of her parents in a shuttle accident or under the stress of suddenly being in charge of the Agency and caring for thousands of patients. Not even the loss of Marsee's sister had caused her this much visible grief, but then she'd been fighting for her own life at the time. He'd grieved with her when she'd lost patients over the years, what healer hasn't, and supported her through the mandatory review with each death. On the few occasions where mistakes had been found, and even when there hadn't, he'd watched his partner spend months of her own time becoming an expert in those areas, so that she would never make those same mistakes again. It's what made her such a phenomenal healer. He personally thought her gifts were wasted out in this desolate community, but she'd grown up here and her patients weren't just patients, they were family, friends, and neighbors. But all of that paled in comparison to the state she was in now. He was terrified she would harm herself, or worse, take her own life for her role in this crime, whether the case went to trial or not, and she wasn't even remotely considering the legal consequences of her actions. He wasn't even sure he understood what the consequences would be. It had been so long since rape had occurred on his world that they just glossed over it in training.

After reviewing all of the evidence and making sure he thoroughly understood the medical scans, he hugged Myra for several minutes and sent her to her office to wait until he called her. He watched her walk down the hallway, tail dragging on the ground, until she was out of sight, before shutting his office door quietly. He looked out his window for a long time and then sat down at his desk and just stared at his tablet and Senior Councilor Tabor's contact information, desperately trying to figure out a way to save his family and friends.

He had been a councilor for this district for close to fifty years, had trained for it for close to forty more, and spent decades as an advocate before he'd been elected. As judge and juror he'd ruled over many complex and difficult cases in his career. Intentional crime was rare, but accidents did happen, and people sometimes lost control of their instinct and emotions in stressful situations, and it was his responsibility to ensure that reparations were fair and just, and ensure that a crime hadn't actually occurred. He never once thought he'd have to make a decision like this, and certainly not against his own partner.

Nearly half an hour passed before he finally made up his mind. Only one option stood a chance of saving them all. So, with a shaking paw, and heavy heart, he placed the call to Councilor Tabor, and called for an emergency session, knowing full well he might be sentencing the love of his life, his partner, and the mother of his children to death, or far worse.

The session lasted well into the night. Needless to say, the entire council had been at an uproar the moment he announced the reason for the meeting. It had taken Councilor Tabor nearly twenty minutes to calm everyone enough to begin deliberations, and examine the evidence. Both his partner and daughter had been called upon to give their statements. Marsee had been absolutely terrified at being questioned before the Council and had bolted out of the room, tail fully poofed, the moment they were done questioning her. Myra had been questioned for hours. She hid nothing from them, even going so far as to take full responsibility for what had happened, in an attempt to save the other healers at the Agency and the Council from the consequences. He was terrified that they would do just that. They had all watched the video, and he had scanned Little Flower's sketchbook as evidence of her accusation. Finally, Councilor Tabor called an end to the session, with plans to reconvene at the next scheduled meeting. Time was needed to gather additional information before any further decisions could be made.

When Jeran signed off from the meeting, he buried his head in his paws and sat there for a long time before forcing himself out of his chair to find his family. He finally found them in the garden along with Little Flower, who was lying down and watching the small fish that inhabited the pool. Marsee sat nearby with a plate of fruit that looked completely untouched. Jeran noticed that Little Flower was not wearing her harness and then saw the shredded remains of it on the ground next to his partner.

"I don't care what the Council says, after everything we've put her through, and everything else she thinks we've done, I'm never putting a leash back on her again. No one will ever force her to do anything again. Not ever. Not on my watch," Myra stated, when she saw his questioning glance.

He smiled sadly at his mate in understanding. Going against the Senior Councilor's orders would add to the list of charges against her, but in this he fully agreed, and they wouldn't find out from him. Besides those consequences paled in comparison to the ones they were already facing. He was still furious that they hadn't dropped that restriction tonight, even though he and Marcus had fought hard for it. They could deny it all they wanted to, but Little Flower was sentient, of that he had no doubt. And sooner, rather than later, she would prove it to them. "How is she?" he asked.

"I don't know," Myra answered truthfully. "When Marsee brought her down, I made a point of taking off the harness and tearing it up.

She didn't respond and Marsee said she wouldn't speak to her either. Afterwards, she just turned and walked away. She wandered around for a while, but she's pretty much been over by the pool ever since. She's not eating again, but she did have something to drink."

Marsee looked up when he'd arrived and started to stand up, but he motioned for her to stay where she was. He needed to talk to Myra alone first. Marsee sat back down, and started wringing her tail, a sign of real distress and worry in their kind. He sighed at the sight and tilted his head to Myra to indicate she should follow him. They wandered off into the garden to find a quiet spot to talk alone, tails and paws intertwined for mutual comfort.

"So, what did the Council decide?" Myra asked when they were alone, and far enough away that Marsee wouldn't be able to hear them.

"Not a lot, to be honest. Logistics mostly. The Council is still split on whether she is sentient or not, and what that means for the actions that occurred, and we still don't have a majority, even with all the progress we've made in communicating with her. More than half the Council is *still* undecided. In light of the accusations, and our inability to decide in her favor, the decision will go before the Full Council. As we expected, several on the Council believe that if they are capable of forcing one of their kind, then they aren't sentient and should be treated as such, requiring no form of reparations. Most seem to believe that since we've somehow tricked them into thinking that they had no choice but to breed as captives for their survival, we can't base their status as sentient based on an act that we caused to occur, intentionally or not. A few...also thought that she wasn't fighting but that that was a normal mating practice, since if the male was capable of mating with her, she must have been in heat."

"That was not a normal mating practice. She wanted nothing to do with him and tried hard to get our attention, and to get away," Myra growled.

"I agree with you," he said, trying to calm his partner's growing anger. "Anyway, a trial has been scheduled a month from today to vote on both her species' sentience and the charges she's made."

"A month?! That's not nearly enough time! How are we going to be able to prove sentience in only a month? Marsee and Little Flower barely have a few dozen words between them."

"I don't know and I agree, but that's the furthest out we could make it," Jeran replied.

"Why is that?" Myra asked.

"Because we can't sentence her rapist until she's been deemed sentient and has accepted membership into the Consortium, and in a case of this magnitude her rapist should be held in solitary confinement so he can't be given the opportunity to harm anyone else, but as Councilor Marcus reminded everyone, our penal code says we can't hold someone in solitary confinement for more than two weeks. Which means we are legally bound to pass sentencing within two weeks as well. Tabor compromised and agreed to extend the trial date by an additional two weeks to give Little Flower more time to prepare, as long as her attacker was given daily supervised visits with others of his species, although..."

"That's far more than he deserves, and it still doesn't give us nearly enough time to get her ready," Myra interrupted with a growl.

"I won't disagree with you there. Thankfully we don't have to do it all on our own," he said.

"What do you mean?" Myra asked.

"Marcus agreed to be her advocate for the trial."

"Can he do that? Wouldn't that still be a conflict of interest?" she asked.

"Marcus resigned his position on the Council," Jeran replied.

"He did *what*?!" Myra exclaimed, turning to face him.

"He resigned his position, effective as soon as his replacement can be elected, or the morning of the trial, whichever comes first. That will hopefully give his district time to vote in his replacement, and if not, Tabor will promote a junior advocate as acting councilor at the time of the trial, until the vote is finalized," Jeran said, and then snorted. "I just realized, by resigning, Marcus may have saved us from full censure as well, since whoever is elected to replace him can't be charged with accessory or collusion, and they may end up as Senior Councilor when this is all said and done. They could very well be the only one left on the Council." Jeran shook his head at his brother's deft maneuvering. *He may have very well just saved our planet from many hard years to come, whether that had been his intention or not. Knowing Marcus, it probably was.*

"But isn't he still going to be accused along with everyone else?" she asked.

"Yes, but it's complicated. There technically isn't anyone who meets the requirements to be her advocate that hasn't already been implicated by her accusation. We discussed asking for a volunteer from one of the other worlds, but the Charter requires that her advocate be someone who fluently speaks her language, or if not available, a language she is fluent in. Since no one speaks her native language or can even hear it, the Council decided that sign language would be her official language, at least temporarily, and the only people who speak that language are members of our world. Which brings us back to requiring that her advocate be a member of our species. And, as an advocate for a full council trial must be a member of the Council, it didn't leave us with a lot of options," Jeran tried to explain.

"But if he steps down, how can he be her advocate?" Myra asked, still confused.

"It was a compromise. As he's advocated for her in the past, there was precedent, and by stepping down, he gave up his right to vote at the trial. Plus, he's been a councilor for longer than just about everyone in any of the councils. He could have been Senior Councilor decades ago but chose not to."

Jeran paused, and Myra glared at him suspiciously. "What aren't you telling me?" she asked.

"Honestly, I wish you could have seen it. I'll show it to you later. Marcus's speech was brilliant. He stood before the Council, informed everyone there that he adamantly believed that Little Flower was sentient, and called everyone cowards for refusing to admit what they all knew was true, just because they were scared to face the consequences of their actions. Then once Councilor Tabor put a stop to all the growling and hissing from the outraged councilors, Marcus vowed before the Council, that if they let him be Little Flower's advocate, he would not only step down from his position to avoid any conflict of interest, but promised to do everything in his power to ensure she was granted sentience, including becoming fully fluent in sign language by the trial...under penalty of death should he fail to prove her sentience."

Myra just sat there and stared at him for several minutes. "He just signed his own death warrant, didn't he?" she said finally.

"Quite possibly," Jeran admitted, with a worried sigh.

"I was expecting you to be her advocate," Myra said after a while.

"I offered but Tabor refused, and rightly so." Myra looked at him in confusion so he continued. "The other councilors only have to worry about their own hides, and what happens to our planet if everyone is kicked out. I have to worry about what happens to you. It's going to be a hard enough decision for me to make as it is," he said quietly.

"You'll vote for her sentience, regardless of what might happen to me. She deserves it. They all deserve it. Whatever the Council decides my punishment should be, I deserve it, and I won't fight it. Promise me," she demanded.

Jeran stood and walked over to the other side of the clearing, unable to look his partner in the eyes, or answer her. "I can't Myra," he finally said, looking down at his paws and flexing his claws, claws he knew he might be forced to use.

"Jeran, I don't care if I get kicked out of the Guild, or what reparations I have to pay to her, Little Flower deserves her freedom and so do her people," Myra said, walking up beside him, and wrapping her tail around him.

Jeran turned to face her, and grabbed her paws in his. "Myra, you're the love of my life, and the mother of my children. My greatest joys in this world have all come from you, but you don't know what you're asking me to do. It's been millennia since this has happened. I don't even know what the punishment will be, but all of our laws are based on equal reparations. If I vote for her sentience and they find you..." he swallowed hard, "...guilty of colluding in her rape, then you would be given the same or equal punishment as him, and frankly the evidence is not in your favor. You took full responsibility in front of the Council, and they may very well hold you to that in order to save themselves. They could sentence you to experience what she went through, force you into another heat after beating you, which we both know would kill you, or they could even sentence you to death, since if Brice hadn't stopped him, he could very easily have killed her. Still might with the risk of giving birth so young. Either way I'd be voting for your death and I can't do that. I just can't."

"Yes, you can. Jeran those punishments are all fair and just for what I did to her, and if her freedom means my death, then so be it. What's one life, freely given, to ensure an entire species their own freedom?" she said quietly.

"But it's not just one life I have to think about. It's Brice's, it's Marcus's, it's every single person on that Council that could also lose their lives, and every single person on this planet that could suffer massive sanctions until a new Council is elected. Marcus was right, I am a coward and I'm terrified of the consequences."

"And what of the consequences if Little Flower is denied her sentience, and she's thrown back in her cell for our people to do with as we please? How long before she kills herself, or the rest do, and we doom their entire species to extinction? Marsee had it right the other day. 'What makes our species more valuable than theirs? There are millions of us and only a few hundred of them. Every one of their lives is far more valuable because the loss of even one life could mean the extinction of an entire species'. Jeran, I couldn't live with myself if my life was spared at the cost of her freedom, and frankly I've thought about ending my own life at least a dozen times since I realized what I've done to her. Jeran, you can and you must vote for her sentience, whatever the consequences. I won't fight it, and neither should you. Promise me," Myra demanded.

"Dark moons, Myra. Please don't hurt yourself. I don't know what I would do without you." He pulled her in for a hug and held her for a long time, shaking with his own fear before pulling away. "It kills me to have to put you in danger like this, but you're right. She deserves her freedom. I promise I'll vote for her sentience, but whatever happens, I also promise you won't have to go through it alone. Even if...even if that means I'm the one..." He couldn't finish.

For the first time in his life, Jeran wished he'd never joined the Council, or run for office when he'd completed his training. He was good at what he did, and worked hard to see that the people in his district had what they needed to thrive. As judge and jury, his people liked and valued his decisions, enough so that he'd been reelected three times with vast majorities, but never once did he think he'd have to fulfill his role as executioner. Even in the case of psychosis, Tabor and the Guard took care of it. It's why he'd turned down the nomination for Senior at the last election. That wasn't something he thought he could do. They stood there in silence for a very long time, just leaning on each other for comfort.

"So, what else happened?" Myra eventually asked.

Jeran sighed. "Well, several of the councilors called for your immediate removal as head of the Agency, but..."

Myra sighed. "I fully expected that, and already had my resignation letter ready if they hadn't. I can't believe I didn't even consider this a possibility. At the very least I should have examined the footage from the fight, and not just taken Brice's word for it. As talented as she is, she's still only a journeyman and rape isn't something you're taught about until you've earned your masters. She wouldn't have been trained to look for that possibility, but I have. I should have known better and I should have considered that a possibility before..."

Jeran interrupted her. "*But* you were not removed from your position, and Councilor Tabor has even ordered that any Guild repercussions for you and Brice, be held until after your guilt or innocence is established. You weren't the only one that didn't look at the footage, none of us did. My brother was the tipping point, *again*. Marcus argued that since Marsee is the only one that has managed to form any sort of relationship with the bipeds, your removal, as well as returning Little Flower to the Agency, would actually end up further harming the cub, and that your role in disseminating Marsee's findings and bringing them to the Council, is actually of far more value to the cub and her species, than removing you would be. That you came straight to the Council with this information, rather than trying to hide it, showed you were more interested in helping Little Flower than avoiding consequences, and he pointed out that the vast majority of the other species, including the other bipeds, are not only recovering but thriving without issue, thanks to the information we've been able to learn in just the past few days alone. Plus, he stated, punishing someone prior to a guilty verdict was against the law."

"We really should invite him over for a meal when this is all over," Myra said.

"I agree, assuming any of us are alive at that point, although I fully expect he'll be over in a few days to meet with Little Flower. As it is, I'm heading over to his place tomorrow to plan and help with research."

Myra nodded. "What else?" she asked and looked at him warily when he didn't immediately continue.

"Well, after Tabor agreed to extend the trial date, several in the Council expressed their concern about the bipeds mental state again, assuming they are found sentient, and expressed their desire to see the quarantine lifted further, which of course visibly upset Parner and his group, as well as several others who were worried that something like this might happen to someone else. We couldn't come to a consensus on that, so Tabor suggested that all of the bipeds, except Little Flower, be placed in stasis until such time as we are properly able to fully communicate with them, and their sentience is established. The Council agreed. They also want a full workup of all the other females, as well as an independent review of all unsupervised interaction between the bipeds, to ensure this has not happened to anyone else."

Myra sighed. "I've already ordered the investigation and review. Witherspoon said she will be assigning people tomorrow to start reviewing the footage, and I have teams already running scans on the other females. I can see why Tabor would suggest putting them in stasis, but we don't know the effects long term stasis will have on them and we've had problems in the past, both with the male who died and with two miscarriages early on. We don't know yet if that had anything to do with being in stasis or just their injuries. We could lose the entire species if something goes wrong. Stopping a heat for us has almost always proved to be fatal. I have no idea what it would do to them, and, well, that puts an awful lot of pressure on one little cub to determine the future rights and freedoms of her entire species."

Jeran frowned at this added information. He hadn't considered that there would be further risks to putting them in stasis. He hadn't been aware of the miscarriages or the affect stasis had on his own species during heat. As the male had been old and it had been the first replacement heart they'd tried to transplant in the species, he'd agreed with the suggestion to keep the bipeds from suffering while they figured out this mess.

"It does indeed," he replied, taking her paw in his again. "Which is why I need you to stop blaming yourself for what happened, and focus on doing everything you can to help her and the others. I know you never intended for anything like this to occur, none of us did, and you weren't the only master at the Agency, and frankly many of them have as much, if not more experience than you do. Any one of them could have said something, but they didn't. As for the stasis order, send me your complaint in writing along with any documentation you have to support your concerns, and I'll submit a formal complaint to Tabor over the order. It's the best I can do."

"Will do. I still don't see how we're possibly going to be able to get her ready in a month, even with Marcus's help," Myra said, with a hopeless sigh.

"I honestly don't know either," Jeran replied, with a matching sigh of his own. "But I've seen you do the impossible before, and if anyone can get her ready, it's you."

"Well, there is one thing I do know," Myra stated. "It's far past time Little Flower knows what happened to her world, and that's something I can do right now."

# CHAPTER 3

# Jessica: Finally Some Answers

Jessica lay on the large flat stones that bordered the pool, and gently trailed her fingers in the water enjoying the coolness. The little octorays nibbled at her fingertips, and scurried away when she wiggled her fingers, but soon came back again. Before long, they let her touch them, and seemed to enjoy it, turning all different colors in the process. It wasn't lost on her that she was seeing things none of her people had ever seen before, and she took enjoyment in her situation where she could. It helped to balance the pain a little.

She was still reeling from the emotions that had overwhelmed her earlier, she and wasn't sure what to think anymore. Marsee had left the room with her sketch books, and hadn't returned for some time. Jessica had curled up around Fuzzy, and surprisingly fallen asleep for several hours, although she hadn't felt much better when Marsee had woken her up. Marsee had looked nearly as pathetic as she had the other day, if not more so, and motioned for her to follow. Jessica had sighed, but done as requested, figuring they'd just pick her up and carry her, if she didn't.

They'd made their way to the garden, and Jessica had been surprised to see all of the doors wide open, not just to the garden, but to the outside as well. Marsee's mother had met them there, and approached with a look that had been just as pathetic and sorrowful, if not more so than Marsee's had been. Jessica had glared up at the giant gold cat, full of hatred and loathing at the cat she now knew had held her captive for so long. But to her surprise, Myra had slowly reached down and unclipped her harness, and before her eyes, had shredded the thing into tiny little pieces with ease. She'd been slightly horrified at how easy it had been for the giant cat, but then Myra had motioned that she was free to go where she liked.

Surprised, Jessica had raised a brow, and had immediately turned and walked out of the garden, to see if they'd follow her. They had not. She wandered at random for a while, looking out at the vast desert for a long time, but had eventually ended up back in the garden and by the pool. It was by far the nicest place in the castle, and as much as she loathed them, there just wasn't anywhere for her to go. She was out of the hated harness, but was she really any freer than she'd been before? Marsee had been ecstatic to see her return, and immediately brought over something for her to eat and drink, but Jessica had just glared up at her, and flopped down by the pool, leaving the food untouched.

Marsee had returned to her spot looking absolutely dejected, and Jessica sighed. *It's not like she would have had anything to do with what happened to me,* Jessica thought, and took pity on the kitten, and had something to drink. She was thirsty, but she had no appetite. Her stomach was still in knots. She watched as Jer entered the garden and had left with Myra moments later, hands and tails entwined, both looking worried. Frowning, she went back to trailing her fingers in the pool and trying to make sense of their reactions, which hadn't been what she'd expected at all. They were acting far too upset, as if they'd not known what had happened to her, but that didn't make sense. It was obvious from the number of times that Healer Morningstar had shown up, moments after she'd been sick, that someone was watching her, and from what she'd learned earlier, Myra ran the Agency. *Had Brice acted on her own?* Jessica wondered, *or were they just now figuring out that she wasn't an animal that they could just breed, and that's why they'd removed the leash?* She wasn't sure if that made it any better or not.

Nor could she figure out why they'd destroyed her planet and taken her captive, if it wasn't to breed her like an animal and keep her as a pet. *Surely, they must have known we weren't just some wild animals. Our homes and technology aren't all that different.*

Her brain kept spinning and eventually she just sighed and tried to forget it all. She didn't have the words to ask the questions, and they hadn't provided any answers to the ones she'd already asked. She'd just about fallen back to sleep, lulled by the warm evening air, when she was tapped on the shoulder. Looking up with a scowl, she was surprised to see that it was Marsee's mother this time. *Now what?* she wondered, and was confused when the giant cat sat down beside her and handed her a tablet. Jessica sat up and Myra tapped the screen.

A video started and showed a view from above and behind several of the big cats in a large room, all focused on various panels and instruments, and the large screens in front. On the center screen was a planet, half in shadow. The side screens showed images of what she thought were spacecraft, although she couldn't be sure as they looked nothing like the small shuttle she'd seen. As she watched, the planet on the center screen grew and came into focus. "That's Earth!" she gasped as she recognized her home planet, and looked up at Myra, who nodded and motioned that she should continue watching.

Suddenly, there was a flurry of activity, and the monitor panned away from focusing on Earth, to focus on another location out in space. The image zoomed in to show a tiny blurry object in the center of the screen. The image zoomed in again and she realized what it was, an asteroid, slowly tumbling through space. The monitor changed to what looked like a 3D map, with a round circle in the very middle. A second smaller circle was added to the grid. As the smaller shape moved, a curving swath of color was drawn from the smaller shape to the bigger one, the swath going from yellow to blue and back to yellow again. Part of the outer yellow covered the bigger circle. She'd seen enough hurricane maps in her life to figure out what it meant, even if it was in three dimensions and not two. The smaller circle shifted slightly closer to the planet and the swath narrowed. However, now the larger circle was completely within the yellow band, with parts of it touching blue. A moment later, the screen refreshed again, and now the blue band completely covered the planet, and Jessica swallowed hard.

The video changed again to show a much closer image of her home, still partially in darkness, along with another object partially lit like the planet, that she realized must be the moon. She could make out the ocean through the clouds, and what looked like Europe, and the distinctive boot shape of Italy. Then in horror Jessica watched as the asteroid appeared on the screen, veered slightly as it just missed the moon, and crashed into the dark side of the planet. An explosion bloomed out of the side of the planet, with debris lit up from both the blast below and the sun, as parts of what she realized must be Australia, were now being ejected far out into space. Then a ripple appeared, traveling through Asia and then Europe, and around the planet and back again, as the shock wave traveled from the site of the impact to make it all the way around the planet to where she had been. The tails of all the cats on the screen were straight out, and poofed to three times their normal size.

Remembering the explosion that had sent her flying and destroyed her school, she realized that if it had been that bad where she was, that there was probably nothing left anywhere else on the planet. Covering her mouth with her hands, she stifled a cry and kept watching.

The image changed again to show the ship diving through the atmosphere, blue lights flashing on either side of the big monitors, the side monitors now red with the heat and flames of re-entry until the ship paused, hovering a few hundred feet above the rubble, and a topographical map of the area was displayed on the front screen. Moments later a number of different colored dots began appearing on the map, as well as one triangle shape in the center. The triangle moved to the center of a small cluster of dots, and the ship landed.

She realized as the video continued, that the ship landed not just anywhere, but in what was left of her local hardware store's parking lot, just down the street from the intersection where she'd been picked up, as the video panned, and her image, covered in dust and blood, picking her way over some rubble, appeared on the screen. *How did I miss a spaceship landing right in front of me? Was I injured that badly?* she wondered, then remembered how little visibility she'd had from the ash and smoke. Dozens of the large cats suddenly exited the craft at nothing less than a full run, one coming straight towards her, other's angling off in other directions. She watched as she saw the cat, screamed, and turned to run. They raised something towards her, and a blue glow raced towards her, hit her in the back, and then she crumpled into a heap. The cat ran over to her, scooped her up, and ran back into the ship.

The image changed again to another room where she was now being placed on a table, where another cat quickly stripped her of her clothing, and examined her wounds. The first cat bolted the moment she was on the table. This was part of the video she'd seen the day before, but it continued on past what she'd been shown. The medic slapped a bracelet on her wrist and wrapped something around her arm, completely enclosing the visibly broken bones. They slapped a bandage of some sort on a large gash on her head, and then moved on to the next person who had been brought in, then a dog and two cats, several birds, and then even a horse! *Where did they find a horse in the middle of town?* she wondered. Another of the alien cats picked her up and carried her away.

The image changed again to a large open room, at least twice the size of her school gymnasium where she was placed in a corner. Other casualties were soon placed next to her. In the background she could also see several other cats frantically throwing items out an open bay to the ground below. *They didn't just save her species. They were grabbing anything they found alive,* she realized. *So much for kangaroos and koala bears,* she thought sadly, but then wondered, *what are they throwing out? Oh! They must be throwing out their own supplies to make room for survivors!* People, plants, and animals of all kinds, all of which were scorched, bleeding, and covered in ash, were brought in and laid out side by side. Then the video switched again to an ocean view and strange creatures, somewhat reminiscent of the octorays but far bigger, and more humanoid in shape, swimming in and out of another ship, bringing back small whales, fish, dolphins, lobsters, jellyfish, and many creatures she'd never even seen before. Then it dawned on her, not only were they rescuing Earth's ocean creatures, but there was a second alien species doing the rescuing! *How many species are there?* she wondered, then remembered that Marsee had said there were five worlds. *Did she mean five species too?*

Footage shifted to another ship, where three of yet another unknown species, hard shelled like an armadillo, were digging into the rubble of a building, moving mangled metal beams with ease. One reached down and pulled out a toddler, alive and wiggling, and handed the child off to another armadillo, who started running awkwardly back to their ship, while the first two kept digging. She watched in horror as a massive earthquake hit, knocking all three creatures to the ground with the force. The video jerked wildly, until apparently the ship lifted, and the video stabilized. As the quake stopped and the dust cleared, she saw the one with the child uncurl from the protective ball they had formed around their charge, and turn to back to look for the others only to watch as the remains of the building teetered and collapsed, completely burying the two in a cloud of rubble. The one with the child stood there blinking, took two steps towards where the others had been, then stopped, looked at the child in their hands, and turned and ran back to the ship. A second quake nearly took the armadillo off their feet again, as they scrambled into the ship that had lowered again to pick up its crew member. Just as the creature made it back to the ship, a massive crack in the earth formed directly under the ship, forcing it to rise up into the air again. She watched as the crack traveled to where the building had been, widened, and swallowed it completely.

*They lost people too,* she realized with horror, and wondered how many had died or had been injured trying to save even a small portion of her world.

The final image was one taken again from space as the craft exited the atmosphere and sped away from the planet. What had once been a serene marble of blues and whites, was now a hellscape of red, as the crust of the planet crumbled and hot magma covered the land, leaving nothing in its wake.

When the recording was done, she just sat there stunned for a long time. They hadn't captured her, they'd rescued her. Not just her, but all that they could from what little remained of her planet. *How many species had they saved? How many people? Was there enough to rebuild a population or were all of the species of Earth doomed to extinction? Is that why they were breeding her, to repopulate the species? Did that make it right? No,* she decided quickly; *not even close.* Then a thought that brought a small sliver of hope. Had her parents been one of the ones rescued, or anyone she knew? There had been dots on the map in the part of town where her mother's bakery had been. She shoved that question aside and locked it behind the broken and shattered remains of the door in her mind. As long as she didn't ask, there was still the hope that they were rescued too.

After a while, Marsee's mother handed her the sketch book, and waved Marsee over to help translate. Jessica just stared at the book trying to make sense of everything she'd just seen, and figure out what she wanted to ask, and how to ask it. She just didn't have the words to say it. Finally, she drew pictures of the earth, of the asteroid, and of the ships, and had Marsee look up the signs for the asteroid and ship, and did her best to communicate her questions, but it took several hours to get through them all, and make sure she understood their responses.

While the video clearly implied that the damage was done by an asteroid, she had no idea if they'd somehow caused the asteroid to hit. Although, based on their poofed tails, she doubted it. Still, she asked anyway, to try and find out what their intentions were and why they'd been there in the first place. "Did you send the ships to hurt my world?" she signed or at least that was her intent. What she actually signed was more like 'You - ship - hurt - me - world' but Marsee seemed to under-stand and translated for her mother.

Marsee's mother shook her head no then through Marsee, "No. The asteroid hurt your world."

"Why were the ships there?" she asked.

In response, Myra wrapped her tail around Jessica's side and gave her a light squeeze. "Hear your world. See you and Marsee play, happy."

*You heard us and came to see if we could play and be happy? To be friends?* Jessica deciphered, and then spent several minutes figuring out the signs for friend and enemy. Jessica used a similar sketch of Marsee and her on the balcony for friend, and a quick version of the cat shooting her in the back for enemy. Myra confirmed that they wanted to be friends.

"Why was I at the Agency? Was I a prisoner?" she asked next, drawing a sad looking picture of her locked in a cage with chains on her hands and feet.

Marsee's mother shook her head hard. "No. Your sick hurt me. My sick hurt you. See danger," came Marsee's translated reply.

This confused Jessica for a bit. She hadn't been sick, she'd been injured, outside of her infected arm, but that had been healed quickly. Then she remembered watching War of the Worlds, and how the aliens had been killed by viruses and remembered the pandemic when she was little. *Doh! I was in quarantine! Is that why Doc never stuck around? She was afraid we'd get sick? So, if I'm out of quarantine is that not a concern anymore?*

"Curious - my - sick - danger - you?" she repeated using Marsee's signs.

"No. You sick no hurt me. My sick no hurt you," Marsee replied.

*Well, that's something,* she thought. *At least I don't have to worry about catching a case of the kitten pox from them.* "Why leash?" she asked after drawing a sketch of her wearing it.

"Tabor - sign," Marsee replied after a look passed between her and her mother.

"Why?" she asked again, demanding an answer. Marsee and her mother spoke for a while. Jessica wasn't sure if they didn't agree on how to answer the question, or if they just didn't know how to answer the question. Marsee looked up something on the language site and taught her the word for 'think'.

"Council think you no think. Council think you chenzie," Marsee had finally answered. "Council think you hurt you."

"I think. I no chenzie," she said, furious that they thought she was an animal, but Marsee and her mother both nodded their agreement, which caused her to calm some. Their worry that she might hurt herself had been valid though, since she had tried to take her own life. Taking a deep breath, she asked the question she really wasn't sure she was ready to talk about, but she needed to know. "Why was I in the cell with that man?"

Marsee's mother looked very sad at that question. "You sad sick. I want heal sad sick. I want see you happy. I see you and man play," Marsee's mother said.

*I was sad sick? Does she mean depressed? She was trying to make me happy? She wanted us to play so I would be happy?* Jessica struggled to understand with the few signs they had. *By 'play' does she mean have sex or play like Marsee and I do with the drones,* she wondered.

"Play cub, or play drone?" she asked next.

"Play drone," Myra replied.

"Did you want me to have a baby with that man to repopulate my species?" she asked, not sure if she got the question across or not.

"No!" Marsee's Mother shook her head vehemently, and then with an expression of deep sorrow, nodded her head slowly yes, and tried to explain. "I want heal your world. I want heal you. I no want harm you."

Jessica nodded, that made sense.

"You cub. When you adult, you choose cub," Marsee's mother continued.

*Yeah well, I didn't exactly choose that,* Jessica thought glaring and very deliberately replied. "I choose no cub. I choose no man. Man hurt me."

The anguish on both Marsee and her mother surprised her, and then Myra picked up her tail and started twisting it. Marsee reached out and put a paw on her mother's arm to stop her, before translating her words.

"I hurt you. I big big big sad I hurt you," Marsee's mother said.

*Is that an apology?* Jessica wondered, *but why is she saying she hurt me? Because she runs the Agency and is taking responsibility for what happened, or because of some other reason?*

"Healer Morningstar put us in that room together, and he hurt me, not you. Why are you saying you hurt me?" she asked, or tried to.

"I say you and man. I choose man. Healer Morningstar say no man. I say Healer Morningstar you go man," Marsee translated. "Big male, little female."

It took a while to understand the last bit and after some drawing, she realized that there were more men than women rescued and that was the best pairing they'd been able to come up with the people under Healer Morningstar's care.

*So, you gave the order for the two of us to be together,* Jessica deciphered, and thought back to the rest of the conversation. *She wants to save our species, but she doesn't want me to have a baby because she thinks I'm still too little to have one? My parents would have to be short. Do they think I'm still a baby? But what did she think would happen locking us up in a room together and leaving us alone? Is rape not a thing for their world if you get to choose your sex as an adult? I guess that could be possible. The females of their species are significantly larger than the males, so maybe it just doesn't happen. Was this all just a horrible mistake on their part?*

"Why didn't you come when I called for help?" she asked.

"No hear Little Flower sign help," Myra signed sadly. "Healer Morningstar help little cub. Cub no..." Marsee made big breathing motions. "Food knife," and then pointed to her neck.

*She hadn't come, because she hadn't heard her call for help, because she'd been busy trying to save a choking baby,* she deciphered.

Suddenly all of her anger drained, leaving her feeling empty and hollow inside. Her anger and hatred had been her constant companion for so long, that she didn't really know what to do without it. She hadn't been captured; she'd been rescued. She hadn't been held a prisoner, she had been held in quarantine to protect both their species, and she hadn't been put in that room to be raped or to repopulate their species, but to try and help her get over her depression from being stuck in quarantine for so long, and it had been working until that no-good bottom-dwelling mud-sucker had raped her. She was still furious with him, and what he'd done, but the time spent with him prior to that was the highlight of her time at the Agency, and her emotions conflicted greatly within her. She had cared about him deeply, might have even come to love him someday, if he hadn't forced himself on her, but that wasn't Myra's fault. He was responsible for his own actions. She had told him no, multiple times, and he could have backed off and waited until she was ready, but he didn't.

"You did not harm me. The man harmed me. I am mad at him, not you," she told the giant cat beside her, and then reached over and wrapped her arms around the giant cat's sides in a big hug.

Myra reached down and scooped her up into her arms, hugging her tightly, almost completely enveloping her in her furry arms. Jessica realized the cat was shaking, not purring, and looked up to see that her eyes were shut tightly, ears and whiskers pressed flat to the sides, and her whiskers were twitching. The big cat's reaction surprised her. Had Myra been that upset about her being raped, or did Jessica's forgiveness mean that much to her. Could it be more than that? *What are the cultural and legal implications of rape on this world?* she wondered.

There was really only one other question she needed answered right now, so she tugged gently on Myra's fur to get the cat's attention. "Little Flower cub?" she signed, and then put her hands over her belly.

Marsee's mother took a deep breath and nodded sadly. "Yes."

# CHAPTER 4

# Marsee: Promises

After finding out that she was pregnant, Little Flower demanded to be set down, picked up her sketchbooks, and walked out of the garden without another word. Marsee didn't know where she was going, but her mother stopped her from following.

"Let her go. She needs time to think, and she needs to know she's free to go where she wants," her mother ordered.

"How much were you able to tell her?" her father asked. He'd purposely kept his distance, not wanting to overwhelm Little Flower, and hadn't approached them until he'd seen the cub walk away.

"Enough," her mother answered and stood up. "I...I have work I need to do. I'll be in my office if you need me."

Marsee and her father watched silently, as her mother left the garden, in the opposite direction Little Flower had taken. "Is Mama okay? I've never seen her like this," Marsee asked.

"She will be. It'll just take time," he answered, but Marsee caught a hint of hesitation in his reply, and it worried her. What wasn't he telling her? "Now why don't you teach me some of that sign language?" he said, turning to her with a smile.

Marsee spent the next hour teaching her father the signs they'd learned that day and talking about everything else that had happened.

"I think that's enough. Any more and my brain is going to explode," her father teased. "Seriously though, I'm impressed at how much you've picked up. The best thing you can do to help Little Flower right now, is for the both of you to become as fluent as possible in this new language, so she will be ready for the Council meeting."

"How is she even possibly going to be ready in a month? It's one thing to tell someone you're hungry or need to pee, how is she possibly going to be ready to answer questions before the Full Council?" Marsee asked.

"With a lot of help from her best friend," he replied.

"Best friend? Me? I'm not even sure she likes me anymore. She wouldn't even talk to me tonight. Every time I tried, she just glared at me or turned her back to me," Marsee said.

"Nonsense! She's just upset. Once she's had time to process everything, I'm sure your friendship will be stronger than ever. Look how close the two of you have become in just a few days, and that was when she thought we'd attacked her planet, captured her, and forced her to mate. Now she knows we were only trying to help. You'll see."

"I suppose," Marsee sighed, not really convinced.

"Trust me. If she can forgive your mother for her role in what happened, then she's already forgiven you. For that matter, I don't think she was ever mad at you. I think she was just mad at the whole situation, and you just happened to be the first person she could talk to about it. I've seen it many times, and have had many people yell at me, when really, they were mad at the situation, or the person who had harmed them. Now, I need to talk with your mother. Why don't you work on learning more of that sign language? That way you can teach us all more words in the morning, and then try to get some sleep." He gave her a quick hug and left, leaving her alone in the garden.

Marsee did as he suggested, and spent some time studying and going back through and filling in the words for the other languages. She hung out next to the pond for another several hours and watched the flicker flyers until she started yawning and decided to call it a night, seeing as no one had returned. Climbing wearily up the ramp to her room she looked out at the horizon from her balcony.

*I wonder what she thinks of our world now,* Marsee thought, before turning and heading into her room. She looked over at the cub's nest but it was empty. *She's not back yet. Should I let Mama know? No, she said to let her be. She'll come back when she's ready, or not.* With a heavy sigh, she jumped up onto her bed to wait and rocked slowly. In just the few days she'd been with them, she'd surprisingly gotten used to having Little Flower around all the time. Now, her solitude felt incredibly lonely, where once it had been her haven and all she'd ever wanted.

An hour later, Marsee was half asleep when she heard the tiny pitter patter of footsteps making their way up the ramp. Marsee opened her eyes and watched as Little Flower stopped and looked out at the horizon for a long time, just as Marsee had done earlier. Little Flower let out a massive sigh and entered the room. They made eye contact and Little Flower nodded once, before walking over to her nest, putting away her items, and stripping down to her under-things. To Marsee's surprise, instead of climbing into her little nest, she grabbed her blanket, walked over, and dragged a table next to Marsee's hanging bed and climbed in next to her. Marsee shifted over, giving the cub some space without saying a word. They would talk when Little Flower was ready and Little Flower looked just as worn out as she felt. Within minutes though, now that her friend was safely by her side, Marsee fell deeply asleep.

Sometime in the night, Marsee was startled awake by the sounds and twitching of Little Flower, caught in another night terror. Marsee shifted and gently laid her arm over Little Flower's side and started purring to comfort the cub. A moment later the cub let out a sigh, and settled back down into an easier sleep.

The next time Marsee woke, the suns were starting to rise, and what had previously been a cool night was quickly changing to what looked to be another hot day. *Not that there were anything but hot days this time of the year,* she thought. Little Flower had crawled out from under Marsee's arm, and was now sprawled out on her stomach, an arm hanging off the side of the bed and a thin sheen of that odd liquid was forming on her skin again. Marsee tried to crawl off the bed without moving it and waking the cub, so she could close the doors and turn on the cooling unit, but that was a lot harder than she realized.

Little Flower woke and sat up, rubbing at her eyes, and chittered quite a bit at her.

Marsee didn't understand what she said of course, so after she finished whatever it was she was saying to her, she signed, "Little Flower angry Marsee"?

"No. I sad. Sad I hurt Marsee's nose. Sad-sick, scared, no angry Marsee," came the reply, and then after a pause, "Hungry."

Marsee nodded her understanding, relieved that the cub was no longer angry with her. Depressed, well that would take time, and she had every reason to be depressed and scared, but hungry was something Marsee could easily fix. "Nose no hurt. Eat, drink, play," Marsee replied back. Little Flower smiled, hopped down off the bed, and started putting on her protective clothing. Marsee walked over and picked up her carry harness and hearing aids, but decided she didn't want to wear them today. She wanted to be able to hear her friend, and that was far more important than not hearing the lights and hydroponics units. Plus, for the first time in her life she'd experienced what it was like for the world to be too quiet. So, she tossed the harness and hearing aids on her bed, and they left to find something to eat.

They were about halfway down the ramp when Little Flower tugged on her fur to get her attention. She stopped and turned to look back. Little Flower held up two fingers and then pointed at the sun. "Two suns?"

Marsee turned and looked, sure enough Octavius was just barely visible in the early morning light. "Yes, two," she replied.

The little cub tried to say something, then tossed her hands up and continued down the ramp. Clearly, she didn't have the words yet to ask. Just then she saw her father's shuttle leaving, and wondered where he was going. Neither of her parents had mentioned he was leaving the night before, and she thought they were still in quarantine, although maybe not, since Ellie and Ammond had both come here. She left Little

Flower in the family room, propped up on the window seat drawing, while she went to the kitchen to find something for them to eat. She found her mother already there, preparing their meal.

"Morning. Where's Papa going?" she asked.

"He's left to talk with Marcus about Little Flower," her mother informed her, as she chopped up several pieces of fruit.

"Is that allowed? I thought our travel was restricted." Marsee grabbed another knife and kicked the steps out so she could help with the food preparation.

"Didn't your father tell you?" her mother asked, handing her several un-chopped pieces of fruit.

"Tell me what?" she asked, as she started chopping.

"Your uncle resigned his position so he could be Little Flower's advocate at the Full Council meeting. As her advocate, she has every right to go see him, and he to see her, and the Council can't stop it."

"I couldn't think of a better advocate for Little Flower than Uncle Marcus, but why would he have to resign his position?" she asked, stopping to look up at her mother.

Her mother set her knife down and turned to face her. "I'll try to explain, but your father is probably the best person to ask, since he understands all of the implications." Her mother paused and thought for a moment. "Basically, because the Council made decisions that ultimately led to Little Flower's rape, they will all likely be held accountable if Little Flower is deemed sentient. It's why this is now going before the Full Council. The risk is too high that her freedom would be denied just so our Council could avoid the consequences. By resigning, Marcus is giving up his right to vote."

"What would the consequences be?" she asked with a frown. She hadn't realized that anyone outside of Little Flower's rapist would be held accountable.

"Well for starters, every single councilor who voted, will lose their position on the Council, including your father, except for maybe Marcus's replacement. The Senior Council could decide to make that replacement Senior Councilor for our world, but more likely they will insist that we wait until a majority of seats have been filled. Either way, without a majority, governance would likely shift to the Full Council, until new officials could be elected, which could take months, even with emergency elections. In that time though, the Full Council would have every legal right to heavily sanction this world for the bipeds care, rather than having it be the joint effort of all five worlds as it has been so far. They could even go so far as to give ownership of parts of this world to the bipeds, regardless of who already lived there," her mother explained.

"Three moons!" Marsee whispered and her mother nodded. "Wait? If she could charge the Council does that mean she could charge you and Healer Brice too?"

Her mother nodded again. "Yes, and she did. She has an even clearer case against your father and I since we were the ones that were advocating for the change in isolation. As for Brice and I, we will most likely be found complicit in her rape, and face pretty severe consequences, since we were in charge of her care. You need to know that your father and I have both decided we will not fight the charges, and we will stand by whatever decision the Council makes."

"What will happen?" Marsee asked, now very worried for her parents.

"I don't know. Honestly, what happened to Little Flower hasn't happened on our worlds in thousands of years. That's why your father went to see Marcus. They're trying to figure out if there is any precedent to follow. I suppose it all depends on what she wants in compensation. At a minimum, I would be kicked out of the Healers Guild, but she could demand a lifetime of care for her child, which I would gladly give, or even demand that I experience what she went through. Our laws are based on equal compensation for harm."

"How would that even work?" Marsee asked, baffled. "You've already been through your second heat."

It's no different than a second heat," her mother explained. "All they would really have to do is turn off the implant, and a week or so later, I would be in heat."

"But a third pregnancy would kill you! You almost died having a second litter as it is!" Marsee cried.

"It's the same risk she's in now being so young and not fully grown, even more so since we know so little about their species, and we would have a difficult time saving her if something went wrong," her mother explained.

"Can't you stop the pregnancy before it gets to that point?" Marsee asked.

Her mother didn't answer for a long time. "It's complicated," she finally said. "Technically, maybe, but I could be putting her at more risk than she would be in, if she carried the cub to term. We rarely have to perform the procedure on our own kind, and usually that's only when something has gone very wrong with the pregnancy, since no one ever chooses to get pregnant now if they don't want cubs."

"Like when you had me?" Marsee asked.

Myra nodded. "We had to make the awful choice to give up your sister, in the hopes that we could save you. It was the hardest decision of my life. My healer did not want me to continue with the pregnancy at all, and we both almost died because of it."

"I had a sister? You never told me," Marsee said, stunned by the news.

"I tried several times, but I just couldn't. We named her Hope. Hope that you would make it long enough to survive being born. She lived for two days. She was the smallest cub I've ever seen, but perfect in every way. She just wasn't ready to come out. She's buried next to my parents. I spent the next twenty-three days in the intensive care ward fighting to keep you alive long enough to be born safely, and against every recommendation of my healer. My heart stopped three times, but yours never did," her mother said, looking away to try and bring her grief under control.

Marsee gave her mother a tight hug. "Thank you for telling me," she said.

Her mother took a deep breath and continued. "Legally though it gets even more complicated. If she decides not to go forward with the pregnancy, I could perform the procedure saying that it was medically necessary, due to her age and size, but that might be seen as tampering with the witness to try and get rid of the consequences of my actions. If we wait until after the trial, neither of us may have the legal right to make that decision. And if something went wrong and she died during that procedure, I could be charged with her murder."

"So, you can't perform the procedure even if she wants to end the pregnancy? The risk to you would be too great?" Marsee asked.

"Let me be perfectly clear. If Little Flower chooses not to go forward with this pregnancy, I will ensure that it happens, whether by my paws, or by another healer, before or after the trial, even if it means that I end up being sentenced to death for murder afterwards."

"But you can't!" Marsee cried.

Her mother kneeled down to look at her face-to-face. "I can, and I will. If it comes down to it and Little Flower dies because of my negligence, the Council will not have to order it. I would not be able to live with myself for what I've done to her, and what I may have done to others. It's hard enough now as it is, knowing how much I hurt her."

"No!" Marsee cried. "No. I won't allow it! I need you! We need you! Little Flower needs you! Promise me you won't take your life or hurt yourself in any way!" Marsee wailed.

Her mother looked down and didn't speak for a long time. "I don't think I can make that promise," her mother finally said in the barest of whispers.

"Promise. Me. Now!" Marsee yelled. "We are not leaving this kitchen until you promise me you will not harm yourself." Marsee's tail was straight out in pure fear.

"Marsee, the Council may…"

"To the ends of the universe with the Council! I will fight everyone one of them myself if I have to. You did nothing wrong. That male did. He should pay for his crimes, not you, not Papa, not anyone on the Council. You were only trying to help her and her species. You didn't force her, he did," she growled, her tail lashing in fury now.

"Marsee. By holding them so long in quarantine, and by locking them in that room together, we essentially gave that man the impression that he had no choice but to mate with her in order to gain his freedom," her mother tried to explain.

"He had a choice. You would choose death over hurting someone else like that, any of us would. If he truly believed that, then he chose his own life over hers. She said no, and he still chose to hurt her. Not only did he rape her, he knocked her out so he could do it, and if you look at his face in the video, he enjoyed it. He wanted to do it. He did it, not you. If you brought me somewhere and someone there harmed me, without you knowing about it, it wouldn't be your fault, it would be theirs. IT WAS NOT YOUR FAULT!" she yelled at the top of her lungs.

Her mother slumped to the floor, her back leaning up against the kitchen cupboard and grabbed her tail, twisting it hard.

"It was not your fault." Marsee reached over and carefully pried the tail out of her mother's grasp. "It was not your fault," she whispered, wrapping her arms around her mother's neck. Her mother grabbed her back and hugged her fiercely. "It was not your fault," she whispered again and again and again, until her mother stopped shaking and pulled away from the embrace.

A noise at the door made them both turn to look. Little Flower was standing in the doorway watching them, a worried expression on her face.

"Marsee's Mother hurt?" she asked. "Ear big sign."

Marsee assumed she meant she'd heard her yell at her mother, and nodded. "Mother sad-sick. Mother want harm mother," Marsee signed back, absolutely loathing the idea of having to look up the word for suicide, or even worse, create it.

"Why?" the cub asked.

"Mother think Mother hurt Little Flower. Mother think mother bad," Marsee signed, disgusted at her mother for not putting the blame where it really lay, on Little Flower's rapist.

The same look of fury that Little Flower had directed at her the day before, clouded Little Flower's tiny face, and she marched in and walked right up to her mother and glared up at her. "MAN HURT LITTLE

FLOWER, NOT MOTHER! she signed with large angry and very deliberate motions. "MAN BAD. MOTHER NOT BAD. MOTHER NO HARM MOTHER!"

Marsee translated, word for deliberate word. "See! Even Little Flower says it's not your fault! Now promise us both, because you do *not* want to see what she does when she's angry!"

The absolute ridiculousness of this statement caused her mother to burst out laughing, and Marsee relaxed slightly.

"Promise?" she asked.

"I promise," her mother said with a sigh and a nod of her head.

"Good, we're holding you to that promise. Little Flower needs you to help fight for her freedom, and for you to care for her and for that baby, should she choose to have it," Marsee said.

"I, Myra Beth Chenzira, do hereby promise that I will do everything in my power to fight for Little Flower's life and freedom, and to always care for her, her offspring, and the rest of the survivors of her world. I promise to not harm or kill myself regardless of what happens in the future," her mother vowed with formality. A pledge given with your full name was sacred to their people and legally binding. No one broke a vow, ever. Marsee shuddered with a sigh of relief.

"Good, now pull yourself together. We have a sign language lesson with Sina at noon, and I expect you to be there," she ordered, and then stormed out of the room, her tail still poofed and shivering with her emotions.

Marsee went back to the family room and sat down on the floor next to the window seat, and pulled at the scruff on the back of her neck trying to calm her frayed nerves. A few minutes later Little Flower appeared with their breakfast, which she'd left behind, completely for-gotten. It looked ridiculously oversized in her tiny paws, but she didn't seem to have any issue carrying it. Marsee's tablet dinged with a message from her mother. Opening it, a picture of a tiny cub hooked up to wires and other medical machinery was displayed.

"Who is that?" Little Flower asked, after climbing up on the window seat and tapping on her shoulder for attention.

"My litter-mate," she signed back, still trying to come to grips with the news that she'd had a litter-mate. She'd always felt like something or someone was missing in her life, and now she knew what it was.

"Where litter-mate now?" Little Flower asked.

They hadn't learned the words for dead, so Marsee just shook her head and signed 'knife'. Little Flower seemed to understand and leaned over and gave her a hug. Marsee leaned in and purred, grateful for the support.

"What's her name?" Little Flower asked.

Marsee opened the reference and looked up the word. "Hope," she signed.

"What does 'hope' mean?" Little Flower asked.

Marsee thought for a while and then signed. "Want happy tomorrow." It wasn't quite the right definition, but Little Flower nodded anyway, after Marsee explained what the sign for 'tomorrow' meant.

Half an hour before the scheduled meeting with Sina, her mother joined them in the family room with the noon meal. "Better?" Marsee asked. Her mother's normally calm expression was back in place, but Marsee didn't believe it for a second. It was too raw around the edges.

"Yes. Thank you. What's all this?" her mother asked in return, motioning to the table. There were small pieces of paper scattered everywhere.

"It was Little Flower's idea. I'm not sure what to call them, but on one side of the paper is our word for something and on the other hers. That way she can look at a word, try to remember what it is and flip it over to see if it's right, or I can hold it up and she can sign the word and I can do the same looking at her words," Marsee explained.

"She's learning to read? Already?!" her mother asked, surprised.

"And write, although she's having a much harder time with that. Her letters are all flipped around." Marsee picked up a piece of paper that had the word 'fruit' written on it a dozen times. Several of the letters were written backwards.

"I see what you mean. Have you asked Ellie if they have any primary school books you could use for her?" her mother suggested. "I remember you having a book that you could trace the letters in when you were first learning to write. Maybe that will help her."

"No, I haven't, but that's a great idea! I'll do that after we meet with Sina, speaking of which, I'd better give her a call."

Sina picked up right away.

"Hi, Sina. This is my mother, Myra. Mama, this is Sina." Marsee introduced and signed.

"Good morning," Sina said and signed back. "It is nice to meet you."

"The same. Thank you for agreeing to teach us," her mother said. "It is far more important than you might realize. Little Flower only has a month to learn to speak fluently, as she will be going before the Full Council to represent her species for rights as a sentient species."

"Forgive me. I am deaf and can read lips, but sometimes it is hard to make out what someone is saying. Did you say she will be going before the Full Council in a month?" Sina asked.

"Yes," Myra replied.

"That is an incredibly short amount of time. It would be one thing if she already knew how to write, then it's easy enough to learn the signs, but to communicate the concepts that go along with the signs will be difficult. It can take deaf born people years to learn sign language, just like it takes hearing children years to become fluent."

"I understand, but Little Flower does not have years," her mother said.

"In that case, we will need to meet more than once a day. And you will all need to immerse yourself in sign language. From this moment forward, consider yourself deaf, with no other way to communicate except in sign. Outside of these sessions your family should avoid speaking as much as possible. Make it a game if you have to. The first person who speaks loses. Look up words if you don't have them. It's okay if Little Flower doesn't understand the meaning. She'll start to pick up the meaning by the words she does know, just like a cub would."

"What do you think, Marsee?" her mother asked. "The person who messes up the most has to clean the sand out of the compound for a month, no cleaning drones?"

Marsee just looked at her with a conspiratorial glint and nodded 'yes'.

"Good. Let's start by seeing how much you remember from our last session," Sina said, and they went through the words and phrases, making small adjustments where necessary, then moved on to all of the words that they'd picked up on their own. Sina expressed her amazement at how much they'd already learned. When that was done, they covered basic greetings which required some creative acting to convey the meanings to Little Flower and learned the phrase "What is the sign for..." By the end of the session, they'd added several new drawings to the sketch book and their matching signs, and had agreed to meet again at noon the next day. Sina had plans for the rest of the day, but she would clear out her schedule to add a second session after the evening meal going forward.

Marsee texted Ellie asking for primers for Little Flower, which she agreed to bring with her next delivery, planned for the following evening. After that, they took a nap, and then spent the rest of the day practicing and playing games. That evening, her father texted to say that he was spending the night with Marcus, and they let him know about the language lessons, and the bet they'd made. Both her father and Marcus agreed to join in the bet and they would both call in for the next language class.

Later that evening when she was back in her room, and Little Flower had fallen asleep, Marsee called her father to talk to him about what had happened in the kitchen that morning, and to find out if what her mother feared was true. Her father confirmed it and explained some of the nuances, and other possible outcomes. He also thanked her for letting him know, and for making her mother promise not to hurt herself, and then he made the same promise to her as well. After she hung up, she wrote down everything that had happened in her journal, but for her report to the Council and Agency she kept it short.

**Biped Observations**
**By Marsee Bet Chenzira 10165.11.10**

**Summary:**

- Our family is engaging in a full immersion sign language course led by Sina Greyfoot.

- The bipeds have a detailed written language.

**Details:**

We've been able to successfully communicate what happened to the bipeds world. It is my belief that sign language should be learned by everyone on all five worlds, as the modifications we are making for Little Flower's differences in anatomy, such as not having movable ears and tail would make for a wonderful universal language between all of the species. I'm adding the words I know for the other languages, so that others may start learning on their own. This reference document is attached.

I am also uploading Little Flower's drawings and written word for each sign, and we are both starting to learn each other's written language. At this point, she is easily recognizing words and correctly matching them to the sign but is struggling to write them. I've reached out to the Senior Guild Master for primary school supplies, and assistance in teaching her to write. I've also included samples of both her written language, their alphabet, and her attempts at writing ours. As you can see, she is flipping many of our letters.

When she was done, she set her tablet aside and sprawled out on her bed. *Has it really only been five days?* It felt like the little cub had been with them for months. So much had happened in such a short time.

# CHAPTER 5

# Jeran: The Ancient Archives

Jer sat in his shuttle, contemplating all of the decisions in his life that had brought him to this very moment, unable to find the will to leave the shuttle and find out from his mentor just how much trouble they were all in. He hadn't slept a wink the night before, just lay there, curled up next to Myra, wrapped in her strong arms, and listening to the sounds of her breathing. He had missed her so much while she was stuck in quarantine, and had prayed to the Ancient Gods to protect her from whatever unknown illnesses the refugees might have brought with them. Now that he finally had her back, he was quite likely going to lose her again, and this time he wasn't just putting her in harm's way, he was the harm. For now, he could hope that it wasn't as bad as he remembered, but the moment he left the shuttle, he would have to face the reality of what was going to happen in a month.

He heard the swish of the shuttle door as it opened, but didn't turn around to look, and just let out a heavy sigh instead.

"You won't be able to save her if you stay in the shuttle," his mentor said quietly from behind him.

"No, but if I stay in the shuttle, I won't have to be the one to kill her, either," he said quietly back.

"You wouldn't be. We're all going to be lined up next to her. It'll be one of the other Senior Councilors," Marcus said.

"Do you honestly think I'd be able to stand there and let someone else do that to her, Marcus? They'll have to kill me first."

"I suppose that could be arranged," Marcus said dryly. "Do you want me to do it, or have Clear Seas zap you? Probably better if I did it. I hear electrocution is a painful way to go."

"Ha. Ha," Jer said, without a hint of humor and swiveled in his seat to face Marcus, who he found leaning up against the side of the open shuttle door, arms crossed, and looking at him. "So, how bad is it?"

"I don't know. I'm still looking. Ten thousand years of archives is a lot to dig through in less than a day."

"Are you telling me, my mentor, the mighty Marcus Surellis, doesn't know everything?" Jer asked with a mock gasp, clutching his heart dramatically.

Marcus snorted. "I know, shocking isn't it. Just think, now you get to die happy knowing you've seen the impossible. That should be of some comfort to you at least. Now come on. We have a lot of work to do." Marcus nodded in the direction of his compound and walked away.

Jer rubbed his face with his paws, groaned, and followed reluctantly after.

Marcus's compound was quite a bit smaller than Myra's family home, but just as ancient and far less modern than theirs. Where Myra hoarded plants, Marcus hoarded books, most of which, including the entire compound, had once belonged to their grandparents. When they'd died, they'd left the entire thing to Marcus, an avid historian as well as councilor, and Marcus had happily remained here ever since.

Uncle Marcus's was one of Marsee's favorite places to visit, and the moment she showed up, she almost always disappeared into the library. On more than one occasion, Jer had been forced to carry Marsee out by the scruff in order to get her to leave. And like Myra thought, he was pretty sure she'd move in if given half a chance. Marcus led him through the main compound into the library and wound through the stacks until they arrived at a locked door, one he'd rarely been allowed access to. Marcus placed his palm on the keypad to open it, and they entered.

"You know, if you don't leave this place to Marsee, she's going to dig you up and make the healers bring you back to life, just so she can kill you again," Jer teased.

Marcus laughed. "Well thankfully, that's one less thing I have to worry about. She's been my beneficiary since the day she picked the first lock I had on this room."

"Seriously?" Jer asked, not sure if he was more surprised to find out Marsee had picked the lock, or that Marcus had made her his beneficiary.

Marcus turned to look at him. "For all your brilliance, Jer, sometimes you can be an absolute fuzz-brain. Marsee's already been through half of my public library. Where do you think she gets all those books she reads? She walks off with half a dozen or more every time she visits. For that matter, who do you think arranged her meeting with Darvo?"

"Seriously?" Jer asked again.

Marcus rolled his eyes. "I had to make sure she knew how to properly take care of these when I'm gone. I'm not exactly getting any younger." Marcus tossed him a pair of gloves that were thickly padded on the tips to ensure that they wouldn't accidentally damage the ancient documents with their claws.

"Well, that might distract Marsee long enough to get over being mad at us. I just hope you lined up someone to drop off meals for her on a regular basis too," Jer replied, as he slid the gloves on.

Marcus chuckled, tilted his head, and raised his brow, as if making a mental note to do just that.

"Seriously though. She picked the lock?" Jer asked.

Marcus chuckled. "That she did. When she was about ten, I think. Not that it was a very good lock. Thankfully, she didn't do any damage. I found her curled up over there in a corner with an old book of myths and legends from before the Great Awakening. She was absolutely distraught about not being able to finish it, until I told her I had copy she could borrow. I fully intend to give her that book when she earns her masters."

"Well, let's just hope you have the chance to do that in person. Why didn't you say anything though?" Jer asked.

"Last I checked, reading isn't a crime, and she thought the room was locked to keep everyone else out, not family," Marcus replied. "That was her excuse anyway. She never tried again, once I explained how fragile these books are, and showed her where the copies were."

Jer snorted and shook his head at his daughter's audacity. "So where do we start?"

"*You* are going to start by trying to find a record of any case in which a healer accidentally triggered a heat in one of their patients. I spoke with the Healers Guild last night. While the implants sometimes break, due to injury, there are several fail-safes to keep that keep a healer from triggering it by accident. They figure that if it ever did happen, it would have been back when they were perfecting the gender assignment procedure, and that would have been right at the beginning of the Great Awakening, since they only had a single generation to fix the damage we'd done to our species. So, you my boy, get years 1 A.G.A through 300 A.G.A," Marcus said, pointing to a stack of thick volumes, and then carefully pulled one off the shelf, and brought it over to the table in the center of the room for him.

"This isn't the original, is it?" Jer asked, looking at the ancient cover.

"Moons, no. This is a copy, although it's nearly as old. I'd work from the copies, but I don't know when that precedent was stripped. The original is kept in the Ancient Archives and only the Senior Archivist and Senior Council have access and I didn't find anything in the digital archives." Marcus said with a sigh. "My only regret in life is not getting in to see them before I die."

"You know, if you'd accepted the senior councilor position the last five times you were nominated, you'd have been in there already," Jer teased.

"And if I had, you'd have never been able to drag me out of there to run a single resource allocation meeting ever again," Marcus replied.

"True," Jer agreed with a curl of his tail.

"Besides, you know why I wouldn't do it. Same reason you turned it down last time too, if I'm not mistaken," Marcus replied, with far less amusement.

"Fat lot of good that did either one of us," Jer muttered, sitting down and opening the archive. "So, what about you?" Jer said, nodding to the stacks.

"I'm going to keep looking for that moon's forsaken case. I could claw our ancestors right now for conveniently 'forgetting' what the punishment was, instead we get one line in our curriculum 'The punishment for murder is death, within one day of conviction...'" Marcus started.

"'And you don't even want to know what the punishment for rape is,'" Jer finished with a growl.

"Barring any luck with that, we'll research medical malpractice cases where death resulted, failing that, we'll see if we can find any record of councilors being accused. I know of a few but those were all for minor crimes, and the consequences were all pretty much the same, stripped of their position and payment of some form of compensation. I don't think we'll be able to reduce the sentence any further than accessory for us, but I would like to try and find a case where collusion was downgraded to accessory for precedence on our part. We'll research that last though, as I've been informed the Archives are packed right now, as everyone else is looking for the same. As far as Little Flower's sentience is concerned, we have the records of all of the other sentience trials to refer back to, and we know that their cases weren't cut and dry either. The Water World had a lot of their 'issues' swept under the table to allow them to join the Consortium. Many of those issues still exist simply because we can't easily communicate with them, and they rarely leave their home world. Those that do are careful to follow our laws. We may ultimately have better luck finding precedence in the archives of one of the other worlds."

Jer nodded and started reading. They took a brief break for the noon and evening meals, and Jer took a few minutes to check in with

Myra and let her know that he was going to spend the night, and then stepped out again when Marsee called later that evening. They'd had a long conversation about some of the possible consequences, and what she told him made his heart sink. When Marsee asked him to make the same promise, he did, but the entire time his heart was screaming at her. *You're asking me to make the wrong promise, Marsee.* He couldn't say it though, because he knew he'd have to break it.

After that, he took a walk outside for some fresh air to clear his head, before calling Myra. She'd been reasonably upbeat and pleased with the progress Marsee and Little Flower had been making with sign language, and he'd been shocked to hear Little Flower was already learning how to read and write. After the call he'd sat outside for a long time, staring up at the stars, and praying to moons to help him find a way out of this mess, before making his way back in to continue reading, and inform Marcus about Little Flower's progress.

Marcus was elated. "That'll certainly make it easier to prove her sentience. When's the last time you've heard of a chenzie learning to read and write? Even Paxton will have to acknowledge that," Marcus said.

Jer shrugged and rolled his eyes. "Knowing Paxton, we could have Little Flower stand in front of the Council and recite the Charter and he'd still deny it."

Marcus frowned and then tilted his head. "That's actually not a bad idea, especially if Little Flower is already learning how to read. We could have the Senior Council pick a section and have her read it back to them, or perhaps a cubs book, depending on how fluent she is by the trial."

Jer nodded and they went back to work. It was well past midnight when they finally gave up for the night and went to bed.

The next morning Jer woke to find Marsee's report, which he shared with Marcus over breakfast. "Marsee's suggestion of a universal language using sign is intriguing too. I'm sending that on to the Senior Council for consideration. Regardless of what happens, I'm sure Clear Seas will be interested," Jer told his mentor.

"That he will. That could have a huge impact on his people and their ability to interact with the rest of us," Marcus said, as he absently read the latest news. "Looks like we might get that storm after all. I'm going to lock up the compound before we get started, just in case. Why don't you bring your shuttle around to the back bay. That one is far more secure. I don't have shields, just old-fashioned stone walls, and I could use your help to shutter up the external windows.

"Let me guess, you still haven't automated any of it?" Jer asked.

"I like the antiquity of my compound. Why waste electricity on modern conveniences when a little bit of effort will suffice?" Marcus replied.

A little bit of effort ended up taking both of them more than an hour of work to complete. Marcus apparently also liked having a lot of natural light in his ancient compound too. They were just bolting the last shutter in place when the wind started to pick up. Jer turned to look in the direction the wind was coming from, and reached back and tapped Marcus on the shoulder. "I think I'm going to be staying here for a while."

Marcus turned. "Yup. Sure looks that way."

"Have you ever seen a storm front that big before?" Jer asked, marveling at the wall of sand in front of them.

"Once when I was a small cub. It lasted almost a half week if I remember correctly. Still, this old compound can easily withstand whatever that beast has in store for us. On the plus side, it'll give us more time to read."

They made their way around to the front door just as the first of the sands started to ping. Safely back inside, Jer returned to the small living room where they'd been eating breakfast to grab his tablet, and saw both a message and a missed call from Myra, and frowned. Something had happened, he just knew it.

"I've got a missed call from Myra, I'll meet you in the Archives after I've spoken with her," he told Marcus. Marcus nodded and left to give him some privacy. Taking a deep breath, he placed the return call to Myra.

# CHAPTER 6

# Jessica: Truce

Jessica only partially woke from another nightmare, to feel her grandfather's old cat Skittles settling in beside her, its weight warm and comforting. She hugged the old cat and listened to the windchimes out the open window, the curtains dancing in the light of three moons as she fell back to sleep, feeling both safe and secure.

When she fully woke up some time later, it took her a long time to realize she was no longer in her grandfather's old farm house, and that it had all been a dream. The soft fur at her side was not the old yellow tomcat, who had died many years before, but the end of Marsee's fluffy tail, and the windchimes nothing but the memory of a sound she would never hear again. Stifling a sob, she sat up and made her way down to the hole of muck, careful to not wake Marsee. She was thrilled she no longer had to wait for Marsee to take her, and was pretty sure that was the best thing that had happened so far, but her emotions were all over the place.

Climbing back up the steep ramp, she sat on the edge of the balcony, legs dangling off the side for a long time, just staring out at the strange landscape lit up by the three moons. After the long conversation with Marsee and her mother the other night, she'd sat for a long time on the outside of the compound, leaning up against one of the massive outer doors, looking out at the desert, and trying to decide what to do.

Gather supplies and run away, stay and make this her home, have the child or not?

It was pretty clear they were trying to let her know she was free to come and go as she pleased. There was still a big part of her that wanted to just walk out into the desert and let some creature fly off with her, because it would be far easier than dealing with everything she'd learned. She'd been holding out hope that she'd be able to find her way home again someday, but now she knew there was nothing left to go back to. Everyone and everything she'd ever known was dead and gone, and she was pregnant.

*Pregnant. What a horrible life-altering word,* she thought. Raising a child hadn't even been on her radar before the asteroid, and she'd never really thought about whether she wanted kids or not. She'd been praying she wasn't, but now she had no idea how many of her species even remained. Would she doom her species to extinction if she didn't have the baby? Would they even allow her to terminate the pregnancy if that's what she decided she wanted? Would they allow her to keep it? She wasn't an adult yet, or at least she didn't think she was. She still had no idea how long she'd been kept in quarantine. How could she care for a child when she barely knew how to care for herself. She was small for her age, small enough that the cats had thought she wasn't old enough to conceive. Would she be able to give birth safely? What if something happened? Would they know how to save her?

She had absolutely no idea what to do. All she knew was that it was entirely up to her what she wanted to make of her life now, and she had no idea what she wanted there either. Exhausted, overwhelmed, and chilly in the cooler night air, she'd returned to the warm comfort of her friend's room, unable to decide what to do. She'd just felt too raw to make any kind of decision at that moment.

Now, a day later, she found herself sitting out on the balcony, woken again by a nightmare she barely remembered, and looked down at the ground far below her wondering if she should just slide off and end it all. She had no more of an idea about what she wanted to do now, than she'd had the day before, but the day had been one of the best since she'd arrived. Without the ever-present hatred for them clouding her thoughts, she found she really liked spending time with Marsee. Their ability to communicate was improving by leaps and bounds, and Marsee's mother was starting to learn too. They were trying to make her feel welcome, and were no longer treating her like an animal or prisoner, but as a guest. Marsee's mother had clearly been distraught over her role in her rape, and that had eased her anger significantly. She no longer blamed anyone but *him* for raping her. From the halting conversations she'd had with Marsee's mother the other night, it was clear that while they wanted to save her species, they did not want it to be done like this.

As she sat there on the edge of the balcony, she reflected on her time on this world through the lens of this new information, trying to decide if this was a world that she wanted to be any part of. Could she live with these people, trust them, raise a child. If what they said was true, then yes. The video they'd shown her had clearly been spliced and edited together, to show a very specific narrative. The real question was whether or not she believed it. She couldn't figure out any reason why they'd lie about it though, or why their Council thought she was an animal.

The Jessica of her childhood was gone, buried in the ashes of Earth. She'd been freed of the Jess of her captivity, and now had a new name. *But who was this Little Flower?* she asked herself. *What did she want?*

Her thoughts eventually began to drift, lost in memory and the grief of the family she knew in her heart was dead, when a long ago, almost forgotten memory popped into her head. She'd been visiting with her Grandpa Ben and Uncle James at their farm across the lake one summer, and they were all sitting on their big front porch. Her grandfather and uncle were rocking gently in two brightly painted rainbow-colored wooden rocking chairs, shucking the peas they'd just gathered from their garden. Jessica sat on the step, her back up against the railing trying to help, although likely eating far more of the yummy peas than made it into her bowl. She'd only been maybe four or five at the time, she thought, and her grandfather was explaining how James was not really her uncle but was going to become her Grandpa James when they married the following month, and how they wanted her to be their flower girl for the wedding.

"Family isn't about who you are born to, it's about heart, and about the people you want in your life. Some people have abusive parents or spouses, and that's not family. Family is the people you love and who love you back. It's about who takes care of you when you're sick, and who you can't wait to share the day's adventures with. It's the people who make you a better person by being around them, who bring you joy, friendship, and laughter. When you find those people, make them your family and hold them close, even if the law says otherwise. That's what we did with James. Since I couldn't marry him, we did the next best thing at the time, which was a civil union. We've just told everyone he's my unofficially adopted brother because it was safer for both of us. Now, I get to make him family in the eyes of the law, not just in my heart," her grandfather explained.

"I'm glad Uncle James is going to be family for real then!" she'd replied, with the immediate acceptance of a young child. "He has the bestest heart!"

"I think so too, child," Grandpa Ben had said, reaching out to hold her uncle's hand and look at him with love.

Wiping tears from her eyes at the memory, she turned and saw Marsee sound asleep on the strange, but fantastical hanging bed. *Well cat, you're all I've got. Does that make you my family now, or is all of this just temporary?* She wondered what was going to happen to her and her people and shook her head at the millions of still unanswered questions she had.

Shivering slightly in the cool night air, she let out a heavy sigh, stood and carefully climbed back into bed, snuggling into Marsee's warm fur. She smiled as the big cat shifted and laid her warm furry arm across her side, holding her secure, and purring. Safe and protected, and most importantly, not alone, she was soon fast asleep.

# CHAPTER 7

# Marsee: Out on a Limb

The next morning, they both woke early, long before her alarm went off, scrounged up some food, and at Little Flower's request, made their way out into the garden to eat. It was a beautiful morning. Not quite the scorcher it would likely soon be, and the garden, cool and peaceful. Once there, Marsee picked a shady spot by the pool and placed the tray of fruit and drinks on the ground, before flopping down next to it. Little Flower sat down next to her in that pretzel-like pose she seemed to prefer, the one that made Marsee's hips ache just to watch.

"How you sit?" Marsee signed, and did her best to cross her legs the same way, which didn't even come close to what the cub was doing.

The little cub just shrugged and popped another piece of fruit in her mouth, and then grinning shifted so her legs were sticking straight out to the side. "Good sit?" the cub replied and shifted again, this time with her legs going straight out in front and back. "Good?"

Marsee just stared at her. "How?" she signed in disbelief.

The cub laughed and just returned to her original position. Marsee shook her head. She'd never seen a creature with bones that was so flexible in so many different directions, and she wondered what evolutionary purpose that served.

When Little Flower was done with her breakfast she stood, stretched her back and started wandering around the garden. Marsee watched while she finished her own breakfast, her thoughts distracted and jumbled with worry for her parents, and concern for the little cub. *She seems to be in a better mood today, at least,* Marsee thought, as Little Flower smelled the flowers, examined the statues, and climbed onto the giant stabilizer roots to walk along the top of them. She eventually wandered back over to the pool and stuck her feet in it for a while, laughing, as the fish tickled the bottom of her feet.

Marsee wished she'd brought her tablet with her, as it would have made a wonderful video to share on the guild board. *Maybe she'll draw the scene later,* Marsee thought. *If not, maybe I will. I haven't painted anything in a while.* The illustrations she'd been fixing in the old books took precision and delicacy to match the style, and were fun and challenging to work on, but they weren't her works, and outside of inventing clothing for the cub, and the puzzle boxes, Marsee hadn't done anything creative or strictly artistic for a while, and her paws twitched. *Maybe I'll try out my new tablet and see what it can do.*

She briefly wondered if the cub was going to jump in the water and swim. She didn't though, and after a while Little Flower put her foot protection back on, and instead started examining the bandala tree and the spigots that dripped water into the pond. After taking a tentative sip, Little Flower shrugged and proceeded to start walking around the tree, checking out the vine covered feeder roots, and peering up into the tree. *It must seem so big to her,* Marsee thought. *It's got to be at least a hundred times taller than she is.* The bandala trees were the tallest tree on all five planets as far as she knew and this one was ancient and massive, both in height and diameter. Little Flower was nearly on the other side of the tree, almost out of Marsee's view when she grabbed ahold of some of the roots near the edge of the pool and pulled a little, apparently seeing how sturdy they were, because before Marsee could fully realize what she intended to do, the little cub scampered up the lattice of roots and into the base of the tree.

Marsee blinked in shock at how quickly and easily the cub had climbed them, and then ran over and peered up after her. "Little Flower, get back down here!" she yelled as loud as she could, hoping the cub could hear her, since she'd heard her yell at her mother the day before. She was absolutely terrified that Little Flower would fall. *She doesn't even have claws to hold onto the tree with!* If she heard, Little Flower didn't show any sign of it. She just kept climbing until Marsee couldn't see her anymore. She scanned the branches frantically, and then another thought crossed her mind: *The fruit! It's poisonous!*

Unsure of what else to do, Marsee tried to figure out how to climb up after her. She reached up to grab one of the feeder roots, but it easily snapped under her weight, so she shifted over to one of the bigger support roots and awkwardly scrabbled her way up. She hadn't climbed anything in years, not since she was a little cub and had to climb onto all of the furniture, and her paws ached with the strain of supporting her much bigger body. She finally made it to the base of the canopy and grabbed one of the branches to pull herself up onto. Once on the branch, she stopped to flex her aching claws, and looked down to find she was directly over the pool and much higher up than she'd realized.

Before she could decide on her next move, the branch she was on suddenly snapped, and she yelped in surprise as she fell, landing with a splash in the pool. Spluttering and in a panic, she started thrashing in a desperate attempt to make her way over to the side of the pool. She didn't know how to swim. *I'm going to drown!* Marsee thought, as she started choking on the water in her panic.

***Stand up, you idiot!*** her instinct chided her.

Ears back in surprise at the unexpected advice, and laughing at her own stupidity, she stood. The water only came up to her shoulders. She sloshed her way over to the edge and climbed out. Shaking her fur hard to remove as much of the water as she could, she started pacing around the tree looking for another way up. Picking another spot, where there were larger branches, she tried again, this time trying to keep her weight off of the branches, but she didn't get very far before her claws, unused to climbing, went from a dull ache to screaming with pain. She tried to put just some of her weight on a branch to relieve some of the strain and it snapped too, sending her skidding back down the tree. She leapt off before she ended up in the pool again and briefly checked her claws to make sure they were still attached. Torn and scuffed but still there, she looked up in horror at the giant tree. She couldn't climb up after the cub and had no idea how to get her back down safely. Heart in her throat with worry, she bolted out of the garden to find her mother, praying she might have some idea how to rescue the cub.

She checked her mother's office first, but the door was wide open and the room empty. Then she ran to her parents' room. She wasn't there either. "Mama?!" she yelled, over and over again, checking every room she thought her mother might be in. *Where is she?!* Unable to find her mother, she ran back out in the courtyard on her way back to the tower to grab her tablet and looked up to check on the cub. She was pretty sure her heart stopped beating at the sight. Little Flower was almost all the way to the top of the massive tree, sitting out on a branch overlooking the garden and courtyard. Little Flower saw Marsee down below and waved a paw at her.

"Little Flower, no!" Marsee signed and then pointed down.

"No. Little Flower happy!" came the distant reply.

*Happy? How can she be happy that high up? I'd be terrified. That branch could break at any moment!* Marsee thought, praying it was strong enough to support the tiny cub's weight, where the bigger branches lower down clearly hadn't been strong enough to support her own.

As if sensing her thoughts, the wind blew, causing the branch Little Flower was on to sway. Little Flower grabbed ahold of it to steady herself, and let out a high pitched terrified screech. Marsee turned and bolted up the ramp to her room, running faster than she'd ever run before. Careening off the doorway with a thud she knew would leave a bruise later, she slid to a stop in her room, her already battered claws screeching on the stone. She frantically looked around for her tablet but couldn't find it. *Where did I leave it?* Finally, she remembered using it that morning to turn off the alarm and tossing it down before getting off the bed. She ran over and scanned the bed but didn't see it. Grabbing Little Flower's blanket, she yanked it off the bed. *There it is!* She grabbed the tablet and flipped it open with such haste that she fumbled and almost dropped it.

She frantically called her mother as she walked back over to the balcony. *Pick up, pick up, pick up!* she thought as the tablet rang and rang. Marsee looked up, scanning the tree that towered above her, to find Little Flower still sitting on that branch. *At least she hasn't fallen. Where are you, Mama?! Pick up!*

Thankfully, a moment later, her mother finally answered. "Hello!" her mother signed with a smile.

"Not now, where are you?" she asked.

"I'm in the storage bay, why?" her mother asked, then seeing Marsee's panic on the screen, "What's wrong?"

"It's Little Flower. She's stuck in the tree!" Marsee explained in a rush.

"She's what?!" her mother exclaimed.

"Little Flower is stuck in the tree," she repeated slower. "She climbed all the way to the top of the bandala tree and now she's stuck out on a branch!"

"I'll be right there," her mother said and hung up.

Marsee tossed her tablet back on the bed and bolted down the ramp at a full run on all fours, tripped at the bottom, and almost crashed into her mother as she tucked and rolled to a stop.

"Where is she?" her mother asked, as she helped Marsee up from the undignified sprawl that she'd landed in.

Marsee looked up and pointed. "There!"

"How under the thrice forsaken dark moons did she get all the way up there?!" her mother exclaimed in utter amazement, tinged with terror. To Marsee's astonishment, her mother's tail was fully poofed, something she'd never seen before. Marsee's was as well, so much so that it hurt. Little Flower was several stories above than Marsee's balcony, out on a tiny branch that didn't seem even remotely big enough to support her. A fall from that height would surely kill her. Marsee knew she couldn't survive a fall that high without serious injury.

"And why are you all wet? Did you have another issue with your instinct?" her mother asked, looking back at her.

"No, she was wandering around the garden and climbed the tree before I could stop her. I tried climbing up, but the branches wouldn't support my weight and I fell in the pool," Marsee explained.

Little Flower looked down, saw them both watching her, and waved again.

"Little Flower get down here!" Marsee signed again.

"No! Little Flower happy play fun!" came the reply and then a screech as another breeze caused the branch to sway again, causing her to grab ahold with both arms this time.

"Is she too scared to come down?" her mother asked, not as good at all of the signs yet.

"No. The little hairless star-fruit-drinking tree-climbing daredevil doesn't *want* to come down. She says she's 'having fun'," Marsee translated in absolute disbelief. Marsee liked heights, especially the height of her tower, but that was solid and secure, not a fragile branch that bucked and swayed in the breeze. Marsee's stomach did a little flip at the idea of being out on that branch and she was almost sick.

"Mama, what are we going to do? What if she falls or eats one of the fruits?" Marsee cried.

"Little Flower, please come down!" her mother yelled out, but of course Little Flower didn't hear, and didn't even look in their direction. Her mother tried again, raising her deeper voice as high as she could, still nothing.

Marsee waved her arms frantically trying to get Little Flower's attention. It worked and Little Flower looked down at them. But then she turned her head and looked at something off in the distance, and frowned as another gust made the branch sway even more this time. This time Little Flower didn't screech. Her eyes stayed locked on whatever it was she saw in the distance.

"Marsee, look. Danger!" Little Flower signed and pointed. Marsee turned to look at what Little Flower was pointing at. She was pretty sure her heart skipped three beats, stopped, skipped another two, and then dove under a rock to hide.

"Mama..." Marsee barely squeaked, "...sandstorm," just as her mother's tablet blared with warning of the impending storm. Her mother turned to look where Marsee indicated. A massive wall of sand took up the entire western horizon. Flashes of lightning flickered as the sands caused electricity to spark along the front. Sandstorms were common this time of year, but this was the biggest storm Marsee had ever seen.

"Where did she go? Did she fall?" her mother cried.

Marsee turned and looked back up at the tree. "There! I see her! She's moved back to the inner part of the tree and is climbing down," Marsee cried with relief, and she and her mother ran into the garden and circled the base of the tree to try and find her again.

"There!" her mother pointed, spotting her first.

They watched anxiously as Little Flower made her slow way down. She was about a quarter of the way down, when a massive gust caused the tree to sway violently. Little Flower screeched as her foot slipped, and she slid down the side of the trunk, unable to maintain her grasp.

"Little Flower!" Both Marsee and her mother cried out as the cub fell, hitting a branch hard with a scream before sliding off that one, and falling another twenty feet and bouncing off of several more, before finally being able to grab onto another branch and stop her fall. Dangling from one arm, she swung her body until she managed to get her other paw on the branch. They watched in a mix of horror and relief as Little Flower swung a leg up and pulled herself onto the branch and sat there for several moments, catching her breath.

Another massive gust rocked the tree but Little Flower maintained her grip this time, hugging the branch tightly as the tree bucked and swayed beneath her.

"Marsee, I need you to go lock up the compound and cover the hydroponics units. I'll stay here with Little Flower and make sure she gets down safely," her mother ordered.

"But Mama," Marsee whined, not wanting to leave Little Flower's side, as she waited for the cub to resume her climb down the tree.

"I can't turn on the static shields until she's out of the tree and the outer doors are shut. I don't know what would happen if I turn the shields on while she's still up there. And if we don't have the doors closed and the plants covered when the front hits, we could lose all the crops and the hydroponics units."

This was only partially true, but Marsee didn't know that. It needed to be done, but Myra really just wanted her daughter out of the garden, in case Little Flower slipped again, and fell to her death. She didn't want her daughter to see that. It had been horrible enough seeing Little Flower fall the first time, and judging by how the cub was now gasping for breath and holding her sides she'd been injured when she hit those branches, which meant she would have a much harder time climbing down, if she even could.

Marsee hesitated, torn between her need to see her friend safely down to the ground, and preventing the loss of the crops, which fed many of the families in their area.

"GO!" her mother commanded with a fierce growl.

Marsee ran. There was no arguing with her mother when she used *that* voice. She ran through the inner courtyard archway and out to the hydroponics units. There was an emergency switch on the far wall. Running so fast she slid into the wall with a thud, she flipped open the protective covering and pulled the lever. Turning she saw each of the hydroponics units were going into shut down mode. Large shields made out of the same fabric used for the main sun shields, were being raised up and over each unit to form a protective arch. The fabric would help block the wind and sands, but they wouldn't hold up for long, not against a storm that size. They were designed more to help deflect the settling sands after the other shields were up, and to protect the delicate crops from the heavy rains in the spring.

A light next to the switch flashed blue, indicating a problem with one of the units. Marsee ran through the courtyard looking desperately for the malfunctioning unit, finally finding it on the other side. It was the one she'd thought sounded funny, and that she and Little Flower had both heard. In all the craziness of the past few days it hadn't been fixed. The shield was stuck halfway up and flapped madly in the growing breeze. Marsee ran over to it and yanked on the frame of the shield. It didn't budge. She pulled as hard as she could and then kicked the motor hard.

"Take that you stupid, brain-itching, piece of squeaky machinery!" she yelled in frustration, as she continued to yank on the shield with everything she had. There was a loud grinding noise, and then suddenly the shield came crashing down, tossing Marsee on her butt.

Picking herself up, Marsee ran to the nearest door to the inner garden, and hit the switch to close it. They rarely used this door, but her mother had opened every single door in the compound the other night in order to let Little Flower know she was free to come and go as she pleased, and hadn't bothered shutting them yet. The door didn't budge. She hit the override, and then using everything she had, she slammed the first half of the door shut. These doors were at least four thousand years old, weighed nearly twenty times her own weight, and based on how slowly it moved, the hinges likely hadn't been oiled in years. Once she finally had the second half closed, she turned the wheel that put the massive locking bar in place. She ran to the next and to the next, and thankfully those closed without issue. She only left the one they normally used open so that her mother and Little Flower could exit.

The inner garden protected as much as possible, she ran to close the four outer storm doors to the compound. They would need to be shut before the sun shields could be deployed, or the wind from the storm would get underneath and just rip them off. Even still, if she didn't get the doors shut, her mother couldn't turn on the static shield that surrounded the compound, and without them, the sun shields wouldn't last ten minutes in a storm this size.

She made it to the first door and hit the switch, but nothing happened. She swore, running outside to manually shut them. As she did, she realized that they'd just been locked in place to keep them open. She flipped the lock off of both doors, swallowing hard at the approaching storm front that was nearly upon them as she did, and ran back inside to hit the switch. They shut without issue and Marsee swung the locking wheel to bolt the doors in place and took off for the second door, which was the one closest to the storm front.

Just as she made it to the second door, the edge of the storm front hit and sand nearly blinded her, getting into her fur and stinging her eyes and palms. She quickly ducked outside, shielding her eyes with her arm, and wishing she had Little Flower's eye protection. She undid the locks and ran back inside to hit the switch but nothing happened. "Not you too!" she swore at it and hit it again. "Come on! Close already!" The door didn't budge. "Dark moons!" she spat, and flipped the manual override and started to pull. The door still didn't budge more than a few inches. Looking down, she realized that sand was already starting to drift against the base. She kicked at the sand and pulled again. It shifted about a foot and then got stuck by the sand again. She kicked and pulled until it had closed enough that the wind shifted from fighting against her to slamming the door shut with such force that she was thrown back, landing hard on her tail.

Marsee stood slowly and checked that her throbbing tail still worked, before digging at the sand on the other half of the door. The sand was even deeper now and it took her several minutes to get the sand cleared enough to budge the door, as the wind kept blowing more against it. Eyes firmly closed and ears pressed tightly to the side of her skull to protect them from the stinging sand, she kicked and pulled until the storm took over and sent her flying again. She was expecting it this time, and managed to tuck and roll. Picking herself up off the ground, she locked the doors and started running down the hallway for the third entrance.

Making her way carefully out into the storm again, she felt her way along the wall until she found the lock. The moment she unhooked it, the door slammed shut, caught by the wind. She made her way over to the other side and unlatched it and quickly ducked back inside and hit the switch, praying it would work. The door slowly closed, bringing in a good foot of sand with it. She had to kick some of the sand out of the way before the door would completely shut, but the moment it did, she quickly bolted them in place and ran for the final door.

Sand swirled down the hallway through the still open inner doors, but she ignored them as she needed to get the outer doors shut first. When she came to the final outer door she was nearly blown off her feet as she entered the hallway. Eyes closed and ears pinned, she felt her way outside and around the wall of the compound. Now slightly protected from the force of the winds, she opened her eyes just enough to quickly find the latch and unhooked the door, turned, and made her way across the opening, covering her eyes with her paws so she could keep them open, just enough to see to make her way across, now worried she'd lose her way in the storm. She couldn't see more than a few feet in front of her now and if she got turned around, she'd never find her way back. Thankfully, she made it safely across, found the lock, and forced her way back inside to hit the switch but nothing happened.

She cried out in both frustration and fear, and made her way back out into the storm to try and manually close them. Here though, the sand wasn't drifting against the door, but the moment she made it half-way, she was having to pull against the full force of the wind that was now howling through the tunnel of the hallway. She had to close both doors in order to lock them, but she couldn't hold them in place long enough to lock the doors down. The third time the doors were ripped out of her paws and she found herself thrown to the ground, she just lay there, panting from exhaustion and fear, as thunder and lightning crackled all around her. If she was struggling this hard, poor Little Flower stood very little chance of climbing down the tree safely, and she howled in her grief and despair for the friend she was sure she had lost.

# CHAPTER 8

# Jessica: Storm Front

Panting heavily from both her fear and pain, Jessica gripped tightly to the tree branch, and struggled to take a full breath. Her lungs hitched in pain with every inhale, and it was making her dizzy. She held on with everything she had as another massive gust tried to knock her off again. Her side hurt horribly, her hands were raw and bleeding from the bark of the tree, and she'd somehow lost one of her shoes. Her hat was long gone, but her sunglasses had miraculously stayed on her face. Deep in her stomach, she felt the distant rumble of thunder, and looked up again at the approaching storm front, now significantly closer than it had been. Lightning danced along it, confirming the sound she thought she'd heard.

She'd climbed the tree, both because she'd always loved climbing trees, and because she had a feeling it was the one place in the entire compound the big cats couldn't go. She didn't think the smaller branches would hold their weight and as neither Marsee or her mother had climbed up to get her, she figured her suspicions were correct, but for her it had been an almost perfect climbing tree, the way the branches weaved and twisted around each other. That fact had saved her life as those very same branches had slowed her fall enough for her to catch one again, but she was now paying dearly for her small act of defiance and few minutes of blissful freedom. The view had been awe inspiring, but now made her nauseous when she realized how much further down she had to go to reach safety.

Terrified, in pain, and far more cautious than before, she started descending again. Each step down caused her shoulder, which had been wrenched hard while grabbing for the branch to stop her fall, and her side, that had taken the full brunt of her impact on several of the branches, to scream in pain, but she did her best to ignore it. If she didn't get down out of the tree quickly, she would be dead, either from being blown off or from lightning hitting the tree. When she realized she had a better grip without her shoes, she flicked off the second one and watched it flutter to the ground. It felt like it was taking forever as she made her way down the tree but she didn't dare rush, afraid she'd fall again.

The wind continued to pick up, and gritty sand started pinging off her sunglasses. Thankful for their protection, she kept her grip tight and her focus only on the next branch and the next. She nearly slipped again as another massive gust of wind caught her clothes and tried to pull her off, but she managed to hold on until it eased some and kept going. She had to stop twice, dizzy with pain, to wait until she felt safe enough to move on. Eventually she finally made it to the canopy line, where only the twisting lattice of roots remained. The storm had strengthened and lightning flashed all around her now. A loud clap of thunder made her jump, unused to hearing loud noises, or anything for that matter. She had no idea how she hadn't been electrocuted yet. The tree should have been a massive lightning rod. *Then again, maybe the lightning was hitting it, and not being affected. Who knew what such giant alien trees could have for defenses,* she thought. *They must be common targets for storms.*

She looked down and Myra held her arms out to her to jump, but Jessica shook her head and signed hurt, touching her side. Marsee's mother frowned and motioned for her to hurry as another burst of lighting lit up the sky. Jessica carefully shifted onto the lattice but had only made it a few feet when another gust of wind caught her, pushing her away from the tree just as the branch she was holding onto snapped. She screamed as she fell, bracing for the hard impact of the ground, more than forty feet below her, but instead of the ground, Myra caught her and cushioned her fall.

Jessica yelped with pain from the impact and Myra's paws as they curled around her sides. Myra quickly set her on the ground and lifted her shirt up and frowned at the nasty bruise that was already forming and quickly examined the cuts on her hands. Jessica didn't bother with mentioning her feet and shoulder. Myra frowned, and tried to pick her up again but Jessica shook her head no as being held had hurt far worse. The cat sighed, and motioned for her to follow. She did her best to keep up with the fast-moving cat, but a slow jog was the best she could manage, trying to breathe through the pain. Exiting the inner garden, Marsee's mother slammed the massive stone doors shut, locking them in place with a spin of an equally massive wheel, and then looked up at the sky before motioning her to follow again, and taking off across the courtyard.

Sand was blowing everywhere now. Jessica pulled her shirt up to protect her nose and mouth from the sand, and started to cross the courtyard to catch up, when she saw something fly out of Marsee's room. Realizing that the doors to Marsee's room had been left open, Jessica took off at the fastest run she could manage, ignoring the pain in her side. She thought she heard something but didn't stop to look back.

She was gasping for breath by the time she made it to the top of the steep ramp, the pain in her side a constant agony now. The wind barreled through Marsee's room and nearly sent her flying over the balcony as the full brunt of the storm front hit. Sand stung her eyes, getting in and around the sunglasses, and reduced her visibility to only a few feet in front of her. Entering the room, her vision cleared slightly, and she saw several of Marsee's items had been blown over and scattered across the floor. The crates she'd used to store her clothing were knocked over and one of her new shirts flew past. Sand covered everything. Several items flew off the wildly rocking bed and she realized it was Marsee's hearing aids and tablet. The case with the hearing aids started sliding across the floor, pushed by the gale force winds. Jessica ran and grabbed it and then the tablet, shoving them both in her overly large pockets for safe keeping, then fought her way over to the door facing the storm and tried to shut it but it wouldn't budge. Suddenly the door started moving, and she looked up to see that Marsee's mother was there. Once all four doors were secured, the giant cat carefully scooped her up avoiding her side and started working her way back down the ramp. Jessica didn't fight her this time as she wasn't sure she could keep from being blown off the tower with the force of the wind, and buried her head in Myra's fur to escape the stinging sands.

At the bottom, and out of the worst of the wind, Jessica looked up and saw that the shields were closing across the courtyard but flapped hard, as a door still remained open to the outside. She could see Marsee struggling to close the door, the wind too strong even for her. She watched as Marsee was thrown to the ground, the doors ripped from her paws. Running over, Marsee's mother shifted Jessica and grabbed her with her tail, swinging her around so that she was now pressed against the big cat's back. Jessica grabbed fistfuls of fur to hold on and yelped from the pain of Myra's tail, but Myra didn't let go of her and used both hands to force the massive doors shut, so Marsee could lock them in place.

Jessica couldn't see what was going on, with her head pressed into the big cat's back, but she could feel the mighty cat's muscles bulging with the effort to fight the wind. The suddenness of the wind stopping almost made her lose her grip, but before she could slide off, Myra peeled her off her back, and plunked her into Marsee's waiting hands. Jessica winced as her side was battered again in the transfer but just looked up with a grin and smiled at the two cats, not sure if they were mad at her for climbing the tree or not. Marsee seemed ecstatic to see her safe and hugged her tightly, making her yelp in pain, but her mother seemed upset and the tip of her tail shivered.

After shutting the inner doors to the courtyard, the three of them made their way to the shower room, or whatever the heck the device was, and Marsee and her mother both used it, before Myra had her remove her clothing. Jessica frowned, not having anything else to wear, but it was all badly ripped and torn anyway. Only her sunglasses were really salvageable. As far as Jessica could tell, they hadn't even been scratched. It was probably the only thing that had kept her eyes from being gouged out by the sands.

*I really need to thank my fairy godmother for these,* Jessica thought, as she set them down and started to pull off her shirt. She winced with the effort to undress, and looked up to see Myra with her ears flat to her head and her tail lashing. *Oh crap. I'm in trouble now,* she thought, but to her surprise the big cat calmed herself and just kneeled down next to her, to look at the growing purple bruises on her side and the cuts that covered her from head to toe. A gentle touch to her side made her wince and step away. Myra's tail twitched twice. Jessica wasn't sure if she was mad about the bruise or because she'd moved away.

With another frown, Marsee's mother led her over to stand in the circle that indicated where the shower was. Once Myra left the circle, a clear shield started to close around her. Suddenly a gust of wind wrapped around her, causing her hair to stick straight up in a spiral, then drop suddenly as the wind stopped. Then something passed over her causing her skin to tingle and vibrate, but when it passed over the bruises on her side she yelped from the pain it caused. As the light passed below, the vibration caused the cuts on her hands and feet, which had mostly stopped bleeding, as they were packed with sand, to open up and start bleeding again as the sand was removed. She hissed from the pain but stayed put.

When the clear shield lifted, Marsee picked her up with exaggerated care to avoid the massive bruise on her side. Myra frowned at the blood left behind and picked up her feet, scowling at them before saying something to Marsee. Marsee carried her to her mother's office, leaving the tattered remains of her clothes behind and laying discarded on the floor, and set her down on the padded table. Myra grabbed her bag of medical equipment and brought it over, setting it on the table beside her.

Pulling out her scanner, she examined the massive bruise on her side and frowned at whatever it was she saw. Marsee must have said something because moments later, the big monitor in the room turned on and she could now see a very detailed scan of her body that showed the bruise, then descended through the muscle to the bone where a very visible crack could be seen in two of her ribs. *No wonder it hurts to breathe,* she thought. Marsee held the scanner where her mother indicated, keeping it pointed at her side, while Myra picked up another device, before wrapping one of her massive paws around Jessica's other side and back, holding her firmly in place. Pressing the device against her side she pushed a button that caused a light to appear on the monitor.

Moving the light to where the crack was, she pushed another button and Jessica screamed. The pain felt like she was being stabbed with a hot knife. She couldn't breathe and tried to get away but Marsee's mother held her so tightly she couldn't move, and flexed her claws in warning that she needed to stay still. Jessica closed her eyes and gritted her teeth as she endured the treatment. Gradually the pain lessened to a dull throb. Opening her eyes and wiping away the tears that streamed down her face, Jessica saw on the screen that the broken ribs now had a white line where the cracks had been. *Healed or just repaired?* she wondered. Still, it didn't hurt as bad to breathe and she could sit upright again.

Setting the two devices down, Myra grabbed a jar, which she hoped was more of that miracle pain cream, but instead scooped out a much thicker and bright green substance that reminded her of the ooze or putty she used to have when she was a kid and motioned for her to spread her fingers out wide. Myra gently spread it out on her palm and fingers, covering the ragged and bleeding cuts, but didn't rub it in. It hurt to open her hands fully and the goo stung, causing her to hiss but she didn't pull her hand away. Myra picked up a small device and ran a blue light over it. This changed the putty from green, to light green, and then finally to white. When the putty had turned white, Myra turned off the device, and motioned for her to open and close her fist. She did and realized the putty had attached to her skin, feeling kind of like a tight rubber glove, grippy but not sticky. She took a nail to the edge, but it didn't come off her skin. *It's a bandage!* She realized it must be the same thing they'd used to treat her wounds at the Agency, and as she examined it, the pain in her hand went away. *A bandage with built-in pain killers! I could really get used to this planet,* she thought.

Myra did the same with her other palm, both feet and a couple of the larger cuts on her side. *I wonder how well this stuff holds up to heat and sand. If it holds up, maybe I could just get this permanently applied to my feet so I don't have to wear shoes.*

Jessica pointed to her shoulder, which was the last remaining major injury. With everything else treated it now throbbed. She was honestly surprised she hadn't dislocated it. Myra scanned her shoulder as well, frowned, and pulled out another jar out of her bag. This time it was the miracle pain cream. Myra spread it carefully over shoulder, the massive bruise on her side, and the dozens of smaller bruises and cuts that covered her that hadn't been covered by the other bandage goop. The relief nearly made her cry.

She felt much better now although she was embarrassed to be naked in front of them again, but if they didn't seem to care she decided not to either. The harness and gloves Marsee had made didn't really count as clothing, and hers were likely all ruined or halfway across the desert by now. *Well, it was nice while it lasted. I wonder if my fairy godmother will send me another Intergalactic Amazon package?* Her stomach took that moment to grumble, suddenly starving and very thirsty, even though she'd just had breakfast, and she turned to Marsee with a grin. "Hungry. Star fruit juice?" she asked.

Marsee burst out laughing, and then told her mother what she'd said. Myra's tail curled and then she started laughing too. She joined them until her sides started hurting, which didn't take long. Her comical wince somehow only made them laugh harder. Crisis averted, they all walked to the kitchen to find something to eat.

# Myra: Waiting

Myra's tablet dinged with a message from Brice, asking her to call when she was in a private location, so Myra left the family room with her half-eaten breakfast and made her way back to her office. Sand was swirling in the hallways, leaving intricate designs on the floor. The shields blocked most of the wind, but they didn't block everything, since they still needed to breathe. When she was in her office, she shut the door and placed the call to Brice, throwing the call up on her wall monitor. Brice answered immediately.

"Problems with the storm?" Myra asked.

"No, the shields are managing fine. I called because the scans are complete. It's not good and I figured you should know right away," Brice replied.

Myra opened her tablet and pulled up the results. She flicked her way through scan after scan after scan before moving over to her chair to sit down and lean her head against her paw as she continued reading. "How many?" Myra finally asked.

"All of them, except for the two mothers," Brice said with a sigh.

"*All* of them? Dark moons," Myra swore. "Are you sure?"

"The scans are all the same, massive increase in the uterine lining, changes in hormones similar to the ones we've seen with Little Flower. They're all definitely in heat although we've only been able to confirm fetal cells in two of the females. It could just be too soon depending on when they mated, if they did. We won't really know for sure until they're back out of stasis."

Myra leaned back in her chair and rubbed at her face with a groan. "I'll let Healers and the Council know," Myra said. She hung up and swore for a full five minutes at the Council, and more specifically Senior Councilor Tabor, who had overruled her objections. Tabor had contacted her directly and ordered her to move everyone into stasis within the hour. She'd tried again to convince the Senior Councilor that it was dangerous, but had been overruled again, and informed that if she didn't, she would be removed as Senior Healer for the Agency, and she would find someone else to do it. Myra had submitted a formal complaint with the Healers Guild that she was complying under duress and against her better judgment, before ordering Brice to move every-one into stasis. Brice had made the same formal complaint, as had many of the other healers. *The Council may have just doomed the entire species with that order*, Myra thought.

She sent her partner a message to call her as soon as possible, and then sent a message to Nerissa Witherspoon, the Senior Healer for the Guild, sending along the scans for review. An hour had passed and Jer still hadn't called her back, so she called him. There was no answer. Frowning, she left a message for him to call her back as soon as possible, and set her tablet down on the desk. He'd been at Marcus's, so he should have been available to pick up; that he hadn't worried her. *Had he left there already and was now caught out in the storm?* Jer was a competent pilot, but there was no way the shuttle would be able safely navigate a storm of this magnitude, even with the autopilot. Her parents had been killed in a storm far smaller than this one. The beast of a storm continued to rage and howl outside. The hiss and ping of sand hit her office window, even through the shields, and flashes of lightning and thunder lit up her office and made the window rattle. No rain though. *Rain would be nice*, she thought, *that would help clean up some of the sand that would be everywhere by the time this storm was over. Then again, maybe not. Then we'd just have mud everywhere.* She tried calling Marcus, but he didn't respond either.

She took a sip of her drink and stood, walking over to the window to peer out at the storm. She couldn't see anything but vague shapes made by the swirling sands. She honestly wasn't paying much attention, her mind churning over the scans from the Agency, Little Flower's injuries, and the coming trial. "What a day!" she muttered, then snorted. *Day? I haven't even finished breakfast yet! What else was that miniature dust storm going to get herself into next? Climbing trees for moon's sake! Who does that? Why would she do that?* Then a horrible thought crossed her mind. *Was she trying to hurt herself?* She shook her head. *No, Marsee said she was having fun. I really need to learn more sign language.*

Her tablet chimed, and she spun to pick it up, hoping it was Jer. It was not. *Just a weather update,* she sighed, and then scowled as she read it. The storm they weren't supposed to get in the first place had stalled over their valley, trapped between the conflicting air fronts of the mountains and the distant sea. The current estimate now showed it could be days before the storm fully passed. She shifted the weather map to confirm that the storm front had hit Marcus's home as well. "Great, just great. This is all we needed," she muttered to herself. *Jer, where are you? Please be safe,* she prayed to the moons.

While Marcus lived in a separate district, he didn't live all that far away by shuttle, as they both lived near the border. It was how she and Jer had met. She'd gone to Marcus's grand opening of his public library with her parents, and Jer had been there. She'd been an in-betweener home on break from her studies with the Healers Guild, and Jer only a few weeks short of his adulthood ceremony. Myra chuckled at the memory. For someone who was now a councilor, Jer had seemed anything but Council material when she'd first met him. He'd wanted nothing to do with being there, and had been dragged by his own parents to the party. She'd found him hiding in one of the back stacks, curled up on a pillow reading. *He was a lot like Marsee back then,* Myra realized. Shy and introverted, he'd wanted little to do with the Council, and the profession both his father and older brother excelled in, although she'd come to realize it had far more to do with feeling like he wouldn't live up to their expectations and example. To be fair, both had set a very high bar for decades at that point.

Myra had known who he was immediately, as he looked just like his father, although his father's coat was more of a dark bronze than copper and had blue eyes, instead of green. She'd stood there watching him for several minutes, before he'd looked up from his book. Her instinct purred and demanded she curl up beside him. She'd been thoroughly surprised by the reaction. Still decades out from her first heat, she shouldn't have had any sort of reaction, but he'd been beautiful, and her instinct had recognized the potential in him. Her species mating instinct always chose the strongest and most powerful mate available. Jer was still an awkward in-betweener, but she somehow knew one day he would be both. Perhaps it was because both Marcus and Frederick commanded the room with their innate power and grace. When he'd finally looked up at her with his beautiful green eyes, he'd been equally transfixed with the sight of her. She'd raised one brow at him and walked away, flicking her tail at him dismissively. He'd followed her back out to the party, and eventually all the way back to Council City, where he'd tried every guild looking for a fit, before eventually giving in and joining the Council, as they all knew he would. Ellie had teased her about it for weeks.

He'd grown into that potential too, and known at a very young age that he wanted to be male, and had chosen to go through his growth spurt early to be ready for her, and their matings had both been glorious. She purred at the memory. *Well, if they do force me to go into heat, at least I'll get to experience that feeling again before I die. I wonder if they'll let me choose him for a mate, pick one for me, or just trigger my heat and make me suffer with the urge until I die?* She sighed and frowned again in worry, both for what her punishment would be and for her partner. *Where is he?* she wondered.

She was about to toss her tablet back down when it chimed again. This time it *was* a call from Jer and she answered, throwing the call up on her main display. "Finally! I was starting to worry!" she exclaimed.

"Sorry Myra," he apologized. "I was helping Marcus close up his compound before the storm hit. He doesn't have anything automated. He says he likes the antiquity of his compound and sees no need for modern conveniences when a little bit of effort will suffice." Jer rolled his eyes and shook his head in bewilderment, which made her chuckle.

"Ha! That sounds just like him. Tell him he'd like it a lot less if he had to close everything up *in* the storm instead of before. I'm going to be picking sand out of my fur for weeks," she complained, giving another hard shake of her fur, filling the air with dust motes as proof.

"Is everything okay there?" he asked, looking worried by her remarks.

"Define okay," she replied, shaking her head, and filled him in on the morning's adventures with Little Flower. When she was done, she rubbed her paws over her face. "I don't know what to do, Jer. How are we going to protect a species that sees nothing wrong with climbing trees a hundred times taller than them and racing into sand storms without any regard for their own safety?" She stood and paced. "We're lucky she had nothing worse than a couple of cracked ribs. I'm worried though, that's the third time in less than a year that she's broken the same ribs. They didn't heal well this time and the bone knitter shouldn't have hurt her, but if you'd heard her scream..." She let her voice trail off and her ears pinned back at the memory. "I don't know what I would have done if those ribs had poked through her lungs again, or if she hadn't been able to catch a branch when she fell. I barely caught her when she fell the second time. I don't have the kind of medical equipment I would need to repair that kind of damage here, and it would have taken far too long to get her to the Agency in the ground crawler. And if she'd died..." Myra left unspoken what they both knew would happen if Little Flower died before the trial.

Jer frowned. "Do you think it has more to do with her species or her age?" he asked. "Remember what our cubs were all like when they were little. They had just as little regard for their own safety and Marsee climbed everything."

"She didn't climb the tree," Myra growled, and then sighed. "Honestly, I don't know. Why would anyone climb a tree in the first place?" she asked.

"Why would anyone climb to the top of a tower, or a mountain, or fly off in a ship to an unknown world?" Jer responded with a question of his own before answering. "For the sake of doing so and to see further than they have before. Maybe she was just trying to get a better view of her new world or figured it was the one place we couldn't go. Or maybe her kind likes to climb, sounds like she was good at it and doing just fine until the storm approached."

"Good at climbing?" she snorted in disbelief. "Jer, they don't have claws to hold on with, their feet can't even flex enough to grab ahold of anything, and their skin is so fragile that the bark just sliced right through it. Her paws were so mangled, I'm surprised they still function. How under the three moons could they possibly be good at climbing?"

"She seemed to have had no problem with those limitations before the storm hit," Jer reminded her. "As for running off into the sand storm, that actually speaks pretty highly of her."

"You've got to be pulling my tail," Myra snorted again.

"Hear me out. Where did she run to?" Jer asked. "Marsee's room, right? And what was she doing?"

"She was trying to shut Marsee's door. Not that she had a moons' forsaken chance of moving it, as small as she is. I had a hard time, and she was nearly blown off the balcony in the process," Myra answered.

"Why though?" he prompted.

"How should I know?" she replied, throwing her paws up. "Maybe to go hide in her nest? Maybe she was afraid of the storm, or afraid she'd be in trouble with us?"

"I don't think so," Jer replied. "The room wouldn't have been a safe place to hide, and she's smarter than that. If she hid anywhere, it would have been in the compound, somewhere out of the storm, like the storage rooms, or even a kitchen cupboard if she was truly scared of us, which I don't think she is, not anymore anyway. I think she saw Marsee's door was open, and that Marsee's things were flying out and being damaged by the storm. I think she was trying to help save Marsee's belongings."

"Huh." Myra stopped pacing and considered.

"If that's the case, it shows she was smart enough to understand the dangers of the storm, that Marsee's door was open, and that no one had noticed. She cared about how Marsee would feel if her stuff was lost or damaged, and that she was willing to put herself at further risk, even though she was already injured, to protect her friend," Jer continued.

"Marsee would have been far more distraught if Little Flower had been lost or damaged," Myra replied.

"As would we all. Still, it might be something we can work with. I'll discuss with Marcus, since I'll apparently be spending the next few days here. Do you need me to pick up anything on my way home?"

"Yes, I'll send you a list, but Little Flower isn't why I called," Myra said, and walked over to her window, looking out at the howling storm.

"What's wrong now?" Jer asked, with a weary sigh.

"The Agency scans are complete. All of the biped females are in heat and we've confirmed two pregnancies," she said without turning around to look at him.

"All of them?" Jer whispered. Myra nodded and Jer swore. "Dark moons. This is bad, isn't it?"

She nodded again and turned back around. "Jer, we have to take them out of stasis. You have to convince the Council. I don't know how, but if we don't, we could lose them all. We've never tested stasis on a female in heat or pregnant of our own species, and the few that have been placed there because of an emergency didn't survive. The risk is just too high for our species, and if stasis had anything to do with those other two biped females miscarrying, we could lose the cubs and I have absolutely no idea what this will do to them in heat. It could already be too late, but the longer they're in stasis the greater the risk there is."

"I'll talk with Marcus and let you know. It might be a few days though. The Seniors are all on their way to the Water World to discuss how the Full Council is going to work with all of the added complications. Tabor's ship just jumped this morning, and we won't be able to reverse the order without her approval."

"We might not have a few days, Jer," Myra said, knowing that if push came to shove, she'd disobey Council orders to save the species.

Jer seemed to realize that as well. "I'll see what I can do. Please don't do anything yet," he begged.

Myra nodded and Jer sighed with relief.

"Well, I'd better get back to my research. I love you, Myra," Jer said.

"I love you too, Jer. Be careful, and give my regards to Marcus."

Jer nodded and hung up. Myra turned and looked out the window again at the storm, sighed, and then picked up her tablet, checked the time and went to join Marsee and Little Flower for their next language lesson, wondering what the next major catastrophe was going to be, and how soon it would hit. Lightning cracked loudly nearby and she jumped. "Moons! Enough already! That wasn't a challenge," she told the Ancient Gods, thoroughly unnerved by the coincidence.

# CHAPTER 10

# Marsee: The Best Medicine

Marsee pulled herself away from watching Little Flower, who was now curled up on one of the cushions in the family room, sound asleep. Between her ordeal with the tree and the effects of the bone knitter, Little Flower had fallen asleep in the middle of eating her second breakfast and they decided not to wake her for their lesson. She needed the sleep to heal. They'd canceled their language lesson with plans to meet again that evening, and instead she'd practiced with her mother, to help get her caught up with everything they'd already learned.

The cutest and tiniest of snores was coming out of the small cub's mouth. *It's a good thing she's so cute when she's asleep,* Marsee thought, *because she's a real handful when she's awake.* She was worried about how much trouble Little Flower seemed to be able to find, and how easily she got hurt. *Is this what it's like having small cubs? Always worried about them getting into trouble, and trying to keep them from getting hurt?* She shuddered. She thought giving birth was bad enough, but having to constantly worry all the time just seemed exhausting. *Why would anyone want cubs? It can't just be because they're cute when they're young. I wasn't this bad when I was a cub was I?*

Marsee shrugged and brought the remains of their meal to the kitchen, and then remembered Little Flower's wrap that had been left by the cleaner. *She'll want her sketchbook and pencils when she wakes up,* Marsee thought and left to retrieve them. Picking Little Flower's torn clothing up off the floor, she took a good look at it. *It's really not very good at protecting her, is it? This thing is completely destroyed. Then again, most of the damage she took was on her hands and feet, if you didn't count the broken ribs. That fall would have hurt any of us too,* she thought, and made a point to send a message to Ellie about using tougher fabric in her replacement clothing, and maybe add in some gloves. She started to take the items out of the carry sacks which had amazingly held up, but stopped in surprise as she pulled out her hearing aids. *What are you doing here?* she wondered. In the other sack she found her tablet. *Well, that's useful at least, but why did you have them?*

Items removed, she used the remains of the clothing to wipe up the blood that had dripped on the floor, trying hard not to breathe in the scent, as the beast inside her drooled at the smell. The moment she was done, she tossed the shredded and bloody clothing in the recycler and bolted out of the room. When she found the external door the farthest from the family room, she sat and leaned up against the door for a long time until she felt calmer and safe enough to return. Her instinct had saved her from drowning but still continued to see her friend as as prey. It hadn't tried taking control again, but she could feel it wanting to run and hunt. Her very skin felt like there were crawlies underneath trying to get out. Eventually the feeling settled and she made her way back.

While she had been gone, Little Flower had rolled over, exposing the angry purple and blue bruises on her side. She winced in sympathy. *That must have really hurt. Maybe now she will be a little more cautious and won't climb the tree, or at least maybe not so high? I know I'm going to have night terrors of her falling for weeks.* Grabbing a few of the cushions, she made herself a comfortable nest of pillows next to the window seat, kneaded them a few times, winced and examined her shredded claws, that she'd completely forgotten about, shrugged and settled down for a nap too, knowing how much work it would take to clean up the compound once the storm had passed. *I'll have Mama look at them later,* she thought, and was soon sleeping just as deeply as the cub.

Myra checked in on them, and watched quietly for a long time from the open doorway, but they never knew. Sometime after Marsee had fallen asleep, Little Flower must have woken and climbed onto Marsee's nest and was now fast asleep with Marsee curled protectively around her. Little Flower was holding Marsee's tail securely in her arms and using it as both a blanket and a pillow. Myra snapped a picture with her tablet, sending it off to both Jer and Ellie, and left the two sleeping, determined now more than ever to do everything she could to save the tiny, exasperating, bewildering, daredevil of a species. If such a creature could risk their own life for the sake of the growing friendship with her daughter, as Jer thought, after everything that had happened to her, that they, that *she* had done to her, could she do any less? She may have made that promise to her daughter, but she still felt responsible, and probably always would, and she was bound and determined to find a way to make amends.

Several hours later Marsee woke, gave an enormous yawn, and half-awake realized something was grabbing her tail. Instinctively she reacted, thinking it was one of the creepy crawlies, and flicked her tail hard to send it flying. There was a squeak followed by a startled 'oof' as Little Flower went flying through the air and landed on a cushion on the far side of the room.

"Little Flower!" Marsee yelled and ran over to the pillow to find Little Flower laughing, but also gasping and holding her sides. "Are you hurt?" she signed ready to run to find her mother, yet again. *Three moons! She can't even sleep without getting hurt!*

"No," Little Flower signed. "No hurt. Surprised. Fun!"

Marsee slumped to the floor in relief. *Thank the moons!* She had not been looking forward to telling her mother that she'd accidentally thrown Little Flower across the room. Marsee checked the cub over carefully anyway. The bruise seemed significantly smaller than before, mostly yellow and green, and none of the angry purple it had been when she'd gone to sleep, and she didn't see any new injuries. *Mother's salve must be working on the bruise,* she thought, *but I should probably make sure.* "Side hurt?" she asked.

"No," Little Flower said, and crawled off the pillow and made some silly motions to prove she was indeed not hurt. "Play?" she asked, and then held her arms up as if she wanted to be picked up.

*What kind of play does she want to do, and why does she want me to pick her up?* Marsee wondered, but picked her up anyway.

As soon as she did Little Flower signed "play" again and then pointed to the pillow.

Marsee set her down gently on the pillow, now even more confused.

"No," Little Flower signed, sliding off the pillow.

"No? Confused Little Flower want play," Marsee signed.

In response the cub scrunched up her face thinking, and then walked over and picked up one of the small pillows, nearly as big as the cub, and tossed it on the bigger pillow, following it with more throwing motions, then walked over to Marsee to have her pick her up again.

Marsee did, completely baffled by what Little Flower wanted. Little Flower pointed to the pillow and then made the same throwing motion. "You want me to throw you on the pillow?" Marsee asked aloud in disbelief. "You just fell out of a tree, broke two ribs, and now you want me to throw you? What is wrong with you? Did you hit your head when you fell?"

Little Flower didn't answer, just pointed at the pillow and made the throwing motion again. *Okay,* Marsee thought. *This creature is either absolutely crazy, or I am for agreeing, but here goes nothing.* Marsee very gently tossed Little Flower onto the pillow.

"Yes, happy!" Little Flower signed, slid off the pillow, walked further away, and held her hands up to be picked up again. Marsee obliged. This time tossing her a little higher and farther. This time Little Flower screeched like she had on the tree branch. "Yes, fun, happy!" Little Flower signed again.

Marsee threw her again, this time causing Little Flower to roll off the pillow laughing. She stood up, wobbled a bit, and then walked over and started pulling on another cushion that was far too big for her to move on her own. Marsee helped her move the cushions together, so they were all in a big pile and then picked up Little Flower and threw her again and again and again, her tail curling at Little Flower's laughter and evident enjoyment of this bizarre activity.

"Cursed eclipse! What under the dark moons is going on in here?!" Marsee's mother yelled from the doorway, just in time to see Little Flower flying through the air, hit the pillow with a screech, and roll off. Marsee turned to see her mother in the doorway, tail lashing, and with an expression on her face that said Marsee was in serious trouble. Marsee shrunk herself down as small as she could, and tucked her tail between her legs. She'd never seen her mother this mad, ever.

Marsee looked back at Little Flower, who was dizzily struggling to climb to her feet, back to her mother's lashing tail and furious glare, and then back at Little Flower, at a complete loss for words. *How am I going to explain this?* she thought frantically, knowing 'she asked me to' wasn't going to be a good enough answer, not with the way her mother's tail was lashing.

Little Flower met her eyes and started giggling.

Absolutely astonished that Little Flower could laugh at a time like this, Marsee's tail started to curl at the ridiculousness of the situation. Little Flower's giggle turned into full on laughter. Marsee's tail curled some more and she started to giggle too, although perhaps more in hysterics than humor, fully expecting to be clawed by her mother at any second. She tried to stop laughing but she couldn't, now fully hysterical, and clamped her paws over her mouth. She looked back at her mother who was now looking at her with a completely exasperated and dumbfounded expression on her face.

Looking up at the sky, her mother sighed. "Ancient Gods protect me! You two are going to give me a heart attack! You know what? I don't think I want to know. Whatever it was you were doing, just stop!" Her mother growled, turned, and stormed off, tail whipping behind her. It was too much. Marsee and Little Flower both collapsed onto the pillows laughing until Little Flower's aching sides hurt too much to breathe and Marsee's tail was starting to cramp from how tightly it was curled.

# CHAPTER 11

# Jeran: Triple Eclipse

The storm raged outside, but deep in Marcus's stone bunker Jer could barely hear it. The storm inside him raged far louder. His stomach was in knots with the news Myra had just shared. It was all he'd been able to do to put a positive spin on what Myra had told him about Little Flower's ordeal. *Thank the blessed moons, Little Flower was alive and relatively unhurt. If she'd fallen to her death, it would have been Myra's death too and probably Marsee's for not having the leash on when Little Flower was outside.* Disobeying a direct Council order had serious consequences on its own, but half the reason he couldn't get the Council to rescind the leash order was because they were afraid Little Flower would try to take her own life. As it was, if the Council found out Little Flower had been hurt, there might not be anything he could do to protect his family.

But it was Myra's other news that had him reeling. *Two more confirmed pregnancies and the rest in heat! We don't stand a chance. One charge, we might be able to downplay, but two hundred? We're all as good as dead. Well, might as well go tell Marcus the wonderful news,* Jer thought, and heaved himself out of his chair.

Marcus took one look at him and sighed. "That bad?"

"Do you want the good news or the bad news first?" Jer asked as he sat down, rubbing at his face.

Marcus leaned back in his chair. "Start with the good news."

"Little Flower climbed to the top of the bandala tree and fell," Jer stated.

"*That's* the good news?!" Marcus asked in shock. "Is she okay?"

"Myra says she managed to catch herself, but not before breaking two of her ribs, nearly dislocating her shoulder, and mangling her hands and feet. Myra's bandaged her up and she should be fine," Jer said.

"How under the three moons did she even get in the tree? Wasn't she leashed?" Marcus asked. Jer just looked at him and Marcus sighed. "Explain."

"Myra destroyed the harness and leash, after we found out Little Flower had been raped," Jer finally said, although he'd been very tempted to say the little cub had just unhooked it and run off before Marsee could stop her.

"Moons, Jer. Is your partner trying to get herself killed? For that matter, was Little Flower? Is that why she climbed the tree? Was this a suicide attempt?" Marcus asked.

"No, Marsee says Little Flower climbed up for fun, although I wouldn't be surprised if it was because it's the one place in the compound we can't go. Marsee was watching her but she climbed the tree faster than she could stop her, and she couldn't climb up after her, although she tried. Little Flower was still in the tree when the storm hit, and her foot slipped when trying to make her way down."

"Moons. I'm afraid to ask what the bad news is," Marcus said after a while.

"The test results are back from the Agency. Two confirmed pregnancies and the rest are all in heat," Jer said dryly.

"*All* of them?!" Marcus squeaked.

Jer chuckled. If nothing else, he'd now seen two impossible things. His mentor was never surprised. He'd lived too long, seen too much. "Yup. All except for the two existing mothers."

Marcus gulped.

"How many times do you think they'll be able to resurrect us, to kill us again?" Jer asked. "Two hundred seems a bit much. I'm thinking after the first fifty there won't be much of anything left." Jer started chuckling. He was too scared to cry.

Marcus rubbed the back of his head and started laughing too. "Well, it was nice knowing you, Jer," Marcus said eventually.

"What under the dark moons are we going to do, Marcus?" Jer asked.

"I'm not even sure the Ancient Gods would know what to do. Could it even get any worse?" Marcus asked.

"Oh sure, Myra says if we don't take the bipeds out of stasis, they might all die," Jer added, trying hard to keep his face blank.

Marcus threw his paws up. "I just had to ask, didn't I?"

"You did," Jer laughed.

"Anything *else* you'd like to add to this wonderful triple eclipse?" Marcus asked, shaking his head.

"Nah, that's it for now. Figured that was good enough for one day," Jer said with a slightly manic smile. He was pretty sure he'd officially lost it.

"You're so kind. I always knew there was a reason I liked you," Marcus said sarcastically. "Well, come on then, Cub. We'd better get back to the books."

Myra called to let them know they were skipping the language lesson, as Little Flower had fallen asleep from the effects of the bone knitter, so they spent the next several hours reading. Jer was pretty sure he was going cross-eyed from trying to read the tiny ancient script. He yawned, and was about to take a break, when Marcus gasped. Jer looked over at his brother and his heart dropped to his feet and fell through the floor at the horror he saw on his brother's normally stoic face.

Marcus finally finished reading, and looked up at him, before slowly turning the ancient book around to face Jer so he could read. "I'm so sorry, little brother, so very, very sorry."

Jer closed his eyes and took several long slow breaths, trying to control his growing panic and then started reading. He was shaking by the time he finished, his blood alternating between boiling rage and ice-cold fear. When he was done, he laid his head in his arms and wept. "No..." he whispered.

"Jer…"

"No!" He looked up and growled at his mentor, ears back and tail lashing. "I will not allow anyone to do that to my children and grandchildren, Marcus. This is not fair or just. Tell me how this is fair or just?" Jer said, standing up and banging his fist on the archive. "How would doing this to Marsee make amends for what happened to Little Flower? How?" he cried.

"Jeran…"

"I swear Marcus, on every moon in the universe, if anyone does this to my children, I will rip their throats out with my claws." Jer started pacing, his claws flexing in his fear and rage as the beast inside him screamed to protect his cubs and grand cubs at all cost. He knew he was very close to losing control but he didn't care.

"JERAN, SIT DOWN!" Marcus roared, grabbed him by the scruff of his neck, and physically threw him back down into his chair and pinned him there with a growl. "I will pretend I didn't just hear you threaten the Senior Council, but if you don't shut up and listen, I will have no choice but to report this."

Jer growled back at him, but remained seated and rubbed the back of his neck, momentarily distracted by the pain, and the instinctive reaction to relax, that grabbing the scruff had with his people. The beast inside him paced, but recognized the authority that Marcus had over him. They might be brothers, but Marcus was his mentor, and had spent months risking his own life to establish dominance over him, in a last ditch effort to save Jer's life when he had lost control of his own instinct, and Jer would never be able to repay that debt. Now both he and the beast inside him prayed that Marcus had a way out of this horrible mess.

"Now listen to me very carefully," Marcus ordered, tense and clearly ready to fight, if it came to that. "The actual punishment is less important than the precedent that was set that day. What happened to Little Flower and what happened to that mother and her cubs are completely different, and that gives us something to work with. That this happened before the Great Awakening also helps, because we can argue that this isn't fair or just with the standards of today's society, because you're right. It's not."

"Go on," Jer growled, fighting hard to contain his fear, and eventually the beast inside calmed to listen.

Marcus relaxed slightly as Jer brought his instinct back under control. "One, we can argue that 'ending the genetic line' as they put it, can be done in a safe and painless way. People do this electively all the time. Your children and grandchildren will probably hate you for the rest of their lives, but they'll live. And two, they gave the victim the opportunity to choose the punishment. Which means we just have to figure out a punishment that would satisfy the Council as being comparable, one that we can all actually live with. Do that, and we can try to convince Little Flower to suggest it, and pray that she's truly forgiven us."

"How under the three moons are we going to find something equal to that?" Jer asked. "It's a death sentence, Marcus, a painful, ugly, death sentence. We might be able to downgrade the Council's involvement and the other healers to accessory, but Myra and Brice are going to be found complicit, and you know it, and neither Brice's children or mine deserve that punishment. I'll take whatever they do to me, but not at the expense of my children, or hers."

Jer's tablet took that moment to ding with a message from Myra. He and Marcus both took a deep breath afraid something else had happened as he unclipped his tablet to look, but he took a shuddering sigh of relief as a picture of Marsee, wrapped protectively around a battered and bruised Little Flower appeared on his tablet. He held it up to Marcus. "I can't do that to her. I don't care what my vows were to my people or to this planet. I can't. I *won't* do that to her, and I meant what I said. I will kill anyone who tries. So, you'd better help me find a way around this. Help me find a way to save all of them, or you might as well just kill me now," Jer told his mentor.

Marcus stared at him for a long time and then nodded. "I reserve my right to kill you later, but for now, we have work to do."

# CHAPTER 12

# Myra: Shish Kabobs

As the storm worsened and buried the solar panels, the lights flickered and went out momentarily, as the compound's primary solar batteries died, and automatically switched to the reserve backup system. Myra shut down all non-essential systems in the compound except for the air conditioning and filtration in the large family room and the refrigeration units to keep the food from spoiling in the heat. The outer sonic shield that protected the compound from the worst of the storm took massive amounts of power to run. The reserve system could easily power the shield and full compound for half a week, but the latest weather report indicated the storm could last anywhere from eight to ten days based on a few of the current predictions. A second major storm was moving in and all signs indicated it would follow the same path, if not merge with the existing storm entirely. If it did it would mean having to reduce power in the shields and potentially cause significant damage to the compound, including the loss of most, if not all of the crops, many of which were close to harvesting. In a storm like this they would normally shut the air conditioning down as well, due to the amount of power it drew, but Myra was concerned about it getting too hot for Little Flower during the day. The buildings were well insulated, but she didn't want to take that chance. Still, she raised the temperature to reduce the drain on the systems, and so far, Little Flower seemed to be managing without issue, although she was drinking far more than normal. They juiced several more trays of star fruit to compensate.

Myra checked on Little Flower's injuries before the evening meal and treated Marsee's shredded claws and bruised tail. The cub's broken bones were healing but not as quickly or as well as she'd like. It wouldn't take much for those ribs to break off again in the future, and she was still furious with her daughter for throwing Little Flower around. *What was she thinking?* Myra wondered, not quite able to keep the shiver out of her tail. She wasn't sure if the bone knitter would work a fourth time, and was debating braving the storm to bring Little Flower back to the Agency to surgically repair them. That came with its own risks, and with everything else going on, she wasn't sure if she dared to operate. Eventually, she sent the scans off to the other masters at the Agency, who specialized in the bipeds care, for their thoughts.

The massive bruise on her side was half the size it had been, and while it probably didn't need it, she applied another large dose of the nano cream to the bruise and her shoulder anyway. Little Flower said she wasn't in any pain, but Myra wasn't taking any chances. The cuts on Little Flower's hands and feet were probably healed as well, but she decided to keep the bandages on and check them in the morning instead, as they didn't have the power to run the cleaning unit again, until after the storm passed, and she didn't want the sand to get in them if the deep cuts hadn't fully healed. They should have been sutured, but she hadn't thought to bring a suture wand with her from the Agency, and hadn't found the one she thought she'd left in her office. It had been almost a year since she'd treated anyone in her home, so it was any-one's guess where she'd misplaced it. She was worried though because, even though the cub was eating and drinking again, she was still losing weight and muscle mass, and she needed to gain weight if she was going to safely carry a cub to term, should she choose to keep it.

"Pausing the bet for a moment," she told her daughter. "We really need to get Little Flower's weight up. I'm pretty sure she's omnivorous and that's part of the reason why she's losing weight. But she, like all of the other bipeds have refused to eat any of the protein sources we've provided. She's still losing muscle mass and with all of the activity and food she's been eating the past few days, she should be building it, not losing more, even with the effects of the bone knitter."

"To be fair, I wouldn't want to eat any of it either," Marsee replied.

"Same," her mother answered. "But she needs it. If not for her, then for her cub. I don't think they can metabolize the protein in the plants and fruits like we can, or at least that's the current hypothesis."

"I'm pretty sure she's going to say 'no'," Marsee stated.

"I'm pretty sure that's all she knows how to say," Myra muttered.

Marsee chuckled. "So, are you really sure about her being pregnant then?"

Myra nodded and pulled up the images on her scanner. "Right now, there isn't much to see, just a collection of cells, but in a few weeks, the cub should be easily visible on the scans."

"What about the fall? Will that cause a miscarriage? She hit really hard," Marsee asked.

"I don't think so. She would have by now if she was going to. For us at least a fall wouldn't be dangerous until later in the pregnancy. But that is something we are going to have to explain to her. No more tree climbing, or throwing her across the room." Myra glared disapprovingly at her daughter, with a tail thwap for emphasis.

"Yes, Mama," Marsee said. "I'm sorry."

"What were you thinking?" Myra finally asked, after another several seconds of glaring, to make her point.

"I'm guessing 'she asked me to' wouldn't work as an explanation," Marsee said with a shrug.

Myra just raised an eyebrow, and then listened as her daughter explained what had happened.

"They clearly have absolutely no sense of self-preservation," she muttered, shaking her head in disbelief, but then let out a heavy sigh, completely at a loss as to how to keep the little tree-climbing imp alive when she seemed bound and determined to put herself at risk. Giving up, she left to find something for them to eat. She returned a short while later with Little Flower's favorite fruit juice, a collection of random fruits and vegetables, and a bowl full of dried bandala chips as a treat. She also had the small stasis unit that contained the various protein sources she'd brought with her from the Agency. She set everything out, and poured a small glass of juice for Little Flower.

Little Flower took the offered drink, setting it down next to her, and scanned the trays before taking one of the chips. Myra knew she hadn't eaten one before, as none of the bipeds had, although her scanner claimed they should be safe, and watched as Little Flower took a tentative bite and crunched. She seemed to be enjoying it, but then started breathing hard, panting, and making strange noises. Her face changed to a bright red, and water started streaming from her face. Myra's heart raced in instant panic. *Was she having an allergic reaction, had she just poisoned her? Three moons! Can't this cub go ten minutes without a life-threatening illness or injury?* Myra grabbed her scanner and checked the cub over carefully. The scanner said nothing was wrong, but she could clearly see something was. She glared at it in frustration.

Little Flower was now guzzling the fruit juice, paused, grinned, and signed something to Marsee.

Marsee's tail curled. "It's okay Mama. She said it's hot. The chips must be spicy to them."

Then to Myra's absolute astonishment, Little Flower grabbed another chip. Myra tossed her hands up. "Ancient Gods, I give up. She clearly has a death wish. Hers or mine, I'm not sure," she muttered, hoping they could do what she couldn't, and tossed the med scanner back on the table. Marsee's tail curled further with the comment. Opening the stasis unit Myra took a piece of fish out and tried handing it to Little Flower.

The cub skittered back, hands up, making a horribly disgusted face and shaking her head no.

"Told ya," Marsee snickered.

"So you did," Myra replied and put the fish back in the stasis unit with a frustrated sigh.

They had barely started eating when the lights flickered again. Myra checked the power reserves on the backup system and frowned. The shields were using far more power than she'd estimated, but then they'd never had a sandstorm this big either.

"I'll be right back," Myra signed and left the room. The air outside the family room was stale and gritty with dust, making her sneeze several times. She made her way over to the storage bay and grabbed several emergency oil lanterns and the lighter next to them, and carried them back to the family room.

"The shields are taking too much power. I'm shutting off the lights and air conditioning," she told Marsee as she set up the lanterns around the room, lit them, and sat back down to eat her meal.

"You didn't sign!" Marsee grinned. "Point!"

Myra pursed her lips at losing the point, although technically they hadn't restarted the bet yet, but her tail curled in amusement as she sat back down. Before Myra had even managed to grab a bite to eat, Little Flower stood up, walked over, and tapped on the stasis unit, surprising both of them. Myra opened it back up and handed the slimy piece of raw fish to the cub, who took it and walked over to one of the lanterns and started trying to open it.

Marsee ran over and stopped the cub. "No, Little Flower. Danger!" Marsee signed and then grabbed her tablet and found the sign for fire. "Fire," she signed and pointed to the lantern. "Fire hot. Danger."

Little Flower nodded. "Little Flower fire fish. Little Flower want fish hot," she signed.

"Pause bet. What is she saying?" Myra asked. Her ability to sign was far less than Marsee's still, and she wasn't sure she believed what she was seeing.

Marsee tilted her head as Little Flower continued to sign.

"Little Flower happy hot fish. Sad cold fish," the cub signed.

"I think she wants to burn the fish," Marsee answered tentatively. "Why would she want to do that?"

"She wants to do what?!" Myra asked, just as confused, although pleased she'd understood what the cub was saying, even if she didn't understand why.

Marsee shrugged. "Burn the fish." Marsee told her mother exactly what Little Flower had signed.

"Odd, but worth a try I suppose. I'll do whatever she wants if she'll just eat it, but I'm not letting her hold it over the flame with her bare paws. I'll be right back, *again*," she told her daughter, and went back to the kitchen. *I need something to hold the fish over the fire so she doesn't burn herself,* she thought, as she scoured the kitchen for an idea. She then saw the wooden sticks they used sometimes to string sliced fruit and vegetables together for easy transport, and grabbed a few, as well as a knife to cut up the fish into smaller pieces. *No point in burning the whole thing if she still won't eat it.* Returning to the family room with those items in hand, she took the fish back from Little Flower, cut a small piece off, stuck it on the end of the stick, and handed it back to her.

Little Flower smiled and signed 'thank you,' before opening the lantern and sticking the fish in the fire. The flame sizzled when it came in contact with the fish, filling the room with a very interesting odor. Not the smell of rot or burnt skin like she'd expected, but something very different. They sat transfixed as the small cub rotated the fish, keeping it from burning until it started to fall away from the stick. Pulling it out, the cub brought it over to her plate that had already been emptied of half its fruit, shoved the rest to the side and set the fish down on the plate. Little Flower grabbed another stick and used it to push the piece off the first one and then used the two to break it in half. The cub examined it closely, then using the sticks together somehow picked it up, sniffed at it, blew on it, and then carefully took a bite and chewed, and to Myra's relief and utter astonishment, swallowed.

"She ate it!" Marsee exclaimed.

"So she did!" Myra replied, just as excited.

Little Flower picked up the other half of the piece, blew on it again, but instead of eating it, paused, put it back down on her plate, grabbed one of the chips and crumpled it into tiny pieces, and then sprinkled the pieces on the fish. She then picked up the fish and took a bite and sighed. "Yes! Little Flower Happy!"

Myra wasted no time in cutting up the rest of the fish and placing them on the remaining skewers. She brought two of the other lamps over by the first and handed a skewer to her daughter. "Here, you too. Let's help her get these heated up." The three of them sat around the small flames, roasting fish for Little Flower, until the entire fish was cooked. It took them a few tries to get it to the right consistency that Little Flower wanted without burning it, but they eventually figured out the trick. Little Flower crumpled up several more chips, dusted the fish with them, and started eating.

When Little Flower had eaten her fill there was still quite a bit left, so Marsee, apparently curious, reached over and took one. She sniffed at it, commented on the change in texture, popped it in her mouth, and cautiously chewed. It's not that their kind couldn't eat meat, they had for millennia, but since the Great Awakening, they'd chosen not to. "You know, it's actually really good," her daughter commented.

Myra, ever the scientist, took a bite as well. She knew what raw fish tasted like. It was actually part of her medical training. She'd taken a course on nature survival, and knew how to identify the plants and animals that were edible in an emergency. She'd absolutely loathed the taste. This however was completely unlike anything she'd tasted before. Fluffy on the inside, crunchy outside with the chips adding both texture and flavor. The enjoyment she had at the novel taste, warred heavily with the moral implications of cooking and eating meat. "Maybe we shouldn't tell anyone how good this tastes," Myra said to her daughter. "And you'd better not have any more."

Marsee nodded in understanding, but then took a deep breath and closed her eyes as her hunter's instinct flared.

"Focus Marsee," Myra ordered and then grabbed a piece of the vile smelling uncooked fish and shoved it under Marsee's nose.

Marsee snapped her head back in revulsion. "Thanks, I needed that. What is that anyway? It smells like the compost heap," Marsee asked.

"I'm not really sure. Some sort of giant water crawly from the Water World, I think," Myra said, relieved that her daughter had snapped out of it.

"They eat bugs? Ugh, remind me never to visit," Marsee said.

Little Flower had been looking out at the storm the entire time, and had missed Marsee's flare up, but then turned around and took one of the empty skewers and placed a piece of star fruit on it and stuck that in the fire. When she took it out, she didn't even bother removing it from the now charred skewer, just blew on it to cool it, and took a tentative bite and groaned. She took the rest off, tossed it in her mouth and closed her eyes and sighed as she leaned back into her pillow and chewed.

Myra and Marsee looked at each other and then simultaneously reached for a piece of the star fruit, cooked it and then when done tried it at the same time. They echoed Little Flower's reaction. It was by far and away the best thing either of them had ever eaten. The three of them spent the next hour trying everything they had over the small fire, minus the fish, amazed at the change in texture and taste, until all three of them were so full they could barely move.

By the time Myra had found the will to move again and picked up the remains of the meal, it was time for their language lesson with Sina. Rather than using the big monitor, Marsee propped her tablet up on the table, using the built-in stand.

"Wait, when did you get your tablet? I thought you left it in your room," Myra asked her daughter.

"I did leave it in my room, but I found it in the remains of Little Flower's clothing along with my hearing aids," Marsee informed her. "She must have grabbed them when she was in my room."

Myra flicked her ears back in surprise and passed that little tidbit on to her partner, who joined them shortly after for the evening lesson. Both Marcus and Jer had their councilor masks on tightly, and that worried her. *What did they find?* Myra wondered, but when she asked Jer later, he had simply stated they were still looking. Myra had been surprised at how much Marcus had already learned on his own, as had the others, but then she reasoned that if his life depended on becoming fully fluent, she knew he'd put everything he had into making it happen. Even if it hadn't, Marcus took his role as councilor and advocate very seriously, and had been a councilor for longer than she'd been alive.

That he was putting so much effort into this reassured her. If anyone could find a way out of this mess it would be him.

That night, Myra lay awake watching the cubs sleep for a long time, worrying about both of them, and trying to decide what to do about Marsee. *She shouldn't be struggling this badly controlling her instinct at this age. None of the healers at the Agency had any problems around the bipeds, so why is Marsee?* As a master healer, she was bound by oath to report any incidents where she even remotely suspected an adult was struggling with their instinct, much less lost control completely and hunted. She'd not told anyone, including Jer, about it since Marsee had been able to stop before the cub was hurt. That a single taste of meat triggered her instinct to flare so quickly was terrifying, although it had been really good. Even her own instinct had agreed and had wanted more, although she hadn't had any difficulty controlling the urge.

*Is she losing control? Or is this just brought on by the unusual circumstances of being around something their species would have identified as prey before the Great Awakening? Moons, please let this just be a flare up and not the first signs of psychosis.* As part of her healers training, Myra had seen a video of someone with psychosis and they had lost all ability to communicate, and had paced in their cell like a wild animal, attacking anyone that entered. There was no cure, and the Council and Guard had been called to put the poor creature down. *No, this has to be related to the bipeds, maybe a pheromone or scent change due to her pregnancy? And besides, Marsee snapped out of it quickly, and look at them now. Marsee's wrapped around Little Flower like a protective mother, not a predator. If this were psychosis or even pheromone related, Marsee would still be struggling right now,* she thought, and decided to watch and see if there were further signs before reporting it.

# CHAPTER 13

# Marsee: Hunger

*I should have never tried that piece of fish,* Marsee thought as the beast inside her drooled. She'd had a hard enough time with the smell of Little Flower's blood, but had managed to remain in control as the beast circled around, looking for a way to break through her defenses, and attack. The fish was an entirely different story.

Her mother made her cut up the slimy fish, and help with cooking it over the flames the next day. The uncooked fish was revolting, but the smell of the fried fish sizzling over the flame made the beast drool and circle the imaginary shield she'd raised around herself, and barrage her with non-stop nudges and demands that made her head hurt from trying to fight it.

***Let me in. That smells wonderful,*** the beast begged as it clawed at a weak spot in her shield. It felt to Marsee like the beast was clawing at the inside of her skull and it was all she could do to keep from flinching.

*No, you can't have any of this. It'll make your hair fall out and your skin turn blue,* she told it.

But the beast just laughed. ***You know that's not true. Remember how good it was? Soft and tender, with just the slightest hint of spice and crunch from those chips. One more bite won't hurt,*** it pleaded.

*NO!* she said, and took a deep sniff of the pieces that remained uncooked and nearly gagged at the smell.

The beast dug at the sands around her shield, looking for a way in. *Of course, if you don't want fish, there's always that delectable little snack sitting over there...*

Marsee blanched and thickened her shields, and the beast yelped as they stung it. *Go away and leave Little Flower alone. She's not prey! I've told you that. She's my friend!*

*Your loss. I bet it would taste amazing roasted and rolled in those chips too...* the beast remarked as it walked away. *Let me know when you change your mind.*

*Never!* she promised it.

*Never is a very long time, but I'm patient. You'll change your mind eventually, and when you do, I'll be waiting.*

Marsee swallowed hard and hurried to finish grilling her share of the fish, hoping her mother hadn't noticed just how badly she was struggling, and wondering for the millionth time what was wrong with her. That night, when Little Flower curled up beside her, she wrapped herself protectively around the cub, triple checking that her claws were sheathed. There was no way she was letting the beast have her, but she didn't know how to protect her either.

Her instinct remained quiet, but as she slept, the beast snuck up and kept digging at the base of her shield looking for a way in. It was hungry and frustrated at being kept out, and from being denied what it wanted. And sooner, rather than later, it knew it would eventually succeed in taking control, and then they would become the fierce predator they were destined to become. Eventually, it found a small crack in her shield, and let out a feral grin as it kept digging. *Yes, soon, my delectable little snack, we shall find out if you taste as good as you smell.*

# CHAPTER 14

# Myra: Guild Review

Myra jerked awake as the cub began screaming. It was almost dawn and more than enough light for her to see by. Marsee tried to comfort her, but that only seemed to scare her more and she bolted for the door and began leaping for the switch, which was far too high for her to reach. Myra walked over and turned on the light but the cub didn't seem to notice as she just kept jumping for the switch. Myra hit it and the cub bolted down the hall the moment she could slip through.

"Stay here," she told Marsee and followed after. There wasn't really anywhere the cub could go, even if she was stuck in a night terror, but there was always the chance a crawley could get in, and she supposed that maybe the cub needed to use the waste room as that was the direction she was heading. *I should put crates down so she can get in and out easier,* Myra thought as she followed the cubs tracks, keeping out of sight.

The tracks ran straight past the waste room and she was nearly three quarters of the way around the compound when she found the cub curled up in a tiny ball, shaking hard, by one of the exits. Myra sighed and slowly walked over, trying hard not to scare her, not sure if she was awake yet or not.

Little Flower looked up at her as she approached, tears streaming down her face.

"No danger," Myra signed. "You hurt?"

"Sad sick," Little Flower replied. "Sleep scared."

Myra nodded her understanding of the night terror and sat down across from her. "You no danger. I see," Myra signed. It was the closest she could come up with to tell the cub she would protect her, and then held her paws out, offering another hug. Little Flower climbed in immediately and Myra began purring. They stayed there for a long time. Myra gently stroked the cub's soft head fur and rocked her until the cub climbed down on her own. She still seemed scared and tense though.

"Talk sleep scared?" Myra asked.

Little Flower didn't say anything for a while, but eventually nodded. "Male Agency. I no out. Scared."

Myra nodded. It didn't surprise her that the cub would be afraid of being trapped in a room again after what had happened to her. "I fix. Come," Myra said, and stood, motioning for the cub to follow.

She led the cub out into the courtyard. The storm howled above them and sand drifted down through the shields, making the fur on the back of Myra's neck raise, but the cub calmed immediately and let out a sigh of relief. It wasn't truly outside, but it was apparently enough. The sand wasn't healthy to breathe for very long, but for a short time it was okay. She led the cub over to the shed and rummaged through until she found half a dozen large crates that she thought would be tall enough and stacked them together and carried them back out. Little Flower followed and Myra shut the shed door with her hip before walking back over to the inner door she'd left open enough for her to squeeze through, trying to keep as much of the sand out of the hallways as possible. Once they were both back inside, Myra placed a box near the door and motioned for Little Flower to climb on and see if she could reach the switch.

Little Flower awkwardly climbed up and could just barely reach it without having to jump. She turned and grinned at Myra. "Thank you," she signed.

"Little out. Storm danger," she told Little Flower, who nodded her understanding and jumped down. Myra proceeded to walk around the compound, leaving a crate at her office, the kitchen, the waste room, and one for either side of the family room.

Marsee was sitting up waiting for them, a look of concern on her face, but she sighed with relief when Little Flower walked back over and climbed back in beside her. Marsee curled around her protectively and began purring. Myra turned off the light and laid back down on her own pillow, but didn't go back to sleep. Instead, she lay there, watching them sleep, until it was time to get up and make breakfast.

After breakfast and their morning session with Sina, she made her way to her office and called the Agency to check in, as Brice hadn't sent her an update yet this morning, which was unusual."

"Everything okay?" Myra asked when Brice finally picked up.

"Not really, no. Between the shields, environmental units, and stasis units, we'll be out of power in another two days," Brice replied.

"Take the bipeds out of stasis and raise the temperature to the highest we've determined as safe for each habitat and species. And I want around the clock monitoring of all of the females. If they so much as sneeze, I want them fully scanned," Myra ordered.

"But the Council's orders?" Brice asked.

"I will deal with the Council. Even that fool Parner will see that keeping the shields and environmental systems running is far more important than not dealing with the moral implications of keeping a sentient species locked up. And if they have problems with it, they can take it up with me and add it to the list. I can't exactly get in more trouble than I'm already in."

"Are you sure?" Brice asked.

"Positive," Myra replied with conviction. If she was going to die anyway, she'd face the Council's wrath to keep the species alive for as long as she could.

"Good, because I already took them out of stasis last night, when I realized we wouldn't have enough power. They're all being sedated for now. I figured that was a reasonable compromise until I spoke to you." At Myra's look of astonishment, she continued. "I'm in just as much trouble as you are, and if we waited for the Council to make up their idiotic minds, it would have been too late."

Myra nodded. "Change your log to indicate I ordered you to do it, and take them off the sedative."

"What log?" Brice said with a wink.

"When they lock us both up, will you share a cell with me?" Myra asked.

"Nah, you snore," Brice replied with a snort.

"I do not!" Myra said with mock indignation.

"You most certainly do too. I could hear you through the walls. Anyway, how's Little Flower? Has she recovered from her fall?" Brice asked.

"She's mostly recovered. I took the bandages off last night and the bruise on her side is almost gone. At least without fur it's significantly easier to see and treat her injuries. Mentally though, she's still struggling. She had a pretty bad night terror this morning and woke in a full panic and took off. When I finally found her, she was curled up next to one of the exits shaking hard and crying. She didn't fully calm down until I took her out into the courtyard."

"Claustrophobia?" Brice asked.

"Looks that way. I have crates by several of the doors now, so hopefully that will help. On the plus side, we've been able to improve our communication significantly. It's incredible how quickly she and Marsee are both learning. I can barely keep up."

"Speaking of that, Ammond is starting a language class with the healers tonight and I've had copies of the drawings you sent printed out and placed in each of the bipeds habitats, so they'll be there when they wake," Brice stated.

"What about the video I sent? We need to make sure they're all shown it, once they're awake. They need to know what happened."

"I sent it out to everyone this morning. I'm planning on sticking around after the language lesson to see if anyone wants to talk about it. It's not an easy video to watch, and I figured everyone should see it before it gets shown to the bipeds."

"Too true. What about teaching the bipeds sign language? Did you and Ammond hatch any plans there?" Myra asked. Impressed at how well Brice was handling the situation so far. There were other, far higher ranking healers at the Agency, but Brice had stepped up to manage the day to day needs of running the place in Myra's absence.

"In a day or two, once they're comfortable using the picture dictionary, we thought we might bring them together in small groups with their healer and have Ammond start teaching them together. That way they'll have supervised interactions with a bigger group, to help combat their isolation sickness without risk that someone else will get hurt."

"That's a really good plan. Keep me informed how that goes. No, actually, send me the schedule. I want to observe a few of the sessions."

"Do you want me to conference you in?" Brice asked.

"No, I'll just connect and observe passively. I don't want to distract from the lessons. I'm assuming you're planning to use one of the conference rooms?" she asked.

"I am. What do we do about the females in heat though?" Brice asked.

Myra sighed and thought for several long moments before answering. "If a female appears to want privacy with or shows a desire to mate with one of the men, let them have it, but observe on the monitors. If they give any indication that they want to leave or you see any signs of violence, separate them immediately. Watch for signs of fighting among the males too. Who knows what will happen with that many females in heat at the same time."

Brice nodded her understanding, and they discussed a few other issues before signing off. Myra was sitting there thinking when her tablet dinged and she frowned at the subject of the calendar invite from the Senior Guild Healer: 'Mandatory Guild Review: Little Flower's Rape.' With a heavy sigh, she accepted and fired off a message to Jer, letting him know.

She spent the entire next day in review with the Healers Guild over her actions and the decisions that ultimately led to Little Flower's rape. While the Healers Guild had been banned from doling out punishments until after the trial, by order of the Council, Myra was torn to shreds by the review board. She'd been through this process many times throughout her career, but never one this thorough and lengthy, but then again, her actions had never warranted it before, and this report would go to the Council for official evidence. She was even more convinced now than she had been before, that she was fully responsible for what had happened, and from the tone of the review board they were too.

Afterwards, she'd sat alone in her office with the door locked and lights off, sitting on the floor by the window, just listening to the storm and watching it rage for several hours. She couldn't move as she was locked in a silent battle with her instinct. She had lost the will to live and her instinct had locked down on her ability to move in order to save her life. *It would be so easy,* she thought. *Just up the dose on the sedative...*

***And who will protect your cubs if you do? Or the others?*** her instinct asked.

Almost as if in response to her instinct, Marsee knocked on the door. "Mama?" Myra just looked at the door, unable to move or do anything else, and didn't answer. Marsee rattled the ancient doorknob and found it locked and knocked again. "Mama, are you in there?" her voice sounded a little worried and she knocked again. Myra couldn't answer, couldn't find the words, and eventually she heard Marsee walk away. A little while later her tablet dinged and she recognized the tone of a message from her daughter. It was all she could do to turn her head and read the message displayed on the tablet that lay on the floor by her side.

"You promised," was all the message said.

Myra stared at the message for several minutes before deciding and heaving herself off the floor to find her daughter. Now, or in a month from now, the results would be the same. She had no doubt now that the Council would order her execution. For now though, she would honor her oath, and try to give her daughter the very best month that she could, and do everything in her power to save Little Flower and her people.

# CHAPTER 15

# Jessica: Mail Call

Jessica woke early and carefully climbed out from under Marsee's warm arm, trying not to wake her friend. She stretched and peered out at the storm that had been raging non-stop for days now. The sky had lightened to the same eerily orange hue that it had been for the past few days. One of the stone sculptures that she could still see occasionally outside of the window had a large drift of sand against one side. *I wonder how long these storms last?* she thought. *On Earth I think they only lasted a day or two, but it's been five days now and it doesn't seem any weaker than before.*

She turned to find Myra watching her. "Morning Mother," she signed. Somewhere in the past few days, she'd shortened 'Marsee's Mother' to just 'Mother' for expedience.

"Good morning, Little Flower. Did you sleep well?" Myra asked. While Marsee's mother had been stuck working all of one day, she'd made up for it the next day by doubling down on learning sign language and the effort showed. She could now speak with Myra nearly as well as she could Marsee.

"Yes. Thank you. I'll be right back. I need to use the hole of muck," she informed the big cat as she stretched, and then climbed up on the crate Myra had placed next to the door for her. That small change had made a huge difference, and she no longer felt trapped like she had the other morning, nor had she been woken by nightmares since, which was a welcome relief.

The hallway air felt stale and hot, and there was a fine layer of sand on the floor that deepened as she approached one of the doors to the inner courtyard where the sand was blowing under. After doing her business, she dragged one of the crates over to the window and peered into the courtyard. Everything was covered in a thick layer of sand that drifted down through the shields and piled up against the sides of the raised gardens. She peered up at the shields covering the courtyard, and saw that they were sagging with the weight of the sand on top of them. One had split during the night, dumping its load on several of the raised beds. *That can't be good*, she thought, and jumped down to run back and inform Myra.

"Courtyard fabric is torn. Big sand on plants," she signed and motioned for Myra to follow her. Myra climbed off of her pillow, and followed her back down to the window, where Jessica pointed out the damaged shield and the buried beds. Myra let out a sigh and her shoulders, tail, and ears drooped. "Mother fix sand on food?" she asked.

Myra shook her head. "No. Wait. Fix when storm is over."

"Why?" Jessica asked. It didn't look bad in the courtyard. Yeah, there was sand drifting down but nowhere near as bad as it had been the first day.

"Sand makes you sick when you breathe long time. Need save power. No use clean drone," Myra replied.

"Wear clothing over your nose and mouth. No breathe sand. Use hands fix sand," she replied, making shoveling motions.

"Clothing over your nose and mouth?" Myra asked, intrigued.

"Little Flower show. Need fabric," she signed back, and started walking towards the storage bay. Myra followed, and opened the door for her. The lights flickered on as they entered. Jessica wound her way through the tall stacks over to the shelf with all the fabric on it, and carefully climbed her way up the shelves to get to the selection of fabrics above her, checking each one out. Tapping one, she jumped down as

Myra pulled it off the shelf, and then demonstrated the size she needed for her head. Myra used a claw to slice a section off, and Jessica took it from her, folding it diagonally and then wrapped it around her face before tying it in the back.

"World had big big sick when Little Flower cub. Wore face clothing so others, Little Flower, no sick when no quarantine," she explained.

Myra's ears flipped back in astonishment. "Face clothing make no sick?" she asked.

"Yes. Fabric for sick," she signed and then tugged on the bandana. "Some help. This not fabric for sick."

"I want learn more. We fix sand on food now," Myra signed back, and then tore off a bigger section of the fabric and tied it around her head, as Little Flower had done. It took some adjustments to make it fit around the different shape of her face, but once it was in place, she took a couple of big breaths to test it out before motioning to follow. Myra shoved open the courtyard door enough to let them enter, and then shut it behind them to keep the sand out of the hallway. They trudged through the sand to get to the tool shed. Myra, seeing that Jessica was struggling through some of the bigger drifts, reached down and picked her up to carry her the rest of the way. Once there, Myra used her feet to shift the sand out of the way of the ancient door, pulled it open, and entered.

Jessica waited and watched as Myra grabbed a shovel, which was at least twice Jessica's height, and then trudged their way back out to the torn section of shielding and buried raised beds. Jessica looked up at the torn shield and saw that the storm was raging above, but somehow wasn't hitting the shield. The fabric flapped slowly in the breeze. *How was it that there wasn't a gale coming through that hole?* she wondered.

"Mother, why storm no go through fabric for courtyard?" she asked the big cat, pointing up.

"No see fabric for courtyard. Use big power. Why no lights," Myra explained while forming the shape of a dome. *Oh, so there's another shield I can't see. Cool!* she thought, wondering how that worked.

"I help?" Jessica asked.

Myra shook her head no and started shoveling, so Jessica just stood back and watched as the powerful cat quickly unburied the raised bed, revealing that the shield underneath was still intact. Half an hour later the other beds were all uncovered. Only one suffered any damage.

"Need get food from garden?" she asked Myra.

"Yes, later. Eat breakfast first. Sign with Sina, then get food from garden," Myra signed back. When they were back in the hallway and the courtyard door was shut, Myra motioned for her to back up and then she let out a huge shake of her fur. Sand went everywhere and Myra's thick fur poofed up in the process.

Jessica couldn't help but giggle.

"What funny?" Myra signed.

She didn't have the words for static electricity so she signed back, "small power make Mother's fur go big," Jessica signed back and then went "Poof" with her hands and giggled some more.

Myra's tail curled, clearly amused, and Jessica followed the big cat on their hunt for breakfast. When they finally made it back to the family room with the results of their successful hunt, Marsee was still sleeping, so Jessica threw a pillow at her to wake her up, and then ran and hid behind Myra when Marsee woke with a ferocious snarl. Myra laughed and picked Jessica up with her tail and dumped her on a pillow before setting the food down on a table. Marsee tossed the pillow back at Jessica, but she ducked out of the way.

"You missed!" Jessica signed, and stuck her tongue out and made a face at Marsee.

"Enough you two. Eat," Myra signed, although her tail stayed curled in humor.

After breakfast and another language lesson with Sina, where she learned the words for shield and static electricity, among many others, they made a bandana for Marsee, and the three of them trudged their way back out into the courtyard. With the sand on the shield providing additional insulation from the sun, as well as the storm overhead, the courtyard was cool enough for her to walk barefoot and unclothed even during midday. Myra claimed the powered cart, while Marsee and

Jessica took the hand cart and they went off in opposite directions. Opening each shield individually, they harvested if appropriate, checked the status of each unit, and unclogged the filters on the water system where needed. Three trips to unload the cart later, they met up with Myra on the far side of the compound, where another tear in the shield had occurred. That tear had not only torn the shield of the unit the sand had landed on, but had also bent the frame supporting the shield, such that it would only open halfway before getting stuck.

"Worried more shield tear," Myra signed. "Sand big." They didn't have words for heavy or light yet. Jessica made a note to look those up later.

"Remove shield? Take sand down?" Marsee signed back.

Myra nodded. "Put carts in shed. You and Little Flower go inside. I do." So, carts put away, they went inside and peered out the window to watch as the shields shifted, one end tilting so each section was now at an angle, causing all of the sand to come crashing down in the aisle between the units. Once most of the sand was off, they flipped all the way down to get the rest. Jessica could now see the storm fully as it raged above the courtyard flowing in a dome around something invisible. Sand slowly drifted down as it passed through whatever barrier was keeping most of it out. After a few moments, the shields were raised back into position and they watched as the rest of the sand settled. What had been a few inches of sand, was now a good three feet deep. High enough that she'd be able to easily reach the gardens herself if she wanted to.

Myra trudged her way through the sands, and cleared out the section by the door so it would open enough to let her squeeze in, and they returned to the family room to rest from the hard morning of work. "Face clothing work good. Little Flower. Thank you," Myra signed, when they were settled down with their lunch.

"Welcome. Sand make big mess," she signed back. "Big work clean later."

"Drones clean when storm over. Big work pick food later. Big sand no use cart," Myra signed back.

"Use cart no wheels on sand," Jessica suggested, not having the word for the floating cart.

"I do not understand," Myra replied, so Jessica drew a picture of the cart.

Myra shook her head. "No power."

Jessica nodded, and drew a picture of a sled instead. The other two looked at it with interest, as if never seeing one before.

"Sled fun in cold. When hard water from sky fall on ground," Jessica explained, and drew a picture of herself bundled up in winter clothing sledding down a hill on a toboggan.

"Hard water from sky?" Marsee asked, so she added pictures of snow falling from the sky. Marsee looked up the sign for snow and showed them.

"Home had big snow, like sand in garden. Play many games in snow." She added pictures of people skiing, skating, building a snowman, and throwing snowballs at each other to her drawing.

"Here little snow. Snow only in mountains," Myra signed back.

She nodded. "When storm over?"

"I don't know. Three or four days. More," Myra answered.

"Big storm!" Jessica signed back.

"Biggest storm," Myra replied. "Storm one or two days no eight. Myra no see eight. Biggest four. Storm no move. Bad."

"Are we safe?" she asked, worried.

"Yes, safe. Shields fall when storm ten days. Lose garden. Walls strong. Safe inside," Myra replied and held her paws apart to indicate they were thick as well. Marsee looked up that word and shared it, which they both dutifully copied, although it wasn't much different than what Myra had motioned.

Jessica nodded her understanding and went back to eating.

When she was done, she decided to continue trying to learn how to read. Myra had grabbed several of the children's books from the nursery for her to practice reading with. Unlike learning to read English, she couldn't sound out the words to figure out what they meant, so she had to memorize the whole word. Every new word she laboriously wrote down, adding to her stack of flash cards, and they worked through the meaning. Their script was even harder than English, and she was constantly getting the letters switched, but she was bound and determined to learn how to read again. She was better at reading than she was writing, but after expressing frustration, when she continued to swap letters and write them backwards, Myra had written to Ellie, who had put them in contact with one of the primary school instructors, who had sent them several digital workbooks. Apparently, it was a very common problem among their children. Myra printed out one page at a time as she worked through them. Unlike working with her parents, they never seemed to get upset that she didn't get it right, and instead congratulated her when she did, and continually worked to find solutions when she still struggled. Their efforts were working too, and Jessica wondered what her education would have been like if her parents had taken her as seriously. Marsee was working just as hard to learn her written language too. Although by consensus, they were focusing most of their efforts on learning to sign.

She'd been at it for a while when Myra sat down beside her, tablet in hand, worry etched on the gold cat's normally calm face.

"What's wrong? Why is Mother sad?" she asked.

"Little Flower's people write words. We do not understand. Do not have enough words. You help? Could be sad, angry. I do not want Little Flower sad," Myra explained.

*Letters!* "Yes!" she signed back with excitement. "I want help!" *Maybe one of them would be from her family.* She carefully shoved her hope down, not wanting to get too excited.

Myra nodded and handed her the tablet. On it was a scanned letter.

She read it and then thought for a bit on how to translate. "They look for cub, son. Want outside," she signed. Myra nodded and switched to another letter. "Same. Look for mother and male, like you and Father. What word?"

Myra flipped open the online sign language dictionary and found the words. "Partner or mate," she signed.

"What difference?" Jessica asked.

"Partner help, love, live together. Mate have cubs. Mate not always partner. Jer my mate and partner," Myra explained.

"Partner. Not know they mate or have cubs," Jessica signed.

Myra pulled up the next letter and Jessica had to laugh. "Say stomach sick. No like food. Bed hard. No pool. Zero star. Would like to leave now."

"Zero star?" Myra asked.

"When go away. Need room to sleep. We tell room good or bad after. We say zero star bad, five star good," Jessica explained.

"Agency not good. Need pool." Myra nodded her understanding and flipped to the next letter.

> *Hello,*
>
> *In the video you showed us was a young girl being rescued. That looked like my granddaughter Jessica. Please. I need to know if my family is safe. I have a husband, his name is Ben and he has two children Alice and David. They would have been picked up in the same area you found Jessica.*
>
> *Thank you for saving us and caring for us all this time. I understand why you have kept us in quarantine. We would have done the same.*
>
> *James Richard O'Neil*

She read the letter a second time, praying this wasn't a dream, and ran her fingers lightly over her uncle's name. *It has to be him,* she thought, *It just has to be. Could he really be alive?*

"What's wrong?" Myra asked, as Jessica started crying and looked up at her.

She wasn't sure how to explain her grandparent's relationship, or know how these people would even react, so she just signed, "My father's father. I want to see bad! Please! Please let me see!" she begged.

Myra's eyes widened at the news, and took the tablet back from her, and immediately called Healer Morningstar. Something was said and the screen went dark again. A minute later a call came in and Myra threw the display up on the big screen. There in amazing beautiful glory, was her uncle.

"Uncle James!" she cried out and ran to the big screen.

"Jessica!" came the mouthed response, tears running down both their faces.

"I can't hear you. I've lost my hearing," she said, hoping he could hear her. He nodded and turned to grab paper and pencil. He was wearing, of all things, a bright pink dress with purple flowers.

"Are you okay?" he wrote.

She nodded. "Yes. Are you? And what *are* you wearing?" she asked him with a grin.

"I'm fine. This is the latest fashion dahling. You like?" he said, then did a little ballerina twirl ending with an absolutely over the top stereotypical gay flounce, that was so unlike him, that Jessica could barely breathe from laughing so hard.

"It shows off your eyes beautifully! Grandpa Ben would love it!" she said when she could finally talk again.

"Have you heard from Ben or your parents? Are they safe?" he asked, with worry etched on his face, humor gone in an instant.

"No. I don't know. You're the first I've found," she told him.

He nodded sadly, and then looked around at the rest of the room in confusion. "Where are you?" he asked.

"I'm at the home of one of their doctors. I'm pretty sure she runs the place where you are," she replied.

"Why are you there and not here? Are they treating you okay?" he asked.

"Yes, they're taking very good care of me," she responded and then hesitated.

"What's wrong?" he scribbled, frowning.

She couldn't answer, just shook her head.

"Tell me. What have they done," he ordered.

"It wasn't their fault," she finally said.

"What wasn't?" he demanded.

"I was depressed from being alone for so long..." He nodded his understanding. "So, they tried putting me in a room with someone else." She looked down, unable to look him in the eyes. "He...he raped me when they weren't watching and I'm pregnant," she whispered and then looked up.

Shock, horror, anger, and then love for her all crossed his face in a matter of seconds. "Oh God, Jessica. I'm so sorry," he wrote. "Is that why you're there?"

"Kind of. After it happened, I didn't want to live anymore, and refused to eat or drink. I think they brought me here to try and help with my depression. I've made friends with their daughter and they're really kind. They take really good care of me and I'm learning to speak their sign language. I can even read and write a little now. I don't think they knew what had happened. When I had enough words to ask them, they were really upset," she told him.

"How could they not know?" he asked.

"I'm not completely sure, but from the conversation I had, I don't think that kind of thing happens here. If understood correctly they get to choose to become male or female and the females are significantly bigger than the males. Plus, it sounded like they were helping someone else at the time."

Her uncle frowned and raised his eyebrows at this, but nodded. "Are you okay? What are you going to do?"

"I guess. I don't know. I haven't decided. There are so few of us left. Before I knew what happened I would have said no. I didn't want to bring a child into captivity. But these people have shown me so much kindness, that now I honestly don't know. I think we could be happy here. I just don't know if I'm ready to be a mother," she said.

"You're far too young to be a mother. But whatever you decide, I'll support you. I love you and will love your child should you choose to have it," he replied.

She nodded, looking away as her eyes threatened to tear up again.

"I wish I could give you a hug right now," he wrote and then, "Will they let me come see you?"

"Me too. I don't know. Let me ask," she replied, and turned to Myra. "Can I see father's father?"

"Yes. After storm," Myra signed back.

"She says yes after the storm passes," she told her grandfather.

"What storm?" he wrote.

"There's a massive sand storm right now. This place is a big desert, very hot and sandy. She said it's going to last another four or five days at least."

"Wow! Is that what that noise is? Are you safe? Will I be able to talk to you again before then?" he asked.

When she asked, Myra replied "Yes. Get you and father's father tablet, talk any time. Show how to write words."

"Yes, I'm safe, and she says yes, and that we are going to get our own tablets so we can talk any time, and they're going to show us how to send emails or text, it sounds like."

They talked for a little while longer, but long before she was ready to say goodbye, Myra told her that Healer Morningstar needed her tablet back, and that they needed to call Sina for their evening language lesson.

"I'll call you back as soon as I can. I have to go to sign language class now. I love you and can't wait to hug you in person!"

"I love you too," he said, and put his hand on the screen. She reached up but the monitor was far too high for her to reach. Myra picked her up and brought her close to the screen so she could touch it back.

After the call was over, Jessica turned to Myra and gave her a big hug. "Thank you, Mother. I look at more letters after Sina," she signed.

# CHAPTER 16

# Myra: Miscarriage

"What are the odds that she would have family among the survivors? They were picked up in two different areas," Healer Brice said later that evening.

"I know! I'm so happy for her though," Myra said. "She needed some good news after everything that's happened to her."

"That's for sure. Do you think there are others with family? We never even considered that, since they were so scattered, and the two of them don't share any genetic markers," Brice said.

"It's entirely possible. Perhaps her grandmother had another mate, or someone was adopted. Either way they've all lost someone. I've already worked with Jer to set up children's accounts for both of them. See if you can find a spare one floating around for her grandfather. We should have a few backups in storage. If not..."

Brice held up a tablet. "Already found one. He's in sign language class right now. I'll bring it over in the morning."

Myra smiled at her protege. "Good. The Senior Guild Master already has techs working to update the programming with their language and alphabet, but that will take some time. Call me when you're in his habitat tomorrow. Little Flower can help translate instructions on how to use it. Do we have the images for the fostering program yet?"

"Yes. We just finished taking them," Brice replied.

"Excellent, I want them shown to every biped, and if they react positively to any of them, put them in the same habitats, with supervision. They need to know if any of their friends or family survived. Little Flower went through all the letters and they were all pretty much the same, looking for news of their family and asking to leave. Well, that and one request for a pool. Apparently, we rate pretty poorly right now," Myra said with a roll of her eyes.

Brice snorted at the obvious understatement. "I'd be surprised if they don't all hate us by now, but we're probably going to have far more grieving than celebration. What are we going to do if they start falling into a depression like Little Flower did?"

"That's a very real possibility, but I'm hoping the sign language classes will allow them to start building a community again. Let's make sure they have time to socialize after each lesson. Schedule a second session each day where they can just interact with each other. Maybe bring them into the recreation room so they can get to know us better too," she suggested, thinking about how much fun Marsee and Little Flower had playing games together. "But keep 326 under close supervision. I don't trust him at all."

"Agreed. He has guards posted at his door now, in case you didn't know. What about the Council?"

"To the dark side of the moons and back with the Council. I care about the well-being of the bipeds. There is absolutely no doubt in my mind that they are a sentient species, and should be treated as such. They have a written language for crying out loud, and have asked for their families. To do any less *would* be criminal. The Council will understand, and if they don't, they aren't fit to be on the Council. My orders, Brice. I'll take full responsibility. And as soon as the storm is over, I am sending Jer over to pick up Little Flower's grandfather and bring him here, and the rest of her family, should we find any," Myra said.

Brice snorted her amusement at Myra's response and nodded. "I'll send you the images once I'm off the call."

Later, when the collection of images came through, she deleted the image of 326. *Little Flower does not need to see that face again,"* she thought, and then left to find the cub.

Twenty minutes later, Little Flower was a sobbing mess on Myra's lap. Only her grandfather had been rescued, and she didn't recognize any of the other survivors. When her grief overwhelmed her so much that she was having a hard time breathing, Myra gave her a sedative. Little Flower was soon sleeping soundly under Marsee's protective arm.

"Mama, can we cancel the bet for a little while? I want to talk," Marsee asked.

"Of course, love. What do you want to talk about?" she asked softly.

"Little Flower. Is her grandfather going to come here to live with us too, or is she going back to the Agency with him?"

"I don't know. That's up to Little Flower and her grandfather to decide, assuming the Council doesn't decide for them. Why?" Myra asked.

"I don't want her to go back to the Agency. I want her to stay here with us. I like having her here, even if she does get into a lot of trouble. She's the best friend I have, and well, it's almost like she's a litter-mate at times," Marsee said.

"I care for her too," Myra replied. "If they want to stay here with us, I'm perfectly fine with that. We'll need to talk to your father of course, but I have a feeling he will feel the same way. But if they want to leave, I won't keep them here, and will do everything in my power to help them get settled wherever they want to go."

Marsee nodded. "I'm really glad she found her grandfather."

"I am too," Myra replied softly.

When it was all said and done, there were only seven joyful reunions. For the rest, it was a long and heart-breaking night. Many, like Little Flower, had to be sedated. A few actively tried to hurt themselves in their grief. Others showed no sign of emotion, as if they'd resigned themselves to the loss a long time ago. Myra read the report and sighed. Hopefully tomorrow would be a better day, and they could start form-ing a new community, and comforting their peers. For now though, her heart wailed to rival the storm outside, both in sympathy for their loss and Little Flower's broken heart. She lay there watching her cubs sleep long into the night, for though she hadn't admitted it to herself, or to anyone else yet, she was starting to think of Little Flower as Marsee's litter-mate too, and hoping the strange little cub would both choose and be allowed to stay with them.

Before dawn she was woken by a call from Brice. "Just a second," Myra said groggily, as she climbed off her pillow in the family room, where they were all sleeping, to walk out in the hallway so she wouldn't disturb her sleeping cubs. "What's wrong?" she asked, when the door was shut.

"The bipeds are miscarrying," Brice said.

"What?!" Myra asked, fully awake now.

"The sensors started indicating a fairly substantial hormone change a couple of hours ago in several of the females. We were trying to figure out what that meant when one of the bipeds triggered the call button we installed. When we arrived, she was covered in blood. We cleaned her up and brought her in for treatment. Her uterine lining has started to detach. In the last hour, four more of the females have also begun bleeding, and all but two of the others are showing the same hormone drop."

"Send me the scans," Myra ordered.

"Already sent," Brice replied.

Myra flipped to her messages and pulled up the information. "Have you tried upping the hormones?" Myra asked.

"We did, but it didn't help. I'm guessing the initial drop was enough to trigger the miscarriages," Brice replied.

"Dark moons. If this is happening across the board, it must be because of the cryo-stasis. The stress from grieving I could see maybe affecting a few, but not all of them. I was worried that putting them in stasis would cause problems. Ancient Gods, please let them have more than one heat. Do your best to care for them and then administer the hormone blockers after it's over. We can't risk another heat until we know what's going on. If they start to show signs of going into shock or that their bodies are shutting down, call me immediately."

Brice nodded and hung up.

She immediately checked the monitor of Little Flower's vitals. Everything looked good, still, she quietly went back in and took a full scan. Aside from the mild sedative still in her system, everything looked normal. Sitting back down on her pillow she watched the monitors closely until Little Flower showed signs of waking. Setting her tablet down, she reached into her bag and dropped a couple of anti-nausea tablets into the water, so it would be ready for her when she woke, knowing the sedative would likely make her dizzy. A few minutes later, her tablet dinged with a message from Brice. All but the two with the confirmed pregnancies mentioned before were now bleeding. *Oh, those poor women! To lose their family and their cubs on the same day...* Myra prayed that Little Flower's cub would be safe since she hadn't been in stasis, but she had been sick with grief.

# CHAPTER 17

# Jessica: Morning Sickness

The next morning Jessica woke slowly from the sedative and lay unmoving, eyes closed, and enjoyed the soft warmth of Marsee's fur. The grief from the night before was still there, but distant somehow. She'd known that finding anyone in her family alive was a long shot. That she'd found her grandfather was nothing short of a miracle, and that she was safe and warm in the embrace of her new best friend helped a great deal more. She was not alone in her grief, and that made all the difference in the world. *So, what happens next?* she wondered. *Can he come and stay here, or now that I've found him do I have to go back to the Agency? I never want to go back there, but I want to see him so much. What about the others? What will happen to them, or to the other species that were rescued?*

Jessica slowly sat up. Marsee moved her arm as Jessica shifted, and then rolled over and went back to sleep. As usual with the sedatives she was queasy, but at least this time she knew it was coming. Myra looked up from her tablet on the other side of the room. "Good morning. How do you feel?"

"Sad-sick but better. I do not feel good. Stomach yucky. Head..." She didn't have the sign for 'dizzy' so made a circular motion with her finger.

Myra nodded, and poured her a drink from a thermos that was sitting on the table beside her.

"Drink. You feel better," Myra signed.

Jessica took the cup and slowly drank. As before, it tasted like water, but immediately calmed her queasy stomach.

"Better?" Myra asked, when Jessica set the empty cup down.

"Yes. Thank you. Mother, what will happen to father's father and the others?" She really needed to have Marsee look up the sign for grandfather, she thought.

"I don't know. It hasn't been decided. Depends on you," Myra replied.

"What do you mean it depends on me?" she asked. Myra sat there for a while not responding.

"I do not have the right words," she finally signed. "What do you want to happen?"

"I want to see father's father. I do not want to go to the Agency ever. Here is better," she signed.

Myra nodded. "After the storm, Jer will bring father's father here."

Jessica smiled at the news. "Thank you!" and then frowned. "How long can father's father stay?" she asked.

"As long as you want. Make home here with us if you want," Myra replied.

Jessica nodded. She would talk to her grandfather about it. "The others?"

"You need to show the Council that you are people, not animals. Then decide how to share our world, how to save the others," Myra finally signed after thinking about it for so long that Jessica began to worry that Myra wasn't going to answer. "You show, you choose. You don't show, the Council chooses."

*Oh great. They still think we're animals to be locked in cages,* Jessica thought. "I am not an animal," she replied emphatically, to which Myra nodded her head in agreement. "How do I show?" she asked.

"At month end, you talk with the Full Council, for five worlds," Myra signed.

"Wait, what?!" she stammered and then signed, "Me? I am not an adult. Why me? Why not others?"

"You are an adult. You can have a cub. That makes you an adult. They know you. They need to know what happened with the man at the Agency. They need to know if your people are good or bad, care, or hurt others."

Jessica blanched. She was going to be questioned about her rape in front of the leaders of all five of their worlds, in less than a month, to try and prove that her species was good enough to get the right to choose for themselves what happens to them? *We're officially doomed,* she thought, with a heavy sigh.

"I cannot show. My people are bad. Hurt others. Most are good, but not all. Many like that man. I don't know the others rescued. They could be more bad than good."

"What do you mean?" Myra asked with a worried expression.

Jessica struggled to explain war and crime. "Some take from others, like to hurt others to feel big and strong. I do not have the right words. Some take ground, homes from others with big knife. Make others do what they want. No choice. I thought damage was done to my world from my people, not asteroid, before you come. My people are bad. Not all. Some like my father and father's father are good, help others, try to stop the bad. My father try to stop people, like the man at the Agency, from harming others. Father's father too."

If Myra's face could blanch, it would have, but she did swallow hard. As Jessica continued her explanation, the cat's eyes went wide and her ears flattened, and she sat there for a long time without answering, after Jessica finished explaining. At some point in the conversation, Marsee must have woken up, because the two had a quick spoken conversation before Myra nodded and then turned her attention back to her.

"I understand," she said. "Your people, some are animals, some are people. We had the same thing many, many years ago. Lost our world too, many animals, many plants. Many bad years. We come here, learn, start new as people, not animals. Your people can learn too. We can help."

Jessica nodded, and then her stomach rumbled. "My stomach better wants food now. Eat food then talk with father's father?" she asked. Myra smiled, nodded, and left to find food for her grumbly tummy, while she ran off to go use the facilities, but when food arrived it smelled funny, and three bites in she felt sick and made it halfway to the door before throwing up.

Myra grabbed her scanner, which she kept in the family room now, and frowned.

"What's wrong?" Jessica asked.

"What's wrong is nothing's wrong. I do not know why Little Flower is sick. Nothing shows on the scanner," Myra said, holding it up.

"Sleep stuff makes me sick," she signed.

"No. Sleep stuff out of your body. Not why you are sick. Stuff in water stops all stomach upset. Food not bad. No sick. Are you in pain?" Myra asked and then Jessica realized what it must be.

"It's morning sick," she signed, trying to calm the worry in Myra's face. "From pregnancy."

Only this caused the big cat's ears to pin to the side of her head and her tail to shiver. She scanned her again. If anything, Myra looked scared. "Not see anything wrong with pregnancy. Why sick?" Myra signed.

"I am not sick. Normal with pregnancy for Little Flower's people, first three of Little Flower's months or more. Food in the morning makes mother sick. I do not know why. I am not a healer. Eat later. Sometimes mother only want one food, lots of one food," she tried to explain.

Marsee had left and gathered cleaning supplies while Myra checked her out. Returning, she handed them to her mother, and then left the room looking a little sick herself. This made both of them chuckle, but Myra sobered. "I find why Little Flower is sick. I fix. I do not like when Little Flower is sick."

"You fix. Little Flower's female people love you for a long time, maybe even forgive you for time at Agency. Little Flower's people find no fix." At least she wasn't aware of any cure for it.

Myra's ears flicked back in astonishment at that, and nodded her understanding. She started cleaning up the mess, while Jessica climbed back up on her window seat and stared out at the storm as she contemplated her traitorous body and what Myra had told her earlier. A little while later, she cautiously tried eating something again, and this time it stayed down, to both their evident reliefs.

After breakfast, Myra handed her a tablet, and showed her how to call her grandfather and put the call up on the big screen if she wanted, as well as send messages. They didn't have the ability to text with her language yet, but she could draw on her tablet and it would show up on his. Once they were comfortable using the devices, the others left to give them privacy to talk, with the excuse that they needed to deal with the mess in the garden.

Her grandfather looked tired and sad, probably how she looked too. "Did they show you the pictures?" she asked, wondering if he knew about the others yet.

He nodded, and they sat there for a moment in their shared grief. After a while, he signed, "How are you?"

"Hey! You're learning to sign!" she exclaimed and then signed back. "I'm good. You?"

"I'm good. Sad," he replied back, and then wrote on the tablet. "They took us out of the cells yesterday after you called, and started teaching us sign language. I don't know a lot yet, but I'm going to practice hard so we can talk easier."

"I'm sad too. I've got news though. I talked to the judge and you're getting released on good behavior once the storm is over. Marsee's dad has been stuck at someone else's house because of the storm, and will stop by and pick you up on his way home."

"That is good news! I can't wait to see you. What's it like there?"

"It's amazing. I feel like Jack in the Beanstalk though. Everything is enormous. The kitchen sink is big enough to swim in and this place is like a castle. It even has a tower! There's probably enough space to house everyone here. Lots of empty rooms. Marsee says they're for guests, and for her siblings when they come to visit. In the center of the castle there's this tree. I can't even explain how big it is. It would make the redwoods look small. The trunk alone is at least twice the size of your house and it's got to be the best climbing tree in the universe. The trunks and branches are all woven together, and the leaves are purple and the size of a car. Around the tree is this most amazing garden, like straight out of Avatar, with glowing plants and animals. There's this thing that looks like a puppy with wings. I call them fairy dogs. Wait! Let me show you."

She jumped down from her seat and picked her sketchbook up off the table, and flipped through until she found the drawings that she'd done the other night. "See! Aren't they adorable! And their wings flash all sorts of different colors too! I think that's how they talk." She flipped to another page. "They have strange fish. I call this one an octoray. They like to play fetch!" Flipping to another page. "They even have giant six-legged pink wooly mammoths. Oh, and they have three moons and two suns!"

"Sounds incredible! I can't wait to see it. How does two suns even work?" James wrote.

"Not a clue. Haven't gotten that far. You have to try the star fruit. It's so good. I don't know why they never gave us any of that in quarantine though. Maybe it was out of season. Anyway, fried over a flame, they're better than s'mores."

"Not possible!" he wrote.

"I swear. I'll make sure we have some the first night. I don't think they know how to cook, or they didn't anyway. I'm pretty sure I invented it for them. They eat everything raw, and I think they choose not to eat fish or meat, only fruits and vegetables. Once I showed them how to cook meat, they let me cook that, but except for the first day, when they were curious, they've not eaten any themselves. They love the fried star fruit though."

"That must be why we started getting cooked meat with our meals. Thank you!" her grandfather said.

"Yeah. Marsee's mother says I need more protein for the baby. I've lost too much weight in quarantine. Apparently, we can't process the protein we need from their fruits and vegetables. At least that's what I think she meant."

"Well, that would make sense. As big as they are, they probably didn't need to cook meat like we did to survive. Cooking makes it easier for us to digest. I'm just glad they found something we can eat," James wrote.

"I learned something else this morning..." she started and paused, trying to find the right words.

"Oh?" he asked when she didn't continue right away.

"At the end of their month, I have to go in front of their worlds' leaders to prove we're people and not animals," she finally blurted out in a rush.

"Wait, what?! Why you? And why would we have to prove we're people?" he asked.

"Because of the man who raped me. Apparently, they don't have crime or wars here anymore. They did in the past but they ended up destroying their own world and moving here, and to them, apparently, we aren't people if we can hurt others like that."

"I wouldn't disagree with that. The man who hurt you is definitely an animal, and should be treated as such. But are you comfortable going before their leaders to talk about this? That won't be easy."

"Do I really have a choice?" she asked, but before he could answer, the others returned.

"It is time to call Sina," Myra signed.

"Can father's father come too?" she asked. Myra nodded and Jessica grinned.

"It's time for my sign language class. They said you could join in if you want," she told him.

In response he simply nodded yes. So, Myra conferenced him into the call along with her father, Councilor Marcus, and the Senior Guild Master, who also ended up joining them that day, although she'd clearly been learning on her own. Introductions were made, and the first sign they all learned was the proper sign for grandfather. By the end of the session, James's official name sign had become 'GrandFather'. He was pretty far behind everyone else, but Myra told her that he would have another lesson later in the day. Ellie had grumbled good naturedly when she realized that they'd given her the name sign of 'Senior Guild Master'.

"Well, it could be worse," Myra teased. "It is your title."

Jessica nodded emphatically in response. "When Marsee first told me my name, I'd been worried you all had called me something like Hairless Crawly or Stinky Butt, which had caused everyone to laugh. "But if you don't like Senior Guild Master, how about something like 'White Heart' or 'Pure Heart' for the patch of white fur on your chest, or 'Fairy Godmother'? That's what I've been calling you in my head." After trying to explain fairy godmother, Jessica told them a quick version of the story of Cinderella, to Ellie's evident delight.

"Well, those are all much better names. Sadly though, I've been 'Senior Guild Master' for almost a century now. I doubt that's ever going to change, unless I make up a new rank. However, Little Flower, I give you permission to call me Fairy Godmother, any time you want." Ellie moved her paws in the same motion Jessica had, and signed. "Poof!"

They'd also given more official name signs to the others, as while 'Marsee's Father' was perfectly good at home, it wouldn't exactly work well for him before the Council. They'd decided on a combination of the sign for chenzie and the letters for the sound 'ra' in their language for Jer, and Healer Chenzie-ra for Myra as it was fairly close to how their family names were spelled.

Marcus had been perfectly happy with having the name sign of 'Uncle Sun', at least until they decided on the official name signs for their world's primary sun, since his family name was the same. In their language, Jessica learned that 'uncle' was also used as an honorific for their parents' male mentor, not just their parents' siblings. Mentors became part of the family and were in many ways far more important than one's parent, as that relationship was both earned and chosen, not given by birth, and there were both legal and cultural expectations from a mentor.

After the lesson they raced the drones around the room, with Myra even joining in for a bit. She was surprisingly good and easily trounced both of them. After lunch, Jessica leaned back against the window seat and looked out at the raging storm, her thoughts as wild and drifting as the winds and sands she saw. After a while she picked up her sketchbook and started drawing again. Marsee was leaning up against the seat next to her, hand sewing some new clothing for her, since the stitcher tool was locked in Marsee's room, and set it down to stretch her paws after a while. Jessica had figured out how to make a wrap out of some of the fabric for use until she finished, but she wasn't wearing it now. It was too hot in the room and it was awkward. She kind of wished she still had the harness to hold everything in place.

"Can I see your drawing?" Marsee asked when Jessica paused to look out at the raging storm again.

Jessica handed it over. It was a picture of the old farm house, based loosely on that long ago memory of her grandparents. Grandpa Ben and Uncle James sat on their rockers shucking peas, while she sat on the stairs leaning up against the banister eating them, their old cat curled up at her feet. Her mother sunbathed on a blanket on the lawn, and her dad played fetch with her grandfather's border collie, Rufus. In the background the apples were ripening on the trees while their horse Buster grazed peacefully behind a white picket fence.

"GrandFather and Little Flower. Who are the others? Marsee asked, pointing to the people she recognized.

"This is my mother," she signed, pointing to the drawing. "My father, and my other grandfather."

"Mother's Father?" Marsee asked.

"No. Father's father," she said. This confused Marsee so she tried to explain, praying they didn't have any prejudices against people of the same sex being partners. "My father's father and GrandFather partner after my father's mother got sick and died."

"Is this why you do not have the same...same inside skin, same blood?" Myra asked, seemingly not at all concerned about the idea of two men being partners.

Jessica nodded. "Family by choice, not blood," she signed back.

"GrandFather's skin is all dark brown. Your skin is all light brown. Why do you not draw your stripes?" Marsee asked.

"Stripes? What stripes?" Jessica signed, confused.

"The stripes on your skin," Marsee answered, looking just as confused by her question.

"I do not have stripes on my skin," Jessica replied, looking down to confirm she hadn't suddenly developed some when she wasn't looking.

"Yes, you do," Myra said, walking over and tracing lines down her body. "Stripes here, swirl here. It is very pretty."

"I do not see stripes. Some dots," she said pointing to a few of her freckles. Skin all the same light brown." Marsee and Myra both looked at each other and they had a quick conversation. Myra took her tablet and flicked on the big monitor and pointed her tablet at Jessica, and apparently must have taken a picture because that went up on the screen a moment later. She then did something to the image and suddenly lines started to glow all up and down her body in stripes, with the occasional swirl.

"Little Flower draw colors all wrong. Missing many colors. Colors we see," Myra said. "Little Flower see sharper, farther, but fewer colors than us."

"That is what you see?" she asked.

"Pattern yes, color no. Not the same. Shifted so you can see the stripes. You look better. Pretty. Like the moon on water at night. Bright," Myra replied.

*Oh great,* Jessica thought. *Not only do I have zebra stripes but they sparkle like a freakin' vampire. Well, at least they think it looks pretty, since I can't see it.*

"GrandFather's skin is dark. Not many at the Agency have dark skin. Most are light, like you," Myra stated. "Your skin was darker when you were rescued, lighter now. Is your skin sick?" she asked.

Jessica shook her head. "Dark skin helps protect my people from sunburn. My skin will get darker with more sun but not as dark as GrandFather. GrandFather was born with dark skin. GrandFather's long time father came from a place with more sun. My long time father came from a place with less sun." Myra nodded and seemed to be happy with the answer, but Jessica had more to say. "Some people think dark skin is bad, light skin good. They hurt people with dark skin like GrandFather. My long time father took GrandFather's long time father from home, hurt, forced them to do what they wanted, treat them like animals. Some still believe dark skin people are animals but that is not true. It is just skin color. Mother, watch the others please. Protect my people with dark skin from them. Many also think male who partner with male is also bad, like an animal, or female who partner with female. Not true. Love is good, not bad."

Myra flicked her ears back in surprise but nodded her agreement. "I will protect GrandFather and others for you."

# CHAPTER 18

# Marsee: Goldilocks and the Ten Chenzies

The storm had raged on for eight days now with no signs of stopping. As expected, a second storm had followed right behind the first, joining forces with the first one and was even stronger now than it had been before. Forecasts now showed they expected the storm to last another several days. Lightning struck outside the window causing Marsee to jump.

"I wish this storm would hurry up and end already!" she signed. With little to do but sit and wait, they'd spent most of their days in lessons with Sina and the others, tending the garden, playing games, and studying. The amount of progress they'd made in being able to communicate via sign language was astounding. Little Flower had even managed to make her way through her first book and as a challenge Marsee had tried translating it into Little Flower's written language. Apparently, she'd messed up pretty badly on a few words because Little Flower had been snickering for hours the night before, but refused to tell her what she'd written, saying she didn't have the words to explain it, and she wasn't going to draw it, to Marsee's utter annoyance. So much so that she'd reached out to Ellie about having one of her techs try to put together a search algorithm for the language dictionary so she could look up Little Flower's words. Ellie had replied that they already had people working on that, and had sent her an early copy of the program, but that didn't help her understand what she'd done wrong either as the word she'd accidentally used wasn't in the language dictionary yet.

They kept the bet going even though her mother had stated that the amount of cleanup would be more than one person could do alone and that they would all help pick up after the storm. After that though, it was fair game. So far, her mother was in the lead by one point. They had agreed that medical discussions, emergencies, or conversations with anyone who didn't know sign language were off limits to the game, as well as any deliberate request to stop. And they'd decided that the bet would end when the storm did.

The sand had piled so high in the courtyard that Little Flower actually had the easiest time harvesting, as the sand was all the way up to the top of the raised beds now. So now Little Flower harvested, while Marsee dragged the trays through the shifting sand on an improvised sled. Her mother processed the produce for long term storage, and prepared baskets for delivery to the neighbors. Most of the produce had been harvested and her mother indicated they would wait until after the storm to replant for the next cycle of crops. Her mother expected they were going to be without the outer shields for at least a day based on the current forecast and state of the power reserves, but she hoped that the storm would be lessening in strength by then.

They were planning on heading out with the ground crawler after lunch to bring supplies to their neighbors, after her mother had checked in and found that several were running low on both food and other necessities. They had an off-road shuttle so her mother could make it to her clinic or patients in an emergency. It was far too dangerous to fly in these conditions, but the ground crawlers automated systems should be able to make it through the storm without issue. Sand storms were common, although one of this duration was not, and illness and injury never waited for storms to pass. *Although,* Marsee thought to herself, *it's really two storms in a way, back-to-back.*

"I think that's the last of it. We might get one more day of star fruit but that's it and we completely lost the crop of yellow fang. Not enough sun to ripen, and they've all started to rot on the vines. I shut down the hydroponics units, no point in even trying to water them as most of the filters are packed with sand at this point. We were barely getting a trickle from the pond and I expect we're probably going to need to replace all the filters when this is over," she signed to her mother after she dropped off the last load.

"I'll add that to the list of things to have your father pick up when he returns," her mother replied, hefting a crate. "While I add this to the care packages, why don't you and Little Flower go clean up and I'll meet you in the shuttle bay in fifteen minutes or so."

"Point!" Marsee signed and her mother groaned.

Laughing, Marsee took Little Flower to the kitchen to wash up. Her little paws were sticky with star fruit juice. At the end of the season, they turned mushy and the juice oozed everywhere, which was great for juicing as they were extra sweet, but not so good for harvesting. She was glad that she hadn't had to pick them. Even with the new gloves her fur would have been stained for weeks. Once Little Flower was washed and changed into a clean outfit that Marsee had finally finished sewing, they left to meet up with her mother at the shuttle.

"Do you think they'll like me?" Little Flower asked on their way.

"I'm sure they will. Most of our neighbors are really nice. Mama said they can't wait to meet you," Marsee replied.

Little Flower looked unsure.

"What's wrong?" she asked.

"I just want to make a good impression. So much depends on what people think of me and well...I've always had a hard time making friends. Everyone always thought I was weird. I had one really good friend though. She was with me that day..." Little Flower's hands fell to her sides, unable to continue.

"I'd love to see a picture of her sometime. I bet she was just as wonderful as you are," Marsee said.

"Thanks. She was even better, and a lot like you. She always helped me in school and was really smart. She wanted to go to school to catch the bad people," Little Flower replied.

"Like a guard?" Marsee asked.

"Kind of. More like a scientist or tech for the guard," Little Flower replied. "You know the day it happened I was taking a language test. I'm pretty sure I failed. Now look at me. Speaking a language from another world."

"Language test? Are there other worlds you talk to? I didn't know there were any in your area," Marsee asked.

"No. Languages on our planet. There were many languages, hundreds. I'm not sure how many. Even people who spoke the same language would have different ways of saying things in their area."

"How do you speak with people if everyone has a different language?" Marsee asked.

"How do you?" Jessica asked back.

"There are only five languages. Each species has their own. It is easy to learn them all. Well four are easy. On the Water World they speak with color."

"How? Like the fish in the pond?" Little Flower asked.

Marsee nodded. "Those fish come from the Water World too. Papa brought them home a few years back. They were a gift from their Senior Councilor, when he found out about Mama's garden and pool, and her preference for things that glow. Their skin lights up in different patterns for words, and they use color to show emotion and context. So how do you learn hundreds of languages?"

"Not very easily. Some languages were more common than others, and we had machines to help speak for us. We could type or speak into our tablets and the other language would come out and people living in the same place often spoke one common language, even if they knew others or came from somewhere else. Many people never bothered learning though," Little Flower explained.

"Wow. That must have made things difficult. Is that why people fought?" Marsee asked.

"Sometimes. Say one thing and the other person hears something else," Jessica said. "Of course, that happened with people who spoke the same language too.

Marsee nodded and hit the switch to the shuttle bay, opening the door. Her mother was already there and loading the last of the crates into the shuttle.

"Perfect timing! Go ahead and get Little Flower buckled in. I'll be right back. I just need to grab my medical bag in case there are any injuries that need treatment on our stops," her mother deliberately signed after she shut the cargo hatch.

Marsee grinned and slid open the passenger door. She lifted Little Flower inside, and climbed in after. The crawler was pretty high off the ground to better handle traversing the uneven terrain. Little Flower looked around the crawler curiously, but there wasn't much to see. With three rows of seats, the crawler could handle seven people, three in the back, and two in each of the first two rows, with an aisle in between. The back row was a bench that could be lowered for additional cargo space, or transport of a patient, if needed, but her mother hadn't put it down. The cargo bay in the back was stacked high with supplies though.

"Why don't you sit up front next to Mother. I'm not sure how much we'll be able to see in this storm, but you'll have a better view from there," Marsee said, tapping one of the seats in the front.

Little Flower walked over and Marsee picked her up, setting her in it, and then pulled out and adjusted the safety harness, so it was snug. She was so tiny that her feet didn't even come to the edge of the seat. "The controls here will allow you to move the seat to wherever you want." Marsee demonstrated and Little Flower raised the seat up and as far forward as it would go, so she could better see out the widows. By the time Marsee had strapped herself in, her mother had returned, tossed her medical bag on the back seat, and climbed in.

Once her mother sat down and buckled her safety harness, the ground crawler powered on and a semi-transparent display appeared on the front window. She tapped on an icon and a map appeared with all the nearby dwellings marked. Her mother tapped the location of their nearest neighbor and a line indicating several paths that could be taken. Her mother chose the longer but flatter route, and the main shuttle bay doors started to slide open, letting the raging storm in. The shuttle bay doors were the one exit through the static shields, as it was really the only one they would likely ever use during a storm anyway. Once the doors were open enough for the crawler to drive through, it automatically started moving forward and would drive them to the neighbor's compound without further assistance. If they wanted to, they could manually operate the vehicle, but in this storm, it was far safer to let the crawler drive. As soon as they were through, the bay doors automatically closed behind them.

As they started moving the display changed from the map, to indicate objects in the path or nearby, changes in elevation, and the status of the crawler. Blue warning lights blinked on as the outside wind speed was detected. Her mother tapped the warning to dismiss it. Outside there was little you could see except the occasional stone pillar as the crawler automatically moved around them. There were no roads to the neighbors but the crawler had no problem navigating through the drifting sand and determining if the ground in front was stable enough to drive over. They went slowly though. With the low visibility and shifting sands, even the auto-pilot system was limited in how far its sensors could see through the storm.

Half an hour later the neighbor's complex suddenly appeared in front of them. The crawler brought them around to the other side of the complex and inside their shuttle bay. Once the outer doors closed, the inner door opened and several people came streaming out of the compound to meet them. Her mother opened the crawler's door and jumped out to greet their neighbors, while she helped Little Flower out of her harness and followed behind.

"Thank the moons you made it safely," their neighbor said as they greeted her mother.

"Nothing this old crawler can't handle. Kind of a boring ride to be honest. Couldn't see more than five feet in front of us the whole time," her mother replied.

"Boring is good on a day like today."

"Indeed. Oh, here she is. Everyone, I'd like you to meet Little Flower," her mother said.

Little Flower was hiding behind Marsee. Marsee gently moved her forward with her tail and then left it wrapped around her for comfort.

"Little Flower, these are our neighbors the Manas, their mother Serin and her five cubs, Rowin, Jowin, Sowin, Dowin, and Peep," Marsee told Little Flower. "I don't know the one Serin is holding though."

Little Flower gave a tentative wave. "Hello. It's nice to meet you," which Marsee translated.

"This is my sister's cub. Teena. I was cub-sitting when the storm hit. My sister was visiting our brother in North Beach and Pep is stuck at the Guild. Thank you so much for bringing supplies. We're getting pretty low on fresh food. Pep was planning to stop by on his way back from the Guild, but this storm has been going on forever," Serin said.

"Of course," her mother replied.

Teena was just about the same size as Little Flower, maybe a few inches taller and tentatively signed, "Hello, Little Flower," causing Little Flower to brighten considerably.

"Teena! You've been learning to sign!" Marsee said. Teena nodded shyly.

"We all have. It's given us something to do during the storm, although we aren't very good at it yet. Pep started teaching us the other day. Apparently, the Senior Guild Master has been taking classes, and dragging everyone she can into them." Marsee was keeping a running translation for Little Flower so she wouldn't be left out of the conversation.

"Thank you for taking the time to learn. It makes me feel very welcome and happy that you are trying," Little Flower signed.

"Of course! You're our neighbor now and we want you to be happy here," Serin said after Marsee translated.

"Mom, can we show Little Flower the chenzies?" Peep asked.

"I don't see why not. Myra and I can unload this. I want to talk with her anyway. Stay out of Fluffer's box though. You know how grumpy she gets when she's this close to having a cub."

"Yes, Mama," came a chorus of innocent sounding replies. Then Peep signed "Come, Little Flower," and they all followed Peep out of the shuttle bay.

"Instead of a food garden, they raise chenzies and the grass they eat," Marsee explained as they made their way to the stable in the middle of their compound. Once there, Marsee picked up Little Flower and Peep picked up Teena so they could both see over the walls of the stall. Inside was a large six-legged fluffy tan-colored creature with dark blue eyes, wide floppy ears, and massive curving tusks. To Little Flower it must look huge. The creature was slightly taller than her mother on all fours, but looked twice as wide with the thick curly fur coat that wouldn't be shaved until the rains started. By then it would be nearly twice as thick and begin to shed naturally.

The creature ambled over and wuffed at Peep, who scratched the fuzzy creature on the head. It closed its eyes in obvious delight and then must have caught the scent of Little Flower as it snorted, opened its eyes back up, and took a good look at them. Spotting Little Flower, it came over and wuffed at the tiny cub, sticking its big nose right up against Little Flower, the chenzies massive curving tusks on either side of them. The chenzie's head alone was bigger than Little Flower. Marsee was thoroughly surprised that Little Flower didn't flinch but instead put her tiny paw out and the chenzie wuffed at that as well, causing her clothing to flap a little. Slowly Little Flower extended her reach, leaning out, and started petting the giant creature on its furry nose. It let out a little snort but then closed its eyes, contented with her attention, deciding Little Flower was not a risk. When it had had enough, the creature returned to munching on its feed, and they moved down to the next stall.

"They're so soft!" Little Flower signed.

Marsee nodded. She couldn't easily sign back while holding her. In total their neighbors had ten chenzies.

"This is Fluffers. She's really pregnant. Due any day now. Don't get too close," Peep said and tried to sign.

Marsee burst out laughing. "You just said 'Fluffers has a blue head'," and set Little Flower down so she could sign. The sign is 'pregnant'.

The others all copied dutifully and then she passed along the information to Little Flower. Picking her back up, they peered into the stall.

Fluffers was in the back corner of the stall wuffing and groaning, leaning her big tusks against the wall of the stall. Her tail was lashing and her belly was hugely distended from the baby inside.

"Is she alright? She looks like she's in pain," Little Flower signed. Marsee translated when the others looked confused.

"Yeah, I don't know. Maybe she's having her cub. I'd better get Mama," Peep said, and ran off.

"What do you use chenzies for?" Little Flower asked while they waited.

"Their fur, mostly. Your blanket is made out of chenzie fur, in fact it came from here. It's one of the things we trade for. Sometimes we use the fur as is, like your blanket, other times it gets turned into fabric. I think Sowin made the fabric your garment is made out of too. Most of what we have in storage came from here. When they die, we take the body where the wild animals can get it for food," Marsee explained.

Sowin took a closer look at the material used in Little Flower's shirt and nodded. "Yep, that's mine alright."

"It's very pretty!" Little Flower said, causing Sowin to smile.

"Thank you! I'm glad you like it!"

Peep returned then with his mother and hers in tow. Her mother had grabbed her medical kit out of the shuttle and the two peered in the stall. "It certainly looks like she's about ready to give birth," Serin said as Myra dug through her bag for her scanner.

"Can we get closer? I'm too far away to get a clear scan," Myra said.

Serin nodded and grabbed a lead rope off of the stall door. "Let me secure her first. She gets super grumpy when she's pregnant and she might kick someone she doesn't know well." Serin slowly opened the door and walked in. "Hey, pretty Mama," she crooned. "You look like you don't feel so good. Can I come see?"

Fluffers snorted but didn't give any other indication that she was upset by Serin's presence. Once she approached. She reached out and gave the creature a scratch. Fluffers let out a painful groan and her side rippled.

"Oh, you poor thing," Serin said, and attached the lead and scratched some more until the creature's eyes half closed. "Okay. You can come in now, slowly."

Her mother entered and carefully walked over, let Fluffers sniff her, and gave her a little pat, before running her scanner over the groaning chenzie. When she was done with her exam, she nodded to Serin and walked out of the stall. Once Myra was clear, Serin unclipped the lead from the harness around the creature's massive head and exited, locking the stall door behind her.

"Breech," Myra said when Serin was safely clear and turned for the results of the examination.

"Three moons! I was afraid of that. Can you help?" Serin asked.

"Honestly, all I have with me are first aid supplies. I can make it to the Agency and back in a little under an hour with the equipment I need to cut the cub out but..." Serin nodded her understanding.

"What's wrong?" Little Flower asked.

"The cub is not in the right position to be born," Marsee explained, "and Mama doesn't have the right equipment to cut the cub out. She can get it from the Agency but cutting the cub out would likely mean Fluffers would die, if she doesn't anyway before we get back."

"GrandFather could help," Little Flower signed.

"How could GrandFather help?" Myra asked.

"GrandFather was an animal healer back on my world. This happened often. Maybe help. Worth a try if you're going to lose Fluffers anyway?" Little Flower signed.

Marsee translated for the others.

"Do you think he could help? A breech birth usually means a death sentence for the chenzies. If they've got a way to fix it..." Serin asked hopefully.

Marsee's mother looked at Serin and the cubs who looked back at her with such hope. "I don't know, but we're going to try. Come on you two, we need to go." Marsee picked up Little Flower and took off at a run, following her mother back to the shuttle bay. A minute later they were in the crawler and on their way. Once the crawler was moving, Myra placed a call to the Agency.

"Brice, we have an emergency, a chenzie with a breech birth. Get Nazari, a surgery kit, and Little Flower's grandfather and have them waiting in the office. We'll be there in twenty minutes."

"Little Flower's grandfather?" Brice asked, confused.

"Yes, Little Flower is with me, and she says that he was an animal healer on their world, and they had a way to fix breech births. It's a long shot, but perhaps between Nazari and GrandFather we can save the chenzie. Fluffers has been a part of the Mana family for decades, and if there's even a chance we can save her I want to try. And if it doesn't work, I want Nazari there to do the surgery. She's far more trained than I am to work with chenzies."

"Understood," Brice said, and signed off.

Marsee translated for Little Flower and then explained that her mother had also studied to be an animal healer, when their last one had died, and there wasn't anyone else willing to move out here and fill his place, as there were only a few families with Chenzie herds in the area. It wasn't her specialty though.

Twenty excruciatingly long minutes later they pulled into the Agency. The wind dropped significantly as they drove through the shield's entrance and the sands now drifted down instead of sideways, making it far easier to see. Her mother switched to the manual system once they were inside the shield, and drove between two of the giant wards towards the center of the compound where the clinic used to be. Marsee was astounded by the changes, even though she'd seen video and aerial footage of the place. It didn't even come close to the scale of what had been built, and in only three days too. Her mother stopped the crawler but didn't shut it off when she made it to the clinic, and as she stopped the door opened. A healer Marsee didn't know and GrandFather came out.

When Little Flower saw her grandfather, she unbuckled her safety harness, jumped up to hit the switch to open the door, and practically flew out of the shuttle and across the yard to her grandfather, before either Marsee or her mother could stop her. As soon as he saw her, he went from looking confused to running. When she made it to him, she leapt into his arms, nearly knocking the male over in her embrace. They hugged each other tightly.

Marsee followed Little Flower out of the shuttle, as her mother opened the cargo door, and leaned over the back seat to make room for the medical supplies that Nazari carried with her.

"Little Flower, GrandFather, come on. We have to hurry. You can catch up in the shuttle," Marsee signed.

Little Flower nodded, grabbed her grandfather's paw and practically dragged him back onto the shuttle. Marsee had them sit in the back row, so Nazari could sit up front with her mother. She buckled them both in as Little Flower brought GrandFather up to speed on what was going on. That done, Marsee clipped into her own seat and spun it around so she could translate. Supplies loaded, Marsee's mother and Nazari took their seats, buckled in, and back out in the storm they went.

"Little Flower says GrandFather wants to see the scans," Marsee said once they were underway.

Her mother nodded, and changed the front display, to bring up the scans she took from earlier. The images were grainy on the crawler's ancient display, but good enough to see what was going on. Little Flower and GrandFather talked some more.

"GrandFather says he thinks he can help. Says he will need two long ropes, hot water, and a soap sponge. He then says we need to...what?!" Marsee exclaimed.

"What did he say?" Nazari asked.

"He says you need to use the soap to make your arm slippery, and then you need to stick it through the birth canal!" she spluttered. "And then push the cub back so there is room to grab each leg, and rotate them so they're coming out of the birth canal instead of butt first, and then wrap a rope around each foot to help pull the cub out and keep it from going back inside. At least I think that's what he said."

Myra and Nazari just looked at each other. "Do you think it would work?" Myra asked.

"In theory, it sounds like it should. Do you think the chenzie will stand for it though? That's pretty invasive," Nazari replied.

"We could give her a light sedative," Myra suggested and Nazari agreed it was worth a try.

When they arrived back at the compound, they were met by Serin, who informed them that Fluffers had laid down in her stall, and they'd not been able to get her back on her feet. All of the cubs were hanging on the outside of the stall when they entered the stable. Fluffers was laying on her belly, head resting on the ground when Marsee peered over. Serin entered the stall and Fluffers didn't even lift her tired head, just let out a low groan. Myra, Nazari and GrandFather followed after. Marsee set Little Flower on the edge of the stall so she could see without being in the way, and still translate for her grandfather. Peep ran off to find soap and a bucket of hot water, while Sowin left to locate a clean coil of soft rope.

"GrandFather says he wants to see how her legs move, to know how to turn the calf's legs. He says they don't have six legged animals like her," Marsee translated.

"Tell him to wait. We're going to sedate Fluffers first so it's safe, before he comes close. One kick from her would kill him," Myra said.

GrandFather nodded his understanding after Little Flower translated. Her mother gave the chenzie the sedative, and her eyes slowly closed with another low groan. Once her mother indicated it was safe, GrandFather examined the chenzie's legs, and then with the help of Nazari manipulated them, so he could see how they moved. They were far too heavy for him to lift on his own, especially with how the chenzie was laying. It took all three of the adults to roll the chenzie over, which apparently was where GrandFather wanted her anyway. Both Nazari and her mother seemed surprised and asked for confirmation.

"He says yes, it will be easier for the cub to come out, and to manipulate the feet and calf based on where it is right now," Marsee replied and then did her best to translate GrandFather's instructions. "GrandFather says if we can get the back two legs around and out the cub should come out. He says the cub's left leg needs to come in close to the body like this and rotate before straightening. Rotate the other way for the right leg. And you need to cover the hoof, so it doesn't tear her inside." GrandFather demonstrated until Nazari nodded her understanding.

At that moment Peep returned with the soap and hot water, and GrandFather took his shirt off and started cleaning his arms all the way up to his shoulders. Once done, he went over and moved Fluffer's short tail aside and stuck his arm inside the birth canal. Fluffers raised her head slightly, groaned and set her head back down.

"*Ewww...*" the watching cubs all groaned in unison. Marsee was thinking the same thing but kept her mouth shut.

"Hush!" came Serin's clipped reply.

Several minutes later, GrandFather retracted his arm, washed it and then took the tablet to talk to Little Flower.

"He says his arm is too short. He can't reach," Marsee translated.

Nazari nodded and took the soap sponge, and did the same as GrandFather, but before she got very far, she had to stop. "I don't have enough space to work, my paw is too big," and then pointed to Marsee, "Come here. You try."

"Me?!" Marsee squeaked.

"You're the only one here that's the right size," Nazari said. "Everyone else is either too big or too small. You saw how the leg needs to move?" she asked.

Marsee gulped and nodded.

"Good. Let's get you cleaned up," Nazari said.

A few minutes later, her arm soaked and slimy from the soap, Marsee found herself staring at the back end of Fluffer's butt. "I don't know..." she said. She wasn't sure what was worse, the idea of sticking her paw up the chenzie's butt, or worry about her instinct.

"You can do this," her mother said gently. It's no worse than cleaning the compost bins, less so, since the waste doesn't come out of that hole.

Just go slow and keep your claws curled in at all times. If you don't try, Fluffers will probably die."

Marsee swallowed hard, growled at her instinct to behave, and gingerly stuck her paw in until she was about up to her elbow. "There's something in the way," she said. "It feels slimy."

"That's the calf and the birth sac," Nazari said, watching the scanner that her mother held. "Gently push the calf back and slide your arm along the calf's side. We'll want to get the bottom one first. Keep going until you can feel the front of the leg...almost there. That's it, now slide your hand down the leg until you get to the knee."

At this point Marsee's arm was in nearly up to her shoulder, when suddenly her arm exploded in pain and pressure. "Oww oww oww oww oww!" Marsee started yelling and tried to pull away.

"Don't move! That's just a contraction. It'll pass in a second," Nazari said.

"Oww oww owwwww!" Marsee said, gritting her teeth through the pain. "Three moons!" she swore when the contraction passed. "That hurt!"

"Well done, Marsee. Now there, you should be right at the knee. Move a little further down and see if you can bend it at all. Slowly now, try not to use your claws or tear the sac if you can. That's it! Now follow the leg until you get to the hoof."

Marsee followed the shape of the leg down until it changed and felt hard instead of squishy.

"That's the hoof," Nazari said, confirming her suspicions. "Now, wrap your paw around it and flex it towards you."

As she did, the pressure of her paw against the hoof must have torn the sac because suddenly she was covered in liquid just as another contraction hit. Marsee whimpered in pain and disgust and waited it out.

"It's okay, we'll just have to move quicker now," Nazari said, when Marsee apologized. "Now carefully try to twist the hoof up and back out towards you. Gently, keep pulling..." Nazari coached.

As soon as the foot was out of the birth canal, GrandFather slapped the rope around the tiny three toed hoof, and held it to keep the leg from slipping back inside.

"One down," her mother said. "One to go. You're doing a wonderful job, Marsee. I'm so proud of you."

Marsee took a few deep breaths, and went back in for the second leg. This one was much harder, with the lack of space from the leg that was already out. Two contractions later, and a lot of yelling on Marsee's part, the second leg was out and rope wrapped around. Marsee collapsed back in a heap as Nazari took the ropes from GrandFather and when the next contraction came, gave a gentle pull on the cub. The cub came free with another gush of fluid that splashed everywhere. Marsee scrambled back to get out of the way.

Nazari removed what was left of the birth sack and cleared the cub's nose. When the cub lifted its head and let out a tiny wuff, everyone cheered.

"Alright, everyone out of the stall except for Serin. I'm going to wake Fluffers," Nazari said, pulling the cub away from his mother just in case she got confused or angry as the sedative wore off. Surprising everyone though, Fluffers just rolled herself into a sitting position, looked back at her cub, and heaved herself to her feet with a groan. Fluffers sniffed at the cub and to everyone's relief started cleaning him. Serin unhitched the lead rope, patted the furry beast, and walked out of the stall, giving mother and son a chance to get acquainted.

When everyone was as clean as they could get without a sonic shower, Serin brought them into her family room, and provided refreshments. "Thank you, GrandFather. Without you we would have lost them both. If there is ever anything I can do for you, please let me know and it's yours," Serin said.

"Agreed. And we wouldn't have been able to do it, if Marsee hadn't been willing to proffer up her arm for science, either," her mother added.

"I'm pretty sure my arm won't ever be the same," Marsee said, causing everyone to laugh. "Is childbirth really that painful or was it just that I was just on the receiving end of it?"

"Yes," Serin, Nazari, and her mother all said at the same time.

"Well, it's official then, I'm never having cubs," Marsee stated, and everyone burst out laughing again, tails curled so tightly they must have hurt as much as Marsee's arm did.

Half an hour later, after a quick check on mother and son, they were back in the shuttle and on their way back to the Agency to drop Nazari off.

"GrandFather, if you would like to continue healing animals here on our world, we could really use someone with your expertise to help care for the animals from your world, and I would be honored to mentor you should you like to become a healer for our people or animals as well," Nazari said when they arrived back at the Agency.

"Thank you, I will think about it. For now though, I would like to spend time with my granddaughter, and figure out what this new world has to offer. It has been far too long since I've seen her and we have a lot of catching up to do," he replied.

"I fully understand. Thank you again, GrandFather. You've made a monumental impact for the care of the species on our world, and for that we can never thank you enough," Nazari said, and climbed out of the shuttle. With Nazari dropped off, the four of them made quick work of delivering the remaining supplies and returned home, after a quick call to Serin confirmed that Fluffers and her cub were still doing well.

# CHAPTER 19

# Jessica: Cleanup

They made it back to the compound with just enough time to grab a quick snack and make their way into the family room before the evening language lesson with Sina and the others. With four of them there, Myra decided to throw the lesson up on the main screen, rather than huddle around one of their tablets. GrandFather's arrival at the compound caused quite the stir, and Marsee had to tell her harrowing tale of how she had to stick her arm up the butt of a chenzie, in sign of course.

"It reminds me of the tale of Goldilocks and the Three Bears," Jessica said, so then she had to tell everyone the story, which she decided to act out to everyone's delight and laughter.

Afterwards, Sina decided that for tonight's lesson, rather than go over the planned list of new vocabulary, everyone else would tell a story of their own.

With a lot of help from her, her grandfather told of how he met Grampa Ben, and used Marsee to stand in for their old draft horse Buster, and Jessica as her grandfather Ben, to help act it out and fill in for the words he didn't know.

"I met Little Flower's grandfather the first day I was new healer in town. Ben's partner had just died. He was depressed, but appeared mad and barely spoke to me. Buster was lame, had a sore foot, and was very grumpy."

Jessica leaned up against one the tables, arms crossed and scowling while GrandFather picked up Marsee's back foot. Marsee played along, acting very annoyed, ears pinned back and glaring.

GrandFather nodded. "Yes, just like this. I was trying to find where his foot was sore, but he didn't want me to hold his foot."

Marsee tried pulling her leg back and GrandFather held on, or tried to.

"Buster kicked and I went flying, lost my balance, and fell over a cart full of horse poop," GrandFather said next.

Marsee kicked slowly and GrandFather pretended to go flying into a pillow.

"The cart fell over on me. Horse poop fell all over me. Ben tried helping me up but he was laughing too hard."

Jessica walked over and pretended to try and help him up, but laughing he pulled her down onto the pillow with him.

"Ben fell down and landed face first in horse poop. We laughed for a very long time afterwards." GrandFather smiled wistfully at the memory.

"Okay, you win. That's worse than what I went through today. Not by much, but worse. But between that and what I went through today, I am never becoming an animal healer either," Marsee signed to the amusement of everyone.

"Myra, did you save Buster? He was with me that day," GrandFather asked through her.

Myra frowned and shook her head. "The only two males we saved of that species were born afterwards. I am sorry."

Her grandfather sighed. "That was always a long shot. He was badly injured. I wouldn't have been able to save him. I was looking for something to put him out of his misery when you showed up."

Jessica leaned over and hugged him, trying hard to keep from crying. For a brief moment her hope had flared. He hugged her back just as tightly and rested his chin on the top of her head. *I have my grandfather back, that's more than most have,* she reminded herself.

Myra decided to go next and told an old cub's tale to go along with Jessica's about five litter-mates who kept getting into all sorts of trouble, which soon had them all shedding tears of laughter instead. Marsee was looking at her mother oddly though.

"What is it?" Jessica asked.

"Those are the names of my siblings," Marsee replied.

"That story is where I got their names from," Myra said. "Thankfully, they weren't nearly as bad when they were younger. Most of the time anyway."

Marsee's father snorted, which had the others laughing.

Councilor Marcus told of how he'd had trouble learning Flyer when he was first training to be in the Council, constantly getting the pitch wrong, and how he accidentally insulted the daughter of a Councilor he was meeting with one time, when he tried greeting her in their language, only to accidentally call the Flyer a smelly fish. Thankfully she'd had a good sense of humor, and only acted outraged for a few moments. Decades later, that same Flyer had invited him and several others from her council to dinner after she'd been elected Senior Councilor. He'd not realized she was the same person he'd met all those years ago, but she hadn't forgotten him and had provided the stinkiest fish she could find for the evening meal, and had proceeded to act outraged that Marcus refused to eat, stating that it was a traditional meal and to refuse would mean he didn't trust her and would be grounds for war, and the others had joined in. At the time, he'd been terrified that he'd caused some sort of interplanetary incident and tried desperately to explain that his species didn't eat eat, before the Flyer's had all burst out laughing at the joke.

"Who was the Senior Councilor?" Marsee's father asked, apparently having never heard the story before.

"None other than Senior Councilor Wind Rider," Marcus replied with a grin and then explained to her that Wind Rider was their current Senior Councilor and a consummate prankster, like most of her species.

"To this day, there's always something new in the shape of a fish in my room, every time I travel to Flyer," he added.

Jer laughed. "I always wondered why there was a giant fish over your desk."

When the laughter died down, Sina told the tale of two brothers, an ancient story of heroism, and a great deal of stupidity, that somehow ended up working in their favor, and Ellie told of how she'd once stained Sina's grandfather's fur bright green by accident.

"That really happened?" Sina asked. "I must have heard that story a dozen times as a cub. I thought for sure he was pulling my tail."

Ellie laughed. "Well, I wasn't the Senior Guild Master then, and frankly I was a bit of a clutz. I was going through my growth spurt, and I must have tripped over my own tail at least a dozen times."

"And everyone else's," Myra added, holding up her tail. "You were as bad as my cubs."

After everyone stopped laughing, Jer told of how Marsee had tried to hide a baby doba beast in the tower when she was a cub, not realizing how much they hated heights, and how the poor thing had cried so loudly for its mother that the neighbors heard and had come to find out what was wrong.

"Really Papa? That's the story you decided to tell?" Marsee huffed.

"What can I say? It's a funny story," he said with a shrug. Marsee just growled at him, but her tail was curled, so everyone knew she was just as amused. Jer apparently had a picture saved and brought that up, showing a very young and adorable Marsee as a kitten, and a purple and brown spotted deer like creature that was about the same size.

"I still don't know how you managed to capture it in the first place," Myra said.

Marsee just shrugged. "I don't really remember. I think I found it in the garden. I didn't capture it, it just followed me around."

"We never did find its mother," Myra stated. "And while Marsee begged us to let her keep it, Jer ended up bringing it to an animal rescue in Council City. We didn't have the time or resources to properly care for a baby doba, especially one that was still nursing."

When the lesson was over, Marsee's mother lit the lanterns, and they had fried foods for the evening meal, saving the fried star fruit for dessert. GrandFather begrudgingly admitted it tasted better than s'mores and certainly better than anything he'd had for the past few years. They talked for a while after, but Marsee seemed quieter than normal, and Myra turned the lanterns off early, stating it had been a long day and everyone was tired.

The next morning, Jessica woke up warm and comfortable, wrapped in Marsee's furry embrace. She opened her eyes to see that her grandfather was still asleep on his pillow, the sun shining on his face. She was hardly able to believe he was actually there. She was so happy to be reunited with him, and couldn't wait to show him around the compound. She just hoped the inner garden wasn't too badly damaged from the storm.

*Wait, sunshine?* She sat up quickly and looked out the window. The sun was shining brightly through the big window. The storm was finally over, and far sooner than everyone expected!

She shoved Marsee's side to try and wake her up. "What?" Marsee signed groggily.

"The storm is over!" Jessica signed excitedly and pointed out the window. Marsee shot up and looked out.

"Mama! Wake up! The storm is over!" Marsee called out, or at least that's what Jessica thought Marsee must have said, since she didn't sign.

"Oh good. You just lost the bet. I'm going back to sleep while you clean up," Marsee's mother signed and then very deliberately closed her eyes, and pretended to be sleeping soundly. If Jessica could hear, she was sure the big cat was snoring too.

"Mother! That's not fair!" Marsee cried out.

"Fair's fair," Myra signed, without opening her eyes. "Now hush. GrandFather is still sleeping."

Marsee collapsed against the window seat with a dramatic groan and heavy sigh, which caused Jessica to giggle.

"I'll help," Jessica signed.

"You will?" Marsee signed back, surprised and hopeful.

"Yes. I'll help watch and make sure you do it right," Jessica teased.

Marsee scowled with a positively feral look, grabbed one of the small pillows, and threw it at her. Jessica ducked, came back up and signed 'missed!' before bolting out of the room. Marsee was right behind. Squeals of laughter echoed down the hallway behind them.

To Jessica's surprise though, Marsee didn't chase her for very long, and when she turned around Marsee was nowhere to be found. Cautious and expecting a trap, Jessica walked back until she came to Marsee's fresh trail in the drifting sand. She examined it with a frown. It looked like Marsee had skidded to a stop, circled a few times, and took off in the other direction. She followed the trail back past the living room, where her grandfather and Marsee's mother were now up and talking, past the kitchen, and had almost made it to Myra's office, when she was hit from behind and flattened by a massive pillow. Laughing and crawling out from under the pillow she found Marsee picking at one of her claws with a very innocent expression on her face.

"You know it's not very nice to sneak up on a deaf person," Jessica said, brushing the sand off her clothes.

Marsee flipped her ears back in astonishment. "It's not *my* fault you forgot the hallway goes in a circle. For a prey species you're not very good at avoiding predators."

"That's because we aren't a prey species," Jessica signed.

Marsee burst out laughing, tail curled, and practically fell over. "Good one."

"I'm serious. Think about it. Prey species tend to have eyes on the sides of their heads, predators in the front. Prey tends to eat plants. Predators meat. We can eat both. We were the apex hunter on our planet, capable of taking down the biggest prey. Some as big as a chenzie. We were so good at it, that our chenzies all died out. Just because we aren't born with teeth and claws like you, doesn't mean we didn't know how to hunt," Jessica replied.

Marsee snorted. "Right. You could take down a chenzie. How?"

"We made our own teeth and claws," Jessica replied. "Tell me, how many of us could you take on at the same time if we all had knives?

Ten? Twenty? What if we put those knives on long sticks, so that you couldn't get close to us, or if we threw them at you?"

Marsee stopped laughing and looked at her hard. "You're serious? You're a predator?"

"I am. That doesn't mean that occasionally a wild animal didn't get us, but where we didn't have teeth and claws, we had a brain that figured out how to make up for it," Jessica said. "We may be small and lack natural defenses but my people are dangerous. I just hope that there weren't more like *him* that were rescued, and that we can leave that all behind."

Marsee sat there for a long time thinking before nodding. "Come on, I should start cleaning up." Marsee walked over and picked up the pillow, and thwacked her with it again for good measure, but not as hard. Jessica mock growled at her, causing Marsee's tail to curl, and they walked back. Marsee tossed the pillow back in the family room when they walked past, and they made their way to the nearest entrance to the courtyard. Marsee looked at her hard several times, still lost in thought, but didn't say anything, and Jessica didn't push it.

She waited in the hall, while Marsee made her way in to dump the sands from the shields. Myra and GrandFather met up with them just as Marsee had finished. Once the shields were back in place, Myra activated the swarm of cleaning drones that began removing the sand from the hallways and the courtyard. They were quite a bit larger than anything she was used to, and they were clearly designed to handle large quantities of sand. Jessica figured that would make sense if they had sandstorms regularly. Trying to sweep or dig out the several feet of sand in the courtyard would have been a monumental task.

"Where will they put all this sand?" Jessica asked.

"Normally the drones would empty into the compost, but with this much sand, I've instructed them to dump the sand outside. The wind will carry it off in a few days," Myra told her.

As the drones cleared out around a raised bed, the four of them would knock off whatever sand was on the smaller shield covering each bed, and retract them if they could. Even with all of their efforts over the past few days, several more had been bent from the weight of the sand, and would need to be repaired. They removed the water filters, as they were all packed with mud, and would need work to clean out or be replaced if too badly damaged. Jessica and her grandfather collected the filters, since it was easy for them to reach, and they didn't mind getting wet, while Marsee and Myra took care of the rest. They broke for their language lesson with Sina, and by then the hallway and half of the outer courtyard had already been cleaned. While they studied, the drones returned to their bases to charge. By the time the lesson was over and they'd had something to eat, the drones had finished charging and were back at it. By mid-afternoon, the outer courtyard was clean and Myra propped open the doors to the inner garden, so the drones could begin cleaning in there, once they were fully charged again.

The inner garden didn't have the retractable sun shields like the outer courtyard did, relying on the massive leaves of the bandala tree to provide shade and while the static shield had protected the great tree from damage, the leaves were still coated in sand. Most of the sand had filtered down around the outside of the tree into the outer courtyard, but as the tree swayed in the far gentler breeze, the remaining sand slowly fell to the ground, twinkling in the sunlight that filtered through the leaves.

"Oh wow!" GrandFather said, at his first good look at the garden and the massive tree that protected it. "How far up did you go?" he asked her.

"All the way to the top," Jessica replied.

"I can't even see the top from here," GrandFather said. "But I see what you mean about Ben loving this place. It's beautiful!"

"Wait until you see it at night. It's even better," Jessica told him.

They spent a little time in the garden, but even in the deep shade, it was far too hot for Jessica and her grandfather to remain outside for very long. Marsee joined them on a slow tour of the compound, while Marsee's mother started cleaning the filters to see how many needed to be replaced. This time around, Jessica was able to ask the million questions she hadn't asked the first time. Eventually they made their way back to the family room for lunch and an afternoon nap. When Jessica and Marsee woke, her grandfather was still sleeping, tired out from two very active days, after months of being stuck in quarantine, so Jessica and Marsee quietly left to clean Marsee's room next.

"Ugh, what a mess!" Marsee said as she swung open the doors.

Their belongings were strewn everywhere and a layer of sand coated everything. Jessica started picking things up off the floor, glad to see that not all of her clothing had blown away when the storm hit. Marsee climbed up on the roof and uncovered the small set of solar panels that powered the room, and checked them over for damage. Once they were cleared, she came back in and turned on the cooling unit, and left again, shutting the door behind her. A few minutes later she returned with supplies to clean off the various surfaces and set them down on one of the tables. One strange contraption basically ended up being nothing more than a hand-held vacuum which Marsee used to clean off her bookshelves. Marsee showed her how to use the special sponge for cleaning the wooden tables so that the sand wouldn't further scratch the surface, but several had been damaged by the storm and would need to be re-stained according to Marsee. Jessica couldn't see it but apparently Marsee did and was rather annoyed. When that was done, Marsee stripped her bed, and sand poured off of the sheet onto the floor as she did.

"Put all of your clothing on this pile. We'll throw it all in the cleaner," Marsee instructed.

Jessica gathered her remaining items and tossed them on the growing pile, as Marsee stripped the coverings off of the various pillows in the room, and tossed the pillows on her bed or the tables to get them off the floor. Once the pile was complete and everything else had been picked up and put away. Marsee threw open all four doors to let the remaining sand blow out, and called the cleaning drones in to get the rest. Then, once Marsee had turned off the cooling unit, she gathered the massive pile of laundry, and lugged everything down to the cleaners with Jessica following behind.

Chucking everything in, including Jessica's current outfit, Marsee started the load and jumped into the sonic shower to clean up. She ran the unit twice. "I can still smell chenzie on me," she said, sniffing her arm after the second cycle, but let Jessica have a turn before going in for a third cleaning.

"Maybe you should jump in the pond?" Jessica suggested while she waited for Marsee.

"Eww. Then I'd smell like fish," Marsee complained.

"Better than chenzie butt!" Jessica teased, as Marsee exited the shower and walked over to pull everything out of the cleaning unit. "Are you sure your family name is Chenzie-*ra* and not Chenzie-*butt*?" she asked innocently.

Marsee responded by dumping the entire load of clean laundry on her. Laughing as she dug herself out of the pile, Jessica grabbed something to wear, and helped Marsee pick up the laundry and carry it back up. It didn't take long to put everything away and they were soon back in the family room.

GrandFather was still sleeping, so she climbed up onto her window seat and started sketching scenes from the past few days. The mother chenzie and her cub, handing out food deliveries, and what she imagined the scene when her grandfathers met had looked like. GrandFather, sprawled ass over tea kettle on the ground, wheelbarrow tipped over, Grandpa Ben leaning up against the stall door laughing hysterically, and Buster watching them both with an annoyed face, sore foot, and a piece of hay sticking out of his mouth.

"That's pretty close to what it looked like," GrandFather said as he looked at the drawing. She hadn't even noticed that he'd woken up. "Only there was far more horse manure. Can I have that drawing?" he asked with tears in his eyes.

She nodded, carefully tearing the paper out of the book and handing it to him. "I drew one for you too, Marsee," Jessica said.

"You did?" Marsee asked excitedly.

"Yes," she replied, and with an innocent expression, flipped the page, and held it up for everyone to see. Everyone burst out laughing.

Everyone that is, except for Marsee who growled and threw a small pillow at her. This time Jessica didn't duck in time and it clocked her square in the face. Laughing, she tossed the pillow to the floor and signed, "So you like it then?"

On the sketchbook was a picture of Marsee on the ground with her arm stuck up the chenzies butt, writhing in pain from the mother's contractions.

"If she doesn't want it, I do," Myra said. "It would be perfect for my office." Marsee just fell back on her pillow with a groan.

Marsee's father arrived early that evening having stayed to help Councilor Marcus clean up after the storm, attend a Council meeting from Marcus's home, and then fly all the way back to the Guild in Council City, for supplies to fix the raised beds and pick up a special delivery for Little Flower and GrandFather. Ellie had put together a care package of new clothes for both, as well as shelving units designed for their size to store their belongings. Ones that closed up to protect them from future storms, as well as several large crates full of frames to display, and protect Little Flower's drawings. Marsee showed her how they worked and she took the drawing she'd given to her grandfather and placed it in one, and the one of Marsee and the chenzie in another. Marsee growled good naturedly when Jessica gave it to her mother for her office.

They set up GrandFather in one of the guest rooms, and then Jer and Marsee helped carry her belongings up to their room, with GrandFather following along to check out where his granddaughter was sleeping.

"I'll have to admit you do have the best view in the place," he said, as they sat out on the balcony watching the sunset. Jer and Marsee had left to give them some privacy.

"This place has its perks," Jessica said, leaning up against his side. "The swinging bed is fun, but the plumbing is severely lacking."

"Isn't that the truth!" he laughed and then sobered. "So, how far along are you?"

"I'm not sure. The days have kind of all run together and I don't know how long I was sedated before I woke up here, but fifteen or sixteen of their days maybe, so maybe a month our time. Myra says their days are about twice as long as ours." She shrugged. "Long enough to have morning sickness twice now."

"Have you decided what you want to do?" he asked.

"Not really. It's all still too raw. Every time I try to think about it, I get stuck thinking about that day. I think that if it weren't for how it was conceived, I'd want to keep it. But how can I love a child when all I can see is the man that hurt me?" she asked.

GrandFather put his arm around her, gave her a hug, and kissed her on the top of her head, but didn't offer her any advice.

"Whatever I decide, it has to be soon, though. After the Council meeting, I might not have a say in what happens," she said after a while.

"Have you had any further discussions about the Council meeting? What to expect?" he asked.

She shook her head. "No. Not really. I guess that's why Marsee's father was at Councilor Marcus's when the storm hit. So, what about you? What do you want to do? Go back to school to learn to be a vet here, retire and take up basket weaving? Or I suppose you could give swimming lessons to the locals."

"Not a clue, but swimming lessons sounds like it could be dangerous. Basket weaving does sound fun though. Want to take a class with me?"

"Sure. Why not? Maybe Marsee can teach us. You know, she made pretty much all of the furniture in our room, including that hanging bed. Hey did you know we have stripes?" Jessica asked as the thought popped into her head.

"Yup. They're called Blaschko's lines. What brought that up?" he asked.

"Apparently the cats can see them and say they glitter 'like water on a moonlit pond' or something to that effect," Jessica replied. "Myra says we can see further and clearer than they can, but they can see more colors, and see them differently than we can. What color did you think the chenzie was?" she asked him.

"Nearly as pink as that dress they had me in," he replied with laughter.

"Same. Marsee says they look tan to them."

"I wonder what color they think those tan walls were then. I don't know about you but I never want to see *that* particular color *ever* again," he said.

"No idea, but we can ask later."

They sat there and chatted for a while, using a combination of sign and writing on the tablets to get around her inability to hear, and they talked about everything and nothing until the suns had fully set, and the moons had started to rise. "Oh, wow!" GrandFather said when all three were visible. "I mean, I know you told me about it, but seeing it for real…"

"Yeah. It hit me hard the first time too. We're not in Kansas anymore, Toto."

"No, we most definitely are not," he said, and then laughed as her stomach rumbled. "So, what does a person have to do to find something to eat around here?"

"Just ask. Come on, I bet everyone is waiting for us in the garden." She was right.

When they arrived at the garden, her grandfather stood stunned in the entrance for several long moments. "Oh wow," he said, forgetting to sign, but she had no problems understanding.

"I told you it was something out of Avatar," she said with a grin.

"You weren't kidding. I did not expect anything like this on a desert planet," her grandfather replied, still looking around at everything.

When they finally entered the clearing by the tree, Marsee waved them over to the pond, where she was sitting.

"Come on, I want to show you the octorays, and after supper, we'll see if we can get the fairy dogs to come close." Jessica had to drag him over to the pool, as he was completely lost in trying to look at everything at once. She wiggled her fingers in the water, once they arrived. Moments later the funny little fish showed up to boop her fingers and scoot away.

"What do you think of our garden, GrandFather?" Myra asked, bringing the two of them a tray with a large selection of freshly sliced fruit, vegetables, some cooked fish, bandala chips, and a large glass of star fruit juice for each of them.

"It's wonderful!" he signed back. "But, it's not at all what I expected to see in the desert."

"When the rains come in another month or so, everything will look very different, but many of these plants came from our old world, carefully preserved through the eons. I am thankful we did not lose them to the storm."

"Yes! More potato chips!" Jessica said, grabbing a couple of the chips and tossing them back. "You should try one. They're really good," she signed, mouth full.

So he did, gasped, and took a long swig of the fruit juice, glaring at her as he did. "What did I do to deserve that?" he finally asked, once he was able to breathe normally.

Laughing, she replied. "I seem to remember something about a ghost pepper one year..."

He groaned. "Yeah, I guess I did deserve that. But you're right, once you get over the initial inferno, they're actually pretty good."

"You should try them over the fish. It makes it taste so much better."

# CHAPTER 20

# Myra: Precedent

Myra and Jer retreated to the privacy of their suite to talk about the council meeting that had occurred earlier in the day, and everything he and Marcus had discovered in their days of research.

"So, how bad was the council meeting?" Myra asked when the door was shut.

"Not as bad as you might think. The Council agreed with your decision to bring the bipeds out of stasis to extend the life of the shields and environmental units. Ammond's updated report on the extent of hearing loss suffered by the other bipeds, as well as the different hearing ranges, had most of the Council agreeing that it was the reason for our lack of communication. And the progress in learning Sina's sign language was met with excitement. They are also in agreement with your decision to have supervised visits for the bipeds as well as joint habitation for family members," he answered as he found a comfortable place to sit.

"I'm sensing a 'but'," Myra said, sitting down next to him.

"But Parner and his faction does not believe we've been able to communicate as effectively as we have, and they were furious that we broke quarantine. There was no real hiding of the fact that I wasn't at home and calling from my office, and if we're going to use the chenzie's birth as evidence towards Little Flower's sentience, then I had to admit to taking GrandFather from the Agency, although they don't know about the other stops you made. They're under the impression that you left to treat the chenzie. They considered that emergency enough, since the Agency doesn't have any ground crawlers and no one else would have been able to get there in time."

"It doesn't surprise me that he'd be vocal about you visiting with Marcus, or have issues with GrandFather leaving. What did the rest of the Council have to say?"

"About half the Council was on Parner's side until Marcus quietly reminded them that he was Little Flower's Advocate, and that by our laws, quarantine or not, no person can be denied contact with their representative, and the only reason he hadn't been to visit directly with Little Flower yet was because of the storm. As for GrandFather, he reminded the Council that they'd just agreed to joint cohabitation with family members. At that point, Parner had no real argument. The best part is that one of his cohorts stated that since Little Flower has clearly improved since coming to the compound, and since there have been no other illnesses, full quarantine should be lifted, as well as the requirement for Little Flower to wear a harness outside. And the Council finally agreed, the majority anyway. Paxton is still against quarantine being lifted."

"It's about time," Myra said "Wait, full quarantine? Are they still implementing a partial quarantine?"

"Yes. Now that we've established a basic level of communication with the bipeds, the Council decreed that until such time as they were proven otherwise, they should be treated as sentient. The shields are to remain up for their protection, but the habitats are to be modified such that the bipeds can lock and unlock their own rooms, and go wherever they want within the confines of the Agency. All except for 326. His cell will remain locked and a pair of Honor Guards are being sent to officially arrest and supervise 326 during his excursions from his cell. As 326 will be held for longer than two weeks, and does not have family, his interactions with the others are to be limited to just the language lessons, and should he wish for it, a walk around the compound in the morning and evening."

"That's frankly far more than he deserves, but the guards are already there. Brice told me about it the other day," Myra replied and Jer frowned. "Half the people on the ships were members of the Guard," Myra explained. "They were quarantined there with the rest of us."

Jer nodded his understanding, but didn't continue right away.

"What about the miscarriages?" she asked next.

"Naturally, everyone was upset, but since thankfully none of the bipeds have died, no additional charges have been added, yet. Tabor's waiting to find out the results of the review, to find out if we're dealing with an actual miscarriage, or just a failed heat. Either way, I reminded her that you'd submitted an official objection to the order to put them in stasis, so whatever happens, that decision should sit entirely on the Senior Councilor and the majority that voted yes to it."

"Well, that's one less thing I have to worry about. I suppose," Myra said, relieved.

"Perhaps, however, most of the Council voted for that originally, as did I. Oh, and before I forget, Marcus will be here tomorrow morning. He's planning to stay until the trial."

Myra frowned at his first statement, but nodded. "Marcus is more than welcome, and it'll be good to see him. What about the fostering program? Did that get discussed at all?"

"It did briefly, but after discussing it with Ellie, we just told the Council we were trying to get crafters to donate their skills and supplies towards helping to make our planet more habitable for them. Since it was presented as Marsee's idea, with the Guild Master's full support, there was no major dissent, even from Parner's crew. Most in the Council agreed it would be better if people donated their time and effort, rather than being required to do so. Honestly, I'm leaving that all up to Ellie. We're going to be too busy preparing Little Flower for the trial to deal with any of that. Other than that, not much else was discussed, at least not related to Little Flower and the others."

Myra nodded and let out a heavy sigh. "So, what did you and Marcus find?"

Jer looked away with a matching sigh but didn't answer.

"Jeran, be honest with me. How bad is it?" she asked.

"You don't want to know," he finally said.

"I do. I need to know what we are facing," Myra insisted.

"Trust me, you don't," he repeated, but she insisted again.

Jer, frowned, stood, ran his paws through the fur on the back of his head, sighed again, and finally grabbed his tablet from the desk. Myra had rarely seen him this upset, and it worried her.

"Before I show you this, you need to understand, the last time a rape case was tried for our people was before the Great Awakening. Times have changed and the situation with the last victim was far worse. We haven't found anything that really matches our role in this, but as a precedent, it's not good. But regardless, Marcus doesn't think it will come to this."

"What could be worse than what Little Flower went through?" Myra asked.

He just handed her the tablet and she read. She was shaking by the time she finished reading. Myra opened her mouth to respond, but stopped, stood up, and bolted into their private waste room and threw up.

"I tried to warn you," Jer said, sitting down beside her, and hugging her.

*Ancient Gods, please protect my children and their children. I'll take any punishment you deem fit and right, but please, I beg of you, don't make them pay for my crimes. Please!* she prayed as Jer held her.

"It won't come to that. At least I don't think so, and neither does Marcus," Jer continued.

"How can you be so sure?" Myra asked.

"Because I've worked with most of these Seniors for close to fifty years now. They're honorable people and I think they will be just as horrified. That punishment doesn't fit this crime, and it certainly doesn't fit our role in it, should they even find us guilty of collusion. It's the choice given to the victim that Marcus thinks they will honor, as that is in keeping with our traditions. If so, I don't believe Little Flower would do anything remotely like that to us, certainly not to Marsee. We just need to figure out something comparable as a replacement that the Senior Council will agree to. Now, if she dies from childbirth or from terminating the pregnancy..." Jer took a deep breath and left unsaid what they both knew. If Little Flower died, so would she. "That hasn't happened so all we can do is our best to insure it never does."

"That's always been the risk, hasn't it? I put her life at risk by allowing her to get pregnant," Myra said.

"You did no such thing. He put her life at risk. You were trying to save it and her species. Now come on, get up off that floor, and quit blaming yourself and worrying about what might happen, and start focusing on what you can do to make sure it doesn't happen. You're a senior healer and you've faced greater odds before and won, and it's time you started acting like one." When she stood, Jer wrapped her in a fierce embrace. "We'll figure it out. I promise."

# CHAPTER 21

# Jessica: Advocate

Like usual, Jessica woke long before Marsee the next morning. The longer days and nights made it difficult to sleep as long as the bigger cats did and the early morning was the best time to be outside. Light enough to see, but not the overpowering inferno that the afternoons would become. After carefully climbing down off the bed, she dragged one of the pillows out onto the balcony to watch the sunrise and draw. She was happier than she'd been in what felt like years. The night before had felt like a celebration. Storm over, the hard work of cleanup completed, or as much as had been possible, and her grandfather beside her, she'd spent the evening showing him the garden. GrandFather, still unused to the massive size of the compound, tired easily, and they had retired to her favorite clearing in the hopes of coaxing some of the fairy dogs down. The others joined them eventually, and they'd spent a companionable evening under the bright moons, trying to answer the million questions GrandFather had. She had all the same questions, but had left many of them unasked, waiting until they were better able to speak.

When she'd explained what they were trying to do, Marsee informed them that the small creatures were called flicker flyers. Jessica had attempted to explain the name she'd given the small creature and had drawn additional pictures to both explain the physical words and the name of the creature that had once had a similar name. This had led to GrandFather asking what other species had been saved and Myra had pulled out her tablet and pulled up the Agency records to show the different species. It was a depressingly small list, although they'd both laughed when they realized that a skunk had been rescued. When asked why, Myra had then informed them that they'd found out about the creature's defensive mechanism the hard way, and now wore personal static shields any time they had to work with the creature. The story had left them in tears laughing, as Myra had explained how even the static showers hadn't removed the smell and the poor Healer that had been sprayed had spent weeks smelling like skunk even after shaving off all of her fur. They'd even gone so far as to build an entirely separate enclosure just for that creature, as the entire ward had stunk for weeks. GrandFather informed Myra that the scent sack could be surgically removed and had made an attempt to explain how.

There had only been one lone male skunk rescued so the species was likely doomed to extinction, although Myra had explained that they were attempting to determine if they could clone or genetically engineer the species, along with the others rescued where there had only been one member of the species. This was not the first time in their history that they'd been down to a single member of a species before, and they were hopeful they could still find a way to save them. This had led to Myra filtering the list to just those creatures. Amazingly half of those listed all ended up being different breeds of dogs, which Myra's species had classified as being separate species, and a good portion of the others being fish. Myra had been astounded when GrandFather had explained that the great dane and chihuahua that were rescued were the same species and could mate.

"But...but how?" she'd asked.

GrandFather had shrugged and signed back, "Very carefully," and everyone had burst into tears and tail kinks laughing again.

When Myra had stated that sadly no prairie dogs or fairies had been rescued, Jessica had laughed and explained that fairies didn't exist, that they were a made-up creature, part of their mythology. When Jessica had explained the sign before, she'd explained the word to mean a person who could make things appear out of the air, not knowing the signs for magic. However, this time she'd drawn a sketch of Tinkerbell. Marsee had been super excited and wanted to know everything about them. Apparently Marsee was a huge fantasy book nerd, which brought the conversation back around to how much knowledge and literary history had been lost in the Cataclysm. Myra had suggested that they try to write down as much as they could remember in their own language, even going so far as to try their best to reproduce their favorite authors' works as a legacy to them. Myra had also suggested that Jessica expand on the work she'd started with illustrating the various creatures of her world, not just to preserve their legacy, but because there was a huge demand for her drawings. GrandFather had reminded her that she'd always wanted to illustrate a children's book and what better legacy could there be than preserving the history of the species that had been lost. He'd agreed to help provide details for the book and Marsee had said she'd help translate it, so she'd agreed.

They'd been in the clearing for a while but the flicker flyers hadn't landed. Marsee had stated that they probably wouldn't. She'd been trying for years to get close to them. It had been one of her favorite things to do when she was a small cub. Jessica had replied that she'd had no problem getting close to them the other night, and showed them her drawings. They'd all been astounded but couldn't deny the accuracy of her drawings. Myra had suggested that maybe they weren't afraid of her smaller size, and unlike Marsee had been when she was a cub, she was capable of sitting still for more than five minutes at a time, and not pouncing on everything that moved. This had earned an annoyed tail thwap from Marsee, but chuckling, the big cats had backed off to the other side of the clearing, and Jessica had started drawing like she had that other night.

It wasn't long before her brave little chocolate-colored friend fluttered down, and landed on her outstretched foot to see what she was drawing. She'd been drawing a picture of them cleaning up the hydroponics units earlier in the day. But when she turned it so the little creature could see, it woofed, flashed red, and looked positively annoyed.

"What's the matter little fellow? You don't like my drawing?" she asked it.

In response it puffed itself up like it had the day before.

"Oh, you want me to do another drawing of you?" she said, flipping back to the page she'd drawn before.

The little creature woofed and let off a rainbow of colors, hopping up and down.

"Ok, ok, I'll draw you another picture," she said smiling, and flipped to a new page and started sketching.

He hopped down onto her leg and walked over to watch her draw, and when she was done, she turned it around to show him.

"Is this better?" she asked, and he woofed and hopped up and down again, and then tried to take the sketch book with him in his tiny little paws. "Do you want this drawing?" she asked him, and carefully ripped the page out and handed it to him. He woofed again, flashed a brilliant rainbow of colors, grabbed the paper and flew off with it.

When she looked up, the jaws of all three cats were hanging low in astonishment. Marsee had apparently recorded the entire thing.

"No one would ever believe me if I hadn't," she'd said afterwards.

A few minutes later, the flicker flyer returned carrying with it a shiny piece of glittering stone, and dropped it onto her sketchbook. She picked it up and examined it closely as the creature watched.

"Is this for me?" she asked, and the creature woofed, lighting up in the same happy rainbow colors. "Thank you. I love it!" she said and held it close to her.

The creature woofed and flew away again.

Jer had demanded to know exactly what Jessica had said to the flicker flyer, so she translated as they watched the recording. This had started a massive discussion between the three cats in their own language.

GrandFather had chuckled and wrote her a note. "I think you just broke their brains," he'd written and then signed to the big cats. "What's wrong?"

"The flicker flyer just recognized its own image, clearly communicated its desire for both the content and ownership of the drawing, and returned with a gift in exchange," Jer answered.

"It did," GrandFather replied. "I take it you've never seen this behavior before?"

"GrandFather, those are all clearly defined markers of sentience," Jer had replied, and GrandFather had simply smiled in response.

"Many of our species could or would do the same, with regards to recognizing their own image, and giving gifts in response. But every species is capable of communicating if you're willing to pay attention. Didn't the chenzie communicate its pain and show its understanding that we were there to help?"

Jer nodded. "That's one of the reasons why we have so few domesticated species. We have no way of really knowing if a species is sentient or capable of becoming sentient if given the opportunity to develop. Tool usage has been one of the primary indicators. We have found other worlds with other creatures, but we avoid them until such time as they communicate with us, as your people did initially. That we had been unable to communicate with you afterwards left many of our people believing that we had not saved the sentient species of your world."

"Our people were debating tool usage as a sign of sentience as well. Several of the species you rescued are more than capable of being trained to perform complex tasks, and even communicate in much the same way we did initially with the drawings. One of our species, that you sadly did not rescue, was even capable of learning our own sign language, and several creatures could mimic our words. There was some debate if they actually understood or not. The real question is, are you defining sentience on a species ability to use the same level of technology as you, their ability to think, speak, or *your* ability to understand them? How many species would be capable of the same level of technology if they'd developed thumbs instead of wings, but are not afforded the same rights simply because they can't use a tablet, or haven't developed the technology necessary to leave their planet?" GrandFather replied through Jessica.

Jer nodded, and thought about what GrandFather had said for a long time, but didn't reply. Eventually Myra declared that it was late and they should all get some sleep.

After they'd returned to their room, Jessica had pilfered Marsee's art supplies, since much of hers had been damaged by the storm and not yet replaced. Jessica positively drooled over everything she found, and had spent the remaining time before bed sampling the different supplies to figure out what she wanted to use. When she'd expressed her concerns about being as accurate as possible, and wanting to be able to correct mistakes, Marsee had gone over to another desk in her room and pulled out her drawing tablet, and had shown her how to use it. This thing was positively huge compared to the one they'd given her to talk with GrandFather, and made every drawing app she'd ever used before pale in comparison.

Now Jessica sat out on the balcony enjoying the sunrise, as she started work illustrating the lost creatures of her former world. She'd been there for maybe an hour when a small shuttle approached, circled the compound, and landed in the shuttle bay. Wondering who would be arriving this early in the morning, she stood, stretched and dragged everything back inside. Marsee was still sound asleep and apparently dreaming, as the long fluffy tail hanging off the bed, her paws, and her whiskers were all twitching furiously, so she decided to let her lion sleep and investigate on her own.

Making her way down the long ramp and into the compound, she walked the empty halls, and realized that aside from trips to the hole of muck, and the random wandering she'd done the night she found out she was pregnant, this was the first time she'd really been out and about on her own. The vast empty compound was eerie all alone in the early morning light. The family room and kitchen were both empty. She was thirsty, so she grabbed a quick drink while she was there. While they'd waited out the storm, Myra had reorganized the kitchen, so that there were now cups, plates and utensils in a lower cupboard where she could reach them, and made sure that her favorite items were on the lower shelves of the fridge. Drink in hand, she kept exploring.

Her GrandFather's door was wide open so she peered in. He was sound asleep on the massive bed in the guest room they'd set him up in. It didn't surprise her that he'd kept his door wide open. After months of being stuck in her cell, she preferred having the tower doors open for as long as she could too. She watched him sleep for a while before continuing on, her heart nearly breaking with happiness to have found him after so long. Myra's office door was open as well, but no one was there, so she kept walking, intending to check the shuttle bay on the other side of the compound, and then the garden if she didn't find anyone.

Halfway to the shuttle bay though, she found Jer's office door left partially open, and she peaked inside and froze, unobserved and absolutely floored by the dynamics of the people in the room. She wished she'd brought her sketchbook so she could capture the sight, but she knew she'd draw this scene later. Both of Marsee's parents were there as well as Councilor Marcus. Myra sat on a smaller version of the family room's window seat, her back leaned up against a wall of built-in shelving that surrounded the window, looking out. Jessica had seen a wide range of emotions from Marsee's mother over the past few days, ranging from mischievousness, to fury, and despair, but today she just seemed resigned, as if she'd heard news that she'd been expecting but dreading. Jer leaned up against the front of his desk, tail draped to the side, arms crossed, looking both worried and determined, but it was Marcus that demanded her attention and left her stunned.

He'd attended most of their language lessons, and she'd been amazed at how quickly he'd learned to sign, rarely needing a reminder for each new sign they learned, and she'd had the impression of a quiet, caring, and fiercely determined person, with a wicked sense of humor. But he tended to fade to the background during their lessons, observing and learning, but rarely contributing unless called upon.

Marcus now sat at the end of a long conference table, under a bank of monitors that covered the entire length of the wall opposite of Jer's desk. A bag similar to Myra's sat on the floor unopened beside him. He was speaking to Myra, of what Jessica had no idea, but confidence and authority radiated off of Marcus in a way that she'd never seen before. All of the cats she'd met since coming here had this to some extent, her fairy godmother most of all, but something about Marcus, made them all pale in comparison. Marcus had the confidence of someone who excelled at what they did, and knew it, who had the wisdom that only came from decades of making hard decisions, and dealing with the consequences of those decisions, and who understood power and authority as if they'd been born to it. This was a person who didn't have to prove himself, because he already had. He knew it, and everyone else around him knew it too. And for some reason, she instinctively trusted him, unlike any of the other cats she'd met.

When she'd first asked what Marsee's father did for a living, she'd misunderstood Marsee's response and thought that she'd indicated Jer ruled her world. Marsee had laughed for a very long time at that, and now she understood why. In a different time and place Jer might have been royalty, but he would have only been a duke or a prince. Marcus would have been king, and not just any king, a leader and a general, someone who wasn't afraid to get their paws dirty, who wouldn't ask of anyone something he wasn't willing to do himself, who had made life or death decisions, and who understood real sacrifice. If she were in Camelot, this would be King Arthur, and she wondered why he wasn't Senior Councilor. What must Tabor be like if they didn't choose him? she wondered, remembering the picture of the Senior Councilor, and how fierce she had seemed.

Marcus finished talking. Myra sighed and nodded, and then turned her head to look at him, but noticed her in the doorway instead, and sat up. The resignation she'd been projecting suddenly disappeared behind a mask of calm.

"Little Flower, good morning. Do you need something?" Myra asked, waving her in, and they all turned to look in her direction, as she slipped through the open door.

"No, I'm all set. I saw Councilor Marcus's shuttle land and was surprised to see someone here so early, so I thought I'd come see who it was," she signed awkwardly, holding her juice glass in the crook of one of her arms.

Marcus smiled at her. "I came to see you."

"You did?" she asked, surprised, and he nodded. "Why?" She knew Jer had been at Marcus's to prepare for the upcoming trial, and that Marcus was Jer's mentor, but she hadn't expected Marcus to come visit, especially so early in the morning.

"I'm going to be your advocate for the upcoming trial," he signed back.

"What does 'advocate' mean?" she asked. She hadn't learned that sign.

"I'm going to help you get ready for the trial, teach you everything you need to know to be prepared, and present witnesses to the Council on your behalf," he replied.

*Oh,* she realized. He was going to be her lawyer. That *was* a surprise. *They must be pulling out the big guns for me,* she thought. "Thank you," she said, feeling relieved at first, and then worried. "Why isn't Jer going to be my advocate?"

Jer and Myra both sighed, but Marcus just smiled calmly at her. "Come, have a seat. I'll try to explain," he said, tapping the chair beside him.

She walked over, placed her drink on the table above her, which she could just barely reach, and then climbed up and into the chair, feeling a bit like a toddler with the giant furniture. When she'd made her way up and sat down, feet dangling over the edge, he continued.

"Tell me. What have you been told about the upcoming trial?" he asked.

"Just that I have to go before the Council of all five worlds to prove I'm sentient, and if so, decide for my people if I want to join yours," she replied. "Myra said I should focus on learning as much sign language as possible for now, and not worry about the trial."

Marcus nodded. "That is partly why I'm here. It's my responsibility as your advocate to prepare you so that you can prove your sentience to the Council and worthiness to be a member of the Consortium, and also make sure you fully understand what you are agreeing to, what the laws of our people are, that your people will be held accountable to if you should join, as well as the benefits and responsibilities that come with that membership."

Jessica nodded her understanding.

"If that were all that the Council were deciding then Jer would have been your advocate for several reasons. You currently live in his district, as do all of your people, but also because you are his ward. He has taken the oath of guardianship for you, and is responsible for you until you are seen as a sentient adult, or you are adopted. This was done before we knew about your grandfather, and before we were sure you were sentient, so that you were allowed to leave the Agency."

They had to stop so that Jessica could be sure she fully understood what the signs for 'oath', 'guardianship', and 'adopted' meant, and apparently there was some surprise about this from Myra. Jessica wasn't sure if Myra was more upset about not being informed, or not being included. Of course, this opened up a whole list of other questions she wanted to ask, but she decided to stay focused on her original question.

"So why isn't Jer my advocate?" she asked again when she was ready to move on.

"Because the trial isn't just for determining your species sentience. If you are found to be sentient and join the Consortium, then it's also to determine the punishment of the person who raped you, and anyone else found guilty of involvement. You accused Myra, Healer Morningstar and the other healers at the Agency, as well as Jer and all of the Local Council as being responsible for that rape. The Senior Council will need to decide our level of involvement, and what punishments we deserve. This is why Jer couldn't be your advocate. It's what we call a conflict of interest. There's too much risk that he might give you the wrong information in order to protect himself and Myra from those consequences. He is both my protege and younger brother, and I know he wouldn't do that to you, but those are our laws."

Jessica frowned at him and struggled to solidify the thoughts in her brain after defining half a dozen other signs.

"What's wrong, Little Flower?" Marcus asked. "Would you rather, Jer be your advocate, or someone else? If that's your preference, I will talk to the Senior Council."

"No, it's not that." She slid down off her chair and started pacing, hoping the swirling thoughts in her brain would focus if she moved. After a while she turned to face him. "I didn't realize my rape would be going to trial. I thought I just had to go before the Council because they didn't think a species that could do that would be sentient. I'm not ready to talk about it, not in any kind of detail that would be needed for a conviction, and well I don't understand why everyone else is being charged too. When did I accuse them, or for that matter why is it even going to trial?"

Marcus flicked an ear back, and tilted his head at her for several moments, before he picked up his tablet. "Is this your drawing?" he asked.

He handed her the tablet and she frowned. It was one of the drawings that she'd done in the sketchbook she'd thrown at Marsee. It showed a series of sketches of her being forced down the hall by Brice, naked, and being locked in the room alone with him, several scenes of her rape, what she'd been awake for anyway, while Brice and several others watched from outside, and ending up with a scene of her giving birth, and her baby being taken away from her. It had been a mix of what had happened, and what she feared would happen.

She nodded. "That's my drawing, but I didn't realize that would get anyone charged for it. I was angry and scared when I drew that, and I didn't know what was going on, and I didn't know what was going to happen to me or my cub," she said.

Marcus sighed and nodded. "Perhaps given to anyone else it wouldn't have had the same consequences, but Marsee brought your sketchbook to her father and wrote down a transcript of what you'd signed to her. Jer was legally bound to take it seriously, and in light of the fact that you were only just barely learning to sign, it was presented to the Council as your official statement. As you did not actually name your rapist, the recordings from the Agency were used for identification. There is no question that he raped and beat you. He has already been found guilty. You won't have to go into details on what happened. At the trial, you'll only have to confirm he was the one that raped you. The trial is to determine whether or not the actions of the Council and healers directly led to that rape, and to what extent."

Jessica swallowed hard, as she realized the implications. She'd come to care for these people in the short time she'd been here, and she'd made those accusations before she'd known what had actually happened to her people. "Can I take it back? I only want my rapist punished. I didn't understand what was going on then. I didn't know your people were trying to save mine, or why I was even being held."

Marcus sighed. "Unfortunately, no. Because it happened at the Agency, while under direct supervision and care of your healer, a full investigation into how that had been allowed to happen would have occurred anyway, and ultimately the same information would have been identified, but your statement on what you want for reparations could really help reduce the consequences for everyone involved."

"I would be happy to do that. What are the consequences?" she asked.

"I do not know for sure. That is why Jer was at my place. We were trying to find precedent for this in our archives."

She'd had to stop him to define precedent and archives.

"It has been a very, very long time since a rape has occurred, and never one in which so many people and members of our leadership were involved. This is why it is going before the Full Council. I believe you will be given the choice to decide what your rapist's punishment should be. As for the rest of us, if we are found guilty, then I believe we will be stripped of our positions on the Council and in the Healers Guild, and perhaps be required to care for you and your child. I think we would all gladly take those consequences for the harm we caused you, but the real problem is, that could have very serious consequences for the rest of our planet. What you may not realize is that we all unanimously voted to begin reintroduction and repopulation of your species, and because of that, the entire Council could be removed of their position. If that happens, leadership of our world goes to the Senior Council, until such time as we elect new officials. We were afraid we were going to lose you all to an illness called isolation sickness. It is what happens when a person is kept by themselves for too long. Jer, Myra, and I fought for a long time to get you out of your isolation, and I'm so very sorry that we ended up hurting you far worse in the process," he stated.

"I was very sick," Jessica agreed. "I was so lonely that I would throw food on the wall just to make Healer Morningstar have to stick around for a few minutes longer to clean it up. I would stand in front of the door or refuse to get out of bed, just so she would have to touch me to move me. I would talk to my stuffed animal and there were times I could have sworn he spoke back to me. Do you know what it's like to go months without being able to talk to someone, without being hugged, or even touched? I was so happy the day Healer Morningstar brought me to his room for the first time. I lived for those few brief moments. The rape was bad, but the isolation was so much worse," she replied.

Her arms shook as she told him, reliving the experiences of her captivity. It was the first time she'd really spoken about it. Even with her grandfather she hadn't been able to do more than acknowledge it had happened. Marcus sighed, and nodded his understanding, while Myra climbed off the window seat and picked her up and hugged her tightly, purring fiercely. Jessica leaned in and allowed herself to be comforted by that embrace. After a moment, Myra sat in the chair Jessica had just vacated, and repositioned her so she could continue talking with Marcus but still be comforted by Myra's purr.

Jessica thought about what he'd said. "So, the risk is too high that your Council will choose to vote to save your people's right to vote on what happens to them, over mine?" she asked Marcus, and he nodded. "So, if Jer can't be my Advocate, how come you can, if you're being charged as well?"

"Because I've already resigned my position on the Council. It was the only way we could ensure you had a fair trial."

She sat there stunned for a long time. He'd willingly given up his power and authority to give her a chance. She didn't know what else he'd vowed, and they'd decided not to tell her, and had agreed to not tell her the more serious consequences they expected to be handed down. It was an attempt to keep both her and Marsee from panicking.

"I can't believe you would do that for me," she said finally.

He flicked both ears back in surprise. "I promise I am not lying, but I fully understand why you would not trust me. We have done little to earn your trust."

Jessica blinked. "That's not what I meant. I believe you. I'm surprised. You would really give up all of your power to save my people?"

He nodded. "I would and I did."

Thank you," she replied. "I'm very sorry you had to do that."

"Don't be. I don't think I've ever enjoyed a moment on the Council more than I did when I stepped down. It was worth it just to see the shock on everyone's faces. It's a small price to pay to ensure you and your species are granted the freedoms you deserve."

"Do we, though?" she asked. "My people are not exactly the best people. The person who raped me certainly wasn't."

"You do. Myra told me what you told her about your people. None of us are perfect. We all strive to do better, but we all make mistakes. Sometimes those mistakes harm other people, like the mistakes we made with your care, but that doesn't mean you don't deserve the opportunity to learn from your mistakes, and try to become a better person. You have the same capacity for growth as any of us. You've shown your ability to forgive, and your compassion for others. You put your life at risk to ensure your friend's treasured belongings were saved, and put aside your reunion with your grandfather to save a dying animal and her cub. You've shown the capacity to learn and build friendships, and the willingness to share what you know with us without reservation, and you've done all of that even after we horribly mistreated you."

She nodded. "So, what do I have to do to get ready?" she asked, just as Marsee appeared at the doorway and entered. Marsee smiled at Councilor Marcus, gave him a quick hug, and curled up on the window seat Myra had just vacated.

"To start, we need to translate the Charter into your language, and make sure you fully understand everything in there, so you can make an informed decision. Then we'll need to prepare your official application. After that, we will need to get you ready to answer any questions that the Council might ask you. While we are doing that, we'll need to identify witnesses on your behalf to show your character, and also get them ready for any questions they might be asked as well. If you are truly interested in helping the others accused, then I'll need your help in researching the archives for precedent to acquit the others of those charges."

There were several signs she needed to translate, but after that she replied. "I can't read your language very well yet."

"I'm impressed you can read at all in such a short amount of time. No, what I need is help scanning in some really old documents, so we can index and search them faster rather than having to read them all."

"Oh, I can do that, if you show me how," Jessica said.

"I'll help too," Marsee said. "I've been learning how to handle and repair old manuscripts anyway. This will be good practice."

Marcus smiled at Marsee and nodded. "Good, I have a shuttle full of documents to go through, but Marsee, we're going to need something far more important from you," he said.

"What's that?" she asked.

"Little Flower needs an official translator for the trial. My understanding is that you are fluent in the four spoken languages, and passable in understanding the fifth?"

Marsee gulped and grabbed her tail in worry, but nodded. "I can understand the basics of Water Sprite, but I obviously can't speak it back. I'm far better at reading their written language than understanding their visual one."

"That's okay you won't need to be able to speak their language, none of us can, but you'll need to be able to translate what they say into sign. This will help ensure that there isn't any miscommunication. I've arranged for a language tutor for you with one of the Sprites that lives in Council City. You'll have lessons with her every day until the trial. Those that can't speak our language will have their own translators, but it would be best if you didn't have to wait for those translations."

Marsee gulped again but nodded. Jessica noticed that her tail was starting to poof, but Marsee shifted and tucked it under her in an attempt to keep everyone from noticing just how scared she was.

"Thank you," Jessica signed to Marsee. Marsee nodded but didn't look any less scared, so she decided to deflect the attention off of Marsee. "Marcus, what will happen to my people if we aren't granted our sentience? Myra said your people will choose. What will you do with us?" Jessica asked.

"If you are not successful then we will continue to care for you as we have at the Agency, food, housing, medical care, and the basic items you need to survive on our world, such as your clothing will be provided. We would not abandon you, but you would not have a vote in what happens to you, your people, or the other species from your planet. Our goal has always been to find a way to build your planet's species back up to sustainable numbers, and determine if we could safely reintroduce you into the wild without harm to our own. Some on the Council have suggested finding a new planet still in its infancy, and repopulating it with your kind, others think we should work out a way to make room for your species among our own, if at all possible. If you were not found sentient, you would not legally have a say in where you lived, or even who you mated with, or even when you mated. That would all be done based on the healers' decisions on how to best repopulate your species as it was done before we knew you were sentient," he replied.

Jessica's anger flared. "You would still do that with everything you know now? Would you still force us to mate in order to save our species?"

Myra set her on the table so she could talk to her. "I would not, nor do I think any of the healers at the Agency would. Whether the Council says you are sentient or not, we would not force you to mate with anyone you did not want to, but the Council could order that you be made pregnant through other means, in order to save your species from extinction. I would not do it. I would resign first and I think most other healers would too, but I cannot guarantee that someone might deem saving your species of far more importance than the risk to any one individual."

Jer came over and squatted down so that he was face to face with her. "I promise that if that should happen, I will represent your people and continue to fight for your rights, for as long as I am able, and I will protect you and your grandfather as if you were still my ward, should you want to remain here with us. I will not abandon you or your people, no matter what the Senior Council decides."

"As will I," Myra vowed, nodding her head.

"And I," Marcus stated.

"For the rest of my life," Marsee signed.

# CHAPTER 22

# Myra: Senior Healer

Myra grabbed her bag and exited the ground crawler on the far side of the Agency, just inside the shield that remained up to protect the creatures within from outside predators, and started making her way across, marveling at the changes that had occurred in the last few weeks. Many of the creatures were now in outdoor pens, with bipeds walking around everywhere. Many of which were even helping out with the care of the various creatures. The wards that had once been locked up tight, now had their doors propped wide open, as were the few windows. She spoke with every healer she passed, checking in on how their wards were doing. Everyone had wonderful things to report and she even had the fantastic news that one of the 'canines' had just given birth to a litter of ten 'puppies'. She was struggling to remember the signs that Little Flower and GrandFather had given to the various creatures.

There was a large crowd around the pen with the new puppies and she peered in briefly to check them out. They were absolutely adorable. Ridiculously tiny, as were most of that worlds creatures, but that just made them even more adorable. *Little Flower's cub probably won't be much bigger,* she realized, remembering the two biped births they'd had, and then continued on her way until she finally made it to the old clinic building, which had once been all she'd managed. It seemed tiny and run down now that it had been converted to offices, and had seen such intense use over the past several months. Sand from the storm still drifted against the sides.

She made her way through to the back where her office was located, and found Brice sitting at her desk, head leaning on one arm as she scowled at her tablet. "You look like someone filing out their eight hundredth requisition form of the day," she teased, leaning up against the doorway.

Brice looked up and smiled. "You're not wrong. What brings you in today? I wasn't expecting you," she said, starting to get up from the desk to let her take her seat. Myra motioned for her to remain seated.

"I'm not staying, I just wanted to check in on the biped females in person, and came by to drop something off, well three somethings actually," she said, sitting down in the chair Brice normally sat in, and placed her bag on the floor.

"Most have finally stopped bleeding. One or two still have a little spotting but their hormone levels are all finally returning to normal. I started the hormone blockers this morning for most of them. The rest I'll probably start tomorrow," Brice said.

"How are they taking it?" Myra asked.

"Honestly, surprisingly well. Most indicated they were in pain, but the nanos seemed to do the trick there. We've seen a few crying, but most just seem grumpier than normal, and have been eating far more. They completely decimated our last shipment of star fruit within a few hours," Brice said. "I have another shipment coming this afternoon."

"Little Flower has done the same to our crop. She did mention that food cravings were normal with pregnancy, although frankly, I'm just glad they're eating, and not going into a depression, or worse, suffering medical complications from their miscarry," Myra said.

"Same. So, what did you come by to drop off?" Brice asked curiously.

Myra grinned and picked her bag up off the floor, reached in and pulled out a scroll that had been bound neatly with a fancy ribbon, and handed it to Brice.

"What's this?" Brice asked as she took it.

"Open it," Myra ordered.

Brice carefully slid the ribbon down and unrolled the document, and stared at it in shock.

"Journeyman Healer Brice Morningstar, it is my honor to present you with your master's certificate, for all of the hard work you've put into running this Agency as my second from day one of the Cataclysm. You've shown me time and again just how dedicated and caring you are, and how intensely devoted you are to your patients. As a journeyman you could have chosen to leave just as Kelly did, but you stayed without a moment's hesitation. You could have chosen to just work with the bipeds or just help me run the Agency, but you chose to do both and excelled at it. During the storm you showed everyone your leadership skills, stepping in to run the Agency in my absence, and I have had nothing but excellent reports from the other healers."

"The Healers Guild actually promoted me? After everything that happened?" Brice said, looking up at her in ears-back astonishment.

"They did more than that. I put in the application for your promotion this morning, and they approved it immediately. I just flew to Council City to pick it up. While I was there, I submitted my resignation as senior healer for the Agency," Myra said.

"You did what?!" Brice asked, as Myra reached into her bag again.

"They accepted, and I recommended you as my replacement. They agreed, and it is my further privilege to present you with your certificate for master healer level two," she said, placing another certificate on the table. "And, master healer level three as the new senior healer in charge of the Agency." She placed the third certificate on the desk.

Brice just stared at the two other certificates, not even daring to touch or open them. "But..."

"But nothing, you've earned it. You've had more real-world experience, both in caring for patients, and the efforts needed to run a major trauma center, than I had when all of this landed on my plate. Your years as a staffer have been invaluable and frankly, you should have been promoted to master years ago, and you would have if you hadn't chosen to stay out here in the middle of nowhere with me. But more than that, you were the first to identify the bipeds isolation sickness, out of hundreds of master healers, and you've managed to keep two hundred and eighteen females alive through simultaneous miscarriages. I don't even know if I could have done that, and you've put in more work than every master healer here on staff. You now have the distinction of having the fastest promotion from journeyman to senior healer ever recorded in guild records, by decades. Granted, a few weeks from now, you may very well also end up with the far more dubious distinction of having the fastest demotion on record too, but that's out of our hands, mine or the Guilds at this point."

Brice just stared at her. She tried several times to speak, and then slowly reached out and opened the certificates, laying them side by side on the desk. "Myra, I..."

"Congratulations, Senior Healer Brice Morningstar. This office and that stack of requisition forms are now *all* yours. Enjoy!" Myra stood and walked out of the office.

"Myra! Don't you dare!" Brice yelled after her, panic etched on her voice.

Myra just smiled, curled her tail, and kept walking.

"Myra! Get back here! *MYRA!*"

# CHAPTER 23

# Jeran: Unchartered Territory

Jer sat in his office staring at his tablet and the thousands of unanswered messages and missed calls, the overflowing calendar of committee meetings, and double the normal number of council sessions between now and the trial. The Local Council was trying desperately to finalize the budget for the entire upcoming year, as well as any currently outstanding cases that needed judgment, in order to put their world in a better position before trial. The hope was that if everyone was kicked off, that at least the residents of their world wouldn't suffer too badly for their actions. Although no one really knew if the Senior Council would honor those decisions or not.

Word of the upcoming trial was all that was on the news channels, on *all* of the planets, and their offices were flooded with calls and messages from their constituents. Jer's junior councilors and staffers were working around the clock to manage the sudden influx of communication. In nearly a third of the districts enough people had registered a vote of no-confidence, including his own, that elections were being held as well. His district had been the first, and it had stung to receive the rejections from personal friends, but he understood.

Whether those elections would be done in time for the trial was anyone's guess. Many were considering whether or not they should just resign as Marcus had done, but they had no idea if the remaining members of the Senior Council would honor a newly elected senior councilor from a collection of pro-tem councilors, chosen and sworn in by Councilor Tabor the day before she was stripped of her rank, assuming they were all found guilty. This was all new territory. The Charter covered the loss of the Local Council in the event of a natural disaster or accident, not if they were all found guilty of committing a crime.

Jer had spent most of the morning teaching Little Flower how their local charter worked as what was actually in the Charter was limited. The Consortium Charter stated that each world would have an elected council of four hundred members, that would be elected for a term of ten years, and that those elected officials would choose one representative as senior councilor. Each elected councilor would identify the junior councilor that would replace them in the event of their death for the remainder of their elected term, which the Senior Council could choose to honor for the remainder of their term, pick someone who met the qualifications of that world's local charter, or call for a new election, at their discretion. All adult members of the Consortium were required to vote for their Local Council, unless physically unable to, due to severe injury or illness, and anyone deemed qualified by their planet's local charter could run as long as they were a legal adult, and had not been convicted of any crime.

Outside of those stipulations, it was up to each planet to decide how they trained their councilors, divided up their world into the four hundred seats, and picked who was qualified to run. They had no idea if the Senior Council would honor their chosen junior councilor, if they were found guilty. In the past, the Senior Council had made liberal use of all three options depending on the scenario. But they were all running under the assumption that the Senior Council would call for new elections, as that was the most common precedent used in a situation like this.

Their Local Council ran much like the Guild ranking system, or rather technically the Guild ranking system was based loosely on the charter and their Council, since the Council had come first. Staffers were the equivalent to apprentices, although they all had to be legal adults, unlike the Guild that accepted children. They learned the day-to-day operations of running the planet, and took in depth courses on the local charter, administrative functions, and language. Each staffer was required to complete a ten-year term before being allowed to sit an examination to become a junior councilor, although many chose to remain as a senior staffer instead. Should they pass their examinations, they would then need to spend three full terms under the mentorship of the elected councilor in the district in which they resided. Marcus had been Jer's mentor the entire time, but it was not uncommon for people to move to a different district for any number of reasons. As a junior councilor, they would take additional courses in forensics, culture, and the charters, and in their final year, discipline, where they learned what they might be required to do someday. They would be tested again, and if they passed, given the title of junior advocate councilor, although this was often shortened to just 'advocate'.

From there, they could run for office in any open election they chose. The only requirement was that they move to that district should they win. If they chose not to run for the Council, then they could remain as an advocate in whatever district they resided, and would assist in whatever else the elected Councilor would need, typically running the day-to-day operations of a local city or town as appointed by that Councilor. Only fully elected councilors could be an advocate at a Full Council trial though. The exception was made for Marcus, both because he was a councilor at the time he'd volunteered, but also because he'd been an elected councilor for fourteen terms, one of the longest terms on record for anyone not also elected to the Senior Council.

Marcus was not only his older brother and mentor, but they both came from a long line of councilors. Marcus had joined as a staffer the same day he took his oath of adulthood, and ran for election shortly after obtaining the rank of junior advocate, and he'd won, which almost never happened but he'd been running to fill the space vacated by their father who had decided to step down at the end of his term. As their father had been loved by his people, and Marcus's record had been impeccable as a junior councilor, the people had given him a chance. He'd won by landslide victories every election since, to the point that his junior advocates usually had an advantage in whatever elections they chose to run for. Jer hadn't been ready to run for councilor, for various reasons. Instead, he had spent a few terms as an advocate in the South District, after relocating there to be with Myra, and help raise their first litter of cubs. When the prior councilor had eventually retired, Jer had finally decided to run, and to his amazement had won.

An election period would open immediately at the end of a term, whenever a councilor stepped down, or whenever more than half of the people in their district submitted a vote of no confidence. The clock would start the moment the first person submitted their application, and over the following week anyone wishing to run would submit their name, and what they hoped to accomplish during their term, and the election would be held. Once all votes were in, the bottom vote earner would be dropped and voting would begin again until such time as someone earned more than fifty percent of the vote. Those running for office could elect to give a single interview to the press, post a statement on their public page, and answer any questions that were sent to them either privately or via their public page. All decisions they'd made as an advocate or councilor were public knowledge, and available at any time via their public page, unless marked as private to protect the identity of a minor, or by the Senior Councilor for any reason.

He'd been astonished to find out how the bipeds elections had run, and just how unfair their system had been, favoring those who already had power and wealth. They'd all been shocked and surprised that the people hadn't just revolted, but had then been equally horrified to learn how those revolts had been suppressed, both through violent means and by other methods used to suppress or restrict votes. Marcus had explained how the four hundred districts had been recorded and set in stone millennia ago and how people could easily move to any district they wanted to. All they had to do was go to any junior councilor or higher, submit the appropriate paperwork, and they would be assigned a new home of equal or better value, and that met their current needs based on the number of people who lived there, and be provided with transportation and assistance in moving if they needed it. While people of higher rank could choose to pay for a better home, no one was denied a place to live and every home had to meet specific standards. They'd all been shocked to find out that poverty and homelessness had been rampant on the bipeds world, although they'd also been relieved that both Jessica and GrandFather had been adamant in their desire to move away from such a failed system.

Jer shook himself out of his musings over everything he'd learned about the bipeds so far, and checked on the current voting for Marcus's district and frowned. As there was a very strong chance Marcus's replacement would end up as Senior Councilor at the end of the month, and there wasn't an incumbent running for the position, which in of itself was rare, the election was hotly contested, almost all of the junior advocates had run. Marcus's junior advocates currently all had the lead, but no one was even close to a majority yet, although several rounds had been completed. While the voting was being completed in near record time, there were just far too many people to weed out. Others had withdrawn their name from consideration when the votes of no confidence had started occurring in other districts, and decided to run against the incumbent there. Jer currently had two dozen people running against him. The voting had not started in his or any of the other districts yet and with only two and a half weeks left to go before the trial, time was running out.

Jer growled his frustration. Thirty days was just not enough time to get everything done. He was up before dawn to prepare for the day's meetings. Sign language lessons had been increased to three times a day, and he'd caught himself starting to sign a response in his last committee meeting. Between meetings, he was trying to help translate the Charter into Little Flowers language, which was taking far too long. At this rate they wouldn't have half of it translated before the trial. They were trying to condense nearly four decades of training into three weeks and do it all in a language none of them spoke fluently. It didn't help that half the words in the Charter didn't even have signs to go with them, and then half of those didn't appear to have matching words in Little Flower's language. They had to explain the concepts behind each word, and then the legal implications of every phrase. It was exhausting and they were all struggling.

On top of that, he and Marcus were still trying to find a way to save Myra and Brice, should they end up successfully proving Little Flower's sentience and worthiness to join the Consortium, leaving it up to the other councilors to find a way to save themselves. At this point they'd given up trying to find a way to negate the charges entirely, and were focusing on trying to find a way to downgrade the charges from collusion to accessory. The rest of the time was spent quizzing Little Flower, and everyone else they'd decided to call for witnesses, and determining how to manage the information they were slowly learning about Little Flower's people. The more they learned, the more they were concerned that the Senior Council wouldn't find them sentient enough to join the Consortium, or worse, would find them a danger, which had its own set of challenges to prepare for, and the discussions he'd had with Marcus frankly would have had them executed for treason if Tabor found out.

To his surprise, Ellie and Marcus had both moved in for the duration. Marcus he'd expected, but not Ellie. They'd converted one of the spare rooms into a miniature archive, and set up the environmental systems to keep the fragile documents safe. Ellie spent a good part of her day working with Marsee to help get her over her stage fright, as Marsee would be front and center on the Council floor the entire time, and she was absolutely terrified about it. That was not going well either. Ellie had tried having Marsee give an interview to the press about her fostering program, but that had ended in disaster. The first question in, Marsee had frozen and bolted to her room, and it had taken hours to convince her to come out again. Ellie had salvaged it by giving the interview instead. Thankfully the interviewer had been a friend of Ellies, and had been prepped about Marsee's stage fright and understood, but they all worried Marsee would panic at the trial.

Ellie had agreed to translate as best she could if it came to that, but she wasn't nearly as fluent in sign as Marsee was. Marsee's skill at learning languages was nothing short of astounding, and Jer had been shocked to learn just how fluent she was in the other languages, expecting her to be only passable enough to manage the basics, but they'd had multiple conversations in the other languages with her to verify her skill, and Jer was pretty sure she was better than he was in most of them, and she'd only been learning the other languages for a few months, while he'd been speaking them for decades. She'd always been a fast learner, especially when interested in the topic, but she rarely forgot a sign or word once learned or created. Although to be fair, he was just as impressed with Marcus and Little Flower's ability to learn sign language, and with Little Flower's ability to both read and write. That was going slower, as they weren't spending as much time on it, but that she could at all was incredible. *I suppose when your life depends on it, you're far more motivated to learn,* Jer decided. Jer knew he was working far harder to learn to sign than he ever had with any of the other languages.

Thankfully though, Ellie had also brought with her a team of master's that specialized in restoring old documents, to assist with scanning and repairing some of the damage to the ancient manuscripts. That at least was moving quickly. He spent hours after everyone else went to bed scouring the days scanned documents hoping to find a way to save his family and friends. Both he and Marcus had been astounded at everything that was missing in the digital archives and they both wondered when and why that had occured. Marcus had checked with both Senior Councilor Tabor and the Senior Archivist and neither of them had records of those changes, which meant it must have occured millenia before. The only hint they had was that much of what was missing would not be considered fair or just by current standards, just like the rape precedent.

With all the new people, his home felt far more crowded than it had been in years. Not since his first litter had all moved out had anyone stayed for more than a few days, and it had been nearly a decade since everyone had been back together again. He wished he could bring his family together for at least a few days before the trial but there just wasn't time. Little Flower needed every second if he was going to save her and her people, as well as everyone else. He just hoped his children and grandchildren would understand, although he seriously doubted they would, once they found out what the consequences were.

*Focus, Jer,* he told himself. *You don't have time for wishes. I need to make time, but how?* He looked again at his tablet and scowled. But then an idea occurred to him, and he did some digging. *It's a longshot but it just might work,* he thought. He fired off a message to Samantha, his senior advocate, and let her know that he was forwarding every message from anyone not on his personal contact list to her, to read through and triage, along with a personal statement on his intentions at the trial, that he wanted her to post to his public facing page, as soon as his next council meeting had started, but not a minute before.

She was one of the few that had not put her name in for consideration. He'd spoken to her about it, and she'd said that she had no desire to win an election this way. She wanted to win on the basis of her own merit, and not at the disgrace of someone else. Additionally, she wanted to help in any way she could to ensure Little Flower and her people had what they needed. She also figured there was a chance she'd be promoted anyway, if the Senior Council decided to promote senior advocates into the position rather than run elections. He'd been incredibly grateful for her support, and prayed that her career wouldn't be damaged by association with him.

Message sent and filter configured, his inbox dropped to much more manageable proportions. Scanning the remaining messages, most of those were for committee positions he just didn't have time to focus on anymore. A fifteen-minute warning for the next council session dinged, and he made up his mind, fired off several more messages, placed himself on the docket for the meeting, made a quick trip to the waste room, and then activated his office's privacy shield and busy light before joining the meeting.

The monitors on his wall lit up. The center screen displayed the docket for the meeting, currently changing as Senior Councilor Tabor adjusted the items for priority. The other monitors were set up to display the images of each of the other councilors. As they logged on from their home offices or council desks, their video flicked on in their assigned square, two hundred on each side. Each position was fixed based on seniority, which included both time in office, and a complex algorithm based on committee positions. Marcus was the most senior, next to Tabor, and Jer wasn't all that far behind. Having the Agency in his district had bumped him up significantly in the rankings. Jer watched as his item was dragged to the very top. This had been common of late, as most everything he had to discuss related to the Agency and the bipeds these days, and frankly, half the time he had something to report, it wasn't good news.

When everyone was in attendance, except for one, Marcus, who had indicated a planned absence, Senior Councilor Tabor began the meeting. "Councilor Chenzira you are first on the docket. I am assuming this is in regards to the Agency. Your docket description was left blank," she both asked and chided at the same time. He'd done that on purpose as he hadn't wanted to give anyone warning as to what he was about to do.

"It is and it isn't, ma'am. I am currently assisting Councilor Surellis in preparing Little Flower for the trial, but it's taking far longer than we'd hoped to translate the Charter into her language. I wish to be able to spend more time helping her prepare, and I cannot do so with the current list of committees I am in and chairing. I'd like to resign my positions on all but the Agency Committee, and if the Council approves, I would like to recommend that Councilor Parner be offered first choice of those committee positions, if he is so interested." Murmurs followed his announcement.

"Are there any objections to this motion?" Tabor asked. Surprisingly only Paxton indicated an objection.

"Councilor Parner, you have the floor," Tabor indicated. Jer could tell she was just as curious as to what Parner had to say.

"Thank you, ma'am. Councilor Chenzira, I'm sure everyone here would agree that we have not exactly seen eye-to-eye on just about every issue presented to the Council." Several on the Council chuckled at this comment, and Jer's tail, out of sight of the camera, curled in his own amusement at the understatement. "So, I wish to know *why* you would choose me, of all people, to fill your positions. I'm looking at the list now and most of these are for positions you currently chair, and I don't even qualify to be on these committees for another term, much less chair them."

"You're right, Councilor Parner, we haven't seen eye to eye on much of anything, especially when it comes to the Agency, but you've shown your conviction and tenacity, and a deep desire to protect the people you represent, and I respect that. I don't know what's going to happen to any of us at the end of the month, but right now we need someone who isn't already on half a dozen committees to fill my place. We just don't have the time to take anyone away from their other responsibilities."

Paxton nodded his head in acceptance of this, but Jer continued. "Also, moments before this meeting, I submitted as official evidence that by *my* actions alone, I forced this Council to vote as they did. I have also requested that my Senior Advocate post a public statement to that effect. I cannot say how any of the rest of this Council would have voted, but you Councilor Parner, have been on record from the very first day as being opposed to removing the bipeds from quarantine until the research was completed, and as such, it is my personal belief that had you been allowed to vote without *my* interference, you would have voted no. It is also my hope that regardless of how the upcoming elections go, that the Senior Council will not find you guilty for the crime *I* forced upon you, that *I* forced all of you to commit. It takes a great deal of bravery to stand up against your seniors and tell them no, and tell them that they're wrong, and that's the kind of tenacity needed to chair these committees. But on top of that, you've shown your humility too. You could have publicly berated all of us for forcing you to vote as you did, but you stuck by your vote, regardless of the consequences that came from it, and *that* is why I chose you."

The Council was silent as Parner absorbed Jer's speech and to Jer's amazement, Parner bowed low to him, showing his respect. "Councilor Chenzira, it would be my honor to accept your offer. Thank you for your kind words. They mean a great deal to me."

Jer bowed back.

Tabor was silent for a long moment and Jer wondered what she was thinking. "Are there any further objections?" she finally asked. There were none. She gave a slight nod. "Then councilors mark your vote." It was unanimous, and Tabor adjusted the committee positions. Jer smiled as he watched the tiles on the monitors shift and Councilor Paxton Parner took his place ahead of Jer and Jer dropped down to the bottom of the list of those in their fifth term.

As he sat listening to one of the other councilors drone on, his tablet buzzed. It was a message from his father and he smiled. His father had been a Councilor for nearly seven terms before retiring so he fully understood what Jer had done and what he was now facing. He checked the time and realized the news would have had just enough time to make it to Flyer, where his parents currently lived, and back again. He responded, knowing it would take time for his father to receive.

**I'm proud of you, Kitten.**

Thanks, Papa. Will you come for a visit?

**Your mother and I have already booked passage on the next ship. We'll be there in two days. How can I help?**

I was hoping you'd ask. Fancy some light reading for your trip?

**Archives?**

Ancient. Number one on the top downloads, ten thousand years and running now.

**Ha! Sounds like a relaxing vacation. Send me what you've got.**

Thanks, Papa.

**Anytime, Kitten, and Kitten, whatever happens, we'll take care of Marsee and Little Flower.**

Thank you, Papa. Love you.

**Love you too, Kitten.**

After Jer sent his father the latest batch of scans along with what they were looking for, he sent a message out to his children, asking them to come for a visit a few days before the trial. If they weren't ready by then, he decided, they weren't going to be anyway. That done, he silenced all of his incoming messages and calls and refocused on the meeting at hand.

When Jer signed off, he checked his tablet and smiled. His announcement had gone out and spread like wildfire. Nearly half of the elections had been stopped as people retracted their vote of no confidence, dropping the votes below the required threshold. To Jer's shock, this also included his own, and all but Marcus's Junior Advocates had dropped out of their race.

He had just turned off his busy light and was about to head back to the family room where everyone was working, when Myra burst through his door without knocking. "Jeran Frederick Chenzira, what moons' forsaken cursed eclipse has possessed you? They're going to kill you for this!" she said, holding up her tablet, tail poofed and lashing in a combination of fury and fear.

"You saw my press announcement, I take it?" he asked, trying hard to keep his emotions tucked under his mask and keep a straight face, knowing that laughing would not go over well with her in this mood. He'd likely be clawed if he did.

"Saw?! How could I not see? It's the only thing on the news, and my inbox is blowing up!" Myra yelled. "How could you do something like this without talking to me first?"

"I only did what you did to try and save the other healers. By taking full responsibility, it gives the Senior Council someone to blame. The elections were taking far too long. Marcus's replacement was never going to be elected in time, and frankly neither were any of the others. My hope is that even if everyone else is found guilty, my plea will protect Parner, which will give the Council an elected official, with at least some experience to place as Senior Councilor."

"But why Parner? He's been against the Agency from day one," Myra asked.

"For that very reason. I posted his track record of votes on the Agency, regarding quarantine as evidence. In every one, including putting the Agency at your clinic, he's voted no. He's the only one on the Full Council that voted no for the Agency. The only time he voted yes was the final vote, but he was against it even then. The comments he posted with his vote clearly stated that he only voted yes because he was under the belief that something had to be done to help the bipeds, but that he felt the proposed plan was not the right one. He said, and I quote, 'There is something off about the proposed plan by Healer Chenzira. I am not a healer and I've never worked with animals, or had much contact with them to understand how domestic breeds are managed, but if these are in fact sentient creatures, are we not taking their choice of mate away from them by choosing who they are paired up with? Even to save a species, shouldn't they have a choice?'"

Myra collapsed into one of the conference chairs. "*Parner*, of all people, saw what I missed?"

Jer nodded.

"They're going to go as hard on you as they are me. Who's going to take care of Marsee and Little Flower?" Myra asked with worry etched on her face.

"My parents. They'll be here in two days, and Papa's already digging into the Archives I've sent him." Jer stood and walked over to Myra, handing her the tablet so she could see the texts herself. "I've also asked the cubs to come for a visit before the trial."

Myra looked up at him, and then leaned into his side. Jer wrapped his arms and tail around her. "Are we going to tell them?" she asked softly.

"No. If it comes down to precedent, I want their last memory of us to be happy ones. Maybe someday they'll forgive us. Now come on, it's almost time to call Sina."

Later that afternoon they were all in his office slogging through another section of the Charter, all except for Marsee, who was in Myra's office meeting with Rainbow Scales, her Water Sprite language tutor. Myra's medical monitor was better suited to handle the finer details of their visual language. They'd made it to the section describing the naming of various people, species, and their worlds.

"Let me see if I understand correctly," Little Flower signed. "For every species there is an official language that is used for council meetings and official documentation. This isn't necessarily the language that they actually speak on their home world, since it's not possible for every species to speak every other language. So, our official language would be sign language even if we happen to speak another language because no one else can speak or even hear our words?"

"That is correct. The Water Sprites have chosen to speak our language officially because it's the easiest of the other four languages for them to speak. Even then many of their Councilors need translators because they haven't developed the skills or ability to speak yet. The

Water Sprites physically can't speak any of our languages until they have reached their full adult stage, and even then, it's awkward for them because the sounds they use were only ever used for mating calls or warnings. Many refuse to even learn because it feels highly inappropriate to do so in a public space," Marcus answered.

"I understand. While it varied from culture to culture, on my world, we usually didn't go around without clothing that covered our...parts...unless we were actively trying to mate, or in the privacy of our own homes," Jessica replied, pointing to the various areas as she didn't have the signs for those yet.

Myra slapped her forehead and groaned. "Is that why he thought we wanted you to mate?"

"That's a big part of it, yes. Personally, I think that was just an excuse," Little Flower answered. "Once mature, we can mate whenever we want to, not just when we are fertile. Most do it because they enjoy it, or because they are trying to have a cub. Some did it for power, others to survive." All three of them looked confused. "It's a skill, just like any other," Little Flower explained.

They'd had a big discussion on economics the night before. Jer was still confused at how their system worked with any fairness. From what he could tell it wasn't fair at all, and one of the biggest reasons they struggled so much, but Jer could understand trading skill for skill, as that was the basis of their economy, and the Ancient Gods knew if he could experience that feeling outside of a proper mating with a female in heat, he'd never want to leave his bedroom again.

"So back to the charter. My official name will be Little Flower, even though I have my own name in my own language?"

"Correct," Marcus answered, "Unless you want a different name sign, although most people already know you as 'Little Flower' so if you're good with it, I recommend sticking with it."

"And every other species can translate that into their own language, as best they can, or pick something else if there is no easy translation?" she continued.

"Yes, for any non-sentient species. For your name and your species name and planet, you will be given the opportunity to review what the other species pick before it becomes official, or pick your own if you're fluent in those languages. Either way, we will do our best to translate it, and confirm that it is not a slur, or derogatory in nature, in any of the various languages. Since you cannot hear those words or read those languages yet, you'll have to take our word for it, but I assure you we will do our best to make sure it's respectful. For your own personal name, we try to match as best we can that name in the sounds of your language, or if not, we use your official name. One of the first decisions you will need to make is what signs you will use for the other worlds, and what you will call us in your own spoken and written language. For now, the signs Sina came up with will work for the trial, but they are not official," Marcus replied.

"That is a big responsibility to decide for another species. How did you decide what you called the other species?"

"We chose to go with a descriptive name for each of the species as the sound the Flyer's use for their species name is very similar to the word for purple in ours. The Flyers were the first to join with us in the Consortium. We kept that same policy for the other species as they joined. For the Water Sprites, we chose it because they live in the water and move very quickly when they want to, or 'spritely' and they live on the only planet that is almost entirely covered in water. Only a few small islands are above ground, so 'Water World' just made sense," Marcus said. "For the..."

"Papa, someone's here to see you," Marsee said from the doorway and they all turned to look. Marsee stepped aside and Councilor Parner stepped in.

"Paxton, this is a surprise. What brings you here?" Jer said. He noticed that Marsee immediately started translating for Little Flower and he smiled at her.

"I figured it was time I met Little Flower," Paxton replied.

Jer raised an eyebrow but turned to Little Flower. "Little Flower, this is Councilor Paxton Parner. He's the councilor for the same district where Healer Ammond lives."

"Hello, Councilor. It is very nice to meet you," Little Flower said with a smile.

"Councilor Parner has very graciously agreed to take over my position on most of my committees, so that I have more time to help you prepare," Jer added, amused at the surprise on Marcus's face. Marcus had been working non-stop, and hadn't actually checked the news or his messages, and Jer hadn't told him yet. *That makes three times I've surprised him. I'm on a roll,* Jer thought with a curl of his tail, and a wicked smile at his mentor who glared at him in return. *Just wait until he finds out what else I did.*

"That's very kind of you. Thank you!" Little Flower signed.

"You're welcome," Parner said. "How is your preparation coming along?"

"Slowly. We're still focusing on translating the Charter and it's taking a long time. There are so many signs we don't have, and then I have to make sure I understand the meaning, and figure out how to translate each passage into words my people will understand. I want to make sure I understand exactly what I'm agreeing to, should we be allowed to join your Consortium. We haven't even begun to work on preparing for the actual trial, and Jer and Marcus are still trying to find ways to save everyone from the consequences of my actions. It does not seem fair to me at all, that the actions of one of my species, done only to me, would end up punishing your entire world, and I'm very sorry about that," Little Flower signed.

Parner looked absolutely shocked by her words. "You would really forgive us for putting you in harm's way?"

Little Flower nodded. "You were only trying to do your best for our people and yours, to keep everyone safe. We did not know your intentions, and you did not know our culture to know how your actions were giving us the wrong impression of you. It was a mistake. Accidents happen. What he did though was not a mistake, and he's the only one I truly blame."

Parner scrunched down so that he was at eye level with her. "From the bottom of my heart, I am sorry for the harm I have caused you. I chose not to believe you were sentient because I was scared. Scared for myself and for my people. It is no excuse, but when I was younger, I lost one of my littermates to an outbreak of spotted fur. It's one of the few illnesses that are still fatal to our kind. I could not bear to lose more of my family to an illness we would have no way to fight or defend against. Myra, Jer, and Marcus all tried for a very long time to convince me to relax the quarantine within the Agency, and I fought against it until Myra came to us and showed us how what we were doing was harming your people. I spent a day in isolation to see what you were going through, and I could not stand it. I do not know how you did, and I'm sorry. I'm sorry I was too scared to meet you myself, and passed judgment on you and your species without ever once meeting you. That was childish and wrong of me."

"It was awful, but I understand why you did it. Our world had a similar illness when I was a cub too. Millions of our people died or were left with long term consequences. I was fortunate that I did not lose anyone close to me, but my best friend's mother was a healer, and she lost so many patients that it broke her. I forgive you. You were only trying to protect your people and ours, and I thank you for that."

"Thank you. I promise, you have my vote and support at the trial. It's not nearly enough for the harm I've caused you, but perhaps I can help another way," Paxton replied.

"How so?" Jer asked.

"You need help getting ready. I have lots of questions, and I'm usually the one causing a ruckus at the Council meetings anyway. Perhaps I could question you as I might at the trial, maybe come up with questions you two might not think of, and I have a whole team of staffers that are suddenly not buried in hate mail from my constituents, thanks to you, Jer. Perhaps they might be put to use searching the archives or whatever else you need?" he suggested.

"Your help would be greatly appreciated, Paxton. Thank you," Jer said, trying hard not to laugh at Paxton's understatement, and his mentor's further glare. Jer was going to enjoy that conversation. Even if his ploy didn't work, a death sentence was almost worth it, just to know he'd successfully managed to pull one over on his big brother.

"Well before any of that happens though, I think it's time to take a break for the evening meal. Councilor Parner, would you care to join us?" Myra asked.

"It would be my pleasure," he replied with a smile. "And please, call me Paxton."

Later that evening, after Paxton had been set up in a guest room for the night, Marcus dragged him back into his office. It had been all Jer could do to keep from laughing at Marcus's expression throughout the entire evening meal, and the conversation that night as Marcus clearly wanted to find out what he'd done, but it would be considered extremely rude to pull out his tablet and check when there was company there. A few times when Paxton was distracted, Marcus had tried to get him to explain in sign but Jer had simply responded with 'later.' He didn't want to discuss it in front of Marsee or Little Flower, not with company there anyway.

"Alright, Cub. Spill it. What did you do this time?" Marcus growled.

"I'm pretty sure if you took two seconds to check the news, you'd figure it out," Jer said, crossing his arms and leaning back against the side of his desk, enjoying seeing his brother outmaneuvered and thoroughly flustered.

Marcus glared at him for not answering, but pulled out his tablet. Jer watched as Marcus's expression went from annoyed to full mask as he read and slowly sat down in one of the chairs, nearly missing it. Finally, he set his tablet down on the table and stared across the room not looking at Jer. "You know I won't be able to save you now," he said softly.

"I know," Jer replied just as softly. "But be honest, you were never going to be able to do so anyway. If anything like this had ever happened before, it would have been at the top of our studies. Ten thousand years of history aside, that wouldn't have been forgotten. This way, everyone else has a chance."

"Unless it was forgotten intentionally, like everything else we've found," Marcus countered, but sighed heavily and nodded, still not looking at him. Marcus stared off into the distance for some time. "I'm sorry, little brother," he said finally.

"For what?" Jer asked, thoroughly surprised.

"For not being good enough to save you. For not having the answers," Marcus said, finally turning to face him.

"I'm not asking you to protect me. If I wanted you to protect me, I wouldn't have done what I did. Just do your best to protect my children and grandchildren," Jer said.

"I don't know how, Jer. I honestly don't know how," Marcus whispered.

Jer closed his eyes and wept. If Marcus didn't know how to save them, then no one could.

# Marsee: Translator

Marsee sat alone in the garden under the shade of the bandala tree trying to calm her frayed nerves. She'd tried swinging in her bed with her hearing aids in for a while, but that hadn't helped. She couldn't sit still long enough for the rocking motion to calm her. Finally, she'd bolted and ran around the compound as fast as she could, until she was gasping for breath, and clawed her way gasping and wheezing into the garden to plunk herself down under the shade of the tree. It still hadn't helped. Now she was exhausted *and* overwhelmed.

Ellie had spent the morning working with Little Flower to design the flag to represent her people at the trial, and review Little Flower's clothing designs and measure them for the outfits she and GrandFather wanted for the meeting. They'd all been astonished when Little Flower had indicated she wanted her ears pierced, and Marsee's mother had flatly refused. When Little Flower explained why, Ellie had told her not to worry about it and then took a detailed scan of both of Little Flower's ears, promising her something beautiful to make up for it. Little Flower had agreed.

Then Marcus had decided it was time to start preparing for the actual meeting, as they were now making much better progress with the Charter and were now more than halfway through. Each day they were making more progress than the last, as there were fewer signs that needed to be created and thoroughly explained.

She was actually fairly curious about this as she'd always wondered what her father did every day. Unlike with her mother at her clinic, her father had never allowed her to attend any of his council meetings, although she'd watched a few of the public sessions during school as they were taught about their government. That was until Marcus had decreed that from this point forward, unless there was an emergency, or they were alone with Little Flower or GrandFather, no one but Marsee was to sign. It would be up to her to be Little Flower's ears and voice. To start with, he said, they were going to have a mock trial, so that everyone could learn what would happen. Frederick, Marsee's grandfather would play the part of the Senior Council, her father and Councilor Parner would be the councilors, Marcus the advocate, and her mother, grandmother, Ellie, and Rainbow Scales would be witnesses. Councilor Parner and Rainbow Scales were conferenced in.

She was managing reasonably well and keeping up until Marcus started speaking in Ice Giant, and then her Papa had responded in Digger and started arguing with Marcus. Myra joined in and then Ellie had called Rainbow Scales a purple nosed poop eater, who had responded with outrage and called Ellie an overrated basket weaver. Her grandfather tried to call everyone to order but no one was listening. Her grandmother had responded to Rainbow Scales by flinging out insults of her own switching languages mid-sentence and then stormed out. Tempers flaring, tails lashing, Marsee hadn't known what to do. Had she done wrong by translating what they actually said? And then, completely overwhelmed she'd panicked and bolted out of the room.

"There you are," Ellie said as she entered the garden. "I've been looking all over for you. Are you okay?"

"No, not even remotely okay. That was awful!" Marsee wailed.

"It was intended to be," Ellie said calmly, sitting down beside her. "We planned it to purposely see how far you would go, and what you would do."

"Three moons! You mean you really didn't call Rainbow Scales a purple nosed poop eater?"

"Oh, no, I did," Ellie said with a laugh, "but she knew it was coming, or something similar anyway, and I'm really not very good at basket weaving, so she wasn't wrong there. But you needed to experience what happens when tempers flare, and believe me, they will. This is not going to be a boring, run of the mill, resource allocation meeting. Emotions are high, people are already upset, and it's only going to get worse, and you also needed to experience what might happen if someone mistranslates something."

"That was supposed to be a mistranslation?" Marsee asked.

"It could have been. In a situation like this, rather than translating exactly what you thought was said, you should have stopped everyone and asked for clarification. You'll be placed next to the Senior Council where everyone can see you, and be given the same authority to stop someone from talking as Councilor Tabor, including her. This situation is unusual in that Little Flower's language is not fluently spoken by just about anyone on the Council, and cannot be held in her language, which almost never happens. If you do not understand something, or hear something that you believe will be an issue if translated as you understand it, or if you can't keep up, you'll need to raise your paw and say 'Stop Translate'. Anything spoken after you do will not be allowed as evidence until you indicate you are ready to continue, by saying 'continue'. Not only will this ensure that the right meaning gets translated, but if I *had* called Rainbow Scales an insult by accident, or even on purpose, it would give me an opportunity to apologize before it became an interplanetary incident."

Marsee sighed and nodded. "Moons. I messed up big time, didn't I?"

"Actually, you did far better than I was expecting. You kept up until everyone was yelling over each other, and even then, managed quite well from what I could tell. I'm not nearly as fluent in sign as you and the others are yet, but I didn't catch any mistakes and neither did the others. So, are you ready to try again?" Ellie asked.

"No," Marsee grumbled but stood up anyway. "Not really. I still feel like I was just run over by a herd of chenzies, but I don't really have much of a choice, do I?"

"You do, but you're far too stubborn and caring to quit on Little Flower," Ellie replied.

Marsee nodded and followed Ellie back into the family room, where everyone was still waiting for her. They spent the next half hour going over procedures and making tweaks. Little Flower told them that she'd had a hard time keeping up with who was talking, so Marsee tried stating who was talking, but that proved too slow and was difficult for Little Flower to tell if the person was speaking or if they'd just said their name, so Marsee just pointed to whomever was talking, or if more than one person was speaking at the same time, she'd raise her fingers to indicate multiple people and request to stop, and then work through each before continuing.

By the end of the evening, Marsee was managing to keep up reasonably well. Rainbow Scales only stayed for another hour or so, but said she would be back for their language session tomorrow night. But once she'd left, Marcus started asking the real questions, and everything suddenly got hard again, not because of her ability to keep up with the translation but because of what was being discussed.

Ellie, who was sitting next to her, thwapped her in the back of her leg with her tail any time she started reacting to what was being said, instead of the intent or actual emotion coming from the person she was translating for, and they made her stand through the whole thing like she would have to at the trial. She was tired, stressed, her feet hurt, and the back of her leg was starting to bruise from Ellies tail, but somehow, she made it through the evening. When Marcus indicated they were done, she gave everyone a hug good night and bolted to the safety of her room. An hour or so later, Little Flower climbed in, signed 'thank you,' and curled up beside her. Marsee wrapped herself protectively around Little Flower and purred them both to sleep.

Marsee's nightmares were filled with angry and screaming councilors, and Little Flower being dragged off in a harness and locked up and forced to breed again, and again, and again, because of her, and it was Little Flower that had woken and comforted her.

Over the next few days, they watched the official Council recordings that led to Little Flower being placed in the other bipeds cell, both to see how well she could keep up with the translation and to ensure that Little Flower fully understood the decisions and arguments that were made, and why. Marsee hadn't seen the video her mother had shown Little Flower, so she had been unprepared by the horror she felt watching Little Flower's home world destroyed. She'd actually managed to successfully tell Marcus to stop as they'd practiced, before she'd bolted from the room, shut the door, and been sick in the hall. Her mother had followed her out, and hugged her for a long time before sending her back in and cleaning up her mess. The others had not said anything about it either when she returned, and her grandparents had looked just as sick. That night, her dreams had been filled with nightmares of her own world being destroyed by an asteroid.

When they had made it through all of the Council footage to where they were sure Little Flower understood what had been said, decided, and why, they moved on to Agency footage in the event that parts of those recordings were used as evidence. Marsee had seen many of these recordings during her own investigation, but not all of them. Apparently, Marcus had spent an uncounted number of hours reviewing the footage to find videos of interest. They would watch a scene and then Little Flower would talk about what was going on from her perspective. Little Flower requested a pause multiple times, and spent most of the time watching those videos curled up on her mother's lap as her mother purred to comfort her.

Marsee hadn't seen the footage of Little Flower's defiance and attack on Healer Brice, but having been on the receiving end of Little Flower's anger, she'd actually chuckled at the shocked expression on Brice's face.

"So, what exactly did I say to her?" Little Flower had asked, to everyone's laughter. Once they'd stopped laughing long enough to explain, Little Flower had laughed too. "Well good, that's exactly what I'd intended to say."

It took nearly half an hour for everyone to stop laughing long enough to continue. That evening Marsee and Little Flower called Sina privately and learned how to swear in sign language, and they'd laughed for hours as they taught Little Flower the meaning behind each, and she'd taught them some of her peoples' rude gestures as well. It was then that Little Flower had finally explained the mistranslation she'd done during the storm and Marsee finally figured out what was so funny. She knew she'd never be able to look at that book the same way again.

After they hung up with Sina, they'd grabbed some cushions and were now sitting out on the balcony watching the moons. It was a beautiful night, comfortable and calm, and the stars were plentiful as the moons were only thin slivers tonight.

"I've been wondering for a while. Did you make the puzzle boxes?" Little Flower asked.

"I can't be sure that they were all mine, but many of the toys you came back with were ones I put in there. They were either mine or belonged to my nephlings," she said.

"Nephlings?" Little Flower asked.

"My siblings' children," Marsee explained.

"Ah. Thank you for making them. I really enjoyed figuring them out. It was one of the few things that kept me going. I'm sorry I destroyed them, and I'm sorry you had to watch me do so," she replied.

"I'm glad they brought you joy, both to unlock and to destroy. You needed a physical outlet to your distress, just like I did the other day when I had to run around the compound. Sometimes keeping it in is just too painful. If it helped you cope in any way, then it was worth every second I spent working on them."

Marsee paused for a bit, looking out at the view before continuing. "When I was younger, I had a really hard time coping with people and electronics. I still do, but I've learned to manage it a little better. Ammond's hearing aids really help. Having you around helps more. I never have to be anyone but myself around you, and you've never once corrected my behavior, and even when it's been too much you've been supportive not disappointed. I moved up here to get away from it all, so I could have a place far enough away from my parents that I could scream or throw pillows when things got too bad for me. I couldn't handle my parents concerned and disapproving looks when I lost control around them. This place was a disaster, full of old broken junk and buried in sand almost as deep as the courtyard was, but hard packed and solid. I spent weeks chucking things off the balcony as hard as I could, just to see them explode at the bottom. It was very satisfying. But I do have to say, you have a surprisingly good aim for someone so small," she said, rubbing her nose in memory of the book Little Flower had hit her with.

Little Flower laughed. "I suppose that's not surprising. Our arms are designed to throw things. It's how we used to hunt before we learned to raise animals for food. We would throw sticks with points on the end to kill our prey from a safe distance, the lack of claws and teeth being a real issue and all that. Now we use those skills for sport. For a few years I played on a team where we played a game called softball. We would throw a ball about this big and the other team would have to hit it with a stick, and run around set spots on the ground. Many of our other games involved throwing and catching balls of various sizes."

"Will you teach me?" Marsee asked.

"Sure, but we'll need some equipment. I'll draw something up and see if Ellie can fashion us something similar. I bet the others at the Agency would appreciate it too."

The next day they made it through the videos up to the part where Little Flower had been moved to the other cell. Before they went any further though, Marsee's mother had kicked everyone out but Marcus, and they'd had a long talk with Little Flower before bringing everyone back in. Marsee wasn't sure what had been said, but Little Flower was currently sitting in her mother's lap, with her mother's arms around her and her mother was purring very loudly.

When Little Flower indicated she was ready, they began. The first video was short, showing Little Flower's escape attempt. Marsee was fully unprepared for the scene. The sight of Healer Brice leaping over Little Flower to catch her triggered Marsee's hunting instincts again, as

Brice showed just how easy it was to catch them. Marsee managed to hold the growling beast at bay long enough to ask for a pause, and she quickly left the room, leaned up against the far wall, and shook. The beast had somehow found a way inside her shield and was fighting hard to take control.

*You've seen how easy it is to catch them. One little pounce is all it will take,* her instinct purred.

Her father followed her. "What's wrong, Kitten?" he asked, kneeling down beside her.

She couldn't answer, just looked down at her claws, which were clenching and unclenching uncontrollably, as she fought for control of her own body.

"Hunting instinct?" he asked and she nodded, unable to speak, furious and terrified that it had reared up again, especially in front of everyone. It had been quiet for days. She'd even chased Little Flower a few times while they played and had no problems, so she'd hoped whatever it was that was going on with her had ended. So much of their early childhood was learning to overcome the instinct to rip into anything that moved, and she should have had control over this years ago. It had been bad enough the first time when she barely knew Little Flower, but now the realization that she still wanted to hunt and eat her best friend made her sick, and she felt herself being swallowed and overpowered by the beast inside her and she fought back and tore at the beast, trying to get it to leave her alone.

*Why do you fight me so? You know you want to hunt. It's in your very nature. Why have teeth and claws if you aren't going to use them?* her instinct asked.

*Go away!* she growled at it.

Her father pulled her in for a hug and wrapped his arms around her, grabbing her firmly but gently by her scruff. "Just breathe through it. Nice and slow. Think how awful she would taste. She's nothing but skin and bones, not even worth hunting." She sagged against him and that thought just made her chuckle until she remembered how good the cooked fish had tasted and she started shaking again as the thought of Little Flower stuck on the end of a stick made her gag, while the beast inside her drooled.

*Mmm, that does sound tasty. Why wait? Get rid of this nuisance and return to the other room and pounce. Think how satisfying your prey will feel beneath your claws.*

*Leave them alone!* she yelled and swiped at the beast.

"It's okay, it's just an instinct. It's something you can control and you did. Even if your body wanted to hunt, you didn't, and you took yourself out of that situation. I'm proud of you. Keep breathing," he said gently, helping her through the reaction.

Eventually the beast backed off, and she stopped shaking from the exhaustion of the fight, and pulled away.

"Better now?" he asked.

She nodded and sighed. "Seeing how easily Brice chased her down and caught her, made me see Little Flower as prey, and easy prey at that, and all I could think was, 'I wonder what she'd taste like'. She's my best friend and I wanted to eat her," Marsee cried, leaning up against her father, not wanting to admit how close she'd come to losing control. *What's wrong with me?* she thought, terrified.

"She would taste horrible," her father said.

"Papa, did Mama tell you about when we first found out that Little Flower liked her fish cooked?" she asked.

"Just that Little Flower had asked for the fish and tried to cook it over the lanterns, and that afterwards she cooked the star fruit, why?"

"Mama and I tried some of the cooked fish. I was curious and really liked how it smelled. It was good, Papa, really good. It was all I could do that day not to eat more and every time they cook it, it just smells so good and the beast inside me wants more," she said, looking down at her claws again.

"Ahh, well, let me ask you this. If you ever had a chance to eat fried Little Flower, would you?"

"Moons no!" she yelped, ears back in horror and disgust.

"Well, there's your answer. Instinct is just that, instinct. You however are a thinking, caring person, and not ruled by your instinct. It was a flinch, nothing more. Just because your brain goes 'Prey!' doesn't mean you would or ever could follow through and hunt her. I've seen you chase each other down the halls and you never once tried to hurt her, and I don't believe you ever would or could kill her," he said.

She shook her head. "No. There was one time. The first day Little Flower was here. Didn't Mama tell you about it?" she asked. "I came so very close that day. I scared her so bad she ran and hid under your bed. I'm surprised she even trusts me."

Her father looked at her hard for several minutes and she looked away. He reached over and lifted her chin so she would look at him. "You didn't hurt her, and that's what matters," he said after staring at her for a long time.

She shook her head and looked down at her claws again.

"Do you remember the day Little Flower fell out of the tree?" he asked.

"How could I forget that?" Marsee asked, looking up at him and rolling her eyes.

"That afternoon you fell asleep. Little Flower climbed in to sleep next to you and you wrapped yourself protectively around her, just like your mother used to do with you. Your mother took a picture and sent it to me. You aren't a predator trying to hunt her, you're her protector keeping the other predators at bay. In order to be the best protector you can be, you have to truly understand how the predators think and work, and gaining that experience is never easy. Trust me."

"How can you be so sure?" Marsee asked. Her father didn't answer for a while, and then looked up and down the hallway, before motioning for her to follow him. Curious, she did, and was surprised when he entered his office and not only shut but locked the door *and* put up his privacy shield. He'd never once done that when talking with her before.

"I'm going to tell you something no one outside of the Council knows, and when I'm done, you can't tell anyone, ever. Do you give your oath to me, not as your father, but as your Councilor?" he asked.

"I Marsee Bet Chenzira promise to never tell another person about what you are about to tell me," she vowed, thoroughly intrigued. Her father nodded but still didn't answer right away.

"When we've completed all of our training and have served our third term as a junior councilor, we're given a test," he started.

"I know that, it's a written test and a bunch of mock trials," Marsee said. "We learned that in school."

"That is not the test I am referring to. There's the mock trials and then there's the real one. One that we don't talk about, even amongst ourselves for fear that someone will overhear and not understand why we do it. The specifics of the trial vary from world to world and are geared towards each species individual culture and challenges. I don't know the specifics of those trials, just our own," he said and looked away. Clearly struggling to tell her.

"What's the trial?" she asked.

He sighed and turned back to her. "We hunt."

"You what?!" she asked in surprise. Hunting was banned except in extreme cases where it was needed for survival. Hunting for sport, when well fed, held nearly the same consequences as murder, or at least that's what she'd been told. *If the Council does this, then maybe not,* Marsee thought.

"The junior councilors, along with their current mentor, the Senior Councilor, and a select group of others, depending on how new the current mentor is, take the junior councilor out into the wilds and tell them that they must hunt and kill whatever animal we come across. We usually pick something that is fast enough to trigger our instincts, but is also easy prey, because we want them to catch the creature. Most refuse outright initially, but we goad them and push them, and tell them if they don't, they can't ever be a councilor, that they won't pass. That it's required that they understand what it's like to truly be a predator, and that they have to learn how to kill because one day they might have to, should they have a trial where they have to put the accused to death. Almost everyone eventually gives in and hunts, and in a true hunt, there's no controlling it, not your first time anyway. At least I've never seen or heard of anyone being able to stop before a kill. We do this to show how easy it is to lose control, and to give into our baser instincts. That you were able to stop, means you weren't ever fully seeing her as prey."

"Are you sure? It certainly felt like that. I've never had an experience like that. It wasn't the normal, ooh shiny, pounce instinct when I was a cub. Well, it was at first when I caught her leash, but after that it changed. It was like there was an entirely separate beast inside of me, in complete control of my body, and it was ravenous. It stalked her, it gloried in the scent of her fear, and drooled at the sight of her trapped and cornered," she said, shaking as she remembered what it had been like and the beast surface again.

***She really would make a very delectable snack,*** her instinct purred and pounced, trying hard to take control of her again.

It was a long time before she managed to contain the beast and her father hugged her until she stopped shaking, and then continued to stare at her, considering. "How did you stop yourself?"

She thought about it for a moment before replying. "I imagined hunting the beast instead and beat it up until it ran away, tail tucked between its legs, but..."

Her father burst out laughing at her description. "Then I'm absolutely sure. And the reason I'm sure is because that's only half the test. Occasionally we'll get someone who will choose not to hunt and walk away, after decades of hard work, but that's pretty rare. Almost everyone hunts, and the moment they've successfully completed the hunt and had their first taste, we turn around and hunt them. We chase them down, nip at them, scratch at their flank, growl and hiss at them, until they either give up or turn to fight. This is designed to show them what it's like to be a victim, so they can better understand the trauma of being harmed by someone else."

Marsee looked at her father in horror and started to speak, but he kept going.

"But the real test isn't for the junior councilor, it's for the councilors doing the hunting, because we've had the taste of blood, and the feel of an animal we've sunk our claws into, and the thrill of a successful hunt, and our instinct knows it and craves it, and we have to learn to control it all over again." Marsee watched as her father swallowed hard, his eyes dilated, and his claws flexed for a brief moment, caught in his own hunting instinct, before returning to normal. "And we have to make ourselves stop before we actually kill the people we've come to know and care about. Because, if we have to put someone to death, we will need to be able to remain in control."

"Have you...?" Marsee whispered.

"No. There's a subtle difference between hunting an animal for food and a person, and that's what gives you the ability to stop. You saw Little Flower as a person. If you hadn't you wouldn't have been able to stop. Every newly elected councilor is watched carefully by those with the best control, and should anyone not stop immediately, we fight them until they do. Usually pinning them down by the scruff and biting them is enough to make them snap out of it, but not always. Injuries can and do happen, but as far as I know, no one has ever died. But that is why the Senior Councilor is there, not only to help stop them, but if we should fail and the other person is injured or dies, to immediately administer their punishment, because they've proven they can't control themselves. It's out of those with the best control that we choose the senior councilor, not because they are the best at running our planet, but because they're the best at stopping us from becoming the monsters of our past. It's also why the senior councilor is almost always female even if others are more qualified."

"Did you ever lose control?" Marsee asked.

Her father grinned wryly at her. "You tell me, Kitten. What do you think happened?"

She squinted at her father, and considered everything she knew about him, every experience she'd ever had with him, and smiled. "Once, your first time, and you were so horrified that you've now got the best control out of all of them."

"I always knew you were smart," her father said, ruffling the fur on her head. "Now go on, get back in there, and if it helps, try eating a piece of that fish raw, and see how bad it really tastes. That stuff is revolting. I don't know how she eats it, raw or cooked."

"I might just do that. Thanks Papa," she said, and gave him another hug before making her way back to the others.

Jer looked down at his own claws for a moment, flexing them, before he closed his eyes and sent a brief prayer to the Ancient Gods. He'd lied his fur off. Marsee *had* been hunting Little Flower, really hunting her, and he was astounded that she'd been able to stop, then and now. But she was struggling, and struggling badly to control it. He'd felt how hard she'd been shaking, both out in the hall and again in his office, and she hadn't responded to several of his questions, which frankly terrified him. She'd always struggled with her control, and it had been a major concern of his and Marcus's for the last several years, but he'd thought she'd finally managed to control it. The reports from the Guild had stopped arriving, and he'd not seen any signs of it for almost a year. She'd been right. He'd come far too close to killing his first Junior Councilor and Marcus had been forced to stop him, but he'd never had a problem afterwards, not until that day at Marcus's and frankly that had been as much him as his instinct. Marcus had tested him repeatedly for months on actual hunts to be sure. *So why is she still struggling so hard? Psychosis? Moons, please let it not be that!* But it was the only thing that made sense. By all rights, she should be placed on the watch list, but he couldn't do it. *She's a lot younger than you were, give her time to work through this. If it gets worse...* Terrified it was already too late, he stood up, and followed out after his daughter.

"Is everything okay?" Little Flower asked when they returned.

Marsee nodded but couldn't meet her gaze, and looked up at her Papa, silently begging him to explain.

"Little Flower, one thing you should know about our species is that we are born with a very powerful hunting instinct. For the first few years of our lives, we pounce on anything and everything that moves. It takes us a long time to learn to control that instinct, and as parents we have to be very careful to make sure that our cubs are not anywhere near any kind of crawly, because our cubs will pounce on them, whether they are poisonous or not. We believe it's one of the reasons why we have so many cubs with a litter, because it's far too easy to lose one. We came close a few times with Marsee's older siblings. The sight of Healer Morningstar catching you triggered her hunting instinct for a moment, and she felt horrible about it," her Papa said, vastly understating what had actually happened.

"I would NEVER hurt you!" Marsee signed emphatically. "But my stupid brain went 'ooh, easy prey! You should pounce!' I'm so sorry! Please forgive me!"

Little Flower smiled. "Nothing to forgive. It's pretty obvious to me that you're a species of predators and that we must look pretty tasty to you. I certainly felt like prey in her paws, but you've had more than ample opportunity to bite my head off and you haven't. You've never even accidentally scratched me, even in your sleep when I woke you from a nightmare, or when I pulled your tail to wake you that first time. I should warn you though, I'm really not worth hunting. I'm all skin and bones, not even a decent snack, and I probably taste horrible."

"You pulled my tail? I thought for sure you'd bit me!" Marsee exclaimed.

Little Flower just shrugged. "I really had to pee."

Once the laughter had died down, Marcus asked if they were ready to continue, and Little Flower nodded. They made it through the various visits where Little Flower explained what they were doing and talking about. GrandFather tweaked it a bit in a few spots, where Little Flower had misunderstood due to her hearing loss. And then, they were at 'the video'.

"I think that's enough for today," Marsee's mother said. Little Flower was shaking in her mother's arms.

"No," Little Flower said. "I need to know what he did to me. My night terrors are too full of my imagination."

"Are you sure?" GrandFather asked, looking horrified. Little Flower nodded and spoke something to him. He shook his head and signed "I'll stay," but then walked over to her and sat down beside her, taking her hand. Marsee could see Little Flower's knuckles were turning white from gripping so hard. Her mother started purring loudly, and Little Flower nodded for Marcus to begin. When it was over, the room remained silent as they waited for Little Flower to recover her composure. She buried her face in her mother's fur for a very long time, shaking hard.

When Little Flower finally recovered enough to face the room again, Marcus quietly spoke. "Little Flower, for official evidence, I'm going to need to know exactly what was said between the two of you."

Little Flower blanched. "I can't. I can't watch that again, not now," she signed and then pushed her way out of her mother's arms and ran out the door.

"I'll tell you what was said. It's probably better if I do anyway, since she wouldn't have been able to hear him," GrandFather signed.

Marsee looked towards the open door and back at Marcus and back to the door.

"Go after her, child. She needs a friend," Marcus said, and she didn't waste a second longer and took off after her friend.

# CHAPTER 25

# Marcus: Watch List

Marcus watched as Marsee bolted out the door and down the hall, keeping his mask firmly in place, praying he hadn't made a mistake by letting her chase after Little Flower. With a sigh he turned back to GrandFather, and quickly documented what was said in the video. GrandFather's sign wasn't as good as everyone else's yet, but he wrote a transcript down in his own language as well, so that Little Flower could confirm without having to watch the video again. Marcus's heart broke for the little cub, and he completely understood the fury that was radiating off of GrandFather. The recording was not easy to watch and she'd been under their protection and care, and they'd failed to do so. Marcus had watched it multiple times as part of his investigation, and it still made him sick, but he was a professional and he kept that reaction firmly under control. With a rough transcript now in place, it was even worse, not just for the cub and what had happened to her, but for what the male had clearly implicated by Brice's actions in locking them in the room together and not coming to her call for help.

When they'd watched past where Brice had separated them to make sure the male hadn't said anything afterwards, Marcus stopped the recording. "I think now would be a good time for a break. Myra, Jer, I'd like to talk to you about something privately if you wouldn't mind."

Myra looked away, but both Jer and their father, Frederick, looked hard at him, and he flicked his whiskers forward. His Papa frowned, and looked away and his mother grabbed his father's paw. Ellie stood and walked over to the window to look out. Jer sighed before standing and walking out the door, with Myra trailing behind him, shoulders drooped and tail dragging on the ground. Marcus locked his mask firmly in place at the sight. Myra's office was closest, so Marcus motioned for them to enter and then shut and locked the door behind them. Moments later, Marcus heard the tell-tale crackle of the privacy shield as it activated.

Marcus took a deep breath and turned. "Spill it. Just how badly is she losing control?" he asked with as much command as he could muster, even though his heart broke to ask the question at all.

Myra turned away, refusing to meet his gaze, and looked out her window, grabbing her tail tightly, and Jer collapsed into a chair, grabbing the fur on the back of his head with both paws.

Marcus swore under his breath. "Moons... *That* badly?!"

Neither of them answered.

"Jeran, has she hunted?" he demanded.

Jer lowered his paws down and stared at them, flexing and unflexing his claws. Marcus walked over and kneeled down to be eye level with his brother, spinning his chair to face him, worried that his brother was losing control too, and lifted his brother's face so he could look into his eyes. Seeing his brother's instinct firmly off, Marcus sighed, and lowered his paws. Jer turned away again.

"Jer, be honest with me," Marcus asked again, softer, but with as much command. "Has she hunted?"

Jer refused to make eye contact, but gave the slightest of nods.

Marcus closed his eyes and prayed to the Ancient Gods. "Tell me what happened," he said, with a heartbroken sigh, all pretense of a mask stripped away.

"The first day Little Flower was here, she scared Little Flower by accident with a knife. Little Flower ran and the sight of the leash going out the door triggered it. From the description she gave me today, she was hunting. She had a hard time controlling her reaction today in the hallway. It was even worse when we were talking about it in my office. She told me she's being triggered by the smell every time they cook the fish too," Jer finally admitted.

"Moons," Marcus whispered again, his heart breaking at the news. He stood and turned away, struggling to contain the fear he felt, but then a thought occurred and he spun back around. "How did she avoid hurting Little Flower? Was someone with her to stop it?" he asked.

"No, she did it on her own," Myra replied, not looking away from the window. "I found her curled up in a little ball out in the hallway. Little Flower was hiding under my bed. I thought that since she stopped, that it had been triggered by the unusual situation, and by not knowing for sure that Little Flower was sentient. I swear I didn't realize she'd been hunting. She only mentioned pouncing on the leash, and that was frankly a valid reaction, since she did need to catch her to keep her from running off. Then later, after we found out Little Flower was pregnant, I thought it might possibly be a pheromone that we hadn't identified. Little Flower's people smell good. We never had any reaction from anyone else at the Agency, but then both of the females that had given birth were already much further along in their pregnancy when they were rescued, and everyone there was a fully grown adult with decades of training. Marsee seemed to be doing fine. I only caught her once afterwards, and that was just after trying some of the fried fish. I..."

"You let her eat meat after she hunted?! How could you, Myra? Were you trying to make her lose control? For that matter, why didn't you report it?" Marcus demanded, furious. "You know you could get in serious trouble for this."

"More trouble than I'm already in, Marcus?" Myra cried, spinning to face him. "I needed to know if this was just the unusual circumstances she'd been in before I reported a case of psychosis on my own daughter. She stopped and she didn't hurt Little Flower, and I did send a report to the Healers Guild indicating that a biped had triggered a hunting instinct flare up, so that we could watch for it at the Agency. I just didn't say by whom. As for the meat, I had no idea how good the cooked fish tasted until afterwards, when I tried some myself. It's absolutely revolting raw, and I thought if she tasted it, it would help keep her from wanting more, just like the smell of the raw fish did. I watched her carefully afterwards. She had no problems cutting up the fish or cooking it any time I watched, and seemed just as revolted as I was to handle the raw stuff. I haven't seen any sign of issues since."

"Myra, she was non-verbal in my office for a good fifteen or twenty minutes," Jer said quietly.

Myra looked terrified, shook her head not wanting to believe it, and grabbed her tail again. "Are you sure she wasn't just flustered like she gets sometimes when she's overwhelmed?" Myra asked, and Marcus prayed that was the case.

"I wish that's all it was. She shook in my arms, and didn't respond to any of my questions," Jer said quietly, clearly not wanting to believe it himself. "And her eyes were dilated and claws out," he added at almost a whisper.

Marcus sighed with regret. "She needs to go on the watch list and be tested, Jer."

"Will you give us more time to work with her?" Jer asked.

"You know I can't do that, Jer. If she's already hunted and going non-verbal, she's a danger to everyone right now, not just Little Flower and GrandFather. It's only a matter of time before she loses control completely."

"She stopped a hunt on her own, Marcus. That *has* to count for something. When's the last time you've heard of someone doing that the first time, or ever, if this is indeed psychosis," Jer asked.

Marcus frowned and considered. It was true and Marsee had been in control enough to ask for a break and walk out of the room, but Jer had just said she'd been non-verbal and that was a very, very bad sign. The risk was just too high, and as much as he hated to do it, he shook his head. "She needs to go on the watch list and she should be tested as soon as the Guard and Tabor can arrive. If this is indeed psychosis, we're not going to be able to stop her if she fully loses control, not on our own." What he really meant though was that none of them would be willing to do what needed to be done before someone got hurt. He'd had to call in the Guard on more than one occasion in his long career, and it was by far the worst part of his job. Even if he wasn't the one usually 'handling' the situation, he had to be there for the test, and to sign off on the execution when they inevitably failed.

Jer growled and stood up, tail lashing, and for a moment Marcus was actually worried that his brother was going to attack, and braced himself.

"I am not putting my own daughter on the watch list and testing her. If you think she's that bad, you'll have to do it, because I won't! I can't!" Jer spat, and then stormed out of the room, slamming the door open as he left. The door hit the wall so hard that the family portrait on the wall fell and the glass shattered as it hit the floor.

"Marcus *please*! Give her more time," Myra begged.

"I can't do that, Myra. What happens if she loses control in front of the Full Council? Do you want her put down in front of everyone? Marsee doesn't deserve that."

"I understand needing to put her on the watch list, but can't you wait until she has another episode to test her? Please? Give her at least a few days to work this out. Let us work with her or bring the Guard in and let them work with her. You know they can help sometimes. *Please*?" Myra begged.

"Myra, if she's gone non-verbal, you know as well as I do what that means. She's already too far gone and it's only a matter of time before we lose her entirely. At this stage the Guard never has success. Working with her will just put her over the edge that much sooner. And if we don't do what needs to be done, someone, probably Little Flower, will be hurt, or killed. I'm sorry, Myra. I'm truly sorry, but she's going on the watch list and she will be tested," Marcus replied, knowing full well he was signing his beloved niece's death warrant.

# CHAPTER 26

# Marsee: Heat

Marsee could just see Little Flower as she passed around the corner and Marsee bolted down the hallway after her. When she caught up with her though, there was no instinct to pounce, she realized, not even a little bit, just concern for her friend. As she ran up beside her, Little Flower looked over to see her, tears streaming down her face and kept running. Marsee ran beside her, matching her pace, until the cub dropped from exhaustion.

They'd made four laps around the compound, and even Marsee was starting to feel winded before Little Flower ducked out into the courtyard, and raced across to the garden. She didn't have her sun protection on and even with the shields it was brutal outside, but Little Flower didn't flinch or stop until she made it to the pool under the tree and jumped in with a splash, clothing and all. *She must really be hot!* Marsee thought as she waited for Little Flower to surface.

"I hope it's okay that I'm in the pool," Little Flower signed when she came back up and brushed the wet fur out of her eyes.

"Of course. You needed to cool down," Marsee signed back. "Why wouldn't it be?"

"I don't know. This place has always seemed magical to me, sacred, as if disturbing it would be frowned upon," Little Flower signed as she floated on the water.

"The garden is meant to be enjoyed. If it brings you joy to swim in the pool, you should. Nothing in there will hurt you," Marsee explained. "Feeling better?"

"Yes. Thank you for running with me. It helped," Little Flower replied and dove under again.

"I'm impressed at how far you ran. I'm tired, and I have four feet and much longer legs than you do," Marsee said, after Little Flower resurfaced. She found a comfortable place to flop next to the pool, panting hard with her own exertion.

Little Flower swam over to the feeder roots, climbed up a bit, and turned to sit, half out of the water to talk easier. "Our best athletes could run for hours without stopping. We would race to see who could get there the fastest. I'm not exactly sure, but I think the hallway would be about a mile in our distances." Little Flower used the hand signs they'd come up with to represent her written language. Little Flower had told her they were the signs they'd used for their deaf people. "Our fastest people could run that distance twenty-six times, in about one of your hours. We called them marathons. I'm not sure if I'm just out of shape or if the gravity is stronger here but I used to be able to easily run ten laps. I've never tried a marathon though."

"Twenty-six times?! Seriously?" Marsee asked in astonishment. "I only managed six laps the other day and I was dragging."

"No claws or teeth remember. We had to outrun predators and chase down our prey," Little Flower explained and then dove under the water, coming up on the other side of the tree. Marsee padded over to where she was now.

"I guess that would make sense. I'm a lot faster, but I can't run at that speed for a long time. I'm assuming that at least at the beginning you were running as fast as you could?" Little Flower nodded and climbed out, water dripping off of her and flopped down next to Marsee. "Eww, you smell like fish," Marsee teased.

"Better than chenzie butt," Little Flower laughed.

"Fair," Marsee replied laughing as well, tail curled.

But then Little Flower sighed. "I guess we'd better head back to do that translation for Marcus."

"GrandFather said he'd do it for you."

"Oh, good. Are you okay?" Little Flower asked.

"Me? Why? You're the one that went through it," Marsee asked, confused.

"You had to watch," Little Flower explained. "That must not have been easy too."

"I've seen it before. The first time I'd been told you had been fighting. I didn't understand what was going on. I watched again after you threw the book at me, but I still wasn't sure. I had to talk to Mama about it."

"Why weren't you sure?" Little Flower asked.

"I'm not fully grown. I don't have all the parts inside yet to be able to mate, and we don't usually learn about how mating works until we start our second growth spurt, which won't happen for me for another twenty years or so. I had a long talk with Mama after everything happened to you. It takes about a year to reach Papa's size and it's really painful from what I've been told. We spend most of that year at a special ward where they can manage the pain, and teach us everything we need to know about mating and caring for cubs. When we get to Papa's size, we can stop the process or keep growing to Mama's size and finish developing the parts needed to be a mother over the course of another year, but at the end of the year we go into heat. We can't stop the first one. Mama says they've tried but something goes wrong and people sometimes die, so they don't try anymore. Although people can begin their growth spurt earlier if they've decided what they want to do, rather than waiting for it to happen naturally. After we've had our cubs though, and they're weaned, we can pause things again so we don't go into a second heat unless we want to. If we didn't, we'd automatically go into another heat after our cubs are weaned. There's far more risk with the second heat, so most people don't try for a second litter. Mama really wanted more cubs though. She almost died and we lost my litter-mate. A third heat is almost always fatal. It's why we control it so carefully."

"So, you're all born with the potential to have cubs? Is that what you meant by female not female?" Little Flower asked.

"Yes. Mama says before the Great Awakening we used to be born both male and female, but something happened and then only females started being born. Before they realized it or figured out how to fix it, it was too late. So, the healers did something and now when we get to Papa's size, those that don't want to give birth to cubs are changed somehow into male, and the males can't mate with a female unless they're actively in heat. Mama said it has something to do with the way they smell. Even then the healers have to do something to complete the mating because the 'males' don't have the right parts. Even if we choose to be male, our bodies are still female. Mama says we have an uncontrollable instinct to rub up against everything, so it's super obvious when someone starts their heat, and they have time to get to a mating center with their mate before the pheromones start."

"So, can you stop the process at male and choose to be female later?" Little Flower asked.

"No. It's a permanent stop. Mama didn't go into details about what they do, but we never start the next phase of growth. I guess it's a similar procedure after the first or second heat to prevent the next one from happening but by then we have all the right parts. I asked Mama about that as well. When they reversed the procedure for the males originally, nothing happened, and when they tried to make it happen, people died, the parts didn't grow right or so she was told, so no one tries anymore. If we decide to become a mother, we have about a year to find a mate if we haven't already."

"So, what happens if you want to have cubs but don't have someone you want to mate with?" Little Flower asked.

"That doesn't really happen. If I wanted to mate and have children but didn't already have a partner, all I'd have to do would be to walk outside, and every male within smelling distance would be at my beck and call. Many people still do that because it tends to have a better success rate, and many unattached males will move to live near a mating center if they want that too. Sometimes partnered males will as well, but usually they don't because it would be unfair to the females who never get to experience that again. My instincts would pick the male most suitable to have healthy cubs with. We'd go back inside, and the healers would do their thing, and that would be it."

"That's it?" Little Flower asked with a raised brow.

"Well, Mama says it takes about three days to be ready, and we spend the entire time with our chosen mates. Apparently touch feels really good, better than it does at any other time in our lives, but once we get to the proper hormone levels, the healers come in, sedate us, and do whatever it is they need to do."

"What happens if the male doesn't want to mate?" Little Flower asked.

"They just tell the healers and the healers give them something to block the pheromones and the female goes and finds another male to mate with."

"So, there's no obligation to raise the cubs by the father?" Little Flower asked.

"Father doesn't mean male genetic donor. Father is the person who chose to raise me with Mama, and who has legal responsibility for us. That's what a partnership is. Partner often also means genetic donor, but doesn't have to be, and it doesn't have to be with a male either. Many females partner and raise their cubs together, and males will partner for companionship, or to raise orphaned cubs, and you can have more than one partner too. Many mothers choose to raise cubs on their own, with their friends, parents or siblings help, and others choose to mate with their partners or not at all. When you have litters of five or six cubs at a time, having more than one partner is beneficial. It's very common for litter-mates to be partners to help raise each other's cubs. Papa happens to be both Mama's mate and partner. Mama and Papa were close friends long before either of them were old enough to mate. When Mama's cubs were born, Papa adopted us legally, indicating his intent to raise us to adulthood along with Mama. It gives him legal rights to care for us if something happened to her. If he hadn't, we would have gone to my mother's parents, but they're both dead,

So I would have become a ward of the district. Papa could ask for guardianship, but the Council wouldn't have to approve it, and I could go somewhere else. As my father though, if something had happened to both Mama and Papa before I was an adult, I would have gone to Papa's parents, if they hadn't indicated someone else as a preference or my grandparents indicated they weren't capable of caring for us, due to injury or illness, or the like. Usually though it's the cub's choice, if we're old enough to indicate one."

"I really like that system. Is that a local law or Charter?" she asked.

"Charter for the most part, with some local flair to account for the different family structures and mating practices of each species. I was reading ahead on the next few sections last night. On the Flyer's world, neither genetic donor raises the children. Only a small fraction of the population is female, which is a good thing, because they can lay thousands of eggs during their lifetime. There's no way she could raise them all, so the rest are given to the community and anyone interested in raising a fledgling is assigned an egg to hatch. Interestingly they won't hatch until this happens and can spend years in the eggs. Everyone knows who their nest mother is, but she doesn't have legal rights to any but those she chooses to raise personally. From a legal perspective it's much the same. The 'mother' is the person with the primary legal rights to the child and 'father' anyone who has been granted those same rights by the mother, regardless of their physical sex."

"What if the female doesn't want to spend her life laying eggs?" Little Flower asked.

"I'm honestly not sure," Marsee said. "But there's an awful lot of status on their world for being a nest mother, and more often than not they become councilors, which isn't surprising when you have that many children to look out for. My understanding is that Senior Councilor Wind Rider has laid over ten thousand eggs so far."

"Wow. I can't even imagine what it would be like to have that many children, even if I wasn't responsible for raising them," Little Flower said, and was quiet for a minute while she considered, and then shrugged. "Some of Serin's cubs used the male pronoun though and they aren't as big as your father," Little Flower stated, returning to the original topic.

Marsee nodded. "That's all personal preference until we get to our adult stage. We all start out female, but some people just feel male or female at an early age, while some don't know right up until they have to make that decision. I've bounced back and forth a few times, but male has never fit right with me, even though I've said many times that I didn't want to give birth to cubs. Does that make sense?" she asked.

"It does. I had a classmate like that. She was born male but always felt female and was very sad that she couldn't have cubs of her own. Does your species have specific roles for male and female or expectations outside of whether you can have cubs or not?"

Marsee thought about that for a long moment before answering. "I've never really thought about it before. There are some skills that are easier if you are bigger or smaller, but we don't stop anyone from doing something they're interested in just because we're male or female. There are some areas, like the mating center that are entirely staffed by female healers, but that has more to do with the effect the mating female would have on a male healer, but there are no other restrictions that I'm aware of. The only other place I can think of would be our Council. The Senior Councilor is elected by all of the other elected councilors on our world, and that's almost always been a female, not always though, but most of the time, and the majority of our Council is female, although there aren't any restrictions from males running, they just don't run as often. Our family structure is predominantly matriarchal. Our family names come from our mothers, so I guess it's not surprising that our government would lean that way too. Local and district offices are fairly evenly split though, as far as I know. I asked Papa once why Marcus wasn't Senior Councilor, since he's been on the Council forever, and Papa said it was because he didn't want it and turned it down. He's second in command though, and whenever Tabor is off-world, he's usually designated Acting Senior, and would be promoted as such, if something happened to Tabor until a new election could occur. With all of the committees he's on, he has almost as much authority. From my own experience, I've had more male instructors and have met more female healers, but I think that has more to do with personal preference than anything." Marsee wasn't going to mention what her father had just told her, but it put a new spin on the old information her father had once said, and she decided she would spend more time thinking about it later.

Little Flower must have been getting hot again as she jumped back in the pool. "I still can't believe Marcus gave up all of his authority for me," she said once she'd surfaced again.

"That's my Uncle Marcus for you," Marsee said. "He doesn't see it as having authority. He sees it as having a great deal of responsibility and he takes that responsibility very seriously. My father is the same way and as far as I know so is the rest of the Council. If they didn't they'd be voted off fairly quickly."

Little Flower made a noncommittal grunt. "We had very specific roles for a very long time but that was changing. For instance, we've never had the female equivalent of your Senior Councilor in my district and far too many of our leaders cared only about themselves and they were far too good at hiding it."

Marsee nodded. That much had been evident from their prior conversations.

"What happens if you get to the point of your heat and you decide you don't want children?"

"You stay in heat until you mate. That can't be stopped from what I understand, but the pregnancy could be ended afterwards, although that's pretty risky."

"So, you could be a female without having cubs?" Little Flower asked. "You said before that you couldn't, or did I misunderstand what you were trying to tell me?"

"Yes, I could, and I guess that must happen sometimes, but I don't think I could do that," Marsee explained. "I want to be a mother. What I meant was that I'm terrified of going through it all, and trying to keep five or six squirming cubs alive just sounds exhausting. It's been hard enough to keep you from jumping out of trees. How could I manage five of you?"

Little Flower laughed and purposely climbed up the feeder roots, just to tease Marsee and jumped back in the pool with another splash. Marsee leapt back to get out of the way and splashed Little Flower when she came back up. She laughed and swam over, leaning on the rocks on the side of the pool.

Marsee glared at her suspiciously, but when she didn't splash back, continued. "Plus, I don't have any litter-mates or a lot of friends to help. My older siblings all have families of their own and I wouldn't want to be a burden on them."

"That makes sense. I'm pretty worried about that too. I don't have a partner or siblings, just GrandFather," Little Flower said.

"You have us. We'll help you. Frankly you'd be lucky to have any time holding your cub with Mama around. You should see her with my siblings' littles. Mama wants cubs, lots of them, always has. I think she was really disappointed only having one in her second litter, and then she ended up with me."

"What's wrong with you? I think you're pretty special," Little Flower signed.

"Thanks, but I'm...different. It's hard to explain," Marsee said, not wanting to talk about how close she'd come to losing control today.

"Well, if you're different, the rest of your world must be pretty weird, because I think you're perfect just the way you are," Little Flower signed.

"You too, even when you smell like fish," Marsee said.

"Chenzie butt," Little Flower signed back and splashed her. Mayhem ensued for several minutes until they were both soggy.

"So how does it work with your people? Mating, partnerships, children?" Marsee asked as she shook the water off her fur, deliberately trying to get Little Flower in the process.

"Well for starters, we're born male or female, for the most part, and have all the parts necessary to reproduce when we're born. Like you, we all start out as female but a few weeks into the pregnancy, hormones are released that turn some people male. Some people have both parts but that's pretty rare or have parts that don't work or don't match how they feel. At around maybe four of your years we hit our growth spurt and become fertile. We can have children then, although we usually wait until we're six or seven and are considered a legal adult. We remain capable of that until we are around fifteen, give or take. Every one of our months our body prepares for pregnancy, and if we don't get pregnant, we eject the blood and tissue. It's messy and painful. We can mate at any time, but we're only fertile part of the time, and as you can see, it's pretty easy for the males to force us to mate, although sometimes women can force men to mate too. And it happened to children far too often," Little Flower said with a sigh.

Marsee looked horrified. "You mean to tell me that you could be forced to mate as a child and not be considered a legal adult?"

Little Flower nodded sadly. "They could even take my cub away stating that I'm too young to be a mother, or even prevent me from making the choice of whether or not I wanted to continue the pregnancy, even though it's really dangerous if we're not fully grown. It really depended on where you lived, and what the laws were, and it was one of the biggest moral disagreements we had among our people. In some parts of my world if I became pregnant without being in a partnership, I could even be killed or forced to partner with the male who raped me. I am not considered a legal adult among my people. I'm only five and a half of your years old, give or take. I've lost track of the time. It's not just cubs that are prevented from making that choice though. Many parts of the world, my own included, had laws or were passing laws that would have prevented adult females from making that choice. Some were even arrested for miscarrying because the councilors in those areas believed they had the right to interfere in a person's medical care. Females have fought for equality for a long time on my world, but in my district, we didn't even have the right to vote until about thirty-five of your years ago."

Marsee stared at Little Flower in shock for a long time. "I can't believe they would do that to you."

Little Flower nodded. "Many in our district wanted to go back to when only the white males had any power or say."

Marsee considered all of the conversations they'd had, as they translated the Charter and understood why both Little Flower and Grand-Father had focused so hard on many of the sections that had just seemed obvious to her. "Well, you won't have to worry about that here. Once you prove your species is sentient, you'll be guaranteed those rights, and you'll be considered an adult because you're old enough to have cubs. Those rights are all protected rights in the Consortium's Charter. Removing them would require a unanimous vote by the Full Council and the Local Charters aren't allowed to infringe on them in any way. Anyone who even tried would likely be voted out of the Council immediately. You're serious though? You're only five? I just turned twenty the day you arrived here. How long do your people live?" Marsee asked.

"Twenty-five or twenty-six years was the average. A few people make it to thirty-three, and I think the oldest person ever was around forty. With your science, who knows. GrandFather looks much younger and healthier than he did before, even if he's lost a lot of muscle from being in the Agency for so long. He's about twenty-one or twenty-two," Little Flower signed.

Marsee grabbed her tail and squeezed. "What?! That's not nearly long enough! You might not even live to see my cubs!"

"Well how long do you live then?" Little Flower asked.

"Around three hundred years, give or take. Papa just turned a hundred and twenty-five, Mama's a hundred and thirty two, and Marcus just turned two hundred. We had a big party for him. Our centennials are a pretty big deal."

"Three hundred?! Wow. I don't even know what I would do with that many years. How do you even remember it all?"

Marsee shrugged, distracted as she tried to absorb the news. "Bigger brains maybe? But we need to tell Mama. She'll know how to fix you.

Twenty-five is not nearly long enough!" Marsee reached down, scooped Little Flower out of the water, who responded with an indignant squeak, and took off at a run. Skidding to a stop at the family room, she found it empty.

"Marsee stop. It's okay," Little Flower signed.

"No, it's not," Marsee signed with one arm and took off again. She found her mother and Marcus in her mother's office. "Mama! Help! Little Flower is dying. You have to fix her!" she cried, barging in, not even caring about what they were talking about. Both her mother and Marcus jumped in surprise and her mother ran over.

"What happened, and why is she all wet?" her mother asked, checking Little Flower all over for signs of an injury. Concern radiating off of both of their faces.

"Little Flower says they only live to twenty-five! You have to find a way to fix her!" Marsee demanded, but to her surprise, they both sighed with relief. *Why do they look relieved, this is horrible news!* Marsee thought.

"That's it? How old are you, Little Flower?" Marcus asked, going from worried to curious.

"I'm *fine*, Marsee. Set me down. There's nothing wrong with me that needs fixing," Little Flower told Marsee, exasperated, and then turned back to the others after she'd done as requested. "I'm wet because I jumped in the pool to cool down. As for my age, I'm not completely sure. I lost track of time, but I think I'm about five and a half, maybe six, if I understood how long your years are in comparison to ours and how long I was in the Agency. It's three to our one, right?"

Marcus nodded. "Give or take."

"Moons! You *are* just a cub," Myra said, looking horrified.

"I am not a cub! I've been physically able to have my own cubs since I was four," Little Flower signed, looking very annoyed.

"You're an adult at four?" Marcus asked, surprised.

Marsee didn't give Little Flower a chance to explain. "No, she's not! She said she wouldn't be an adult until she was seven, and that they would force her to have cubs if she became pregnant, and then take her cubs away because she's not old enough to be a mother, and that they might even kill her because she's not in a partnership or force her to partner with her rapist!"

Marsee's mother put her paw over her mouth and sat down in her chair. Marcus walked over and shut the door and then returned to kneel down in front of Little Flower. "Little Flower, are you considered an adult, on your world?"

Little Flower sighed. "It's complicated. The age at which you became an adult depended a lot on where you lived. In my district, I could live on my own at five and a half and vote at six, but there were some things I still couldn't do until I was older. Most of my people wait until we are done with school or at least have finished growing, to start a family. That happens between ages six and eight depending on how much schooling we take and when we hit our growth spurt," Little Flower explained.

"So, we did trigger your heat before you were mature," Myra said.

"No, I told you, I've been mature since I was four. I had my first 'heat' as you call it, when I had completed twelve rotations around our sun. Some start much earlier, at eight or nine of our years. I think I remember hearing about someone becoming pregnant at only five. I just won't reach my full height until later, although frankly, this is probably as tall as I'm going to get. My parents were both short. Anyway, we go into heat every twenty-eight of our days or abouts, until we're around forty or forty-five of our years, but not like you. We don't get pregnant every time, and can mate whenever we want to, or even when we don't want to. I've been told it can be very enjoyable which is why people do it all the time, but I've never..." Little Flower stopped, closed her eyes and took a deep breath before continuing. "I never found anyone I wanted to mate with. I wasn't even thinking about whether I wanted a cub someday or not, much less looking for a partner, although many of my age mates were starting to...I do not have the word. Hang out with the males to see if they were interested in forming a partnership. We are born with all of the parts to mate but we don't start releasing eggs until later. At that age we start growing and our hormones change and we release an egg every month on the off chance that there will be a...a 'genetic donation' as Marsee called it. You didn't force me to become pregnant just because he raped me. That was just bad timing."

"What happens when your heat isn't successful? We stay in heat until a mating occurs," Myra asked pointedly.

"We bleed out the...unnecessary stuff for about a week, our time, and start over," Little Flower said.

"You're absolutely sure of this?" Marcus demanded.

Little Flower nodded. "Of course. I'm not sure why my cycle stopped while I was at the Agency, but I'm glad it did. Trying to manage that in there without the proper supplies would have just made everything worse. It's messy and painful and I often got sick and had really bad headaches. I'd get very moody too. I'd be angry one minute and cry the next for no reason, and I craved sweet foods."

"Oh, Thank the blessed moons!" Myra said, leaning back in her chair and rubbing her face with her paws. Marcus looked greatly relieved as well and closed his eyes as if he were praying. Marsee looked at him in confusion. She was not used to seeing either of them show so much emotion, even in the privacy of their own home, especially Marcus.

"What's going on?" Marsee asked. "Why are you both so relieved? I don't understand."

"We thought the other females at the agency had all miscarried because the Council decided to put Little Flower's people in stasis until after the trial. We had to take them out again because of the storm, and a few days later they all started bleeding," Marcus explained.

"Oh. Oh!" Marsee exclaimed and sat down hard. "Moons. That would have been bad, wouldn't it?"

Before Marcus could reply, Little Flower tugged at her side. "What's going on?" she asked, repeating Marsee's words, and Marsee realized that she hadn't translated Marcus's words to Little Flower and repeated them.

Little Flower's eyes got wide and she turned to Marcus. "You would have been charged for all of them too, wouldn't you?"

Marcus nodded, "The Council would have, or at least those that voted in favor, and it would have been a death sentence. Myra objected over her concerns about what could happen with long-term stasis, but the Senior Councilor overruled it out of concern that you would suffer more continuing to be held without being able to communicate with us."

"What's stasis? And why a death sentence?" Little Flower asked.

"Stasis is like when we sedate you but more. It stops everything. We use it for transporting patients to trauma centers when they are in critical condition," her mother explained.

"As for why it would have been a death sentence, it's because it would have been seen as tampering with the evidence to get rid of the consequences. And because we had no idea if you came into heat more than once, we could have potentially doomed your species to extinction with that order. Plus terminating a wanted pregnancy outside of medical necessity is considered murder," Marcus added, and turned to her mother. "So Myra, that just leaves the two others that are still pregnant, and the third that we confirmed had mated, that we need to take statements from. At least we now know why we couldn't find anything on the scans or recordings. I'll take GrandFather and go interview them to see if they willingly chose to mate."

"I'll let Brice know you're coming," Myra said, and then turned to Little Flower, "As for why you didn't have a cycle, that's because we stopped it out of fear you only had one or two heats like us. We started it again when we began reintroduction in case you chose to mate. In your case, we were hoping you'd continue to mature. We didn't know you could mate if you weren't in heat and we thought you were still a cub, although we weren't sure."

Little Flower nodded. "So, everyone was on the same cycle and that's why they all bled at the same time. That must have been a miserable time for everyone at the Agency."

"You have no idea," Myra replied, and followed up with several questions on how to best care for her people during their heats. Marcus had Little Flower give an official statement on how their heat worked, which he submitted for evidence.

"But, what about Little Flower not living very long?" Marsee asked. "Can you do anything about that?"

"Oh, it's not as bad as that," Myra said, turning to face Little Flower. "Your genetics say we should be able to get fifty to seventy-five years at least, with proper care, and probably more, once we're more comfortable with repairing the effects of aging on your species. If you were only living to twenty-five, that would certainly explain the cellular damage we found. We thought that was all from radiation poisoning, but that was all easily treatable."

It was Little Flower's turn to sit down hard in astonishment.

"The more important question is whether or not we consider her an adult when her species did or when she became capable of having children," Marcus said.

"She's an adult because she's pregnant. A cub can't be a mother," Myra stated flatly.

"So how about adult at seven for the males and whenever the females become fertile, or whichever comes first? That would match with our laws," Marcus said. "What do you think, Little Flower?"

Little Flower smiled wickedly. "Perfect."

Marsee wondered why Little Flower was so enthusiastic about it, and asked.

"The men on my planet have had power and control over the women for far too long. It will be good for them to cool their heels for a few years, and maybe give us a chance to do things right."

This made everyone's ears flick back in surprise and they spent the next hour, after Little Flower changed into some dry clothes discussing her statement.

Afterwards, Marcus flew over to the Agency with GrandFather to meet with Brice and the three other women they'd identified as having engaged in mating during the same unsupervised time frame. Two of which were now very clearly pregnant on the scans. Marcus took official statements from each of the women who all indicated that they had mated without being forced. They had missed and needed physical contact, and in the case of the two pregnant women, they indicated they were both happy to be pregnant, and knew beforehand that was a possibility they might, and were prepared to raise their cub. They were greatly relieved to know that they would be provided resources to help raise and care for their cubs though, and Marcus made a note to talk to Little Flower about that. He also spoke with several of the women to confirm what Little Flower had said about their heats. Marcus submitted his evidence, and the Senior Council agreed that no crime had been committed in the others' mating, and since no actual miscarriages had occurred and the bipeds would go into heat again, that there was no crime there either. It brought the potential crimes down from two hundred and fourteen to one, and everyone breathed a lot easier.

It was late by the time Marcus finished submitting his evidence, so he decided he would wait until morning to call the Senior Councilor to bring the Guard and come test Marsee, after placing her on the watch list. With a heavy heart, he crawled into bed and lay there praying to the Ancient Gods that somehow, someway, Marsee would be the one to pass testing, when no one else ever had.

# CHAPTER 27

# Marsee: Hunt

Ellie left to bring the techs home later that afternoon as they'd apparently finished scanning in Marcus archives, and stated she would return late that evening. That left only family in the compound that night for the evening meal. They'd made quite the party of the meal, frying up star fruit after dinner and joking and telling tales, in an attempt to help cheer up Little Flower, and counteract the difficult day they'd all had. Everyone had their masks on tightly, but Marsee could sense the underlying sadness and stress in her family, even though they were all trying hard not to show it.

Marsee spent most of the evening lost in thought and curled up next to her mother, trying to come to grips with everything that had happened. Her flare up earlier still scared her. It had been as bad as that first day, and there hadn't even been anything to pounce on, and she still felt her instinct clawing and scraping at her defenses. The imaginary shield she'd raised was gone now, useless, as the beast was now well inside. She was hastily trying to build a rock wall around herself but it now felt like an itch deep inside her brain that she couldn't scratch. She was having a hard time keeping still but she didn't need her parents disappointment on top of everything else. She'd gone through years of that. Even still, every time she so much as twiched, everyone, including her uncle looked at her, and her mother would hug her tighter with her tail. Oddly, the hug helped some, almost as if her mother was holding her together.

Her uncle was the first to leave, abruptly stating he had work to do and they all watched him leave in silence. There was a great deal of sadness in his posture that she'd never seen before, and she wondered if it was just the video they'd watched today, or if he was worried about what would happen at the trial. That signaled the end of the party, as everyone remembered their own work. GrandFather and Little Flower had left for a while and had a long conversation. Her mother had been the last to leave but a look had passed between her parents as her father left, that she didn't understand, but didn't ask either. She didn't really want to know. After they'd left, she'd take some time to walk around the garden, hoping that would help, as motion usually did, and it did some, but not nearly enough. Something was very wrong with her and she knew it, but she didn't know what to do about it.

Eventually, Little Flower had returned, sketch book in hand. Now it was just the two of them enjoying the beautiful evening. Little Flower was drawing more pictures for the flicker flyers and handing them out afterwards, and now had a collection of small rocks, flowers, and even a colorful seashell. Where they'd gotten that, Marsee had no idea as the nearest sea was some distance away and she didn't think they flew that far. Momentarily distracted by the scene, Marsee recorded everything and sent it off to both of her parents. While Little Flower drew, they alternated between talking and sitting in silence. After the last flicker flyer left, Marsee stood to pace in the clearing, trying to get her brain to calm and was seriously considering going outside for a run, even though she knew that would be dangerous, this late at night.

Little Flower looked over at her with a serious expression on her face. "Marsee, that first day, when I was scared by the knife, you were really hunting me, weren't you? Not just trying to keep me from running away?"

Marsee's heart sank and she sat with a heavy sigh and nodded. "I'm so sorry! I feel absolutely horrible about that. I could have killed you. I almost did. It's not normally like that. Usually, it's just an instinct to pounce on anything that moves, which is what happened with the leash at first. But that day was different. It changed afterwards and it scared me a lot. It still does. I don't know what's wrong with me. I've tried talking to Mama and Papa about it and they say I'm fine, that I just need more practice, but it's not getting better. If anything, it's getting harder and harder to control. I've *never* reacted to a video before, and even the smell of your food is harder to handle every day. It's like there's a beast inside me trying to claw its way into my brain and take over and I'm losing control, and...and I'll understand if you don't want to be around me anymore. I think it might be best if you didn't. I don't want to hurt you," she said, and grabbed her tail and twisted hard, unable to look over at Little Flower to see her response.

Little Flower walked over to her and then surprised her by climbing onto her lap and purposely wrapping Marsee's giant paws around her, before giving her a big hug. Marsee shook with her own fear and the absolute trust that Little Flower was showing her.

Afterwards, Little Flower moved away so she could talk easier. "I trust you, Marsee. I know you won't hurt me."

"How can you trust me? I don't even trust myself?" Marsee signed.

"Because you didn't hurt me. You just scared the non-existent pants off me. What you're going through sounds an awful lot like how I felt when I first came here. I tried shoving everything that had happened to me in a closet and locking the door, along with all of my fear, anger, and loathing for your people. But it kept sneaking out through the cracks and the door was bulging, and it was all I could do to keep it shut. The day you asked me if I wanted cubs and I threw the book at you, I wasn't just angry, I wanted to kill you, kill all of you. But now you're my best friend, practically my sister, and I'm really glad you're on my side. You're ferocious when you're hunting by the way. I pity the fool that gets on your bad side. They're not going to know what bit them," Little Flower signed.

Marsee's ears went back in astonishment. "Really?" Marsee asked.

"Really. I'll try to be more careful around you. Tell me all of your triggers, like the smell of my food. What can I do to help stop it?

Would it help if I eat in a different room? Do you need to hunt more? Would practicing help, so you can get it better under control?" Little Flower asked.

Marsee just blinked at her. "Are you *seriously* offering to let me hunt you? Are you out of your furless mind? I could kill you!"

"Yes, I am. If that's what you need. We *are* easy prey to you, and I don't want any of my people getting hurt by accident, including myself. I want to know what we need to teach our people so that we don't accidentally trigger a response in your people, and figure out how to protect ourselves if we do. Plus, you stopped without hurting me before, so I know you can do it again."

Marsee thought for a while, twisting her tail hard to stay in control. "Let me go find Papa," she signed. "He should be here for this conversation." It wasn't just that Marsee wanted him there to discuss it. She was terrified that if she started discussing her triggers that she'd lose control again, like she had in his office. Little Flower nodded, and Marsee bolted to find her father, glad for the excuse to be able to run. She eventually found him in his office, still working. He was leaning his forehead on his paw, staring at his tablet when she looked in his open door. She'd never seen him look so defeated before, and she hesitated before knocking, not wanting to add to his worry, but decided saving Little Flower was too important to wait. Something told her that if she didn't do something soon, that it would be too late.

"Papa, can we talk for a minute?" He looked up and nodded with a smile at her, his emotions immediately hidden behind his mask, so she entered and shut the door. He flicked his ears back in surprise when she walked over and turned on his privacy screen.

"What's the matter, Kitten?" he asked, giving her his full attention.

"I was talking with Little Flower out in the garden, and she asked me if I had hunted her that first day. She's concerned that her people are at risk from us, and rightly so, and she wants to figure out a way to keep her people safe. She suggested that I practice hunting her so I could learn to control it better, like you had to." Her father scowled at her when she said that, so she hastily added, "I swear I didn't tell her what you told me. She suggested this entirely on her own. But she's right. I need to learn to control this better. It really scares me, Papa. Something is really wrong with me. I know what you said, but I don't trust myself around her. It's getting worse, not better, and nothing I'm doing is working. I can feel it clawing at me, trying to take control, even now, and frankly even if a cub pounced by accident, they could easily hurt her. I know I struggle with this. I always have. But it's different now, and I can't be the only one to struggle like this. How do we keep them safe? Them or the other creatures we have to care for?"

Her father stared at her for a long time and then pulled her in for a hug. When she pulled back, she noticed that his tail was shivering. She looked closer at him. *Was he afraid?* she wondered. She'd never seen him afraid before, and she sniffed. *Definitely fear scent,* although how she knew that, she still had no idea as it smelled completely different on him than it did on Little Flower. *What is he afraid about? Was she truly losing control?* That thought terrified her even more.

"Practice does make it easier, but I don't know how I feel about you hunting her. If something went wrong, that could be really bad for everyone," he finally said, scratching the back of his head.

"And so would hunting her and not being able to stop," Marsee countered.

He let out a heavy sigh, but nodded. "Where is Little Flower now?"

"She's still out in the garden," Marsee replied.

He picked up his tablet and typed something, turned off the privacy screen, and motioned for her to follow, his body practically vibrating with tension. They found Little Flower right where she'd left her.

"Marsee says you want to let her hunt you?" her father said, sitting down across from Little Flower, although a good distance away. Marsee climbed onto his lap, needing his comfort, and leaned into him. She was scared she was going to hurt her friend and felt far too close to breaking. The beast inside *wanted* to hunt, was excited about this turn of events, and she was nearly shaking with her fear. Her father hugged her tightly and started purring while waiting for Little Flower's reply.

Little Flower nodded. "I want to do whatever is necessary to ensure that Marsee feels comfortable around me, and I want to find a way to protect my people from yours hurting us by accident. Even your cubs could hurt us pretty badly without trying. I want to know every way we trigger that instinct, so we can teach my people how to avoid triggering it by accident, and if possible, how to stop it before someone gets hurt."

"That is a reasonable request, but one that comes with a significant amount of risk, for both you and Marsee," he replied, letting go of her so he could talk. She shifted to lean up against his side instead and he wrapped his tail around her and squeezed hard. She grabbed ahold and held it tighter.

"My life for the past year has been nothing but risk," Little Flower countered, glaring at her father.

Her father snorted, "Fair. Well, we can start with what triggers it and then discuss ways to allow Marsee to practice safely. If we can figure out a way to do that, then I will agree. But because of everything else going on, I will need you to make a statement indicating your permission, and your reasons for doing this, to protect Marsee and everyone else if you get hurt."

Little Flower nodded, and they spent the next hour discussing all of the triggers Marsee and her father could think of, and then they talked for a long time about how to safely allow Marsee to practice. To Marsee's relief she managed to maintain control as they discussed her triggers. The beast seemed content to wait, knowing she was giving in. She wanted to run and hide, but she didn't know what else to do. Eventually they decided to have Marsee sit wrapped tightly in her father's arms so that she couldn't get away and have Little Flower sit up in the tree high enough that neither Marsee or her father could reach her, just in case. And then, she would fully release the beast inside her, rather than trying to control it right away as she'd always done, with the idea being that it needed to be as close to a real hunt as possible. When Little Flower finished recording her statement and everyone was in place, they began.

Marsee closed her eyes and remembered the first day, the flash of the leash, the success of the pounce, the tug on the leash, and Little Flower trapped at the end, and the overwhelming smell of her fear.

*Mmmm, she will make a lovely snack,* the beast purred.

Marsee remembered the taste and smell of the fried fish and her mouth watered.

*Yes! We should hunt!*

She took a deep breath and caught Little Flower's scent.

*Doesn't she smell de...lect...able?* The word practically dripped as the beast drooled.

Marsee, terrified, released the control she'd locked on the beast. and suddenly the beast wasn't beside her, it *was* her, *and they were famished.*

Their eyes sprung open and locked onto their prey, which was sitting on a branch above them, feet dangling and wiggling back and forth, just begging to be torn off and nibbled on. They examined the tree, trying to figure out how to get at their yummy smelling snack, and decided that they could run and leap off the base of the tree and leap up to the branch she was sitting on. Their weight should be enough to cause it to crash down, and they could easily chase after it, if it ran.

*Yes! Now we hunt!* they growled, and started to slink forward, but were stopped. Something had them trapped and they growled and tried to spin around to attack whatever had them, but they couldn't move, and they roared their frustration. Their prey, scared by their roar, jumped, and tucked its feet away, and climbed up further in the tree.

*No! Our prey is getting away!* The grip around them tightened and they growled as they watched their prey climb up onto another, higher branch. They tried digging their claws and teeth into whatever held them but couldn't reach as they were held tightly in place. They growled in fury and heard another growl and felt teeth dig into their scruff, which made them want to relax, but that just infuriated them more. They roared their anger at whatever was attacking them and it growled back, and the bite on their neck tightened causing them pain and started to cut off their air supply. They let out a half strangled roar, now terrified for their own survival and fought harder, but no matter what they did, they couldn't get free, and their vision was starting to fade at the edges.

"You can do this Marsee, I trust you," their prey signed.

***Prey doesn't talk,*** they decided, and suddenly Marsee remembered where she was, and who she was. The beast was still there inside her, but was now completely uninterested in Little Flower and she remembered that her father was holding her in place to keep her from hurting anyone. She stopped struggling and collapsed against her father and gasped for breath as the urge to hunt slowly vanished.

"I'm okay," she gasped out, barely above a whisper, as the darkness threatened to pull her under.

"Oh well done, Marsee," her father purred, instantly releasing his bite on her neck, and held her there until she calmed and regained her breath. It wasn't until she stopped shaking that she realized he wasn't just purring, he was shaking too. When he finally relaxed his grip, Marsee rubbed the back of her sore neck. Her paw came away with blood on it.

"I'm sorry Marsee," her father said. "I didn't mean to hurt you."

"I know," Marsee replied. "It didn't help though. It just made the beast madder. Are you okay? Did I hurt you?" she asked.

"No. I'm fine," her father said and hugged her tightly. She sagged back into his embrace, horrified at what had happened, and thanked the Ancient Gods she hadn't hurt anyone.

"You were absolutely terrifying Marsee!" Little Flower signed from the tree branch, not coming down. "I wasn't sure your father was going to be able to hold onto you. You looked so fierce! So, how did you stop yourself?"

"I didn't. You did. The moment you signed, my instinct completely lost interest in you," she both said and signed, not sure her father could see from behind her. She felt her father take a huge shuddering sigh of relief, and she turned to face him. "It was a real hunt that first time, wasn't it?" she asked him.

"It was, and I've never been prouder of you in my life. You stopped on your own, and I've never heard of anyone who has done that before," he replied before he started signing. "We'll do it again, but this time, Little Flower, the moment you think she's hunting, I want you to just sign 'stop' and see if we can snap her out of it quicker this time. I'm curious if it was the signing that did it, the specific words, or if Marsee just managed to break free of her instinct with enough time."

She was terrified to try again, but they did, after giving her a little more time to recover. This time it was both far easier to get into that state, and out of it. The moment Little Flower signed 'stop', it went away, just like it had before.

The third time she entered that state, she didn't lose sense of herself, like she had the first two times. Even though she wanted to hunt, she had absolutely no interest in Little Flower, and remained in control of her thoughts and actions. She was even able to ask Little Flower to act more like prey and her instinct still didn't see her as a valid choice, although she struggled for some time to shut it off. Finally, she tried imagining Little Flower signing stop and it worked!

"I did it, Papa! I turned it off on my own!" Marsee exclaimed, and they tried again. She had no problems this time and turned it on and off several times just to be sure.

She spun around to face her father when he relaxed his grip. "I did it, Papa! I wanted to hunt, but Little Flower wasn't something to hunt and I had no problems turning it on or off!"

He looked astonished at her. "Are you sure?" he asked. She nodded and flicked the instinct on while facing him, and she watched as her Papa noticed, and he bolted forward to grab ahold of her again, panic clear on his face, worried that she'd go after Little Flower, and she stopped it.

"I'm sure," she said, and he flicked his whiskers and ears back in amazement.

"Well, there's only one way to be sure. We try it one more time and Little Flower has to come within striking distance," he signed. "Little Flower, are you willing to do that?"

"I am. If she says she won't hurt me, then I trust her not to hurt me," she signed.

So, they did. Marsee flicked it back on and watched as Little Flower climbed carefully down from the tree and walked over and stood in front of her, just out of paw's reach. Her father held on so tightly it hurt, but she found it very reassuring. Marsee took a deep breath of Little Flower's scent, that her instinct immediately identified as 'friend' and she smiled.

"Still good," she signed. Little Flower walked closer until she was close enough to reach out and touch her, well within Marsee's striking range. Her father tightened his grip on her even more, but then Little Flower surprised them both by reaching up and patting her on the side of her face. Marsee leaned into it and started purring. It felt *so* good, and she had the urge to rub herself all over Little Flower. That almost surprised her out of the hunting state itself.

"Still good. Let go, please," she asked her father.

Little Flower backed up a few steps to give her room. Her father shifted so he could lunge for her if necessary, and then cautiously let go. Marsee stood up slowly on all fours and carefully padded over to look directly into Little Flower's face. Then unable to resist the urge any longer, rubbed the side of her head against Little Flower's, purring loudly. She had no idea why she was doing that, but it felt like the right thing to do, and it felt so very good. Little Flower reached up and hugged her back, and they stood there holding each other for several moments. Then Marsee took a deep breath, sniffing her head fur, and sneezed as the fur went up her nose. It snapped her out of the state and she fell to the ground laughing and sneezing, tail curled as Little Flower sat down and leaned up against her. She looked back at her Papa who just looked completely dumbfounded at her.

"Marcus isn't going to believe this," her father whispered.

"Marcus watched the whole thing," her uncle said loudly from the shadows.

Marsee jumped, startled by his unexpected voice and sat up, careful not to dump Little Flower on the ground. Her uncle stepped out into the light of the lantern in the clearing, his body tense. Her father stood to face him, placing himself between them, in a very defensive posture, which surprised her. It almost looked like her father was preparing to fight Marcus.

"She's good, Marcus. She has it under control," her father said.

"Marsee, I need you to come over here, now," Marcus demanded, not answering her father, but stopped where he was, never taking his eyes off her. His voice was very flat and controlled and his mask was on tighter than she'd ever seen it before. This wasn't her Uncle Marcus asking, it was Councilor Surellis, the second most powerful councilor on her planet ordering, she realized.

She tilted her head in confusion, not understanding what was going on between her father and uncle, but did as requested. To disobey the direct order of a councilor came with serious consequences, even if they were family. "Why?" she asked as she walked over. Her father stared at Marcus the entire time and Marsee had to walk around him. She almost expected that he was going to stop her. Every muscle in his body was tense and coiled to attack. *What's going on?* Marsee wondered.

"I want you to turn your instinct back on again, and then I need you to stop when I ask, but not until then. Can you do that?" he asked.

"Sure, Uncle Marcus," she said, signing for Little Flower's benefit, and flicked it back on. The scents around her strengthened and the garden brighted to where it almost seemed like daylight, not the middle of the night, yet everything glowed even brighter than it did on the darkest of nights. Her ears picked up the sounds of the flicker flyer's wings nearby, the breathing of the others, the gentle murmur and drip of the water in the pool and streams around her, and the wind chimes and hydroponics units out in the courtyard, which she normally couldn't hear this deep in the garden. She could smell the lingering scents of the rest of her family from earlier, so strong, she could almost see them. Her nose picked up the tang of the ashes left behind from roasting star fruit, and her ears twitched as they picked up the quiet pitter-patter and crunch of someone walking across the courtyard and entering the garden on the far side, but the wind was going in the wrong direction for her to make out who it was. Marcus watched her closely for several minutes as she just sat there marveling at the vibrant world around her, with absolutely no desire to hunt. She had no idea just how beautiful and alive her desert world was, and it was like she was truly seeing it for the first time.

"Can you still understand me?" Marcus asked.

"Loud and clear," Marsee replied, also speaking, and turned her attention back to her uncle. His fur sparkled in the moonlight and her instinct purred at the power he radiated. It recognized him as both family and her protector, powerful, loving, and intelligent. She smiled up in love at him, and let herself purr with the happiness she was feeling in that moment. She felt more alive and in control than she'd ever felt before and the feeling was incredible.

"Good. You can stop now," he said, and she imagined Little Flower signing stop, and it, whatever it was, stopped and the world went back to normal. It seemed bland and dark now, after the vibrancy of before and she almost wanted to weep at its loss. Her purring stopped, but she flicked her ears back in surprise when Marcus closed his eyes and gave a huge shuddering sigh of relief, verging on tears himself.

*Why is he so relieved?* she wondered.

"Thank you, Marsee. Now, I need to know exactly how you did it," Marcus ordered.

Marsee thought for a moment, not really sure how to explain. "I guess I just stopped fighting it. I just let it be part of me and not something I had to contain or control, and once I did, I stopped losing my sense of self, and just became me with a strong urge to find something to hunt, but Little Flower was not even remotely a target, and after the first few times I was fully in control of that urge. It was no different than wanting to go fry up some star fruit, a craving, but one I could control. Her smell was 'friend' not 'prey', someone I wanted to go hunting *with*, not hunt," she explained. "This last time though, it was different. There wasn't even the urge to hunt and everything was so vibrant. I could have sat here all night just marveling at the beauty of the world around me. I have never seen anything like it."

"That, Marsee, was the answer I needed to hear," Marcus said. "Jer, Marsee's hunting instinct is no longer of concern to the Council. I will rescind the watch."

Her father slumped in relief, sitting down hard on the ground. "Thank the bright blessed full moons!" he whispered.

"I don't understand. What's going on?" Marsee asked. "Why is the Council concerned about me?"

"I spoke to your parents about your lapse today, and they informed me of what happened before. While you were able to stop yourself the first time, which in of itself is unheard of, you were still experiencing fairly strong reactions indicating your instinct was not fully in control, and getting worse. Your father said you were completely non-verbal in his office today which is a sign of an illness we call psychosis. When someone your age has issues with their control, it almost always gets worse, not better, and we are left with no choice but to stop the problem before someone gets hurt." Marcus explained.

"By 'stop', do you mean…?" Marsee gulped.

"He does," her father replied. "And it's something we've all been worried about for years."

"I had no choice but to put you on the watch list, and because of your nonverbal state you would have been tested by the Senior Councilor herself, and put down if you failed. Frankly, I've not known anyone to pass in all the time I've been on the Council. I'm sorry. I didn't want to, but the risk was too great that you would hurt someone," Marcus stated softly. "Your father let me know what you were attempting this evening and I followed to observe and…provide assistance in case he needed it."

"Are you saying you would have put Marsee down because she was struggling with her self-control?" Little Flower asked, fuming with indignation for her.

"No, child," Marcus replied. "We would have had to put Marsee down because she would have lost her sense of self. The Marsee you know wouldn't have existed anymore, only her instinct. Long before the Great Awakening, we were nothing but instinct. Eventually we learned to control it, but it took thousands of years before we wiped out what we call psychosis, the advanced stages of hunting instinct that you saw tonight. Before we did, we destroyed our old planet, and most of the people and creatures on it. It doesn't occur very often anymore, usually just in those who have had to hunt for survival, and occasionally those of Marsee's age. It is why hunting is banned for my people, and why we no longer eat meat, unless we absolutely have to. It's not a preference, it's a necessity. Only the Council, Guard, and Healers ever try meat and that's because our profession requires us to be around blood, and in the case of the Council and Guard, possibly kill, and we are watched very carefully afterwards for any signs of psychosis. I honestly thought we'd lost Marsee tonight with that first test, and was just trying to find the will to end it, knowing her father never could, when you snapped her out of it. I'm not really sure how you did it, but I'm very, very thankful," Marcus explained, and then looked at Marsee. "Marsee did you even hear your father talking to you at all that first time?"

"No. I didn't know who or what was restraining me and I wanted to kill him too. You would have been right to do it too," she said, even though she shuddered at how close she'd come to dying. "I wasn't myself and if Papa hadn't been holding me, I wouldn't have been able to stop myself from going after Little Flower, or trying anyway, both the first and the second time," Marsee explained. "It was far more than what happened that first day though with Little Flower. Then I was aware of being pushed out, of not being in control. I knew who Little Flower was even if I couldn't stop what was happening. The first few times tonight, I...I didn't exist, just the beast. We were very hungry and we didn't know who or what Little Flower was, besides prey, and very yummy smelling prey at that."

Marcus and her father looked at each other and Marcus sat down hard, clearly stunned by what she was describing. She tilted her head to look at him in confusion.

"Marsee, to stop a hunt like you did on your own the first time is incredible enough, but this..." Marcus shook his head in disbelief. "I've never heard of anyone ever coming back once they'd been fully lost to their instinct."

"So, you saw me sign, but couldn't hear your father?" Little Flower asked, and Marcus and her father looked at Little Flower with shock on their faces.

"Yeah, that's what snapped me out of it. You said 'You can do this Marsee, I trust you,' and the moment you did, my brain went 'prey doesn't talk' and it was enough to snap me out of it, only it wasn't like before when my instinct was a separate beast I had to contain and control. It was, is still there, but it's a part of me now, not a wild creature I'm trying to restrain with a leash," Marsee signed. "I don't know how to explain. It's confusing. It kind of feels like something snapped back into place. Maybe? I don't know. I feel very different. Less...jagged?" Marsee shrugged and looked down at her paws. "Since I was a little cub, I've felt...shaky, like I'm vibrating all the time or like some small crawley was in my fur, and the only thing that ever really made that feeling go away was motion. Since the day I hunted you, there's been this itch in my brain that I just couldn't scratch as it clawed away at my defenses. Both feelings are completely gone now."

"Do you think it was sign language or Little Flower's faith in Marsee that did it?" her father asked Marcus.

"I don't know, but I'm going to recommend that what you did here be tried next time. If there's any way we could save the next child, we have to try. It's possible that a visual language is processed differently by the brain than an auditory one. Marsee, if you wouldn't mind, I'd like you to write up a report of everything you experienced as well, the more detail the better. Not just tonight, but everything you've experienced. This will be shared with both the Council, Guard, and the Healers Guild but we'll keep your identity hidden. Only the Seniors will know. I know that there's a lot of stigma associated with losing control as an adult, but this could save someone else's life. What you've been able to share is more than we've ever had. No one has ever come back from psychosis to be able to tell us what they experienced. We just know they become wild animals and attack anyone and everything."

Marsee nodded without hesitation and both her father and uncle looked at her with pride on their faces.

"So, what does this mean for my people? Do I need to worry about yours losing control?" Little Flower asked.

"In general no, not from the adults anyway," Marcus stated. "The younger cubs, three and under, you'll need to be careful with, as they don't always have control over their claws when they pounce. Although, more than likely they'll go after your feet anyway. They like anything that wiggles on the ground. Our tails get shredded by the cubs the first few years. By the age of three most cubs have pretty good control over it unless they get surprised. We start to worry if they haven't learned to fully control it by ten. It almost always happens in single cubs, and we think it might be because they don't grow up playing with litter-mates. It's why we've always pushed Marsee to spend more time around others. It's been almost a year since we've had a report about Marsee losing control, or witnessed it ourselves, so we thought she'd contained it until today. Myra didn't inform either of us about Marsee's prior incidents. All we knew was that Marsee scared you and that you'd run and hid under her parents' bed," Marcus explained.

"It was never under control and it was happening all the time, Uncle Marcus. I was just getting better at hiding it, by pretending that there'd been a bug on my guildmate's tail or that I'd tripped. It's why I started staying home from the Guild so much while Mama was away, not because of transportation. I didn't have to worry about anyone seeing it if it happened in my room, and it was easier to control here because there weren't as many triggers, and I could run or swing on my bed if I needed to," Marsee admitted, looking down with her guilt at lying to her parents and uncle. "I know I should have told you, but I was scared."

"I'm sorry, Kitten, I knew you were spending more time here, but I figured you were just missing your mother. I should have paid more attention and made sure you were okay," her father apologized, looking dejected, and looked away unable to meet her eyes.

"We all should have paid more attention, and worked with you more to learn to control it better. I'm very sorry too," Marcus said and reached out a paw to caress the side of her face.

Suddenly there was a ferocious growl, and her mother leapt out of the dark and launched herself at Marcus, knocking him to the ground, snarling. "LEAVE HER ALONE!"

Marsee stood there, completely slack-jawed in shock and amazement to see her mother attacking a councilor, and Marcus no less, although she recognized immediately that her mother thought Marcus had been trying to kill her. In the second it took for her to come to that realization, Marcus flipped and scrambled to get away and fight back, but her mother grabbed him by the scruff with her teeth and pinned him to the ground, growling. Marcus froze, his tail sticking straight out in fully poofed fear.

"Myra! Stop! It's okay. She has it fully under control! Marcus is rescinding the watch," her father yelled, as he scrambled to his feet to try and pull her mother off of Marcus before she killed him. Myra let go of Marcus's scruff but didn't let him up, one paw now planted firmly on his back, and turned and looked back at her father and then down at Marcus, who nodded.

Myra quickly backed off. "Thank the moons!" her mother exclaimed, and then scooped Marsee up into a crushing hug, before glaring at Marcus, who was still laying on the ground rubbing the back of his neck. With a final growl in Marcus's direction, her mother turned and carried her away from the councilor that nearly had to end her life tonight.

Marsee leaned against her mother and purred. *Little Flower might think I'm fierce, but no one is as fierce as my Mama!* To her surprise, her mother carried her all the way back to the nursery and locked the door behind them, before setting her down in the nest and curling protectively around her. Marsee didn't complain about being treated like a cub, but instead snuggled in next to her mother. She needed time to calm down and come to grips with what had happened tonight too. Eventually though, her father knocked on the door to be let in. To her shock, her mother growled and hugged Marsee tightly.

"Myra let me in," he replied. "I promise. I'm not going to hurt her." She did but kept her father at bay, placing herself between them with another warning growl. He sighed but said nothing, just sat there, just inside the door. Marsee sighed and climbed out of the nest and walked over to him. He wrapped his arms around her and hugged her tightly.

"Mama, don't be mad at Papa. He was doing what I asked him to." She then explained what had happened. Her mother was slack jawed with amazement by the time she finished, and eventually walked over and hugged the both, when she realized the immense risk her father had taken to try and save her. Then guarded by both of them, she wrote up her report. To her relief, she had no problems with her control as she described every experience she'd had fighting her instinct, from as early as she could remember. They spent several hours reviewing the report and asking her all sorts of clarifying questions and then after they'd exhausted everything they could think of, her father tested her again, like Marcus had done in the garden, before letting her leave and return to her room.

Little Flower was waiting for her on the balcony, arms wrapped around her knees and rocking. "Are you okay?" she asked as soon as Marsee appeared, and ran over to hug her.

"I am. Better than I've been since I was a cub," Marsee replied afterwards. "Thank you. You saved my life tonight. I don't think I'll ever be able to repay you for that." Little Flower's expression changed, to one Marsee couldn't quite decipher and she sat back down, pulling her knees back in close and started rocking again. Marsee sagged, worried that her friend didn't want her around anymore. She didn't blame her though. "I'll understand if you want to sleep somewhere else."

Little Flower stopped her rocking to respond, "No. I trust you," but then turned and looked out at the valley.

"So what's bothering you then?" Marsee asked.

Little Flower was silent for a very long time. Marsee sat down and wrapped her tail around Little Flower, who leaned into her side. "I nearly lost my best friend tonight," Little Flower finally said. "I...I don't know if I could survive losing you too, and I'm scared about what's going to happen at the council meeting. If they make me go back to the Agency I..."

"I won't let them," Marsee promised with a growl.

"You might not have a choice," Little Flower replied.

"If I have to fight the Council and Guard to protect you, I will. I promise, the fools won't know what bit them," Marsee replied.

Little Flower chuckled slightly at the use of her own words and leaned into her again for comfort. They stared out at the moonlit valley for a long time before Little Flower leaned away and looked up at her. "Marsee, if they vote against me, don't let them take me back there."

Marsee frowned at her. "I just said I wouldn't."

"That's not what I meant. I'd rather die than go back there," she replied.

Marsee flicked her ears back when she realized what Little Flower was asking, but nodded without hesitation. Little Flower had risked her life to save hers. She would do no less for Little Flower. "I Marsee Bet Chenzira promise that you will never ever set foot in the Agency again, unless you want to, no matter what happens, even if I have to kill you myself. However, before that happens, you'd better gain some weight. If I'm going to die for killing you, I at least want a good snack out of it and you're far too bony," Marsee teased with a wicked grin.

Little Flower laughed and poked her with a bony elbow. "Thanks. I'll see what I can do." Marsee gave a little shove back and they sat there for hours, each lost in their own thoughts and worries, until eventually crawling into bed just as the sky started to brighten with the approaching dawn.

# CHAPTER 28

# Jessica: Family Reunion

Three days before the trial, Myra and Jer's extended family began to descend on the compound, and the place was packed with people and laughing children running everywhere. When everyone had arrived between Myra and Jer's extended family, and a few close friends, there were over a hundred people in attendance. There were people everywhere and she was completely overwhelmed by the crowd, having gotten used to the quiet solitude of the place. She couldn't keep track of everyone's name, but thankfully she was able to ask Marsee what their names were without offending anyone.

Myra warned everyone about the potential risk of a hunting instinct flare up around them due to their smaller size, and the adults were careful to supervise the younger cubs, but it turned out that it wasn't necessary. As they were nearly about the same size, and didn't have fuzzy tails to pounce on, the cub's instinct completely ignored them. Jessica had a chance to see this in action with Marsee's youngest niece who had just turned two. Maggie was a rambunctious ball of fur and the spitting image of Marsee, and every tail just *had* to be pounced on, but Maggie didn't seem to be affected by her or her grandfather at all. They'd even cautiously tried wiggling their feet and fingers. Maggie was far more interested in learning *everything* about them, and when she wasn't pouncing on tails, she was pestering them with nonstop questions, sometimes both. Marsee could barely keep up.

At the evening meal they were all sitting out under the bandala tree chatting, and Jessica was watching Maggie go from one tail to the next. The adults would stop her, detach their tails from her claws and teeth, and redirect her onto something else which would last for all of about five minutes before the next tail would be pounced on. Both Jessica and her grandfather were having a hard time keeping a straight face as the distracted adults would jump. When it was Marsee's turn, Jessica couldn't help herself, and she burst out laughing.

"I don't see what's so funny," Marsee scowled as she detangled Maggie's claws and teeth from her tail.

"She reminds me a lot of our cats. They act much the same way when they're cubs too," she signed.

"How do you get them to stop pouncing on everything?" Marsee's older brother Thomas asked.

"Mostly by redirecting them to safer things they can pounce on. They're about this big when they're cubs and only grow to be about this big, so mostly we just thought it was funny. They were one of our most popular domestic creatures, and we liked the antics of our tiny house panthers. We had lots of toys for them. Special structures they could climb or claw, strings, balls, light pointers," she replied. She didn't have the word for laser.

"Light pointers?" Myra asked.

"A small device that would shine a bright red dot about this big. Something about that light drove them wild and they would chase it until they were worn out. It worked best at night."

"Don't forget about catnip," her grandfather laughed.

"Cat nip?" Thomas asked. "Did you bite them?"

"No, it's a plant we used to have," Jessica explained with a laugh. "When they ate or smelled it, they would roll in it and get all wound up and run around like crazy. I'm guessing it made them feel good. I wonder if you collected any of that?"

Myra burst out laughing. "I think we must have. After all the surgeries were done, we started working with the plants, and one day we found one of our healers rubbing up against everything. We were concerned because that's a normal reaction for a female in heat, but he stated he felt better than he had in years. We're researching it for a possible treatment for pain and depression."

"I wonder what Maggie would do with a light pointer," Thomas asked. "I'd give anything to tire her out for even a few minutes some nights."

Myra laughed and stood up. "I'll be right back." A few minutes later she returned with a small device that looked nothing like a laser pointer but apparently did the same. Myra turned it on and focused the beam from a wide beam to a tiny pinprick, and then changed the color until it was red, pointing it on the ground.

"That looks about the same," Jessica said, so Myra handed it to her. "I apologize in advance if mayhem ensues," she said, and then began wiggling it in front of Maggie. The reaction was instantaneous, not just with Maggie but with all of the younger cubs. It *was* mayhem for about all of five minutes when they collapsed from exhaustion and lay there panting.

"That was really fun!" Maggie said. Little Flower wiggled it over by Maggie and she batted at it but with far less gusto.

"Well Thomas, how much is 'anything' worth to you?" Little Flower asked, holding up the laser pointer. The adults collapsed in laughter.

"Name it and it's yours," Thomas answered.

Jessica thought for a while. "Two days of cub sitting for my cub at some random date in the future, when I've had enough of being pounced on and need a break," she offered.

"Deal! In fact, I'll bump it to four days, freely given," he stated, to everyone's continued laughter. She tossed it over to him, but Myra caught it mid throw.

"Nice try. This belongs to the Agency. I'll order you one of your own, and all cub sitting belongs to me. You'll have to find something else to bargain with," Myra stated, but then handed it to him anyway so he could redirect the cubs when they recovered. They tried several other colors and thicknesses but like with cats back home, the small red dot proved to cause the greatest reaction among the cubs. It was the hit of the evening, for both cubs and parents alike. Ellie's eyes gleamed with what could only be described as avarice, and Jessica had a feeling that laser pointers were going to be all the rage very soon.

Ellie left shortly after to return to the Guild, with the excuse that she needed to pick up the clothing that she and grandfather had ordered, but Jessica was pretty sure that Ellie was making plans. She returned early the next morning with the clothing, along with a large crate full of the sports equipment she'd drawn up and sent a while back, in sizes to fit everyone. Jessica had completely forgotten about it. So, after trying on the clothing and deeming them absolutely perfect, she ended up teaching everyone how to play baseball. With so many in attendance they split up into several teams based on size. Everyone Marsee's size and down in one league, and everyone else in another. It turned out the cats could catch really well, but were terrible at throwing or hitting the ball with a bat, even when they'd been adjusted for their sizes. Both she and grandfather could easily out throw even the bigger cats, due to how their arms worked, but were far slower than even the cubs their own size.

After several games, they retired to the garden for refreshments and both Jessica and GrandFather stuck their feet in the water to cool down. Jessica seriously wanted to jump in but decided not to as she didn't want to bother climbing back up to her room for a change of clothing. Marsee's older siblings turned out to be musicians with their own band that toured the five planets, and as a surprise had reached out to Ammond to find out what their range of hearing was, and transposed many of their pieces into a range that GrandFather could easily hear. She found that when they played loud, she could both hear and feel the beat. She and her grandfather danced and the others attempted their steps, and then the others showed off their own dances, which involved a lot of leaping, flipping, and spinning, which neither of them could easily do, but then Marsee suggested that they could throw Jessica and catch her instead. Myra adamantly refused due to her advancing pregnancy, but then picked her up and carried her through one of the dances. For a few minutes, she flew, and it was exhilarating!

After the noon meal, she begged off for a break because it was getting far too hot for her, and she and Marsee went back to their room. Several of Marsee's nephlings wanted to see her drawings, so they all followed her up to the room. Maggie was very talkative the entire way, and had been keeping Marsee busy trying to keep up with her questions as they walked up the ramp, but Jessica wasn't feeling very good. She was really hot and her head hurt, and she really just wanted to just lay down and have a few moments of peace in the cool room, but she was trying to be polite.

"What's your favorite food?" Maggie asked.

"Fried star fruit," Jessica replied.

"Fried?"

"You stick it over a fire until it gets warm," Jessica replied.

"I bet we'll have some tonight," Marsee said. "Mama was talking about it with Thomas earlier."

"Oh, I can't wait to try it. Mines yellow fang. Have you tried that?"

"No, I don't think I have. Have I?' she asked Marsee.

"No, that's the crop we lost during the storm," Marsee explained. "Although I don't know if you had any at the agency."

"Too bad. It's really yummy," Maggie said as they entered the room. "Oh, it's really cold in here," she said and poofed out her fur.

"That's to keep Little Flower cool enough. It gets too hot for her during the day," Marsee explained.

"Oh, that makes sense. Fuzzy!" Maggie suddenly gasped and ran across the room, and grabbed Sir Fuzzleton McFuzzface the Third off of the bed. "They gave you Fuzzy? I'm so happy you got him!"

"What did you call him?" Jessica asked as the room started spinning.

"Fuzzy," Maggie replied.

Marsee's translation was the last thing Jessica saw before she collapsed.

A few minutes later, Myra was there waking her up, scanner in hand. "Hey there, feeling better?"

"No. I'm dizzy and my head hurts," she said.

Myra nodded. "That's not surprising. Your temperature is too high. I think you got overheated with all the games and dancing." Marsee came barreling into the room and handed her mother a thermos. Myra poured her out a cup and handed it to her. "Drink."

Jessica did as ordered, and found she was very thirsty and drank the entire cup and handed it back for more. By the time she'd finished drinking the second cup, much slower than the first one, the room had stopped spinning.

"Alright, everyone out. Little Flower needs to rest," Myra ordered, and everyone started filing out, all except for Maggie who was still holding Fuzzy tightly.

"Are you okay, Little Flower?" she asked, looking very concerned, and handing the doll back to her.

"I will be. Was this your doll? And did you really call this distinguished gentleman here, Fuzzy?" Jessica asked.

"Uh huh," Maggie nodded. "Mama said that there was a really scared and lonely little cub at the Agency that needed a friend, and so I gave her Fuzzy to send over. Fuzzy was my favorite. He kept the creepy crawlies away at night and gave the bestest hugs of all my stuffies, and I asked him really nicely to take good care of you because you didn't have anyone to watch out for the creepy crawlies. Did it help?"

"Oh Maggie, it more than helped. You saved my life. I was so very, very lonely and he was my best friend and he really does give the bestest hugs. But do you want to know a little secret?" Maggie nodded. "The day I met him he *told* me his name was Fuzzy, Sir Fuzzy the Third to be exact and that a very special little cub had sent him," Jessica said. She didn't have signs for "Fuzzleton McFuzzface'.

"Really?" Maggie asked, with wide eyed wonder.

"Really. Do you want him back?" Jessica asked.

"No. He says he's yours now, and he's waiting for your cub to be born," Maggie answered.

"Did someone tell you Little Flower was pregnant?" Myra asked.

"Uh huh, Fuzzy did, while we were waiting for you to show up," Maggie replied.

"Thank you very much, Maggie. I'll take very good care of him," Jessica said, and gave the little cub a hug.

"Welcome!" she said, and then bolted out the door after the others.

"Did I hit my head when I fell?" Jessica asked Myra, after Maggie was gone.

"If you did, so did I. Now come on, you need to rest. Healer's orders," Myra insisted, and scooped her up and placed her on Marsee's bed. Myra gave her something for the headache and she was asleep before Myra left the room.

When she woke up later that evening, Marsee was laying on the bed next to her, watching her with concern. "Are you feeling better?" Marsee asked.

"Much," she replied and sat up. Marsee jumped down and padded her way over to the table where the thermos had been left and returned with another cup of juice for her. Jessica downed it and when she continued to feel good, they made their way down to the garden and joined in the celebration that was continuing, with more music, dancing, and a small fire where they showed everyone how to roast star fruit. It was well past midnight when Marsee carried her back up the tower, too exhausted to even try walking up it, and they sat out on the balcony watching the moons in silence for a while, each lost in their own thoughts of the coming days.

"I really hope I'm allowed to come back here," Jessica said eventually.

"I hope so too," Marsee replied, and Jessica leaned up against her best friend, who wrapped her tail around her, and then after a while, carried her in. As tired as they were, they both failed miserably to fall asleep.

# CHAPTER 29

# Jessica: Witness

The next day was a somber affair as they packed up and said goodbye to Marsee's extended family. It was an incredibly surreal and uncomfortable experience, and far different than she'd ever experienced when her own family left after after a party. She still struggled at times reading their body language, yet it seemed like everyone was saying goodbye as if they didn't expect to see the other person ever again. When she asked Marsee about it, to find out if it was a cultural thing or if something else was going on, Marsee had simply stated that it had been years since they'd seen everyone. Eventually though, she begged off, stating that she wanted to lay down for a little bit before the flight to Council City. Myra had asked if she was feeling sick, and Jessica shook her head. "Just nervous," she'd replied. Marsee had followed and curled around her protectively until late that afternoon when everyone was gone and Myra came to check on her, scanner in hand.

When the scanner proved that she was well, Myra scooped her up into her arms and held her, purring. "It will be alright," Myra said after setting her back down on the bed. "They will vote in your favor. I have no doubt of it."

"What about you and everyone else though?" Jessica asked.

"Do not worry about us," Myra said. "I know you don't blame us for what happened, and that means everything to me, but I still hurt you. Whatever the Council decides will be fair and just. They are good people, as are you, and they will do what is right. Now, come on. We should be going. It wouldn't be good to keep the Senior Guild Master waiting. It's very kind of her to offer to transport us and I've never had the privilege of flying on a personal ship before."

Jessica nodded and jumped down. Everything she was taking had already been packed and loaded on the ship the night before. She started to walk out of the room but turned and walked back to the bed, grabbed Fuzzy, and carried him out. Jessica dared them to say something with a glare, but Myra just looked sad before the expression vanished and she turned, holding out her tail to her for comfort. Jessica let Myra wrap her with her tail in another hug before taking a deep breath and walking down the ramp with the two cats following behind.

Everyone else was waiting for them on the ship, and after tossing fuzzy in her seat, Ellie gave her a full tour, which included meeting her pilots, who were all Flyers, or as far as she was concerned, dragons, beautiful dragons at that. She had chosen to go with the name Sina had picked for the species rather what she really wanted to call them, as it matched the name they already had, but still, meeting an honest to goodness dragon was an experience. The ship master, Petra was a beautiful indigo color, while the other two were both shades of dappled green, darker on the top, fading to almost white underneath. The scales of all three glistened like jewels in the late afternoon sunlight.

"Myra, I always wondered. Why wasn't I allowed on the ship that first day Ellie came to visit?" Jessica asked.

Myra snorted. "Well, lets just say we were bending a few of the Council's edicts by having Ellie here in the first place. We didn't let you on the ship to keep the pilots safe from the consequences of our disobedience."

"Bending?" Jessica asked.

"No one said I couldn't visit," Ellie replied. "Just that Myra's family couldn't leave. Granted, loophole aside, I would have been in serious trouble if Jer had reported me."

"Why didn't you," Jessica asked Marsee's father.

Jer looked up and away, and almost seemed embarrassed before answering. "Well, Ellie has as much power in her own way as the Senior Council. Regardless of the fact that she could destroy this districts economy with a single command, I've always been a little intimidated by her. Ellie's reputation precedes her. You do not want to be on her bad side."

Ellie's tail curled in laughter, but she kept her face serious. "I intimidate you do I? Well good. I've worked hard to earn that reputation. If you think keeping junior councilors in line is hard, you should try herding overgrown pompous guild masters." A look passed between Ellie and Myra and Myra snickered.

"Are you ever going to tell me that story?" Marsee asked.

"No," both Ellie and Myra said in unison, causing them to laugh and their tails curl.

"Now come on, let's get buckled in so Petra can stop twiddling her claws waiting for us," Ellie said.

"I never twiddle my claws," Petra said indignantly. "I wouldn't dare risk losing the second most cushiest job in the universe."

"What's the first?" Jessica asked, curious.

"Nest mother, but that won't be for another year or two. Until then, I get to travel the universe in style, and Ellie takes very good care of us," Petra replied.

"Do you want to be a nest mother?" Jessica asked. "I'm not even sure about having one. Marsee says you'll lay thousands of eggs?"

Petra nodded. "Tens of thousands on average and I do. I don't know how many I'll raise myself, but I would never have to do another thing again, if I didn't want to, which is very freeing in a way. My mother wants me to go into the Council, like her, but I haven't decided yet. I like being a pilot. Perhaps I'll feel differently after my first clutch."

"Who's your mother?" Jer asked.

Petra grinned. "I would think you'd be able to figure that out, Councilor. It's not like just anyone would be able to keep the Senior Guild Master in line."

Jer flicked his ears back in surprise and not being given a direct answer. Ellie howled with laughter and shooed them out of the cockpit. After they were seated and strapped in, Jer raised an eyebrow at Ellie. "Wind Rider?" he guessed.

She chuckled but nodded. "Wind Rider asked me personally if I would watch out for her. Petra is one of the highest rated pilots in the Ships Guild though. I'll honestly be sad when she retires. She's been the best pilot I've ever had. That's for sure. She'll make a good councilor someday too."

Jessica spent most of their trip to Council City staring out the window and thinking about the coming trial. In a normal trial or meeting, the senior councilor of the presiding home world would run the session and have the tie breaking vote. As Senior Councilor Tabor was being tried along with the rest of her council, it had been decided that she would abstain from voting on Little Flower's sentience, admittance into the Consortium, and the complicit nature of her Council. In these decisions there would be no tie-breaking vote. Tabor would still run the session and vote on all other decisions.

Her rapist was flown in by the Guard, but due to the nature of the crimes committed, he would be held in a separate room where he could watch the trial, but not interfere or intimidate her or any of the others. Between her drawings, the Agency footage, and her obvious pregnancy, there was no question that she'd been forced to mate and beaten in the process. They hadn't even needed genetic testing, but that had been submitted anyway. All they really needed was her word. What mattered was how she felt. If she felt that she had been forced to mate, that was all the proof they really needed. Having proof of any kind would be rare in most situations, so her word was taken as the sole proof needed for conviction. Although, if she hadn't been sure who had raped her, or if there had been some other evidence to prove his innocence or question his guilt, that would have been allowed, and he would have been assigned an Advocate. As the consequences of the crime were so severe, none of their people would accuse another if it wasn't true. Additionally, if it was determined at a later date that the accuser had lied to the Council, they would be held to the same punishment that had been given to the accused.

As it was, he'd already been found guilty by a majority of the Local Council the day she'd submitted her accusation. What had not been determined was whether or not the actions of the Council and Agency had tricked him into believing he had no choice but to commit that crime, whether to gain his freedom or save his life. That could potentially affect the severity of his punishment, but not his guilt.

Her drawings and original statement had been taken to indicate that she was accusing the Agency and Council for the rape as well. She'd since given a statement to Marcus about what each drawing represented to clarify her intent, and she'd indicated that many of the drawings had been her attempts to gain answers, and understand why she was being held and had been locked in the room with him, not to formally accuse anyone but him. This had been risky as she could have been seen as lying to the Council with her original accusation, but the Senior Council had decreed that her lack of ability to communicate at the time meant that they'd had to interpret her intent, which was no fault of hers, and they'd accepted her updated statement and accusation.

It would now be up to the Senior Council to determine who, if anyone, had been complicit in her rape. The actions of the Council and Agency were all well documented and submitted for evidence already. She would be required to answer questions any of the councilors had regarding that evidence, on the events leading up to her rape and after, but not the actual rape itself. Should she choose to provide additional details, that statement and any questioning would be done in private, with just the Senior Council in attendance, along with her advocate and translator. She had waived that option, since there was little her statement would do to change the results, and they already had more information than she could provide with the Agency's video, as she'd thankfully been unconscious for most of it.

The official recordings and logs of the Council, Agency, and the Healers Guild already implicated Healer Brice for putting her in the room, Myra for specifically choosing the two to be paired up and ordering the stop to the hormone blockers, and the other master healers for not stopping Myra, or even bringing up concerns of the risk of rape. The Local Council was also implicated for allowing the Agency to begin repopulation and reintegration, since they'd given the Agency full control over that process, and had been provided with a detailed plan on how the Agency intended to manage repopulation among the various species. What was not determined was whether or not they colluded in the rape, which held the same punishment as the rape itself, or the far lesser charge of accessory.

They still had not informed Jessica or Marsee of the expected punishments if they were found guilty of collusion, or of Marcus's vow regarding her sentience, and had purposely left that out of the meetings they'd reviewed with them. The more they'd learned about her people, the more they were concerned that the Council would find them not sentient enough, or far worse, too dangerous to keep around, and had worked hard to craft the responses she would give. This had led to long disagreements that she was still not fully convinced were the right path to take. But at this point, it was in her hands as to what she decided, and would say.

When they arrived at Council City, Petra took the long way around the city to the council building so she and her grandfather could see some of the city before they landed. It was unlike anything either of them had ever seen before. Close to a million people lived in the city, one of the most populated cities on the planet, yet you'd never know it. Much further north than where she'd been living, the climate here was more temperate and foliage bloomed in a riot of color. Most of the buildings, except for the Council, which was a massive sprawling complex of buildings, were no higher than the tower back home and they'd been built to blend in with nature. Shuttles flew through the air along some sort of invisible roadway, while people of every race walked below. There were no ground crawlers, only the personal transport carts for the Water Sprites, so there was no need for roads, only carefully manicured paths that people strolled along. A river wound its way through the city and split off into smaller tributaries at regular intervals that large foot bridges arched gracefully over. The water was both calm and clear, and as they traveled over it, Jessica saw large creatures swimming in the waterways, but she couldn't make out what they were. She pointed them out to Marsee.

"Those are the Water Sprites. They can't walk on land without special carts to hold them, so the water way was created to allow them the ability to access the major parts of the city easily," Marsee explained.

"That's the Guild where Ellie works and your clothes were made," Myra said, pointing it out as they flew past another massive but far more ornate complex of sprawling buildings with small parks and paths in and around them.

"Can we visit?" Little Flower asked.

"Maybe after the trial," Myra said, and Jessica nodded her understanding. There might not be an after.

Eventually they made their way to the Council and they landed in an underground shuttle bay in Ellie's assigned parking spot. They unloaded and Jer led them all to the suite of rooms that belonged to him, as long as he was a councilor. The suite consisted of two large bedrooms, with two beds in each, an equally large common room, a fully provisioned but small kitchen, and a waste room with a sonic shower and small cleaning unit. A short hallway connected to Jer's office suite, where a few of his junior councilors and staffers were currently working. Jer briefly introduced them to Samantha, who he hoped would take his place after the trial, if he was found guilty and Jessica was surprised but pleased when Samantha greeted her in sign.

Jessica, GrandFather, and Marsee claimed one bedroom, while Myra and Jer took the other. Marsee's grandparents were saying with Marcus in his suite, just down the hall. Ellie only lived fifteen minutes away by walk, and Ammond and Brice, who flew in separately in Ammond's shuttle, were given visitor suites, for them and their families.

Jessica unpacked the small collection of clothing she'd brought with her, but since there wasn't a closet or dresser to be used, she ended up using one of the drawers in the desk instead, and hooked the rest on the backs of the chairs. She had several new outfits that had been provided by Ellie at her request. These people had no real concept of formal wear, since none of the other species wore clothing either, outside of similar harnesses or the occasional protective wear, like Marsee's gloves, but she wanted to look her best, knowing that her image would forever be recorded in the history books, one way or another. She hadn't been happy about the idea that images and video of her naked might be shown to everyone, so Marcus had asked and was granted the request that those images and video would be blurred before being broadcast to the community at large. It was the best he'd been able to do as the rest of the Council needed to be able to view the unaltered evidence. Additionally, the video of her actual rape would not be shown to the public, for which she was very grateful.

Marcus, Ellie, Brice, Ammond, and Marsee's grandparents joined them shortly after they arrived for the evening meal, but it was the first time Jessica had been in the room with Brice since she'd left the Agency and it had taken everything she had to contain the panic she felt at her appearance even though Brice had been included on several conference calls in preparation for the trial.

Brice wilted, seeing her expression. "I am truly sorry for the harm I have caused you," Brice signed. "I'll leave. I don't want to cause you more pain."

"No. Stay," Jessica said. "I need to get comfortable around you before tomorrow and I know you didn't intend me harm. Myra has told me how you were the first person to come forward with concerns about my isolation sickness. You did what you could to care for me."

Brice shook her head. "I didn't do nearly enough. I wasn't brave enough, like some of the others, to go against the edicts of the Council. Not until it was too late."

"What do you mean?" Marcus asked with a frown.

Brice hesitated and shook her head. "I don't want to get anyone else in trouble." Marcus just raised a brow and waited. Brice sighed. "You know 84, the cub that was moved into my care."

"The one that was choking when Little Flower was raped?" Marcus asked for confirmation.

Brice nodded. "He did not do well with the transfer to my care and would cry for half the night. I spoke to Nazari about it and she offered to take the night alerts for him, thinking that maybe they imprinted. I watched that first night, on the monitor, curious to see how he would do, and then spoke to Nazari afterwards. It turns out, she's been sleeping in his habitat from pretty much the day they arrived. She wants to adopt him, if none of the bipeds do."

"Huh," Myra said. "That explains that mystery at least. I always wondered why he didn't have any problems with his isolation."

Brice nodded. "She apparently spent more time in all their habitats than she was strictly allowed to as well as did many of the others, when they could."

"I wondered why you spent so little time in my granddaughters room, compared to what I experienced," GrandFather signed. "Nazari was working with me all the time."

"In your case, the observation and physical therapy you needed was warranted," Myra explained. "We had to print you a new heart. You suffered a heart attack from the stunner and we weren't able to start it again. The first biped we tried a replacement heart with with didn't survive. He's still in stasis though as we're waiting to see if you have complications before trying again. We still don't know if there was something faulty with the heart or if something else happened. So far everything looks good with yours, at least according to the last time I scanned you. Little Flower had the same care until her injuries were healed."

Brice nodded. "You were in stasis until a couple of months ago too. Your granddaughter was awake the entire time. For months, I was not allowed in her room for more than a few minutes at a time, and physical contact, unless needed to treat our patients wasn't allowed either."

"Wait, just how long has it been since we were rescued?" Grand-Father asked.

"Almost two and a half of your years now," Marcus answered.

"That long?!" GrandFather exclaimed. "Good god. Jessica, how did you survive isolation that long? I thought the time I was in there was bad, but two years?"

"I didn't," Jessica replied. "I'm pretty sure I went mad for a time. I'm glad they were able to give you a new heart though."

"Me too," her grandfather said and then shook his head. "Who knew being captured by dragons would save my life. I'd just found out about the heart disease I had a few days before the Cataclysm. Is there anything I need to worry about?"

"No. You're fully recovered now. You will want to be careful if you jump between worlds and check with a healer first. Replacement organs don't always do well in the first few months during a jump," Myra explained. "Stasis can be a problem as well during the first six months or so, but since you're still here, that should be fine."

Brice looked away. "I didn't put him in stasis. My report says I did, but I wasn't taking that chance with him. It was too soon. Not after what happened with the other biped."

Myra snorted. "It seems you've gotten over your inability to disregard the Council's orders."

"Only when they're stupid and risk the life of my patients," Brice said. "Are you going to arrest me for that too?" she asked Marcus.

"For what?" Marcus asked. "Saving his life? I'm well aware of the risk a transplant has with stasis and jump. You made the right decision there. The Council will hear nothing from me, about what you did or Nazari." Everyone turned and looked at Marcus. "What?" he asked.

"You, bend the rules?" Jer asked. "I never thought I'd see the day."

Marcus raised a brow at his brother. "The rules are meant to be bent, little brother, especially when it comes to saving a life. I'm honesty furious at Tabor for disregarding all of the medical recommendation Myra made. Half the reason we're in this mess is because of her. We're just lucky that statis order didn't end up killing off the entire species."

Jer shook his head again, in astonishment this time and then shrugged. He stood and peered into the fridge to see what they had for food and pulled out several trays of already prepared meals. They spent the rest of the evening talking about anything and everything but the upcoming trial. After their guests left, Myra ordered everyone to bed but it was a long time before anyone fell asleep.

Myra woke everyone up early the next morning. Jessica was sick twice, even with Myra's new and improved tonic. After finally managing to eat something, she showered and put on her favorite new outfit and combed her hair. The Guild had exceeded all of her expectations and made her a beautiful light blue gown that shimmered in the morning light, with embroidered flowers along the neckline and hem and built-in support for her now growing breasts. There weren't pockets but the dress had an ornate belt similar in functionality to the cat's carry harnesses, that accentuated her waist, which she could use to clip her tablet onto if she wanted. The crafters had invented jewelry for her, and she now sported a delicately handcrafted necklace with a glass blown lily that practically glowed like the flower's in Myra's garden. The crafters had also managed to figure out a way to craft a piece that wound around her ears, displaying a vine of colorful flowers that matched her necklace, instead of earrings, and she loved it. As she expected to be standing for a long time during the trial, they had made her a pair of beautiful padded white boots with an incredibly soft chenzie fur lining that fit her better than any footwear she'd ever worn.

When she was dressed, Marsee wove her hair into an intricate braid and tied it off with a matching ribbon and placed more matching flower jewelry in her hair, pinning everything in place. There weren't any mirrors in the room, so she used her tablet and projected her image up on the monitor in the bedroom to examine her appearance. Her hair was far longer than it had been before, and a few days prior Marsee had carefully trimmed it and applied a bluish/purple dye made from the bandala tree berries to freshen up the remains of the faded color she had left. Her skin had tanned considerably in the past month, local time, and she had a whole host of new freckles. She'd also finally regained some of the muscle that she lost during quarantine, and no longer looked emaciated. She wasn't sure she even recognized herself. *I look a bit like an elf or warrior princess in this gown,* she thought. She had never owned anything nearly this nice before and the other outfits she'd been given were equally as stunning. Her fairy godmother had truly outdone herself.

She flattened the dress to her belly trying to see if she was starting to show and frowned. From what she'd been able to figure out, with the differences in their length of days and what they called a month, or four twelve-day weeks, she was now almost four months pregnant. She sighed, and turned to her grandfather, "How do I look?"

"Like a beautiful young woman ready to take on the universe," he said. "Whatever happens, I'm proud of you."

"Thank you," she replied. "And I think you look pretty dashing in that new suit of yours, although I was kind of hoping you'd wear that pink dress again," she said with a wink.

"Nah, I'm saving that one for a special occasion. I'm thinking maybe the first time you bring someone special over to meet me," he said with an evil grin.

"You'd better! I'll be disappointed if you don't!" she replied.

Laughing, she pulled him in for a hug, then went out to meet the others waiting for them in the common room. After another trip to the facilities, they made their way over to the council chamber. The others all walked slowly, matching her pace, as she did not want to be seen being carried in like a child or pet. Back straight and head held high, she approached the massive entrance to the Full Council chamber. Gilded and intricately carved doors had been propped opened wide, with the local flag hanging from the center, and the flags of the other members of the Consortium hanging on either side.

Two imposing honor guards stood at rigid attention on either side of the door, in the most formal gear she'd seen yet. Everyone but her and GrandFather were wearing carry-harnesses with badges that clearly indicated who they were and their guild affiliation if they had one. The guards' gear wasn't all that different, although they had far more equipment on their harnesses than anyone else she saw, but it was embroidered in colors that matched the local flag, and far more ornate. While they stood stock still, their eyes and ears were everywhere, and it was clear to her that they were aware of them the moment she came into view. However, as they were being escorted by a councilor, and would be the only two humans that would be attending, they were let in without a challenge.

They left Myra, GrandFather and Jer's parents at the visitors seating, where they were checked in by another Guard to confirm that they were on the very short list of people allowed. Ammond and Brice were already there. Due to the nature of the trial, the Senior Council had closed the session to all outside visitors, so only those expected to be called as witnesses were in attendance, along with the press. The trial would be recorded and broadcast on all five worlds, and adult citizens would be allowed but not required to cast a vote on inclusion into the Consortium. The citizens' vote would not be binding, only used for consideration by the Senior Council to gauge the will of the people following the trial.

When they were checked in, Jer led her and Marsee to their assigned seating in the plaintiff's box, where Marcus was waiting for them.

"Welcome to Council City, Ambassador Little Flower," Marcus signed and formally bowed.

"Thank you Advocate Surellis. It's a pleasure to be here," she replied, bowing back, fully expecting this exchange. Marsee, as her translator was ignored. Jessica turned to Jer. "Councilor, thank you for your assistance," she said, formally dismissing him, per the expected protocol. Jer nodded to both of them and took his proper place among his council.

"Are you ready?" Marcus asked her, once the formal exchange was over.

"As ready as I'll ever be," she replied, and climbed up on the raised platform that had been placed under her seat. The Guild had crafted this in an effort to allow her to comfortably see and sit during the proceedings, and so she wouldn't look like a child in their oversized furniture, well more like one anyway, and it honestly felt strange to be sitting in a normal sized chair again.

Little else was said as they waited for the rest of the Council to enter. She took the opportunity to look around the massive room while she waited. It was divided into six equal sections of raised seating that started about twenty feet up so that everyone could see, one section for each sentient world, and another for the various guilds. *I wonder what they'll do if we get accepted? Build a new chamber or just shift every-thing around? As small as we are compared to everyone else, we certainly wouldn't take up much space.*

One of the sections was fully enclosed and filled with water, with Water Sprites swimming in from an opening below. Rather than desks and chairs, they had podiums that they floated behind and strange net-like seats they could tangle their tentacles in to keep themselves from floating off. She watched in fascination as they communicated. Light flickered along their bodies like the flicker flier wings had done, but in a more controlled and rhythmic pattern. Their vaguely humanoid top, with head, torso, and arms, with four webbed fingers on each hand, gave way to a more octopus-like lower body and five tentacles instead of legs. *Would that make them pentacles?* Jessica wondered absently.

Ice Giants, a cross between a massive polar bear and abominable snowman, sat nearest her and she occasionally felt the gust of a cool breeze waft out of their section. Like her, they loathed the heat, as their planet almost never got above freezing on the surface. She recognized the armadillo like Diggers from the video she'd been shown. They had a fairly slow shuffling walk compared to the other species. Ramps, rather than stairs, were used throughout the council building as they could not easily use stairs, nor could the Water Sprites in their carts. Flyers, as she'd chosen to call the final species, sticking with the sign that Sina had developed, rather than dragons, like she really wanted to, glittered in a multitude of different colors. They flew up to their desks, although they didn't bother with actual seats. Every one of the species was far larger than hers, and she found it rather intimidating, since she wasn't much bigger than a young child to most of them. There were Water Sprites closer in size to her, although even the smallest was bigger than she was. Apparently while they grew slowly, they never stopped growing, and some of the older Sprites in the room were close to forty feet long.

In the middle of the room, in addition to the plaintiff's box, where they were sitting, was the currently empty witness box and seating for those not currently testifying. The box where the defendant would normally sit had been removed, as his guilty status had already been determined. Plus there were far too many other people potentially affected by the outcome of this trial to bother with it. Most of the accused healers had remained at the Agency in order to care for their wards, only Healer Brice was in attendance, as they only expected the other healers to be reprimanded at this point for not speaking up against the proposed repopulation plans, and frankly, as they were now the experts in care for those species, removing them would have caused more harm.

In front of her was a large raised platform with four massive desks and an enclosed water-filled box with another of the odd podiums and nets, although this podium was much larger than the others, matching the size of the other desks. This was where the Senior Council would sit to observe and pass judgment. Flags of each of the worlds hung from poles that hovered in the air above each chair. As this trial would also determine her world's inclusion into the Consortium, she'd been asked to design a flag to represent her people. Ellie had taken that design to the Guild, and master weavers had turned it into the beautiful piece of artwork that fluttered above her. *I wonder what my father would say about my artwork now?* she thought absently as she looked up at it.

At a full council trial, every councilor was able to vote, but it was the Senior Council that would take those votes and the comments submitted with each and reach a final decision. They could completely override the will of the other councilors if they felt it was necessary, but they rarely went against the majority. Technically though, the trial wasn't even necessary as the Senior Council, if unanimous, could make any decision they chose, as long as it didn't infringe on the rights of the people. However, with a member of their own on trial, it was highly unlikely that they would vote against the majority. The Full Council's majority of approval was required by law for inclusion into the Consortium, regardless of what the Seniors wanted, although they could choose to leave at any time, and they could be kicked out with a majority ruling of either the Full or Senior Council, if they proved to be untrustworthy.

"All rise as the Senior Council enters and takes their seats!" came a booming voice near a door to the back. Jessica stood as Marsee tapped her on the shoulder to get her attention, and translated, pointing in the direction of the voice. Two more honor guards were stationed by a door in the direction Marsee pointed, and she watched as the four land-based councilors entered and took their seats, while the fifth floated up through an opening in the floor.

When they were all there and settled, Senior Councilor Tabor walked forward. Jessica swallowed hard as they made eye contact, but she didn't look away. The Senior Councilors picture hadn't done her justice and every instinct in Jessica screamed that this cat was both a predator and a threat. She made Marcus look like a bumbling kitten, with the grace, authority, and innate feral power that radiated off of her. This wasn't just someone used to leading and making difficult decisions. This was someone who would kill without a second thought, and from what she'd learned about Marsee's illness, likely had, many times.

"This Council is now in session. Please be seated," she called out and everyone took their seats or sat as appropriate based on their species. "We are here today to determine the sentience of the biped known as Little Flower and by association her people. Should she be deemed sentient we will also be determining whether or not her people should be invited to be members of the Consortium of Sentient Beings, with all the rights and responsibilities associated with that membership. Additionally, should she be deemed sentient, and accept membership to the Consortium on behalf of her people, we will be determining the punishment for the biped who forced her to mate, and determine whether or not the actions of the Local Council and healers in charge of her care at the time colluded in that rape, and their punishments if found guilty. Journeyman Marsee Bet Chenzira please rise."

Marsee rose, head high and shoulders back, trying to project the confidence Jessica was sure she wasn't feeling.

"It is my understanding that you have been requested as the Official Translator by Ambassador Little Flower for these proceedings. Is that correct?" Tabor asked.

"Yes, Your Honor," Marsee replied, signing at the same time.

"Do you promise to translate the words of the Council, and that of the Ambassador, and any that may be called for questioning, to the best of your ability, knowing that should you intentionally misrepresent our intent, you will be held in contempt of council, with possible punishment up to and including the highest punishment decided by this court during these proceedings?"

"I do," Marsee promised.

"And do you promise to remain impartial during these proceedings, regardless of your feelings or relationships with the Ambassador, or any of those accused or found guilty of the crimes being tried?"

"I do," Marsee replied.

"Do you promise to inform this Council if you cannot fulfill a translation due to a lack of words and work with this Council and the members of Little Flower's people to find adequate translations."

"I do."

"Then it is this Council's unanimous and final decision that you are recognized as an official translator for the Council and for these proceedings. Please take your place beside the head podium, Translator Chenzira."

Marsee strode confidently across the room to her designated location and turned to face Jessica. Only those who knew her well would have noticed the slight shiver of her tail as she walked across the room, forcing herself to remain calm and not show her fear at being in front of so many people.

"Ambassador Little Flower, please stand," Tabor commanded.

Jessica stood.

"Ambassador Little Flower, do you wish to be recognized as a sentient being on behalf of your people, with all of the rights and responsibilities that go along with that designation?"

"I do, Your Honor," Jessica replied as confidently as she could project.

"And do you wish to submit your application for inclusion into the Consortium of Sentient Beings on behalf of you and your people?"

"I do," she answered.

"And do you wish to charge the biped, known by the agency as 2A326, with beating you and forcing you to mate?" As Tabor asked this, what she'd thought was only a wall below the first row of seating sprang to life showing her rapist sitting in a room by himself.

She closed her eyes and took several deep breaths to control the near instant panic that rose inside her, as memories and the fear of that day flashed through her mind the moment she saw him. She'd known she would be shown his image for confirmation, but she hadn't expected it to be so large and plastered everywhere. Marcus reached over and placed his paw lightly on her shoulder. She jumped, opened her eyes, and looked at him.

"You're safe," he signed.

She nodded slightly and turned back to face the Senior Councilor. Thankfully the image was already gone and Councilor Tabor looked at her with compassion, waiting patiently for her answer. That compassion surprised Jessica, but it didn't change her answer.

"I do, Your Honor," she signed with barely controlled rage.

"Thank you, Ambassador Little Flower. You may be seated," Tabor stated.

She sat hard and continued to take several deep breaths to get her nerves and emotions back under control, as the Senior Councilor continued.

"Advocate Marcus Surellis, please stand. Do you have witnesses to call forth to present evidence of Ambassador Little Flower's sentience?"

"I do, Your Honor," he replied.

Councilor Tabor nodded and returned to her seat. "Please call forth your first witness."

"For my first witness, I would like to call forth hearing specialist Master Healer Ammond Greyfoot," Marcus called out.

Tabor nodded, and Ammond made his way from the visitor's booth to the witness box, where he was sworn in with a similar oath and consequences as Marsee had been made to give. Once sworn in, Marcus had Ammond give his testimony. He spoke on her species hearing loss, as well as the difference in hearing and vocal ranges that made speech difficult between their respective species, and his recommendation that they be taught the sign language used by the deaf among his people. When asked to provide his reasoning as to why he believed she was sentient, he spoke of how she had been upset about losing her hearing, and how she'd been able to effectively communicate using the picture dictionary that she'd invented, when he'd first met her, and how he could now communicate as effectively with her as he could any of the deaf patients fluent in sign, including his own granddaughter. There were some questions for clarifications on a few of the medical terms and long-term prognosis on his ability to repair their hearing, but no major cross examination, which matched their expectations.

Marcus next called forth Healer Morningstar to give testimony on her experiences with Little Flower at the Agency, including the extent of her injuries upon arrival and her isolation sickness. She spoke of the anger and frustration Little Flower had shown at being held for so long, her demands to be let out of the habitat, and her compassion when she offered to share her meal with her and shared her toys with both her and the other biped. Several videos were shared with the Council to illustrate her attempts to communicate, which they had misunderstood at the time, her ability to follow instructions and solve complex puzzles, her demands to be let out, and her rage at being denied. They also showed video of her multiple escape attempts. She also described the treatment of care that had been required following the suicide attempt she had made after being raped, as well as footage showing the extent of her injuries, both then and when she was first rescued.

Several hours were spent in cross examination, questioning who had given the orders to have them put together and why, why she'd left them alone, what she'd done to mitigate risk of injury prior to leaving them alone, why she'd waited so long to check on Little Flower after the sensors indicated a problem, what she had witnessed when she re-entered the room, and why her initial report did not mention rape or mating.

"When I entered his room to find out what was wrong, I found him beating her. She was already unconscious and the rape completed before I entered. We believe he may have been continuing to beat her to hide his other actions. He had not shown the arousal we had identified as a wish to mate in any of our prior visits, nor was he showing so when I entered. I forcibly separated the two and brought her in for treatment. I missed the signs of mating on my scans as I was focused on treating her broken ribs, concussion, and the cuts and bruises that covered most of her body. We...I thought that her suicide attempt was due to advanced stages of isolation sickness, having fought with the first person she'd seen since being placed in quarantine, and not rape. To be honest, the thought that he would or even could rape her, never crossed my mind. Not only did we believe her to be too young to mate, I had never even heard of the term until Healer Chenzira informed me of Little Flower's accusation. I reviewed the footage and scans and confirmed that a mating had occurred, and that she appeared to be pregnant. Healer Chenzira informed me that rape is something not normally taught about until after we earn our masters. I was still a journeyman at that time."

One of the Water Sprite councilors expressed his disbelief that she didn't know what rape was and pressed her on it.

"Councilor, my species requires significant medical intervention in order to successfully mate, as we no longer have true males. Mating happens only once or twice in our lifetimes, if we choose it, and without the female being in heat our males don't react."

"So, your species can't force a mating?" he pressed, still not convinced, and speaking out of turn. However, Tabor didn't stop it.

Brice hesitated and looked over in the direction of Senior Healer Witherspoon, who was sitting in the guild section. They did not have a vote, but they could attend any session, and as there was a good chance Witherspoon would be called upon to testify later, it was not surprising that she was there.

"You need to answer the question, Healer Morningstar," Tabor commanded.

Witherspoon frowned, and hit her button to speak. Tabor raised a brow at the intervention, but allowed it.

"Senior Councilors, the short answer is yes, it is possible. For more than that, I would respectfully request that this particular line of questioning be continued in private, to protect the members of my species. With regards to Healer Morningstar's comment, she is correct. We do not teach healers about rape, how it can occur, or how to recognize that it has happened until after they earn their masters, as we want to ensure that information is not misused. As it has not occurred for millennia among our species, there has been little need to teach it sooner."

Tabor considered Witherspoon's comments and then nodded. "This Council honors your request. We will take a twenty minute recess. Senior Healer Witherspoon, Councilor Current, please join the Senior Council in our conference room."

The Council rose with the Seniors and Witherspoon walked down out of her guild box and across the chamber, while the councilor who had asked the question disappeared through the hole in the floor. Jessica indicated her need to use the hole of muck and Marcus led her and Marsee, who had crossed the chamber to join them, out of the chamber to show them where the nearest one was. To her utter embarrassment it was a communal room with a dozen dastardly dugouts of doom, and a long line of people waiting.

"Is there somewhere else we can go?" Jessica asked, face red with embarrassment.

"It will take longer to get there than to wait," Marcus said as the line moved forwards.

"It's not that... It's a cultural thing. I can't go in front of everyone," Jessica said.

Marcus frowned. "I don't understand," he signed.

Jessica sighed. "I don't want to get this beautiful outfit dirty, and we don't remove our clothing or expose ourselves in front of others, except with our family or our mates, even to use the hole of muck," Jessica explained. "To do so would be considered very rude and potentially be seen as a desire to mate."

"Oh, that makes so much more sense," Marsee replied. "I always wondered why you wanted privacy for such a natural function."

Marcus pinched the bridge of his nose and muttered something under his breath. "Forgive me, Ambassador. I should have realized. Come, my office isn't far," Marcus said, and then growled something at the other Councilors waiting in line who all looked shocked and highly amused by whatever it was that he'd muttered the moment before, which made Marsee snicker and her tail curl, as did the others.

"What did he say?" Jessica asked, as they followed behind Marcus.

"I'm an idiot," Marsee translated, with another snicker. "And, 'Yes, you heard me right. Even the mighty Marcus Surellis can make stupid mistakes. I allow myself one every hundred years or so. Consider your-self lucky enough to witness it.'"

Jessica laughed and Marcus's ears flicked back. He turned to see if they'd tried to get his attention with a raised brow. Both Marsee and Jessica burst out laughing. Marcus snorted, rolled his eyes, and kept walking. They were both still snickering when they returned to the council chamber and Marsee's tail was curled as she walked over and sat down at her place by the Seniors podium to wait. It was closer to half an hour before the Senior Council returned, and they continued on with the session.

There were no further questions for Brice, so Marcus called forth Myra next, to give her testimony, including her involvement with Little Flower at the Agency, and her assessment of isolation sickness, as well as her experiences with Little Flower in her home and the friendship between Little Flower and her daughter. Myra spoke of the compassion she'd shown in rescuing belongings that she knew were prized by Marsee, at the risk to herself during the sandstorm. She described her help in gathering food, and her suggestion of using face clothing to pre-vent breathing in the sand, and how it could also be used as a low-cost method to prevent transmission of illness, which they were studying to determine the most effective fabric to use, and how those initial trials were proving her information to be correct.

Myra then spoke of her assistance in saving the chenzie, and her suggestion to fetch her grandfather who had been an animal healer on his planet prior to the Cataclysm. That suggestion had saved, not just the chenzie and her cub, but also the lives of several other creatures since, and was being evaluated for use as a possible treatment to avoid having to cut the cubs out on their own species as well.

She also mentioned the laser pointer as a way to stop young cubs from pouncing on tails. Video of Myra's grandchildren chasing the red dot was shown, to the laughter of the entire Council and one Councilor had actually thanked Little Flower on behalf of her currently shredded tail. They'd added this at the last minute in the hopes that it would soften the Senior Council towards Myra's children and grandchildren, should she be found complicit.

Myra was cross-examined for hours about her reasoning behind putting the bipeds together as treatment for isolation sickness, as well as her intentions and involvement in getting the Council to override their quarantine restrictions. She was asked to confirm that as her mentor she'd never taught Brice about rape, and why she had not reviewed the footage of the fight.

"While we regularly dealt with pregnancy at our clinic, we were not a registered mating clinic. The nearest one is in Sand Dune. Brice had more training than most of her rank with regards to dealing with pregnancy, miscarriage, and recognizing someone in heat, as with a nearly two hundred league radius of care and only three healers, she needed to be prepared for anything that might happen, when I was not there, but I never taught her about rape or how to spot it in our species, although she was taught how to recognize signs of physical abuse. The medical scanners are programmed to recognize signs of a potential rape in our species, and flag scans for review by a master level healer. However, for the bipeds, we didn't have a full hormonal cycle yet, or even samples of the males' sperm to program into the scanners to alert on it. I trust my healers to do their job. I've worked with Senior Healer Morningstar for decades, and have never found reason to question her judgment. Her intuition and attention to detail make her one of the finest healers I've had the privilege to work with. When her report indicated it had been a fight, I saw no reason to investigate further and chose instead to reinstitute supervised visits."

"Did you review the medical scans yourself?" the next councilor asked.

"Not until Little Flower's accusation. At that point, Brice was far more of an expert in biped anatomy and care than I was, and she stated that Little Flower's injuries had all been successfully treated, which they were. They were all within her level of authorized care as a journeyman at the time. After that, I was focusing my attention on trying to get the Council to let us foster her and help with evacuating the flyers habitat when their environmental systems failed. Brice found no indication of any physical injuries bad enough to make her stop eating or drinking, so we assumed that she was suffering from a critical case of isolation sickness and depression brought on by her beating. I saw no reason to doubt her."

When Myra left the stand and took a seat in the witness area next to Brice she looked like she'd been run over by a herd of chenzies. The Council had not been kind to her, and it was fairly clear how they felt about her actions.

As his next witness, Marcus called the Senior Guild Master to the stand. She gave her assessment of Little Flower's artwork in use of early communication. They'd carefully curated the drawings to be shown to not only highlight Jessica's skill, but to show her growing friendship with Marsee and the others. They also showed the video Marsee had taken to prove that she was the artist, and pointed out the flag above her. The only question Ellie was asked afterwards was what level ranking she would give Little Flower if she were a member of the Guild.

"Should she ever choose to join the Guild, I would immediately award her level three master artist." This caused quite the stir among the Council and Little Flower was stunned at the praise. Level three was only one rank below a local guild master and something very few people ever earned, if she understood the ranking system correctly.

When Ellie left the stand, Little Flower signed her a quick thank you.

"You earned it. Please think about joining the Guild. We'd love to have you as a member," Ellie signed back, and took her seat, returning to her guild box rather than sitting in the witness booth.

Sina was conferenced in next, as she had been unable to make the journey to Council City, at the orders of her own healer. The day before, while in a hurry as she prepared to leave, she'd stepped on one of her sibling's toys, which had been left on a flight of stairs, and ended up with a badly broken leg. Calling from her room in the Trauma Center, Sina spoke of the sign language she'd developed and started teaching among her local deaf community, and then gave her assessment on Little Flower's language abilities and speed at which she'd picked up sign, and her belief that Little Flower was not merely trained to respond to specific commands like a domestic animal. By consensus, Sina signed her responses, even though she could speak.

"She is no more a trained domestic animal than I am. Little Flower's people have a rich and complex written language, which she has provided us as she's learned each sign. She assisted Translator Chenzira in demonstrating hundreds, if not thousands of new signs that have been added to the language reference in the past month, and used that information to translate the Charter for her people. She's also provided drawings, where applicable, which has proved invaluable when teaching young cubs who have not yet learned to read. Since she does not have the same anatomy as we do, missing a tail, movable ears, whiskers, and claws, we've had to make modifications for the signs we use. Those modifications are being picked up by the deaf community already, as being both far easier to sign and more accessible, as they can be performed by any of the sentient species. Should she be admitted to the Consortium and their official language designated as sign, we would be required by law to include that in our education programs, giving us a universal language that we can all speak. Translator Chenzira has jumpstarted us on that process by providing translations for the four other species as well. This is something I have been trying to bring before our Local Council for the past several years to help our deaf community."

This caused a huge stir in the Council, especially among the Water Sprites, which Tabor let continue for a few moments. During that time Senior Councilor Clear Seas, from the Water World, indicated his wish to speak. It was highly unusual for a senior councilor to ask questions of witnesses in a Full Council trial, to the point where it was almost, but not quite law. They were there to observe and listen, not cross examine. It was even rarer for a senior councilor from any but the host planet to ever speak. This caused immediate and total silence in the room. Tabor did not have to allow him to speak, as the Senior of the hosting planet, but she immediately gave him the floor.

Clear Seas floated up from his seat, and in a slow, yet hauntingly beautiful and melodic voice, spoke. "Following the testimony of the Senior Guild Master, Ambassador Little Flower said something to her. Can you tell me what this sign means?" Clear Seas made a motion with his webbed hands.

"I can, Your Honor. It means, 'thank you'."

"That is as I believed. The recommendation to use sign as a universal language was passed on to me shortly after you began teaching Little Flower, and I have been very curious to see just how effective this language is. I will be honest, I did not expect much past being able to communicate the basics, even after examining your reference that day. But I have been watching the communication between the Ambassador, her advocate, and translator, and I have come to the same conclusion as you. Even without knowing the actual meaning of these signs, this language still conveys meaning and intent. Even a basic version of this sign language would be highly valuable for our species, as we struggle to communicate with our peers from the other worlds. It is very...difficult...for most of us to make the sounds you use to communicate, and takes decades of practice to become fluent in even our official language. The other languages are even harder, as there are many sounds we just cannot make. I wish to say to you, 'thank you' for giving us this language. Regardless of the outcome of this trial, I will be bringing this language back to our people and petitioning for Sina's Language to become our official language as well." The 'thank you' had been signed and not spoken.

She signed back and said "You're very welcome, Your Honor," and then bowed her head in recognition of the honor the Senior Councilor bestowed on her by naming the language after her.

"That is all I have to say," Clear Seas said, and floated back down into his seat.

After that there were no further questions asked of Sina, and Marcus decided not to call his parents, deciding instead to end on Clear Seas ringing endorsement. Neither he or Jer could be called as witnesses, nor could GrandFather give witness for Little Flower since he wasn't recognized as sentient yet, although he could be called for cross examination later. They'd discussed bringing Serin and Nazari forth as witnesses, but decided there was little they could add, that hadn't already been stated, although they had given statements, as had Marcus and Jer's parents.

"That concludes my list of witnesses," Marcus informed the Council.

"With the conclusion of the Ambassador's witness testimony, this session is now in recess. We will return in one hour to begin cross examinations. Dismissed."

"All rise as the Senior Council leaves the chamber!" came the same booming voice from before and everyone rose and waited until they'd left, before beginning discussions on the morning's events.

# CHAPTER 30

# Jessica: Cross Examination

They retreated to the suite for a quick meal and to discuss how the trial had gone so far. At this point they were fairly hopeful that Brice would be acquitted, following the unexpected testimony of the Guild's Senior Healer, although they were less sure about Myra's case. There had been very little discussion about the Council's involvement in the decisions, which surprised everyone, and led Marcus to believe that most were likely taking Jer's public statement of guilt as an established fact, although with the cross examination to come, it was really anyone's guess. Clear Seas' statement though, made them all hopeful that Little Flower would be deemed sentient.

After having a few bites to eat and something to drink, Marsee retreated to her room and put her hearing aids in, trying to recover her strength and composure before she had to go back out on the floor again. The hour was quickly over, and after retrieving Marsee from the bedroom, they made their way back down and took their places again.

"All rise as the Senior Council enters and takes their seats!"

The councilors all walked in and sat down. "This Council is back in session," Tabor announced, without standing. "We will continue with the cross examination of Ambassador Little Flower. Ambassador, please stand."

Jessica stood.

"Are there any councilors who wish to question the Ambassador?" Tabor asked.

The lights on the front of many of the councilor's desks flashed, indicating their desire to speak. The giant monitors changed to display the order in which they submitted their request. As the cross examination continued, councilors could indicate their desire to speak, and be added to the list, or cancel their request if someone else asked their question, and they were content with the reply. They would be allowed one question and then go to the end of the line for their next one.

"Do you believe you are sentient?" the first councilor asked.

"Yes," she replied simply. "I do."

"What do your people call themselves and the planet you came from?"

This was a question they'd expected and she spoke the words 'human' and 'Earth' aloud, but she knew that most couldn't hear it. Marsee had worked carefully with GrandFather to learn how to say those two words and repeated them so that the others could hear, as well as learning how to say her full name, which apparently was a real mouthful and challenge for the cats to say. They could all hear his deeper voice better, and he could hear Marsee reasonably well, but not the others, although he'd told her it sounded mostly like growls and hisses, and he had a hard time telling one word from another.

She'd thought for a long time on the best way to translate it, and the signs she'd wanted to use to represent her people going forward. "Our world had many languages and every language had its own words for our people and planet. Our scientific communities even had their own words as well. In my language, we called our planet 'Earth'" which she spelled out. It roughly means 'soil' or 'ground' in your language. Sometimes we would refer to it as Mother Earth or Terra. For our people, we called ourselves 'human'. The closest translation to the sounds that make up that word, that I've learned so far, would be hue-man, with the first part meaning different colors or shades, while the second meaning people. The scientific term for our species, which was in one of our old languages, no longer spoken, except in the scientific community, roughly meant 'The wise man', or so I've been told, but I think that sounds arrogant. I will be submitting 'hue-man' for our official species name, should we be accepted."

"On the day of the Cataclysm, what happened to you and what did you believe was happening to your planet?"

She took a deep breath to give herself a moment to compose her thoughts. "When the asteroid hit, I was in school taking a test on one of the many spoken languages of my world. I was knocked unconscious by the shockwave and woke to find my school and town utterly destroyed. I was badly injured, dizzy, and confused. I had absolutely no idea what was going on. My best friend had been sitting next to me, and she had been partially buried in the rubble of our school. I unburied her to find that she had been killed instantly. A large beam from the roof had fallen and crushed her head." She paused to push down the grief she felt at the memory of her friend's death and give Marsee time to catch up.

"Running from the horror of my friend's injuries and death, I climbed out of the building onto the street, and tried to make my way to safety, although for a while I walked in a daze, not really seeing any-thing around me. I'm not really sure for how long. There were several large earthquakes but that didn't seem to match the immense damage that I saw. I thought perhaps a volcano had erupted due the ash that started falling. Then I noticed that all of the trees had been knocked over in the same direction. This made me believe that there had been some kind of explosion, so I followed the downed trees hoping to find safety as I got further away. Everything was destroyed and burning. There was ash and smoke everywhere, making it hard to see and breathe. The people I came across were all dead and things did not get better as I had expected. Eventually I made it to the center of my small town and noticed something large flying overhead, but I couldn't tell what it was. I hoped it was someone looking for survivors, so I waved but the shape flew on. A minute or two later a member of your species appeared out of the smoke. At first I thought I was hallucinating from the injury to my head, but then they stopped and raised something at me that I believed to be a weapon of some kind. I turned to run but something hit me in the back, and that is the last thing I remembered until I woke up at the Agency."

Several lights went off with her answer.

"What made you believe it was a weapon?" came the next question.

This was coming dangerously close to questions she did not want to answer, but this was a question they'd prepared for. "Like you, my people have a long history of storytelling for entertainment. As we had never met another sentient species before, we used to make up all kinds of stories about what first contact would be like, and why they would be there, and whether or not they'd be a friend or enemy. One of the most common themes among those stories was that this other species was coming to take our world from us, to hold us against our wills, and make us do what they wanted."

Dozens of lights came on at that answer. Which they'd expected.

"You mentioned that you thought the damage was from an explosion. What did you believe caused that explosion?"

"There were chemicals on our world that were highly flammable and explosive and needed to be handled with great care. Some were used for energy sources. Another was used as part of the process to make fertilizer for our crops. When I was a very small cub a large shipment of this chemical was in one of our port cities and a fire broke out in the building next to where it was being stored. This chemical exploded, destroying much of that city and killing hundreds of people. After your species arrived however, I was fairly certain you had attacked and destroyed our planet."

Several lights went off with this answer and she breathed a little easier.

"Did you ever believe we were there to save you?" asked the next Councilor.

"No," she answered simply. "I had no reason to. My home was destroyed and I'd been shot and captured, and while my injuries were being cared for, I was also locked in my room, like a prisoner."

"Did the idea of quarantine ever cross your mind?"

"No," she replied.

"If not quarantine, why did you believe you were being held?"

"At first, I had no idea. I knew my arm had been badly broken, and I woke to find a strange cast on my arm. I was in significantly less pain than I had been in before, although I was still very dizzy and confused. When Healer Morningstar entered my room, I had no idea who she was or what she wanted, but she was kind and patient, and gave me time to get used to her presence before she treated my injuries, so I guessed she was a healer. I was taken out of my room once, when my broken arm became infected, and treated, and I saw others of my kind being treated, or so it appeared. While I recovered from my injuries, I thought I was just in a very strange alien hospital, but I didn't have any idea why you'd taken me captive after destroying my world and were bothering to heal me. I thought perhaps you intended to put me to work once my injuries were healed. Later, when my injuries were as fully healed as possible, and I was still kept in that room for what felt like an eternity, I was at a loss for why I was still there. For a while, I thought I was being held in a habitat for wild animals, and imagined that people were watching me through the walls, or on cameras for entertainment. I was given more and more complex puzzle boxes and toys to pass the hours, so I thought maybe I was being tested to see how smart I was. I was not asked to do anything or communicated with in any way outside of basic hand signals, and for all but a few minutes a day I was left alone with my thoughts. After a while though, the toys stopped coming. I wasn't sure if I'd failed some test or not, but eventually I stopped caring about everything. One day, Healer Morningstar stayed rather than just dropping off my food and leaving. I thought she was trying to communicate with me, build a relationship with me, so I offered her some of my food as a gesture of friendship. One day, when I was feeling especially lonely, I gathered the courage to lean up against her, and she hugged me with her tail. But the very next day the visits stopped, and I didn't know why. I thought maybe she'd gotten in trouble for doing so, or that maybe I'd done something wrong but I had no idea what. Then one day I was brought to a room with another of my species. We didn't know why we were being held there, but I cherished the time we spent together, until that last day anyway. After he raped me, I believed I was being held as breeding stock and completely lost my will to live. I did not want any child I had to be raised in captivity. I tried to take my own life by refusing to eat or drink. Later, after I'd been brought to the Chenziras, I thought that maybe I'd been held on a ship for all that time and had just arrived at your world. That was until Marsee showed me how close the Agency was to her home. I eventually decided that I was being bred and kept as a pet or domestic animal, as I was being cared for by what appeared to be one of your children, and forced to wear a harness and leash just to go outside and down to the waste room."

Tabor paused for several long moments before calling for the next question and Jessica maintained eye contact with her the entire time. To her surprise Tabor looked away first and called the next name. Jessica wondered what the Senior Councilor was thinking.

"Do you believe that the male who raped you, also believed that was why you were being held, as breeding stock?"

"Yes. He said as much. He tried to convince me to mate with him at first, using that as an excuse, saying we had no choice, that you would keep us there until we mated."

"Were you given any indication by Healer Morningstar that she wanted you to mate?"

"No. Mostly she just observed. Occasionally, she joined in play with us. When she left us alone, she gave us no indication of what she expected of us, and I received no indication from her that she was unhappy with me, when she brought me back to my room after the first few times that she left us alone. In fact, I didn't even know what he was intending when he first touched me. We were both so starved for touch that we regularly held hands, hugged, and leaned up against each other."

"Is that considered normal mating practice for your species?"

"Holding hands and hugging?" she asked for confirmation. The councilor nodded. "Yes and no. Everything we'd done prior to that was something that we would do with close friends and family too. There are parts of our body that only our mates touch. He never touched me in a way that made me think he wanted to mate with me, before that day. It wasn't until he started rubbing my upper leg that I realized what he intended."

"What made you believe that it was the intention of Healer Morningstar and the Agency that you were breeding stock? Was it just what the male told you or something else?"

"We were naked and denied clothing the entire time we were there. For my people clothing isn't just for protection. We cover that area of our body until we mate. How much would be covered depended on the area of the world where you lived. Also, I yelled for help and begged to leave, but nobody came. Many times in the past, when I was sick or needed help, Healer Morningstar would appear and offer treatment without me having to even ask, so I knew I was being watched somehow. Afterwards, she brought another male to my room and I figured it was because...326 wasn't successful in getting me pregnant."

"Were you ever harmed by Healer Morningstar or any of the people who have cared for you since your arrival?"

"No, quite the opposite. They have all cared for me, healed my injuries multiple times, invented clothing to protect me from the heat of your world, and helped me learn to speak, read, and write. They taught me your culture, and helped me prepare for this meeting. The Chenziras have treated me as family from the moment I arrived, even if I didn't recognize it."

"Is rape or violence common on your world or were his actions a novel thing brought on by your long stay in isolation?"

This was the question they were hoping wouldn't be asked. She paused trying to decide what to say. They had argued for days about how to answer this.

"You need to answer the question, Ambassador," Tabor ordered.

"I intend to, Your Honor. I am trying to find the right words," she explained, and Tabor nodded and gave her the time she needed. Finally, she made up her mind and continued. "My Advocate and I have had many long conversations on how best to answer this question. The whole point of this trial is to answer that question, is it not, Councilor? If my people are truly sentient, how could one of my people have done what my rapist did to me? I could stand here and tell you that no it is not common on my world, that his actions were brought on by months of captivity, isolation, and misinterpretation of your intentions, but I would be lying."

This caused a stir as the translation came through. Marcus signaled his desire to speak to her privately, which was granted. "Are you sure you want to do this?" he asked her once the privacy shield was up. "This isn't what we agreed upon."

"I know you all think I should paint my people in the best possible way, but what happens when one of my people hurts someone else? It would be incredibly naive of me to believe that everyone will just change overnight. Are you really advocating that I should lie to the Council?" Jessica asked.

Marcus frowned but finally shook his head. "No. To do so now would be pointless and you would be seen as being in contempt if you tried to take back what you just said. Focus on your desire to change your people for the better."

She nodded and hit the privacy screen.

"Are you ready to continue?" Tabor asked.

"I am, Your Honor. There were close to eight billion people on my world and most of them were good, honest, hardworking individuals, who wanted nothing more than to be able to care for their families and live a long and happy life. There were people who gave back to the communities they lived in, who gave to strangers in need, and who worked hard to secure a better future for everyone. Like you, we had our own healers, teachers, and crafters. We made beautiful works of art, dance, and music. We had skilled scientists and we reached for the stars and put people on our moon. We sent drones to far away planets and sent out calls to see if there was anyone else in the universe, or if we were truly all alone."

She paused to let Marsee catch up and took a quick sip of the drink that had been provided to her before moving on. "You kept us in isolation for months to ensure we were free from disease, but the sad truth is the disease you should have been worried about is not one made of bacteria and viruses. It's one that you would never pick up on a scanner, a disease so powerful that it has killed more of my people for thousands if not hundreds of thousands of years. It is a disease of hate and greed, and a lust for power, a darkness that infects our very souls and can spread faster than any pandemic. We had scientists who studied the past trying to find out where we came from and in every generation, in every legend passed down, and even in the bones we dug up out of the earth there was evidence of this disease, of rape, war, and murder, of holding people against their will and making them do what they wanted. You do not have a word for this or many of the things my people have done in our past, and I wish we didn't either."

She paused as Tabor had to silence the room again, and continued when prompted. "Perhaps there was a good reason for this in our past. I do not know. We are small and do not have the teeth and claws of a predator, so we made our own. Perhaps at first this was only to defend ourselves from larger predators, like the felines you rescued only much bigger, or used to secure food. But over time, we became the most dangerous predator on our planet. So much so, that many species on our planet went extinct long before the asteroid hit. Our scientists who studied the ancient past, found evidence that there was once another species of man on our planet that showed every evidence of being as sentient as we were. They buried their dead, performed surgeries, and took care of their old, weak, and injured. We do not know what really happened to that species. Perhaps they did not adapt to changes in climate and just died off. Some say we mated and became one species. I am not a scientist so I do not know for sure. For much of our history we roamed our world in small tribes, each with their own culture and be-liefs. Often, when those tribes met, they would fight over the resources of the land, like any animal with its own territory. We eventually learned how to raise animals and grow our own food, and as our tribes became bigger so did our fights. The bigger you were, the more powerful. The more resources you could control meant you had a better chance of surviving, but there were many who were ruled by greed, wanting more than they needed to survive. They craved power and did whatever they could to secure that. Nothing was off limits to obtain it, and the more powerful you were, the more you could get away with."

She could see that Marsee was struggling to avoid showing emotion as she translated her words, so she paused and took another drink and only continued when Marsee gave her the slightest of nods.

"But throughout history, there were also people who fought against that disease, who taught hope, love, kindness, and forgiveness. Every tribe had their own...I do not have the word for it...belief in where we came from, who created us, and where we go when we die."

Marsee called for a stop, pulled out her tablet and looked up the sign and showed her.

"Every tribe had their own religion and every religion taught of the fight between good and evil, between hero and villain, to try to teach people to be better, to avoid the darkness and disease of evil, but sometimes even those religions got too big and became just as infected by the darkness. The worst of our leaders would rape and kill their own people, just because they had the power and ability to do so. What they said was absolute law, and there was often very little anyone could do or say to stop it." Tabor swallowed and gave her a slight nod that she understood the implied warning.

"As our tribes and fights grew, we made bigger and deadlier weapons, weapons that could kill from a distance, weapons big enough to level a city bigger than this one in an instant. A hundred years ago, our time, my people used those weapons in the biggest fight our world had ever seen. It spanned the entire world and lasted for four of our years and killed more people than any other fight in our history ever had. My people ended that fight by using those weapons on three of our enemies' cities, killing hundreds of thousands of innocent people in the process. Since then, our world has been at a bit of a stalemate, with fights more localized and people trying to end the fighting through peaceful means, but it was not always successful and we still continued to make deadlier weapons hoping that the horror of the destruction they would cause would be enough to stop the infected from using them. Before your people showed up, I thought that was what happened to my world. Nothing else seemed big enough."

Every single councilor had their light on at this point, but she continued and Tabor didn't stop her.

"For a while my people thought we had beaten back the disease. As technology suddenly allowed us to easily make friends and communicate with people from around the world, we began forming a consortium with our neighbors and signed treaties to dismantle our weapons. We taught our children of the great wars and tried to teach them to be better than the generation before. Many districts came together and started sharing ideas and started learning to treat people as equals not less than because of the place they were born, their sex, their religion, or even the color of their skin, or who they loved. We built great cities with towers that could hold fifty thousand people or more and we called our district the great melting pot, where all people could come together and live in peace. But not everyone wanted peace. Some still craved power but were now just less obvious about it. One day a small group of people took control of four shuttles carrying hundreds of our people and flew them into those towers, into our Council City, and the disease infected our people once more. Hatred at the people who had done that horrible crime spread faster than any pandemic, and people called out for blood, not just of the people who had done the crime, but anyone who looked like them. We spent twenty of our years locked in bloodshed to get back at those who had hurt us, and yet we still lost. Our communities suffered as our resources went into that great fight. People starved as those with power took control of our Council. All in the name of fighting this great evil. But that was just an excuse for those in power to gain more power at our expense. But even in the midst of that darkness, people fought back with love. Communities took in stranded passengers on the other shuttles in the air that day as the air space was closed. Volunteers raced to help dig out survivors from the collapsed towers and treat the wounded. Many died that day trying to put out the fires, but the buildings collapsed on them before they could, and before they could get everyone out. Many on our Council spoke out about the great evil and how we should not meet hatred with hatred, but they were not listened to, and our great melting pot cracked and burned, and our freedoms were stripped away one, by one, by one, willingly given up for nothing more than the illusion of safety."

She turned to face the Councilor who had asked the question. "You asked if rape and violence was common on my world and the horrible answer is yes. Sometimes I think that is all we know. Part of my schooling was how to protect myself from my peers infected with this disease. We would practice hiding, practice how to escape, and how to fight back. A year before the asteroid destroyed my planet, one of my very own classmates was infected and he killed three of my classmates and one of my teachers, injuring several more before he killed himself. We made an artform out of fighting and we even fought over whose artform was better. As a small child I was taught one of these artforms to try to protect me from those that would do me harm, because one in every three or four of our females would be raped or beaten in their lifetime. More often than not these actions were performed by the people they knew and trusted, by people in authority, by our leaders, and even by the very guard that was supposed to protect us, by partners or those you were thinking about partnering with, by family members, and far, far too often children would be beaten and raped by their very own parents. My training did me no good. I was weak and weaponless, locked in a room with no way out, and no way to defend myself, but I fought back with everything I had anyway. It just wasn't enough."

She stopped and clenched her fists, taking several deep shuddering breaths to bring herself back under control. Tabor waited for her to continue.

"I do not know the quality or character of the people you rescued, but I know that some, like my grandfather, are good, honest, caring individuals, that would do anything to help someone in need, who would put themselves in harm's way to stop the evil. His first action upon leaving the Agency was to help a dying chenzie and her cub, after all. But our people are infected with a disease and it's clear to me that at least one individual brought that disease with them, and it would be incredibly naive of me to think he was the only one. By your standards, that would mean our people are not sentient, and are still animals. I believe most of my people *are* sentient, but I cannot guarantee it. I cannot guarantee we did not bring more darkness with us. I have been told that thousands of years ago your people went through a Great Awakening where things like that used to happen, where your people were infected with a disease you called psychosis, where you destroyed your planet and had to move to this one, and yet you managed to come through that, and become the caring sentient people I have grown to know and love in my short time on your world. My people are in the midst of our own awakening, and we could really use your help and guidance to make it through that transition."

All of the lights went off, save one.

"Do you believe that your people are capable of making that transition, if we gave you that help, without infecting or harming us with this disease?"

"I cannot guarantee that all of my people are good, or that violence won't happen in the future, and frankly neither can you. If you could, there wouldn't be guards posted at the doors and around this very room." She pointed in the direction of the two guards stationed around the Senior Councilors entrance. The councilor nodded the point, and she continued. "What I do believe, with all my heart, is that we are all capable of making that transition. I've experienced that transformation for myself. When the Chenzira's took me in I was filled with so much anger and loathing, that I wanted nothing more than to harm the people that I believed had killed my family, that had hurt me, forced me to mate, and kept me in captivity for so long that I almost forgot what the stars looked like. But their infinite patience brought me out of that dark place and replaced it with light and love and compassion. I know it will take time, and I know we'll make mistakes, but I want that same chance for the rest of my people, for our children, more than anything in the universe."

The last light went off and no more came on.

Tabor sat and waited several moments to see if anyone else had questions before standing. "The cross examination of Little Flower is complete. Ambassador, you may be seated."

She sat down hard, her legs shaking from the ordeal. Marcus reached over and put one of his paws on hers and squeezed lightly and she looked up at him. He was tense, but his expression was a calm mask and he nodded slightly. She shrugged. She'd done what she thought was right and it was now out of her hands.

"Does anyone wish to call a witness for further cross examination?" Tabor asked. Surprisingly, none came on and after a few moments Tabor continued. "Then this investigation is now complete and this Council is in recess until all councilors have submitted their votes and the Senior Council has made their decision. Dismissed."

# CHAPTER 31

# Jeran: Duty

J er sat at his desk for several hours, long after everyone else had voted and left the chamber. Only a handful of guards remained to keep him company. They stood silent, watching the entrances, as he stared at his desk, trying to force himself to submit his vote. With a sigh he looked up, praying to the Ancient Gods to give him strength, but instead made eye contact with the guard outside of the Senior Councilor's entrance, and breathed deeply as Senior Honor Guard Kendra Hunt stared back at him. He had seen her kill on many occasions throughout his career, as she usually performed the test for those on the watch list, and dealt with the consequences when they inevitably failed, and more than likely it would be her that would execute the Councils orders. It would be her he would have to fight, not just Tabor, if it came to that.

Almost as if reading his thoughts, her eyes narrowed at him and he looked away. Swallowing hard to contain the sob that wanted to break free and with a shaking paw, he finally performed what he knew was likely his last action as a councilor and perhaps his very life. He shut his desk down and left with a hurry, trying to distance himself from those actions, but took the long way back to his suite, unable to face his family and the decisions he'd made.

He and Marcus had spent hours crafting Jer's response to the various votes, but he had found it almost impossible to submit. On the question of Little Flower's sentience and inclusion, the answer was an easy and obvious yes. As he had not been able to be called as a witness on her behalf, he submitted his own observations, including the severe risk she'd made in offering to help find a way to cure his daughter's psychosis. They had decided not to bring that up during the trial to protect Marsee, but their reports had all been submitted, so it was already known to Senior Councilor Tabor anyway, and the vote itself would be marked as private due to the fact that his entire council was on trial. Only the Senior Council would see what he wrote.

"I don't know if it was Little Flower's friendship and absolute trust in my daughter, or the use of sign language that snapped Marsee out of her psychosis, but Little Flower not only saved my daughter's life, she quite likely saved every child in the future from this horrible disease. Even the hope of a cure is more than we've ever had before. She risked her life to save my daughter and I will never be able to repay her for that. I don't know what will happen to me or to my partner, or if the Senior Council will find Little Flower sentient, but I ask the Council to look out for her and GrandFather, if I cannot, and place their care in that of my parents, rather than returning her to the Agency, if she is not found sentient. I believe that if she were forced to return, she would take her own life. She has shown the capacity for love and kindness and I truly believe her people deserve a chance to grow and learn as she has."

On the question of the complicit nature of everyone else implicated during the trial, and his recommendation for punishment, there wasn't a yes or no answer, but simply an open-ended comment section. He stared at that blank box for hours before copying his answer in and submitting it. He knew he was likely signing his own death warrant and that of his partners, but he prayed that it would be enough to save everyone else. The problem was, he had no idea how the Council would vote after Little Flower's testimony.

Only the guards patrolling the complex were out and awake as he wandered, lost in thought, and for that he was grateful. Passing a small fountain and garden, he sat on the edge and trailed his paw in the cool water, wondering if he would see the garden of his home again, or if it would only be to bury his partner. He knew that if the Council went with precedent, his family would likely never speak to him again. Tears streamed silently down his face as he tried to bring his fear and grief back under control, and failed miserably.

"Councilor, is there a problem?" a quiet voice asked, and he looked up in surprise to see the Senior Honor Guard, looking down at him.

Jer wiped the tears off his face and looked away. "Sometimes, the weight of my oath is just too painful to bear," he said quietly, as Kendra sat down next to him. She did not press, but after a while he continued anyway. "My own death, I would gladly give to repay the harm we have caused, and to ensure Little Flower and her people the freedoms and rights they deserve, as I know my partner would. Even though it broke my heart to do as I swore to do, I fear that our sacrifice won't be enough to save them or my children and grandchildren."

"What do you mean?" Kendra asked.

Jer sat, listening to the water trickle for a long time before answering. He was treading dangerously close to treason with this conversation, and he knew it. Kendra had the authority to kill him without trial if she felt he was a risk, but he decided to take the chance. He didn't know what else to do. "I am terrified that the Seniors will decide that Little Flower and her people are too dangerous to keep around after her testimony today, and I don't know how to protect her or them. And if the Seniors go with precedent, and Myra or I are found guilty of collusion, I don't know how I will save Marsee or.."

"Do you believe your daughter is a risk if they vote for your death? I am aware she was placed on the watch list and have read her report," she interrupted, her voice stern and full of command, insistent that he answer.

His head snapped up, now even more terrified for Marsee. "No. Not at all," he replied emphatically. "She's in full control. Marcus and I have tested her daily. I wouldn't have believed it, if I hadn't seen it with my own eyes, but sign language cuts through where speech does not. I promise you."

Kendra tilted her head in acknowledgement of that statement. "For our children's sake I pray that it is as true as it appears to be. I have seen little today that would make me believe she is a risk," she stated, and Jer sighed with relief. "But we will continue to watch for the standard term, if you cannot, even if she's not on the watch list anymore. We need to fully understand this new development," she added. Jer frowned but nodded his understanding. He'd half expected it anyway. He'd honestly been surprised Kendra hadn't shown up at the compound anyway after Marsee's report had been submitted.

She was quiet for a few moments. "Do you truly believe that the Seniors will harm Little Flower or her people?"

"Yes," he stated. "I do. Especially if the people call for it. What's five hundred and twelve lives of a potentially violent nature in exchange for avoiding the consequences of their own decisions and the censure and economic hardship of a billion people. Either way, Myra and I will likely die to give the Council someone to blame, and with us my children..."

"Your children are not on trial, Councilor," Kendra interrupted again, this time with a frown of confusion.

Jer explained the precedent from the last rape trial. Kendra sat silently, face a complete mask as he explained. "I can only pray that the Seniors will take our suggestions. My children and grandchildren will probably hate us for the rest of their lives, but they'll live. If they don't..." Jer left unsaid what he would do if they went with the original precedent. Their suggestions were bad enough, unfair, and unjust, but precedent, and because of that, law.

Kendra was silent for a long time, and Jer wondered if he was going to be arrested with how intently she was staring at him. *Probably best if she did,* Jer thought glumly and looked away.

Eventually she stood and turned away from him to look at the fountain instead. So quietly he could barely hear her over the gentle murmur of the fountain, she spoke. "Your oath, as is mine, is foremost to protect the people, and that includes from the unjust actions of the Council. Your children and grandchildren are people too, and whether or not the Council admits it, so too are Little Flower's people. All people are innocent until proven guilty of a crime. What crime has any of them committed?"

Jer watched in astonishment as Kendra turned and walked away without a further word. *Is she honestly implying what I think she is?* Jer sat there for another hour contemplating what Kendra said, before deciding that either way, he would do everything he could to protect his children and the Hue-mans, even if that meant fighting the entire Council. If Kendra was impling what she was and backed him, he might stand a chance. With a heavy sigh, he stood and walked back to his suite, where he crawled into Myra's waiting arms, and lay there contemplating treason into the early hours of the morning.

# CHAPTER 32

# Kendra: Ancient Orders

Kendra left Councilor Chenzira in the courtyard. Outwardly her face was a mask, and her pace no different than normal, but inside her mind was racing. Chenzira's words weighed heavily on her, as did her oath. By all rights, she should have arrested him for suspicion of treason. But he hadn't acted on it yet, merely expressed his concerns and that wasn't a crime. He fully believed that the Senior Council would not only harm his children, but commit genocide against Little Flower's people, and frankly, if she were honest with herself, so did she. She'd been wrestling with many of those concerns for the past month.

She knew what the precedent for rape was and why it had been stripped from record, as did the rest of the senior guard. The punishment was far too horrifying to even consider, but it was precedent and therefore law. It had been secretly stripped millenia ago in the hopes that a new precedent would be set, if a rape ever occurred again. She'd been praying the Council wouldn't find that precedent in the archives, but apparently they had. *Marcus would have an ancient copy,* she muttered under her breath. Jer had explained what he had proposed to the Seniors as an alternative. It was better, but no less horrifying or unjust in her opinion.

She was already prepared to deal with that decision though. While she couldn't protect Jer or Myra, as they'd taken full responsibility for their actions, and she knew there was a very good chance they'd both die, by her own claws, she could and would protect their children from an unjust ruling. She just prayed that she'd have enough time to do so before Marsee lost control, as she knew it would be more than enough to put her over the edge, even if she hadn't been dealing with psychosis.

She had also watched or attended all of the Local Council meetings since word of the rape came through, and had gone back and watched many of the meetings prior. She hadn't been aware of the conditions in the Agency, even though she had guards posted there, including her own nephew, as they had not been permitted in the habitats for their own health and safety. By the time she'd found out the Hue-mans were being held in near absolute isolation, the Council had already rectified the situation by giving the Agency permission to do as they saw fit. She'd been under the impression that they were only being quarantined at the Agency, not isolated, and while she'd been aware that their budget had been reduced once the initial build-out had been completed, she'd not realized just how empty their chambers had been until she saw the footage from today.

She was horrified at what they'd been through and how she'd failed to protect them, and she had made changes to ensure that would never happen again. Guards were present at all official Council meetings, but many of the decisions had been made during committee meetings and out of the public eye, where guards rarely attended, unless requested for some reason. She'd been equally horrified and concerned by Little Flower's testimony about the world she'd come from, but impressed that she'd had the courage and honor to tell the Council the truth, and not try to hide it as many would, and as she knew the other species had in the past.

While she didn't know the other Seniors as well as she did Tabor, they had always acted with honor and integrity as far as she knew. She'd been fairly confident that the rest of the Full Council and Seniors would find in Little Flower's favor, as there was little reason for them not to, at least not until today. The other worlds would benefit greatly from her own worlds disgrace and the sanctions they faced, but now they had to weigh the very real risk of harm to their own people.

*Jeran is right to worry about Genocide*, Kendra thought. *In many ways that would be the easy answer. And the Council is right to worry about the threat the Hue-mans pose.*

She eventually made her way back to her office and activated her privacy shield, locked her door. and proceeded to pace for a long time, trying to make up her mind about what to do. Her oath was the was to the people and the people of the Consortium should come first, but the Hue-mans had no one to protect them. If she were to protect them, she would be committing treason, but if she didn't, who would? *Would Jeran? His life is already forfeit. He would fight for them, as would Myra and quite likely Marsee, but...Marsee...What am I going to do about her?*

Kendra shook her head, conflicted by Marsee and everything she represented. She'd read the report seven times in absolute disbelief. It didn't say who it was, but it didn't take much to figure out, not with the information she had, and Jeran had confirmed her suspicions tonight. She was astounded that Little Flower hadn't been killed with Marsee's first hunt. There had only ever been two options when it came to psychosis, you either killed off your instinct, like the guard did in secret, or it killed you. There was no other option for a guard. Training to fight always triggered psychosis. It was only a matter of how long it took.

From what Marsee had written, she should have transitioned, which in of itself would have been practically unheard of. No one transitioned without help. Only one person ever had, according to her knowledge. But Marsee had apparently lost herself completely to her instinct and had somehow managed to find her way back and regain full control of her instinct, at least according to her description. She had seen nothing to indicate Marsee was still struggling or lying about it. Only time would tell if it was sign language that made the difference, but she prayed it was. They lost far too many children to that horrible disease. Still, they had transitioned one guard since the report came in and while that had gone remarkably smoothly, they had transitioned as normal, not regained full control. Still the guard had been able to understand them, which was phenomenal.

She really wanted to test Marsee herself but she had orders not to, ancient orders from The General herself. *Ancient Gods, please let it not be her,* she prayed, not wanting to believe it, but all the signs were there.

Walking over to her bookcase she pulled down a small book and flipped it open to reveal an ornate key hidden inside. Taking the key out, she walked back to her ancient desk and fiddled with it until a hidden panel shifted, revealing a keyhole. After several turns, she heard a faint click and reached down under the desk to the hidden compartment that had popped open. Inside was an ancient piece of paper in a protective case. On it, the last order of their last general, long before the Great Awakening, and long before they'd even come to this world. Kendra had confirmed the handwriting matched the other journals she had from that time and every guard knew about the prophecy, but only the Senior Honor Guard and their second, knew about the orders. She'd been watching Marsee since she was born. Chenzira was a very uncommon name. Kendra ran her fingers lightly over the surface of the short letter written so long very ago and read it again, even though she had every word memorized.

*There will come a day when another bears my name, long after most of us have forgotten about the horrors of war. Thee will know it is her because she will do what no other has done before. Protect her as best you can, but do not test her or bring her into the guard until thee are sure she has transitioned on her own or she asks thee for thy help. Thy oath is to thy people and she is the only one that can save them from the horror to come. Her journey will not be easy but it is necessary if she is to see as I do. In all things follow her lead. If you are not sure of the path to take, do as she would do, and always honor thy oath.*

*General Marsee Ezabet Chenzira*

Even though she'd read it dozens of times over the past two decades, the message hit her harder than it ever had before. The feeling that she must act now, hit her so hard that she fell to her knees gasping. There was no doubt in her mind, Marsee had done what no other had done before in regaining control of her instinct. *So what would Marsee do now?* Kendra thought. *She would protect Little Flower and her people,* she decided. She stared at her orders for several long moments, trying to find the courage to commit treason as the feeling grew inside her to act, and to act quickly, before it was too late. **Your oath is to the people, not to the Council,** a voice in her head whispered, almost like her instinct, gone now nearly two hundred years.

She took a deep shuddering breath with a final look at that ancient document, stored it, and hid the key before sitting down at her desk and opening her tablet. As the Senior Honor Guard, she could access every security camera on the planet. She was the only one who could, outside of the Senior Council, and that included the security camera in the Senior's conference room. She'd never once accessed it though, as it was only there in the event something happened and they needed to gather evidence afterwards. Until now, they'd never needed it. The footage taken was deleted after a day and her access of that information would be logged, but what she didn't know was whether or not the Senior Council would be notified of that access or not, like they would be if she accessed their accounts. *More than likely,* she decided.

She tapped her claws on her desk for several minutes before deciding she needed to make precautions in case the Senior Council was notified, and called her nephew instead.

"Ma'am?" Avery asked when he picked up.

"What's your assessment on Marsee?" she asked.

"I saw no issues with her. I'm honestly more worried about her mother," he replied.

Kendra pursed her lips. The signs for psychosis could easily be mistaken for extreme anxiety, but there was little doubt in Kendra's mind that the Council would find Myra guilty, and Myra clearly knew what she was facing with that verdict. Psychosis or parental instinct, Myra would defend her cubs if the Council went with precedent. Kendra nodded. "My conclusion as well. They know about the precedent."

"I was afraid of that," he said with a frown. "I'll let the other's know. Do you want me to focus on Myra then, with the verdict?"

"Yes and no," she replied. "Let the others know and deal with it, but I want you to take your squad, along with squads five and six back to the Agency. I am worried that the Seniors will harm the Hue-mans after Little Flower's testimony today. If the Seniors should show up at the Agency before the end of the trial, do not let them out of your sight, even if they order you to leave. I will take full responsibility. Scan any shipments of food earmarked for the Hue-mans for poisons as well."

Avery frowned. "Do you really think they would?"

"I honestly don't know, but I'm not allowing genocide on my watch. The Hue-mans might have shown violence and come from a violent species, but so did we, and none of them have committed a crime outside of 326. The violence they've shown so far is directly related to their captivity and isolation, and that is not a crime, that's self defense and isolation sickness," Kendra replied. "Any of us would react the same, if not worse, if held in the same conditions they were kept in."

"And if the Seniors do try something?" Avery asked.

"Stun them and bring them back for trial, if you can," she replied. "If they bring a force with them, do your best to protect the Hue-mans and let me know. I'll send reinforcements. If something happens to me, assume they're planning something and get them out of there."

Avery looked away, considering her orders. She gave him that time. She knew what she was asking him to do.

"You're asking me to commit treason," he said, quietly.

"I am," she replied simply. "I honestly hope it won't come to that, but remember, our oath is to the people, not to the Council, and the Hue-mans don't have anyone else to protect them. They may not be citizens of the Consortium, but they are our wards and under our protection too."

"Yes, ma'am." Avery saluted and hung up.

She stared at the main screen of her tablet for a moment, praying she hadn't just sent her nephew to his death, but that was the risk she took with every order she gave. With a heavy sigh, she hit the icon for the security footage, and began watching the Senior's deliberations. Five minutes in, she grabbed the back of her scruff, in an attempt to contain her horror at what they were discussing. *Ancient Gods, protect them,* she thought, and disconnected and quickly placed another call. "I want guards protecting Little Flower and GrandFather at all times. At no time, are they to be left alone with the Senior Council, under any circumstances."

Quinn Bluestone, her second in command, frowned, and was silent for several moments before twitching his whiskers forward in a yes. "On my honor," he said, and hung up.

With those words, Quinn had just promised to protect them with his life. He was her best fighter. She just prayed that would be enough. One guard against five would tax even his abilities, and she knew full well that Tabor was more than capable of killing, as were the other Seniors. With a heavy heart, she returned to watching the Seniors deliberation, and make plans, trying to decide who else she could trust with this information.

She watched for another hour as the Seniors argued before Tabor suddenly cut them off and said they weren't getting anywhere and called a break for the night. Kendra frowned at the suddenness but it was nearly midnight. When she wasn't immediately arrested, she relaxed slightly. The next two days, Kendra watched when she could, between other responsibilities, and then stayed up late reviewing what she missed. To her surprise they had shifted to discussing the other charges and in many of those areas they were just as split. By the afternoon of the second day they'd come to a few decisions and Tabor put a meeting on the calendar for the next morning to discuss security for the verdict, before they broke for the evening.

The next morning, Kendra arrived at Tabor's office to find the Senior Councilor waiting for her and motioned her in to take a seat. A tray of prepared fruits were on her desk. "Sorry about the early meeting," Tabor said, grabbed a piece of fruit and motioned to Kendra to partake if she were interested. "I wanted to meet with you before deliberation started up again."

"No worries," Kendra replied. "What did you want to discuss?"

"I..." Tabor started, but Tabor's tablet dinged, interrupting her. "One moment," Tabor said, picking it up and looking at it for a moment. "Forgive me. I need to deal with this. Wait here please. It shouldn't take long."

Kendra nodded and watched as Tabor stood and left the office, the door swinging shut behind her. Moments later, she realized her mistake as she heard the quiet snick of the door being locked and the buzz of the privacy screen turning on remotely. She stood and tried the door anyway, but it was locked. She hit the manual switch for the privacy screen in the office, but it did nothing, and when she her comms to call a warning in to Quinn she was met with static. Growling, she opened her tablet she found her entire account had been disabled, something that shouldn't have been possible. Swearing she sent a silent prayer up to the Ancient Gods, that she'd done enough, and sat down to wait as there was little else she could do.

# CHAPTER 33

# Jessica: Deliberation

The Senior Council sequestered for days while they waited for them to make their decision. As both Myra and Jer were charged, they were not allowed to leave the council building during that time unless there was an emergency and guards were placed outside their door. Jessica spent her time drawing or pacing, while the others sat quietly and chatted or watched the news, which she couldn't understand. Marsee offered to translate, but Jessica just shook her head. She didn't really want to know. So instead Marsee curled up on a pillow by the window and read, while she leaned up against her furry best friend's side and drew, but she was so nervous that she even found that hard to do, and eventually just stared out the window for hours on end.

Early the third morning, shortly after breakfast, a guard knocked at their door to indicate that the Senior Council had requested to speak with her for further questioning. So, she and Marsee followed the guard around past the council chamber, and down a long hallway to a door where another guard was posted.

The guard knocked and a moment later, Tabor motioned them in. To her surprise and based on the reactions of the Seniors' theirs, the guard stopped her and entered first, taking up station in the corner.

Tabor frowned at the guard. "Quinn, this is a private meeting."

"I'm following orders, Ma'am," Quinn stated calmly.

Tabor flicked her ears back in surprise and glared at him. "And just what orders might those be?" she growled.

"That Little Flower should not be left alone in your presence," Quinn replied, not looking the least bit phased by her growl. "*You* are on trial for colluding her rape, Senior Councilor. I am here to ensure she is not harmed. If we do not leave this room in one piece, the guards outside are prepared to arrest all of you."

Tabor's brows and ears flicked back in surprise.

"Jennette, sit down," Clear Seas stated. "He's in the right."

Tabor snorted, but shut the door and took her seat at the center of the long conference table, where the others sat, save for Clear Seas, who floated in a wall of water at one end. Tabor motioned for them to stand on the other side of the table and Marsee adjusted so she could translate for her.

"Ambassador Little Flower we have questions…"

"Ma'am, where's Marcus?" she interrupted, not liking the idea that her Advocate was not there, especially after what Quinn had just implied.

"He is not needed today," Tabor replied.

"I am not answering any questions without the presence of my Advocate. I know my rights," she replied and crossed her arms.

Tabor raised a brow but nodded her head. "Very well." She stood again and walked over to the door. "Fetch Advocate Surellis," Tabor said to the guard outside and shut the door again.

"While we wait, would you like anything to eat or drink?" she asked.

"No thank you," Little Flower replied. "I am curious though. What form of magic do you use to keep the water in place?" She'd just seen Clear Seas' reach out of the water to grab a piece of food on a plate in front of him.

Clear Seas's skin rippled with amusement. "It's not magic, it's a static shield. It is specifically designed for my species. I can pass through but you cannot. Not unless you are wearing a mask." He pointed over to a wall where a number of thin, metallic circles were hanging on the wall, high above her. "I assure you, you are perfectly safe. In the event of a failure, the water will automatically drain out. You'll get wet, but that's all."

She walked over and put her hand on the water and she realized it felt the same as the walls of her cell. "What about you? Can you breathe if there's no water?"

"I can, for a short time. More than an hour or two would kill me. My lungs would dry out," he stated and swam towards her.

Before she could blink, the guard picked her up and moved her away from the shield. "Ambassador, please keep your distance from the Senior Councilor. He could kill you with a single touch."

Clear Seas flashed a color, which Marsee indicated meant surprise. "My apologies Ambassador. I didn't mean to scare you or the guard. I simply meant to allow you the opportunity to examine my species closer. I assure you, you are safe. On my oath as a Senior Councilor, I will not harm you."

Jessica snorted. "Guard, put me down please. I am well aware of the danger you all pose to me and to my species. Any one of you could easily kill me, and frankly after my testimony and the severe consequences of this trial, I wouldn't be surprised if you weren't contemplating genocide, to get rid of your...little problem."

As she said this, there was a knock on the door, but no one moved to open it and the guard did not set her down. Instead he backed up further.

Their lack of response told her everything she needed to know and she raised a brow. "So is that it? You've brought me here to kill me?" The guard took another step back when they didn't answer right away.

"No. We've brought you here because we need to understand just how great of a threat your people are," Clear Seas stated eventually. "Right now, your people do not have the resources to be a threat, but you will, if we welcome you into the Consortium, and we want to know how to counter it before it becomes a threat."

Jessica considered his words. The threat was still there, she decided. If they did not like the answers she gave, she was not leaving this room alive, and the odds were not in her favor. Her guard must have come to the same conclusion as he took another step back and one arm shifted to where, what she now knew was a stunner, was located. "Let me ask you this, Councilors. If you *counter* that threat, would you be any better than us?" They all expressed surprise, but didn't speak, and she glared them down. After several moments of silence, she pursed her lips and decided to clarify. "If I were to tell you all the ways we killed each other, what would you do with that information, build bigger weapons? Trust me. You do not want to go down that path. We nearly destroyed ourselves that way. You should let this information die and focus on teaching our people a better way to live. Now, let my Advocate in, or we're leaving."

None of them moved for several seconds and the guard started shifting towards the door, never taking his eyes off of them. Marsee's tail poofed out, but she remained still, waiting.

"Jennette, let him in," Clear Seas ordered.

Tabor stared at her for a moment longer, but then stood and opened the door. The guard on the other side of the door, took one look at the situation and unclipped her stunner, pointing it directly at Senior Councilor Tabor. Everyone froze.

"Guard, lower your weapon and let my Advocate in," Jessica ordered. "There's no problem here. Quinn set me down." The guard at the door glanced over at her, but didn't lower her weapon or back away until Quinn did as ordered.

"Are you all right?" Marcus asked after he entered and Tabor shut the door again.

"I am, for now," she replied, and then turned back to the Councilors. "I will answer anything you want to know about my people and culture, but not our weapons, not unless you do the same, and not until after we are accepted as full and equal members. That is the only defense we have against you right now, and I am not giving that up. I know you are trying to protect your people, but so am I."

Clear Seas considered for a moment and agreed, and so they spent the entire day with them as they asked question after question about her world and its governments, laws, religions, sciences, and the kinds of crimes her people committed, but they honored their agreement and never asked about her weapons. They read back portions of her testimony and asked for further clarification on what she said, at one point spending over an hour on a single sentence. They stopped only briefly for refreshments and necessities, and by the time they were done questioning her for the day, she was so exhausted and her feet so swollen, that Marsee had to carry her as they were escorted back to their suite. Halfway back, she had to have Marsee stop so she could take her boots off. She was crying in pain before they made it back to the room, as her feet swelled even more, no longer confined to the boots.

The room was full and the others sighed with relief the moment they reappeared. Myra fretted over her and slathered her in that miracle cream, while Marcus gave them a rundown of what had been asked, both speaking and signing for her benefit, but the moment the cream took effect, she fell instantly asleep. With the difference in the length of days, it had been nearly a full earth day and she was physically and emotionally spent.

The next day she was called back again, but to everyone's surprise she was not allowed to bring Marsee, and was told a different translator would be provided. The room was tense with apprehension when she left, and she wondered if they were going to kill her today.

When she arrived, they motioned her and the guard back in. She waited nervously next to her guard, who kept his paw on his stunner the entire time, wondering what was going on, until the moment Ellie entered the room. She let out a sigh of relief, knowing they wouldn't try something with Ellie there.

"Senior Guild Master," Tabor began, motioning her over. "My understanding is that you are fluent in sign language?"

Ellie began translating for her. "I am passable, but nowhere near as good as Marsee."

"That is acceptable. We would like you to translate for Little Flower today. We only have a few questions for her."

Ellie frowned, but nodded her agreement. To her surprise Tabor stood and left the room.

"Ambassador," Clear Seas began. "For the following questions, your Advocate cannot be present due to the charges against him and for that very same reason Senior Councilor Tabor has just left the room. I assure you these questions are to protect you from the Local Council and the others accused, and that you will not be harmed. If you have any questions, feel free to ask us, the Senior Guild Master, or the guard before answering."

She frowned but nodded, trusting Ellie's judgment.

"Ambassador Little Flower, did anyone hurt, threaten, or otherwise coerce or bribe you into changing your original accusation to the Council?" Clear Seas asked.

"No sir," she replied, understanding immediately why Marcus hadn't been allowed in the room, and relaxed slightly. "I swear I didn't even know I was bringing charges forward to accuse anyone. I was angry and scared at the time, and just wanted answers. When I drew those particular drawings, I hadn't intended for them to be seen by anyone. They were a combination of what happened and my fears about what was going to happen."

"Why then, when asked if you wanted cubs, did you respond to Marsee with 'No. Marsee's Mother choose. Healer Morningstar choose. Council choose. Marsee's mother hurt me. Healer Morningstar hurt me. Council hurt me. Male hurt me.' Did they in fact hurt you?"

Jessica paused to consider her words carefully. "326 is the only one that physically hurt me, but I was hurting emotionally from my long isolation. I'd only just started learning to sign that day, so I did not have a lot of words to pull from to explain what had happened to me. Marsee and I had just spent the last hour or two as she tried to explain what her family did for a living, using drawings and what few signs we knew. At that time, I had just learned that Marsee's mother was the Senior Healer in charge of the Agency and that her father was a councilor or leader of some sort for her district. I didn't know why we were being held for so long and I didn't know why our planet had been destroyed. What I did know was that Healer Morningstar brought me from my room to his and left us alone, and then later brought another male to my room, but I had no idea why, although I had my suspicions. I hated her for not coming when I called for help and I hated your people because I believed you'd killed mine. I didn't find out until later about the asteroid and how you lost people to save us, and how we were just in quarantine. I didn't know she was busy trying to save a choking baby at that time, and didn't, and couldn't hear my call for help. No one coerced me to change my statement. Just the opposite. Advocate Surellis was concerned that if I submitted an entirely new statement that I might be seen as lying to the Council with my first accusation, but I insisted, and we settled on describing what I had meant with each of my drawings and presenting them as a clarification, rather than a change in my statement. I didn't and still don't want anyone charged but 326. He's the one that hurt me, and the only one that should pay."

Clear Seas was silent for several moments before speaking again. "You're serious? You do not hold the Local Council responsible for the harm they caused you? They knew full well what Healer Chenzira planned with regards to reintroduction and repopulation when they voted to allow the Agency to move forward with those programs."

"Not for the decisions that led to my rape. I believe that the healers and Council had our best interests in mind and were only trying to help cure our isolation sickness and save our species," she replied.

"But you do for other decisions?" he pressed.

Jessica sighed. "Wouldn't you, if you were in my place? Councilor, harm was done to my people, but I don't believe that there was malicious intent involved. Your people risked their lives to save us and care for us and I thank you for that. I am well aware of what the consequences will be to the people of this planet if the entire local council is found guilty of a crime, and I don't want that. I don't want the first action made as a member of your consortium to be one that breeds resentment. My people will need your help for a very long time and I would rather that help be freely given and not at the expense of someone else who did not harm me or my people."

Clear Seas briefly flashed surprise before bringing his emotions under control. "I must admit, I find it hard to believe that you would be so forgiving."

"I suppose that's fair. I don't trust you either. But we're going to have to learn to eventually, if we're going to be part of the Consortium. I'm going to have to trust that you won't hurt my people again and you're going to have to trust that my people won't hurt yours in the future. I can't guarantee the actions of my people or even know how they feel. I haven't spoken to any of them but my grandfather. I can only speak for myself. I promise not to hurt your people and do everything I can to lead my people to a peaceful future. But I will do everything within my power to protect my people, including fighting to save them and giving my life, if necessary."

She purposely strode forward until she was well within reach of Clear Seas. The guard shifted to approach and tried to stop her, but she put her hand up to stop him instead. "Can I trust you, Councilor, with my life and lives of my people?" she asked, and then held her hand out.

He floated there unmoving for several seconds before nodding. "You can, Ambassador. I promise that I will not hurt you or your people, but I will do everything within my power to protect my people, including fighting to save them and give my life, if necessary," he replied, repeating her words, and slowly extended his webbed hand through the shield, but stopped just short of touching hers. Letting her decide.

She didn't hesitate. With a nod accepting his oath, she grasped his hand tightly and held it there for several seconds before letting go.

"You are brave for such a small species. I will give you that," he said afterwards.

She snorted but didn't comment and instead turned to look back at the rest of the Seniors. Their faces were all the same blank mask she was used to seeing on them now. She was curious if the others would make the same promise or not, but they said nothing. She didn't press them either. She had the support of Clear Seas, which was a start and she sensed they were still undecided. At that point, Councilor Tabor was allowed back in the room but to her confusion, Tabor asked her again if anyone had ever hurt or threatened to hurt her besides 326 in her time at the Agency, or while living with the Chenziras.

"No one has ever hurt me but him," she repeated.

"But someone has threatened you?" Tabor pressed.

"No one has said they're going to hurt me either," Jessica replied, confused why they were continuing to push the same question, and she was beginning to wonder if she was missing something with the translation as Ellie wasn't nearly as fluent as Marsee, so she asked Ellie. "Why do they keep asking the same question? What am I not understanding?"

"Your medical report and the report from the Healers Guild states that you were treated for broken ribs and multiple cuts and bruises while you were staying with the Chenziras. What happened?" Tabor asked as clarification.

"Oh. Is that what this is about? That was my fault. I climbed all the way to the top of the tree in the center of their compound before Marsee could stop me. Both she and her mother tried to get me to come down, but I refused. While up there, I noticed the sand storm approaching and tried to hurry down, but I slipped when a gust of wind shook the tree and I fell, hitting several branches on my way down, before I was able to catch one and stop myself," Jessica explained.

"Why did you climb the tree in the first place? Were you trying to take your life?" Tabor asked.

"No. Not then anyway. I climbed the tree because I like climbing trees, and I like being up high. It was the one place in the entire compound where I could be free, where no one could get me," Jessica replied. "I needed the time and space to think after having just learned about the asteroid and my pregnancy."

"But you did consider it?" Tabor pressed.

"Obviously. I did try to take my life after all. I didn't want a child raised in captivity and I was pretty sure I'd lost everyone I ever cared about. I didn't know my grandfather was still alive until several days later," she replied. "I was trying to decide if I could trust your people and make a life here."

The others nodded at her answer but Tabor continued to press. "In the first report we had from Translator Chenzira, she indicated that you were scared by her holding a knife and ran and hid under her parent's bed. What really happened? Did she try to hurt you?" Tabor asked.

She took a deep breath when she realized where they were going with this conversation. She really didn't want to get Marsee in trouble, and realized that was why Marsee had been required to stay behind too, not just because of her relationship with others accused. She knew that Marsee's report had been sent to Senior Councilor Tabor though, so to lie about what happened would be bad, although she didn't know what Marsee put in her report. She carefully explained what she'd wrongly imagined Marsee was doing and why, that first day, blaming her fright on the difference in size of the knife and its similarities to a weapon they had, but Tabor kept pressing.

"So Marsee was not hunting you?" When she hesitated to reply, Tabor pressed hard. "You need to answer the question. Did Marsee hunt you?"

Jessica sighed and nodded. Ellie took a deep breath, looking very worried, and glanced in the direction of the guard, before bringing her emotions under control, so Jessica quickly tried to explain, to try and save her friend. "She said she did but she stopped on her own, and outside of being really scared, I was never hurt. At the time I had decided that I'd misread her intent, and thought that she was only trying to catch me, to keep me from running off. We would run and chase each other in play all the time later, and there was never an issue until one day when we were watching the video where I'd run off down the hall and Healer Morningstar caught me. Marsee had a flare up, I guess, and left the room. Her father followed out and they didn't return for a long time. Afterwards her father told me about your hunting instinct that your cubs have. Marsee replied that for a brief moment she'd seen me as prey and it had horrified her. I didn't think much of it, since I'd felt like prey in that moment, and the creatures we have, that are similar in appearance, like to pounce on everything when they're young too. Later I asked her about it, as I was more concerned about being hurt by one of your cubs, since they're the same size we are. But it turns out we don't trigger it at all, at least not with all the cubs that came to visit us the other day. Anyway, Marsee was really upset and said she was struggling hard and didn't know what was wrong with her. To me it sounded much like how I felt before finding out what really happened to my people and the difficulty I had in containing the rage I felt, so she went and got her father after I suggested that perhaps practicing would help. We spent a good hour discussing all the ways that your hunting instinct can be triggered accidentally, and then discussed ways that Marsee might be able to safely practice and Marsee agreed, wanting desperately to find a way to keep me safe too. I gave a statement as well that I understood the risks and was doing so of my own free will, in case I got hurt. I climbed high up in the tree where she couldn't reach and her father held her tightly so she couldn't get away, and she allowed herself to pretend to hunt me and stop fighting the urge to attack. It worked. It took a few tries, but Marsee learned how to control whatever it is that she was struggling with, but for a while I will admit it was pretty scary. I don't fully understand what was really going on, but Advocate Surellis was there, and watched the whole thing from the shadows, and he said that she had an illness called psychosis, and that normally it's a death sentence because those that get it lose all sense of self and never come back. For a while, it certainly seemed like Marsee had turned into a wild animal, as she roared and fought to get out of her father's grip. Marsee even said that for a while she didn't remember who she was, but she's been fine ever since. Both her father and Advocate Marcus have been testing her every day, although I'm not really sure what they're looking at either, but she's been so much calmer and far less fidgety, even in her sleep. That night she said it felt like something snapped into place, and that somehow sign language cut through, although she couldn't understand what her father was saying. She never hurt me, then or any other time, not even in her sleep, and I sleep wrapped in her arms. I need the physical contact to feel safe. She never once made me feel like I wasn't welcome, or that I was a burden. If anything, she made me feel like a treasured friend. I know she's one of the best friends I've ever had. None of the Chenziras have hurt me. They've only ever tried to help, even if I didn't know it at the time."

She knew she'd been rambling, and Ellie struggled to keep up with the translation.

"So, you no longer feel Marsee is a danger to you or your people?" Tabor asked.

"She is no more of a danger to my people than you are, Senior Councilor Tabor, perhaps less so as I trust her with my life and the lives of my people," Jessica replied with a glare. "What do I need to do to prove it to you? Stick my head in her mouth? Or would you just use that to prove I wasn't sane? Marsee has done everything in her power to help me this past month, has learned two languages so she could be my translator, has helped teach me sign language and how to read. She's held me while I cried and screamed through night terrors, and has shown me how to love, dream, and hope again. If you're expecting me to charge her with a crime, you can just stuff it where the moons don't shine."

Tabor's ears flicked back in astonishment, and perhaps a hint of outrage at the not so implied insults, before bringing her emotions under control.

To her surprise, Clear Seas chuckled, letting ripples of color cross his skin. "She has a point, Jennette. She has absolutely no reason to trust you or your Council, whereas Translator Chenzira has risked her very life for her and her species, if this disease is as deadly as you say it is. I have certainly seen nothing that would indicate the Translator is the risk you seem to believe she is. She has been calm and professional this entire time, far exceeding what I would expect from someone of her age, and she's been forthcoming to the Council about her own actions and experiences, in the hopes that it will help the next person with this illness, at great risk to herself. This line of questioning needs to stop. The Translator is not on trial."

Senior Councilor Tabor breathed out, not quite approaching a huff, but tilted her head in acknowledgement of Clear Seas statement and the others' murmured agreement.

They were both excused after that, and it was all she could do to not run out of the room. They were about halfway back, when Ellie pulled her into an empty conference room and shut the door, leaving their escort outside, although it took Jessica ordering the guard to remain outside for him to leave. Jessica turned to face her and realized that her fairy godmother was struggling to keep her emotions from breaking through, and she couldn't tell if she was laughing or crying. "What is it?" Jessica asked.

"Oh child, I can't believe you just did that," Ellie signed, laughter finally winning.

"Did what?" Jessica asked.

"All of it. Your bravery in offering your hand to Clear Seas for one. I have known him since he was a child. Marsee told us what happened before Marcus showed up yesterday. I find it hard to believe they would have hurt you, but I could be very wrong. You may have just saved your people with that act. I'm fairly certain you just earned Clear Sea's vote anyway."

"I know. I fully believe they intended to kill me yesterday, and probably would have if it hadn't been for the guard." Jessica replied. "I honestly thought that's why Marsee hadn't been allowed back today, until you showed up. I had to do something. If I didn't, I was dead anyway, whether by their hands or mine. If I am forced to go back to the Agency, I will kill myself the first chance I get. I can't live like that again."

Ellie was silent for a while, considering and glanced towards the guard outside. "I don't know what's going to happen, but if that should happen, don't give up. I will use every resource available to me to get you out of there, but it may take time. Please, give me that time."

Jessica nodded. "Just don't take too long."

Ellie nodded, serious, but then her tail curled again. "I honestly can't believe you flat out insulted Tabor and accused her of trying to trick you into doing something that could be used against you. 'What do you want me to do, stick my head in her mouth?'" Ellie repeated, tail now corkscrewing. "I'm not sure if I should be amazed you had the audacity, or shocked you walked out of there unscathed after you swore at her." Ellie just shook her head. "I'm not sure I would dare do that, and I've known her for decades. No one swears at the Senior Council. It's just not done, mostly because she could kill you for even the hint of violence or treason."

"Well, if the Senior Council can't handle a few insults and accusations, then maybe they don't deserve to be on the Senior Council," Jessica stated blandly. "And if they think that was bad, wait till they meet everyone else."

Ellie snorted in humor and her tail curled further, but then she sobered again. "You do realize you just saved Marsee's life."

Jessica frowned. "I get what they were pressing for, but I would never have pressed charges against her for an illness, even if she had hurt me."

"No child. That wasn't what was going on. If you had given even the slightest hint that she wasn't in control, they would have killed her. There wouldn't have even been a trial. No one has *ever* survived her illness before. You would not realize it, but there were double the normal guards in the chamber the other day, and the Senior Honor Guard herself was in attendance and she rarely attends meetings. We thought it was just because the entire Local Council is being charged, but having guards outside of the Seniors conference room when the Council is not in session is very unusual and with Tabor's questioning today, she's clearly not taking Marcus's word for Marsee's sanity. She might not officially be on the watch list anymore, but the Guard and Councilor Tabor still believes she's a risk. But your comment convinced the rest of the Seniors, and with everything else against Tabor and our Local Council right now, she can't try anything. The Guard still could, but they won't unless she shows any signs of loss of control."

"Any sign?" Jessica asked with a frown.

Ellie considered. "She's shown some emotion in reaction to your testimony, but those have all been normal responses that everyone was experiencing, and they've done nothing, so most likely she would have to go non-verbal or start attacking someone in the Council. She tends to shut down when she's scared though, and that could be mistaken as being non-verbal. I don't think she will though. Your assessment of her was spot on. She has changed significantly for the better since that day and if she was going to have a problem, she would have yesterday morning. But if she does, you need to snap her out of it. Get her to speak any way you can, or give her time to recover if you think she's struggling. I also don't think you should tell her what was said here until after the trial. That will just add stress that she doesn't need. Afterwards...if for some reason Tabor or the Guards come after her without just cause, and we're not around, demand that her case be brought before the Full Senior Council and do everything you can to keep her calm. As long as she's not actively resisting her arrest, or trying to hurt someone, she has that right."

"Do you think they would come after her?" Jessica asked. This went against everything she'd learned about this society, but then the past two days had shown her what lengths they were at least considering.

Ellie didn't answer for a long time. "I honestly don't know, child. We have been fighting psychosis for more than ten thousand years. We lost our former planet because of it. Even the barest hint of an issue is snuffed out before someone gets hurt. There's a great deal of stigma around it too. You should avoid telling anyone she had issues unless there is reason for concern. I am legally bound to report any issues by any adult in my guild to the Guard and Council so they can be tested. Not once in all my time as Senior has anyone passed. I'm honestly surprised they haven't brought her in to be tested anyway. My guess is that the only reason they haven't done so is because to deny you your translator this late could be seen as trying to interfere with the trial. That and because Marcus's reputation is impeccable. They have no cause not to trust his assessment, even if she is family. He's had to make that awful decision many times in his career. They've given her a chance they've not given anyone else, but she's not clear, not by any means, and probably won't be for a while. A standard watch is six months. My guess is that she will continue to be watched for at least that long, even if she's not officially on the list."

Jessica nodded. "I can understand their concern. What I saw that day..." Jessica shook her head. "It was truly terrifying. I almost lost my best friend and it would have been my fault for suggesting she practice."

"No, child," Ellie said, "I have read her report and spoken to both her father and Marcus. You saved her life. On her own, she wouldn't have lasted more than another day or two, tops. I've seen psychosis enough times in my life to know just how close she was. I chose to ignore the signs because, like her parents, I didn't want to believe it. But none of that mattered. She wouldn't have been given that time. Marcus had already put her on the watch list and fully intended to call in Tabor and the Guard in the morning. Marsee would have been dead before breakfast and none of us would have been able to do anything to stop it."

# CHAPTER 34

# Jessica: Verdict

Several more days passed before they were finally called back into the council chamber. The Senior Council had finally made their decision.

"This Council is now in session. Please be seated," Councilor Tabor said. When they had, she began delivering their verdict.

"On the question of sentience for the Hue-man, known as Little Flower, let it be known that the Full Council's decision was entirely unanimous and the Senior Council agrees, and it is considered final. From this day forth, Little Flower is recognized as being of sound mind and fully sentient with all of the rights and responsibilities that come with that designation."

The Council erupted into cheers and applause. Councilor Tabor let it go on for a few moments before raising her paw to silence the room. The silence was immediate.

"On the question of offering admittance of the Hue-man species into the Consortium of Sentient Beings, let it be known that the majority of the Full Council and the people agree, and the Senior Council unanimously agrees and it is considered final."

More cheers followed although Jessica wondered just how many people had voted against her. She understood their concerns and knew it would take time for her people to prove themselves.

"As Ambassador Little Flower is now recognized as sentient, and with the expectation that she will accept our offer to join the Consortium of Sentient Beings, it is this council's unanimous decision that the Hue-man known as 2A326 is found guilty of beating and forcing Little Flower to mate, against her repeated requests to stop, resulting in both physical and mental harm to Little Flower and resulting in pregnancy. Sentencing to follow. It is also the Senior Council's unanimous belief that the Local Council decision that led to the two being placed in the same room together was done in good faith and with her best interest in mind, to try and treat her isolation sickness, and save her species from extinction. It is therefore the Senior Council's unanimous decision that the councilors who voted yes to that motion are found not guilty of collusion or accessory in the rape of Little Flower, with one exception. Councilor Jeran Frederick Chenzira, please stand."

Jer stood, head up and back straight, outwardly calm and prepared to take his punishment. Jessica frowned. *If the others were found not guilty, why is he?* she wondered.

"It is the Senior Council's unanimous and final decision that you, having brought forth the motion on the suggestion of your partner, and per your admission of guilt in forcing your fellow councilors to vote as they did, that you be held solely responsible for the vote and are found guilty to the lesser charge of accessory to Little Flower's rape. And as such, that you are henceforth removed from your position as councilor and shall never be allowed to run for election as a councilor, for your people from this day forth, and as long as you should live. As you have been found guilty of a crime, this Council also finds that you are no longer an adequate guardian for Little Flower, and your guardianship rights have been revoked. Please step down from your seat and join your family."

Jer acknowledged his understanding and acceptance of the punishment and stepped down without hesitation. In his mind, it was a fair and just decision, and he was relieved that his gambit had worked. The loss of his council position was a small price to pay to protect his peers and his planet from sanctions. Jessica however, fumed at the injustice. Jer hadn't forced his peers to vote, Tabor had. Jer hadn't even suggested the idea, Myra had.

"Advocate Marcus Rufino Surellis, please stand."

Marcus stood looking fairly surprised to be called out, since Tabor had already indicated the rest of the Local Council was not complicit, as were several others based on the murmurs that traveled around the chamber.

"Advocate Surellis, you have been legally elected by your district a total of fourteen times and maintained the second highest-ranking position among your Local Council and the highest rating of any councilor by your people for several terms, yet you chose to abdicate your position and vowed before the Council, upon penalty of death, that you would prove Little Flower's sentience, as a means to ensure Little Flower was given a fair trial. You did this knowing that should she be found sentient, that you were risking severe consequences and would be giving up your right to vote on that outcome. As no conflict of interest was found by this court, the Senior Council believes you should be reinstated to your rank and position as councilor. However, since your district has already legally elected a new representative, and as your home is very close to the border of the South District, we have unanimously decided that you should be placed as the representative to fulfill former Councilor Chenzira's position to the end of his elected term in five years, should you choose to accept. You will not be required to move to the South District if you do. Do you accept this position?"

Shocked gasps rang across the council floor and Little Flower turned to stare at her advocate, completely blown away at what he'd risked for her. He however was not looking at her, he was looking in Jer's direction and she turned to face him. She couldn't tell what was being said between them with that look but Jer eventually nodded.

"I do," Marcus replied.

"Then by the unanimous and final decision of the Senior Council, it is so. You may take your place in the former councilor's seat or remain by Little Flower as her advocate."

"I will remain here," he stated and sat.

"Thank you for risking your life for me," Little Flower signed to him, and she reached over and gave him a hug.

"It was never a risk. I always knew you'd be found sentient. I knew from the moment I saw you demand to leave the Agency."

"Thank you anyway, for everything," she said. He nodded, but his body language was tense and focused on Councilor Tabor.

When Little Flower's attention was back on Marsee, the Senior Councilor continued. Marsee had not translated her conversation with Marcus, as any conversation between Little Flower and her advocate was considered private, even if the shield wasn't up.

"Healer Brice Morningstar, please stand. For the charge of collusion in the rape of Little Flower this Council has determined that all due diligence was done to ensure the safe co-habitation of the two with the training you had been given at the time. We have also confirmed that you were treating a choking cub at the same time this rape occurred, and that the monitors only showed an elevated heart rate as you mentioned. As no signs of aggression or violence by the male were seen in any prior visit against you or Little Flower, this Council agrees with your decision to give them privacy and to focus on the more life-threatening issue, and finds you not guilty, with no reprimand or demotion allowed by the Healers Guild on this case. This decision is unanimous and final. Please sit down."

Brice's legs nearly gave out with relief as she sat.

"This Council has also determined that the other healers at the Agency are also not guilty of collusion or accessory in the rape of Little Flower, due to the statement given by then Senior Healer Chenzira in the session where the charges of rape were presented to her Local Council. In her official statement she indicated that she took full responsibility for the actions that occurred at the Agency. This Council accepts her statement and desire to take responsibility for those actions and clears the other healers of their charges, with no further reprimand or demotion allowed by the Healers Guild. Healer Myra Beth Chenzira, please stand."

Myra stood, one paw gripped tightly in Jer's for support, both relieved that the others were safe and terrified of what that meant for her.

"It is our belief that by deliberately placing the Hue-mans together in pairs, not just in the hopes that it would cure their isolation sickness, but with the hope that attachment and mating would also occur, and that by deliberately ordering the stop of the hormone blockers, in the hopes that pregnancy would result, and that by specifically choosing the male to pair with Little Flower against the recommendation of her healer, that you effectively took the choice of mate away from her and caused Little Flower to come in to heat which resulted in her pregnancy. On the charge of collusion in the rape of Little Flower, this court finds you guilty. Sentencing to follow. Be seated."

Myra collapsed into her seat. The fur on her back and tail stuck out in full terror, and she grabbed her tail tightly in her paws and twisted hard. Jer wrapped his arms around her and held her close, but did not stop her. He kept his own tail tucked under him. If he hadn't, he would have been doing the same. Marsee's hands shook as she translated the verdict. It was clear to everyone that Councilor Tabor gave Marsee a moment to compose herself as Tabor paused, took a sip of water, and fiddled with the console on her desk for some time before continuing. Beside Jessica, Marcus remained tense, if not more so, and one finger twitched on the desk in front of him.

"It is also the unanimous decision that since Ambassador Little Flower is now pregnant, she can no longer be considered a child and that she should be presented for her adulthood ceremony to become an adult of her species, with all of the rights and responsibilities that comes with that designation. Ambassador Little Flower, please come forward."

Jessica climbed down off of her raised platform and walked forward until Senior Councilor Tabor indicated she should stop, about halfway between her desk and the Senior Council's podium. Far enough that she could still easily see Marsee's translation.

"Ambassador Little Flower. It is our custom that a child be represented on their name day, when they transition from childhood to adulthood, by their parents or legal guardians. As your parents were both killed during the cataclysm that destroyed your planet, and as you no longer have a legal guardian, we are giving you the choice to pick any legal adults among our society to either be your legal guardians or parents, should they choose to accept. Who would you like to designate as your parents or legal guardians from this day forward?"

Without hesitation, Little Flower shifted so she could look over at those who had come with her. "I choose Myra and Jeran Chenzira to be my new parents, if they would have me as their child. They have shown me kindness, love, and far more patience than I deserve, and I can think of no one I would rather have as my mother and father." The Council gasped at her announcement and even the Senior Council looked surprised when she turned to face forward again.

"Are you sure Little Flower, both have been found guilty in association with your rape. That would normally prevent them from being considered as an option as they are seen as unfit by this Council," Tabor asked.

"I am absolutely positive. I cannot think of anyone more 'fit' to be my parents than them. I have thought of them as such for weeks now. 'Mother' and 'Father' are the name signs I use for them. They have taught me your culture, laws, and beliefs. They've taught me to speak and to read and write. They have healed me when I was broken. They have held and comforted me when I grieved and showed me how to love and laugh again. Is that not what a parent does? I want them to be my parents, if they want me as their daughter," Jessica replied.

"Then, as it is the custom of the Council to honor the wishes of the child in this matter, this Council sees no reason to deny your request. Myra, Jeran, please stand," Tabor replied.

Jer had to help Myra stand as she was shaking so badly. "Myra Beth Chenzira, do you consent to being Little Flower's mother, with all of the rights and responsibilities that come with that designation?"

"I do!" she said instantly, her voice breaking with emotion.

"And Jeran Frederick Chenzira, do you consent to being Little Flower's father, with all the rights and responsibilities that come with that designation?"

"I do," Jer said with a conviction that rang throughout the council chamber.

"Then it is the unanimous and final decision of this Council that Little Flower's parents and legal guardians from this day forward are Myra and Jeran Chenzira." At this announcement the Full Council roared their approval and actually caused Tabor to startle. She had clearly not expected that reaction.

Myra, no longer able to restrain herself, ran forward and scooped up Little Flower, nearly crushing her in a hug. Jer followed and soon all three were hugging. Councilor Tabor gave them the time they needed to compose themselves. She more than anyone understood the implications of what was to come later, and she wanted Little Flower to have a moment of happiness to remember before that occurred.

Tabor motioned to gain their attention after a while. "Little Flower Chenzira, please kneel."

Little Flower did and her new mother and father stood behind her.

"Who presents Little Flower Chenzira to this Council to be recognized as a legal adult with all of the rights and responsibilities that go with that designation?" Tabor asked.

"We do," her parents said proudly in unison.

"Do you believe that she is of sound mind and ready to take on all of the responsibilities that come with adulthood?"

"We do," they replied.

"Little Flower Chenzira, do you understand and promise to uphold the laws of our people from this day forth?"

"I do," she replied.

"Do you promise to care and take responsibility for your offspring, should you choose to have them, to the best of your ability, until such time as they themselves reach adulthood?"

"I do."

"Do you promise to provide for your neighbors and community in their times of need whether that be in the form of food, shelter, or protection from harm, to the best of your abilities and without reservation?"

"I do."

"Then it is the unanimous and final decision of this Council that Little Flower Chenzira is an adult with all of the rights and responsibilities that come with that designation, from this day forth. Please rise and let me be the first to wish you a Happy Name Day!"

When the cheers settled again Councilor Tabor continued. "Myra, Jer, please return to your seats. Little Flower, please stay."

They each did as requested.

"Ambassador Little Flower, as the only recognized adult of your species, this Council wishes to offer you and your people equal membership to the Consortium of Sentient Beings, with all the rights and responsibilities that come with that membership. On behalf of your people, do you wish to accept this offer?"

She swallowed hard, but signed with confidence. "I do."

"Then it is the final decision of this Council to welcome you and your people as full and equal members of the Consortium of Sentient Beings."

Councilor Tabor raised a paw to silence the cheering crowd.

"As the sole adult of your species, do you wish to join the Council of Sentient Beings as its senior councilor or elect another legal adult as your representative, for the standard term of ten years or until that councilor steps down of their own choice?"

"I wish to elect a senior councilor," she signed.

This caused a murmur to go through the room. After everything that she'd said about her peoples' desire for power, this was not expected and frankly, who else was there for her to pick? Councilor Tabor raised her paw for silence yet again.

"Who do you elect as your representative?" Tabor asked.

"I elect Jeran Frederick Chenzira as my representative," Little Flower signed, staring at Councilor Tabor as she did.

The roar through the Council Chamber was thunderous and angry. It was so loud it made Little Flower's ears ring and she placed her hands over her ears to protect what little hearing she had left. Even the raised paw of Councilor Tabor did not silence the room.

"SILENCE!" Tabor roared, and let the immediate and lingering silence go on for several moments, to show her displeasure at the Council for their outburst, before turning to Little Flower to explain. "Little Flower, I am sorry, but Jeran Chenzira cannot be your representative. This Council just forbade him from ever being a councilor again."

"No. You forbade him from being a councilor to *his* people again, not to mine." Little Flower paused for Tabor's reaction, but when Tabor just stood there looking at Little Flower with an expression of stark astonishment, she continued. "I understand that he took responsibility for what happened to me, but I ask you, Senior Councilor Tabor, what crime did he commit that was so heinous as to strip him of his rank and position for the rest of his life? Please, read the charge to me again."

Tabor blinked at her, both stunned and confused. *Surely Little Flower understood how her father had been an accessory to her rape,* Tabor thought. She decided to simplify the ruling. *Perhaps there had been a mistranslation.* "He was found guilty for having brought forth the motion that ultimately led to your rape," she said.

"And what motion was that?" Little Flower asked.

"That quarantine restrictions be dropped within the Agency to treat your isolation sickness."

Little Flower nodded. "And how many times did my mother petition the Council to have those restrictions dropped?"

Tabor wasn't sure where these questions were going, but she wanted to make sure Little Flower understood why Jer could not be her representative and returned to her desk to look at her notes. "She submitted four official requests to the Local Council prior to Councilor Chenzira's motion."

Little Flower nodded again. "Are you, or were you ever a healer, Senior Councilor Tabor?" she asked.

"No. I am not. I was in the Ships Guild before becoming a Councilor, but I do have training in emergency care as part of my pilots training," Tabor replied, tilting her head in confusion at Little Flower's question.

"Were you familiar with the symptoms of isolation sickness prior to my mother's requests?" Little Flower asked.

"I was not," Tabor answered.

"Did you talk to a healer or read up on isolation sickness to understand what was wrong with me?" she asked again.

Tabor's ears flicked back as she started to see where this was going and sighed. "No, I did not. The genetic testing was not complete. Ending quarantine would have put our people at risk," Tabor explained.

"Our people? Or yours?" Little Flower asked pointedly.

"Both our people," Tabor replied.

Little Flower just raised an eyebrow at that. "Tell me Senior Councilor, would you have allowed your own children to be held in the same conditions you forced on mine? To be locked in a room with only a few minutes of contact with a healer each day?"

Tabor took a deep breath. "To keep the people of this Consortium safe, I would do whatever was necessary, even lock up or kill my own children, if I felt that they were a danger to others. That is the oath I have taken, or part of it anyway."

Little Flower glared at Tabor for several moments, trying to process that statement. She didn't doubt in the least that she would kill her own children. "Which was it? The people of the Consortium or both our people?" When Tabor didn't answer, Little Flower continued. "So if I understand this correctly, in order to keep us 'safe', you ignored the medical advice of a Senior Healer, forced them to stop treatment when they'd identified an illness that needed treatment, did not even bother to look up what we were sick with, were unfamiliar with your own charter, which you as a Senior Councilor pledged to uphold for every species, a charter which mentions the very illness I was sick with, and the harm it causes, and *yet* you somehow still felt you had the right to dictate my medical care?"

The Council gasped. This was a major accusation being leveled at the Senior Councilor, nearly on par with the rape.

"Tell me again why Councilor Chenzira was sentenced? What *crime* did he actually commit?" she demanded.

"He was found guilty for having brought forth the motion that..."

"Stopped *you* from killing me and every member of my species," she interrupted, and then paused to let the Council settle when Marsee indicated multiple people were yelling.

Tabor just sat there in shock. The rest of the Seniors were just as still.

"That stopped you from denying me the rights I deserved as a sentient being. The same rights that were given to my convicted rapist, following my accusation, yet were denied to me for more than eight of your months, or two *years* of mine. Jer was my legal representative or the closest thing I had to one, and yet I was denied access to him. I was denied pencil and paper. I tried writing out words with puzzle pieces and my food. I screamed to be let out for so long I lost my voice. I tried communicating with the sign language of my world, but *you* chose not to see it. You *all* chose not to see it. Instead, you turned your backs and refused to listen, and said I was not communicating, that I was not sentient, and that I did not deserve those rights. I have watched the recordings of those decisions, Senior Councilor Tabor. *All* of them. I have had those official requests translated. I was denied contact with my family. I didn't even know if they were still alive. I was not allowed outside. I wasn't even allowed a window to look outside. There was nothing in my cell, nothing to look at, nothing to do, and no one to talk to except my stuffed animal. My parents tried to improve the conditions of our cells, but your Council denied them, saying we were nothing but animals and continued to treat me as such even after I was removed from the Agency. In all that time, I went without seeing the sun or the stars. I went without anyone comforting me as I grieved for lost loved ones, or even so much as touching me except to pick me up and move me out of the way. Only once was I given anything close to a hug and that very same day, you ordered that healer to keep her distance. I was starving for touch and slowly going mad, and you allowed it, because you felt that the ends justified the means. That denying a few hundred people their rights was worth it, if it kept *both* our peoples safe. That sounds an awful lot like those infected leaders of my world, Councilor Tabor. Perhaps the darkness was here all along, dormant, and waiting for an opportunity to strike? Councilor Chenzira tried to stop you, and for that, and that alone, you found him guilty. He didn't present the idea for you to lock yourselves in a room to see what it was like for us, my mother did, after being denied and ignored by this very Council. She was even denied her own rights when you ordered her to stop sending those requests because you didn't want to see them anymore and had absolutely no intentions of changing your mind. My father didn't force the Council to choose between locking themselves in their rooms or stepping down, *you* did. He never even spoke that day. But it is easier to let him take the blame for your actions, than to take responsibility for the harm you've done and the consequences of your decisions. Every decision you make, Councilor, has the potential for unforeseen consequences. You chose to be safe. You chose to protect yourself at my cost, but my father fought for me, fought to earn my freedom, and had to find a way to force you to give up control of a decision you should never have been allowed to make in the first place. If your Council had not been sticking their tails in where they did not belong, and trying to dictate something you knew *nothing* about, and hadn't infringed on my rights and my mothers rights, my father would have never had to bring that motion forward. So I ask you again, what *crime* did my father commit, besides standing up to you?"

Tabor just continued to sit there, stunned. She opened her mouth to speak several times, but words did not form. The room was silent and waiting for her answer.

When the Senior Councilor did not answer, Little Flower continued. "When my father found out that I had been raped, not just injured in a fight, he came to your Council immediately, to ensure my proper representation and care, even though doing so meant putting himself and his family at severe risk of punishment. He has fought for my freedom, for my safety, and for my very life. If he and his family had not taken me in, I would have died in that cell. One way or another, I would have found a way to end my life. I would rather be beaten and raped again, rather than spend a single second more in that *awful* room. That is how bad it was. And then, if standing up to you weren't enough, he took responsibility for *your* crimes to try and save *your* people from sanctions and to save the rest of *your* Council from being found guilty of a crime you yourself said a moment ago that they didn't commit. If they aren't guilty, why is he? I can think of no one more dedicated, more driven, more selfless, and more honorable than Jeran Frederic Chenzira, my father, to represent me and my people. So tell me, am I free to pick my own representative, *Senior Councilor Tabor,* or do you still hold the ends of the harness and leash that you forced me to wear?"

Little Flower waited, crossed her arms to indicate she was done speaking, and stared unblinking at the Senior Councilor as the entire room held their breaths in absolute shock.

Councilor Tabor shook with barely controlled emotion, and was the first to look away and turned to the others on the Senior Council to see what they felt, but they refused to make eye contact with her and remained facing forward, expressionless. If they gave any signal of what they were thinking, Little Flower couldn't see it.

Tabor turned back to face her again, clearly still reeling from her accusations. "You are free to pick your own representative, Little Flower Chenzira, of this the Council's decision is unanimous and final," she answered in a quiet but barely controlled voice, and then took a long shuddering breath. "Jeran Frederic Chenzira, please stand."

Jer stood.

"Do you accept sole responsibility for Little Flower's people and the remaining species of her world, to see that they flourish and grow, and that their rights are honored and protected? To represent them in the Full Council for the standard term of ten years, or until you are voted out or step down of your own choice, even at the expense of your own species, self, and family?"

Jer did not answer right away, and Little Flower spun to look at him. He was looking down at the floor, one claw tapping against the side of his leg. He looked up and made eye contact with her. Little Flower couldn't tell what he was thinking, but after a moment, he straightened and turned his attention back to Tabor. His expression changed to one full of conviction and the same hard focus Little Flower had glared at Tabor with, only moments before. "I do," he replied.

"Will you provide fair and unbiased council to all six species as a senior member of the Full Council and will you *uphold* the articles of the Charter to the best of your ability?" Tabor asked.

"I will," Jer said, his voice almost a growl as he said it and there was a slight tremor in his paws. Little Flower glared at Tabor trying to figure out what she was implying, and what he was agreeing to.

"Do you relinquish your citizenship and right to vote as a member of your birth species for the rest of your life, and instead transfer your citizenship to her species, to be recognized as a legal adult of her species and not yours, willingly and without reservation, from this day forth?"

"I do so willingly and without reservation," he said and signed, this time far calmer as the mask of Senior Councilor settled over him.

"Then it is this Council's unanimous and final decision to welcome you as Senior Councilor for Little Flower's people. Please take your seat at the head podium. Ambassador Little Flower, you may be seated."

By the time he had walked from Myra's side to the head podium, after giving both her and Myra a quick hug, a chair and desk had been brought out and placed on the platform, and the flag that had been hanging above Little Flower's desk, moved over to hang above it. The other Seniors shook his hand in welcome.

When everyone was seated again, Tabor continued. "We now need to come to a decision on the punishments for Healer Chenzira and the Hue-man known as 2A326 who raped Little Flower. In this decision the Senior Council was not unanimous but a majority was reached. We have searched the archives for precedent with regards to this crime, but did not find any case that occurred within the time since each species has joined the Consortium. We did however find precedent outside of those boundaries on each of the planets, which varied significantly in punishment. As this rape occurred on this planet, we have decided to follow the precedent set forth by the last trial that occurred here, over ten thousand years ago and..."

"Ancient Gods! Please, no!"

"Healer Chenzira, if you cannot remain silent, you will be removed from the council chamber and the decision passed with or without you here," Tabor growled.

Little Flower turned to look at her mother as the translation came in. She'd slid out of her chair and onto her knees and placed both her paws over her mouth to keep herself from speaking further. Her tail stuck straight out behind her in pure fear and guards approached with the Senior Councilors warning. Her mother looked up to see them and swallowed hard, but nodded her understanding.

*Why was her mother so terrified? They'd only told her that they expected she would be stripped of her rank and prevented from being a healer, bad surely, but not bad enough to cause this kind of reaction,* she thought. She quickly looked back so she could see Marsee's translation of the Senior Councilor's words. Marsee looked just as terrified, and she'd tucked her tail between her legs in an attempt to keep it under control. Her hands were shaking as she continued signing.

"In that ancient case the Council decided to allow the victim to choose the punishment. It was her choice to have her rapist forced to watch as his line was...ended and then be restrained and beaten for the same amount of time she had been held, beaten, and raped, and then sentenced to death so he could never harm another person again."

"Little Flower, This Council has decided to give you the same choice. You may choose this punishment or suggest one of your own. If the Council feels it is equal, fair, and just, we will honor it. How would you see the Hue-man known as 2A326 punished?" Councilor Tabor asked when she had her full attention again.

"I do not understand. What do you mean by 'his line was ended'?" Little Flower asked, although she guessed.

"In that ancient time, we did not have a way to sterilize a person so they could no longer produce offspring. His direct offspring, both children and grandchildren, were…ultimately also sentenced to death," Tabor explained.

Little Flower frowned at the second hesitation and quickly asked Marsee. "Did she hesitate or you?"

"She did," Marsee replied.

"Why did you hesitate?" Little Flower asked.

Tabor didn't answer right away but then sighed. "In the original case, the victims existing children had also been raped and violently killed in front of the victim. She chose to do the same to his children and grandchildren."

"So, what would happen to my unborn child if I chose that punishment?" Little Flower asked with a frown.

"The victim in that ancient day chose to have her pregnancy terminated. This Council believes it is your choice to decide what happens to your unborn child. If you wish to have the pregnancy terminated, medical care will be provided. But if you choose to have the child it is our expectation that you would honor your pledge to raise that child to adulthood as you would any other child, without bias or hate towards the child for the crimes of their genetic donor. We also understand that in a situation like this, you may be unable to honor that pledge due to the trauma you received, and if that should occur this Council will help you find a new home and parents for your child."

"Does 2A326 have any other children that were rescued?" Little Flower asked. She had no intention of hurting someone else for his actions, no matter what he'd done to her.

"He does not," Tabor stated.

Reassured, she did not have to think long or hard about her answer. It was all she'd thought about for the past month. "Many in this room have argued that he only raped me because he thought he was being forced to, but that is not true. He wanted to rape me. He wanted to hurt me, and he enjoyed doing it. On my old world, men like him would not stop, no matter how much they were punished, if they were even punished. Most never were. We cannot afford to have people like that in our new world, or allow behavior like that to ever happen again. I find the Council's suggested punishment both fair and just."

"Then it is the final and unanimous decision of this Council that the Hue-man known as 2A326 is to be beaten for the same length of time that you were, and executed afterwards, to be completed by the end of this day. Little Flower, as is our custom, you may do this yourself or request that someone else do it for you."

"While part of me wants to see him torn to shreds, slowly, I do not want to see his face ever again, or risk his sickness infecting me. Please pick someone else," she answered.

"I'll do it."

"The Council accepts your offer, Healer Chenzira," Councilor Tabor replied before Jessica could turn to see who had spoken.

Little Flower spun to look at her mother again.

"I will make sure he pays dearly before he dies," her mother signed. She just nodded, unsure how she felt about her mother being the one to deliver his punishment. She turned back and caught an expression on her father's face that she couldn't fully decipher before it vanished, and it scared her. For a brief moment, he'd looked terrified.

"Healer Myra Beth Chenzira, please rise. Little Flower, how would you see Myra Chenzira punished for the crime of colluding in your rape? You may choose the same punishment as 2A326, with one exception. The children and grandchildren of Myra Chenzira would be sterilized and not sentenced to death. This court believes that since none of those children were responsible for the crimes committed against you, and that because the technology now exists to safely and painlessly prevent future pregnancies, that ending the genetic line is sufficient. You may also suggest your own punishment. If this Council decides that suggestion is equal, fair, and just, we will honor it."

Little Flower stared absolutely stunned at Tabor's words. Had the Councilor not heard any of her words? What was true for her father was just as true for her mother.

"And if I choose that she not be punished, what will happen?" she asked Tabor.

"Then this Council will deem it insufficient to meet the requirements, and have no choice but to sentence her to the same punishment as your rapist."

Little Flower swore, frantically trying to figure out a way to save not only her mother, but Marsee, her siblings, and their children. She didn't hold her mother responsible for what had happened in the least bit and certainly not her children, and grandchildren, and there was no way she was sentencing her mother to death or taking Marsee's future children from her because of what he did. The thought horrified her. She looked at Marsee. Her sister was shaking so hard that Little Flower had to look away and she caught her father's expression. He was not looking at her but in the direction of her mother. Outwardly his expression was calm, but his eyes told another story. He was petrified.

She turned and looked in the direction of her mother and swallowed hard. The guards that had been standing behind her in warning moments before, now had her held firmly in their grasp. She wasn't fighting them, but she was visibly shaking and her claws were clenching and unclenching, and her eyes begged and pleaded with her to find a way to save them all.

She turned to Marcus and slammed the privacy shield up.

"What do I do?" she asked him frantically. "How do I save them?"

"I am so very sorry," he signed. "I don't know what to tell you. None of us could figure out a way around this that we thought the Senior Council might accept. I am just grateful they took our suggestion to sterilize and not euthanize Myra's children as that was the best we could come up with."

Little Flower sat down hard on her seat, nearly missing it, and buried her head in her hands, practically pulling her hair out of her braids. Finally, an idea came to her, and she prayed it would be good enough to meet the Council's demands. She quickly discussed her idea with Marcus and he shrugged.

"It's better than anything we came up with," he said. "It's worth a try."

Taking several deep breaths, she stood back up, turning the shield off as she did. "Senior Councilor Tabor, as I have stated multiple times before this Council, I do not feel my mother is to blame for what happened to me that day, any more than my father was. I believe she was doing her best to save us all from isolation sickness, and to save our species from extinction. No matter what decision she made that day, I believe it would have ended the same way. Maybe not for me, but for some other person. That male knew what he was doing. I have no doubt that he has raped before, and that he would do so again if given the chance, whether at the Agency, or in private once released. Now though, at least he can never harm another again. The punishment suggested by the Council doesn't just punish my mother for the crimes you believe she committed, but also her children and grandchildren, who had nothing to do with what happened to me. I would never harm my sister Marsee, or take her choice to have children away from her, even if I thought my mother had been responsible. The very idea is just as appalling to me as forcing someone to mate and have children. I only just met my mother's other children and grandchildren a few days ago, and they are all kind and wonderful people. My mother's youngest granddaughter is only two, and she gave up her favorite stuffed animal for me. That was the only thing that kept me alive and going for a very long time. You all laughed at her antics as she chased the laser pointer around, and I honestly find it hard to believe that you feel that *she* should be punished for my mother's crimes. And as such, I choose to suggest my own punishment. This Council found my mother guilty of colluding with my rape because she took my *choice* of mate away. Did I understand that correctly?" Little Flower asked, barely able to keep the rage she felt in control.

"That is essentially correct," Councilor Tabor replied, just a hint of wariness in her voice.

"Then rather than taking that same choice away from her, and her children and grandchildren, I believe that she needs to give me, to give all of us, our choice back. I cannot change what happened to me or who I was forced to mate with before, but she can help me find the partner I want to spend the rest of my life with. I could never step foot in the Agency again, much less live there, and I would never be able to find a partner or even a future mate if they are all there and I am living somewhere else. The oath you asked me to make just a few minutes ago, asked if I promised to provide food, shelter, and protection to our neighbors in need. What my people need more than anything right now is a home, and the Agency could never ever be that, no matter how much it was fixed up. There are too many negative memories there for my people. It will take years to get over the trauma of what happened to us, intentional or otherwise. I ask that the Council require Myra Chenzira to open her home to us, to all of us, to care for us as long as we need a home, or to help us find new ones, to help grow our food, to teach us so we can become valuable members of this new society, and to help me raise my cub until I find that partner and no longer need her help. Their compound is big enough for all of my people with room to spare, and there is so much food that she gives it away to the neighbors. Myra, Jer, and Marsee have provided me with a home, with love and kindness, and have given me my life and hope for a future back. I want that for my people too. If, however, you do not find this acceptable then I beg the Council that you at least reduce the punishment and do not harm her children or grandchildren and take their own ability to have children away. That is neither equal, fair or just, as she has not harmed my child, as was done in that long ago case."

Tabor paused to consider her request and Little Flower took a brief glance at her father while she waited. His body was full of tension and his eyes were looking up at the ceiling, as if he were praying. She added her own prayers to whatever gods were watching.

"It is my understanding that Healer Chenzira currently shares her home with her partner, Senior Councilor Chenzira and their daughter Translator Marsee Chenzira. As such, this request would exceed both the duration and scope of affected individuals, and in good conscience we could not agree with that request..."

"I accept!" Marsee yelled, spinning to face the Senior Council. "I Marsee Bet Chenzira willingly and openly welcome all of Little Flower's people into my home, to share my home for as long as they need it."

"As do I!" Jer said, standing up.

Councilor Tabor looked back at the other Senior Councilors, and like before, as far as Little Flower could tell, they gave no indication of their approval or disapproval, leaving the decision entirely up to her. Tabor twitched a whisker and turned back to face the room.

"Then, it is this Council's final decision that the home of Myra Chenzira is to be converted into a home for Little Flower's people, for as long as they should choose to live there, and that she shall care for them to the best of her ability for as long as she lives. That she shall help them to find homes of their own if they choose not to stay there, and that she shall care for Little Flower's cub for as long as Little Flower requests assistance. This Council also dictates that all of the resources that were to be directed to the Agency for this purpose, be redirected to the home of Myra Chenzira to aid in that effort. This decision is final, and no further repercussions or demotions can be taken by the Healers Guild on this matter. This Council is now adjourned."

Tabor turned and stormed out of the room before the booming voice had even begun to tell them to rise, her tail shivering in barely controlled emotion behind her. She made it to the exit before the Council could even come to their feet and slammed the switch to the door with her paw. The entire Council watched as she disappeared through, her tail now lashing, moments before the door swished shut behind it.

Little Flower turned her attention back to the rest of the Senior Council, who had stood and watched Tabor storm out, almost as if they had forgotten they were supposed to leave too. Their expressions were the same blank mask they'd been before and she wondered just what they were thinking. Only her father's face showed any emotion, and his was one she knew matched hers, absolute relief.

Regaining their composure, they started to make their way out. Suddenly, her father stopped and turned to look back with a look of concern on his face, which quickly turned to fear and he started running back into the room. She turned and looked in the same direction he was running and gasped.

"Mama," she whispered, fear rising in her throat, as she watched the guards as they lowered her mother's limp body to the ground.

# CHAPTER 35

# Little Flower: Aftermath

"Mama!" Little Flower yelled as she bolted across the council floor, where her mother now lay unmoving. Healer Morningstar, who had been sitting next to her, was now kneeling on the floor next to her. She and her father arrived at the same time, but the guards blocked their access to allow the Council's healers to pass. She ducked under his outstretched tail before he could stop her, but suddenly, she found herself being physically picked up and restrained.

"Let me go!" she signed, "Mother!"

Brice said something to her mother and to Little Flower's relief, began to help her mother sit up.

"Mother! Are you okay?" she signed, when she finally got her mother's attention.

"Oh child, my love, I am better than okay. The Ancient Gods have heard my prayers," her mother signed and then said something to the guard, who immediately set her back down and let her go. She raced to her mother's side who crushed her in a hug. "Thank you for finding a way to save my children from being punished for my crimes. Nothing would bring me greater joy than to spend the rest of my life helping you and your people make a new home for themselves, and I will do everything in my power to make that happen," her mother signed, when Jessica pulled back to talk, and then crushed her in another hug.

The next thing she knew, her father and Marsee were there, joining in as well. The people around them backed off as the guard now provided them with a barrier to give them a semblance of privacy, now that they knew her mother was unhurt.

When they finally picked themselves up from the huddle on the Council floor, Little Flower turned to find herself face to face with her grandfather, and he looked at her as if he didn't even recognize her. Was he mad at her for choosing Myra and Jer to be her parents and not him, or any of the other decisions she made today?

"GrandFather, I..."

"I'm so very proud of you," GrandFather signed. "I have always been proud of you, but these past few days you've shown wisdom and compassion far beyond your years, and in doing so secured a promising future for all of us. If this is what you can accomplish on your first day as an adult, I cannot wait to see what tomorrow brings. You are the most amazing, wonderful, intelligent...and stubborn person I've ever had the privilege of knowing. Don't you dare ever change. Happy Name Day Little Flower Chenzira, may all your Name Days be just as happy!"

With a half laugh, half sob, Little Flower crushed him in a hug. "Thank you, GrandFather," she whispered.

After that, the next several hours were spent meeting the various councilors who came to welcome her and her people and offer their assistance. Eventually Jer managed to sneak her and GrandFather out of the council chamber and back up to their suite where Marcus, Ellie, Ammond, and her new mother and grandparents were waiting for them, already having escaped the madness hours earlier. To Marsee's evident relief, they'd managed to avoid the press, but only just barely.

Marsee walked in and flopped face down on the nearest available pillow with a groan. But she ran straight for the waste room to empty her screaming bladder, the excuse they had used to finally break free of the crowd, and avoid the press reporters that had been circling like sharks, just waiting for their turn to attack. When she returned, food, drink, and a large tub of nano cream were waiting for her and her swollen and aching feet. Myra fretted over her and once treated, pulled her onto her lap while she ate. Her feet were sore enough, even with the nano cream, that she didn't complain, and leaned back into her mother's purring side, content to be held.

After grabbing his own meal, her new father sat down on the couch between his own parents, who both leaned in and hugged him.

"Senior Councilor huh? Never thought *that* would happen today," Frederick said, just as her father was taking a sip of his drink.

Her father snorted, barely able to keep from spitting out his drink in laughter, and covered his mouth as his tail spiraled. At Little Flower's question asking what was so funny, Marsee sat up and began translating for her as her grandparents weren't as fluent in sign yet, although they were learning quickly.

"Papa, I thought I was going to die today. Little Flower, you were simply amazing. I've never seen anything like it. In all my years on the Council, not once have I ever seen a Senior Council verdict be overturned," her father signed. "You would have made an incredible Senior Councilor, and thank you for all of your kind words in my defense and Myra's, and for saving our children and grandchildren. I promise I will do everything in my power to make you proud and give you the wonderful life you deserve."

"You already have," Little Flower stated. "If you hadn't I wouldn't have elected you."

Her father snorted. "I don't know how I managed that, but thank you. I'm not even sure if this means my criminal record has officially been overturned or not."

"You can't be a councilor or senior councilor with a criminal record, regardless of that little loophole in the Seniors sentencing that Little Flower found, or the giant hole she dug and pushed Tabor into," Marcus stated with a snort, and followed it up by reciting article and section of the Consortium's Charter. "By allowing you to be promoted, they had to overturn your conviction. I expect that the other Seniors will announce something of the sort once they've had a chance to recover from the bombshell that Little Flower dropped on them. She's publicly accused Tabor and pretty much the entire Full Council of committing a crime for holding her people in isolation, one that she felt caused her more harm than the rape. It'll be interesting to see if they decide to hold another trial, or if they consider the resources being redirected to the compound, and your promotion compensation enough for that crime. I expect that will all depend on the public outcry. Tabor may very well be convicted later though. Have they said anything to you?"

"No. I haven't spoken to them since they left the chamber and I haven't left Little Flower's side since." Her father checked his tablet. "My privileges have been upgraded but I'm not seeing any messages from them."

"Then they're probably still licking their wounds," Marcus replied. "They clearly underestimated the intelligence and ferocity of your daughter."

"I warned Mama she didn't want to get on Little Flower's bad side when she was angry. I guess I should have warned the Seniors that our Little Flower has thorns too," Marsee signed, looking anything but apologetic.

When the laughter died down some, Ellie changed the topic. "So Myra, I'm guessing you're going to need a shipment of pillows for all your new house guests."

Myra snorted. "And a bigger house. I know the Hue-mans are small, but there's no way we can comfortably house everyone and give them the privacy they deserve in my old home. Tabor mentioned resources being provided. What do we have to work with?"

They spent the next several hours discussing plans for retrofitting the compound and what she wanted for her people, until there was a loud knock on the door. Her father stood and answered it. Someone she didn't know was standing there, but the room suddenly got very still and tense as the person spoke, and they all turned to look at her.

"What is it?" she signed as Marsee had not translated.

"The Senior Honor Guard is here to fetch your mother. The condemned is ready for his punishment," her father signed.

She nodded, made eye contact with her mother for a moment, and then walked into her bedroom, shutting the door behind her, without signing another word. Climbing into the massive chair by the window that overlooked the city, she sat and just stared out, watching her strange new world and the people below, who were oblivious to the fact that someone's life was now violently ending, at her command, and tried not to think about anything. An hour or so later her mother returned and sat down beside her. Nothing was signed between them, and yet everything was said that needed to be said.

They sat there together for a long time until Little Flower let out a heavy sigh, and turned to her mother. "It's done then?"

"I keep my promises. He will never be able to hurt you or anyone else ever again," her mother signed back.

"Good. Then I can close that chapter of my life and begin a new one. I would like to see more of this world that is to be my new home. Shall we go explore the city, Mother?" Little Flower asked.

"Nothing would make me happier, my beautiful, wonderful, amazing daughter," her mother replied with a grin and picked her up, crushing her in another hug.

Little Flower sighed as she snuggled into her mother's soft fur. She would always miss her family and grieve their loss, but for the first time in years she now looked forward to the future that awaited her, confident in her own abilities, and wrapped securely in the love of her new mother's arms.

LAURA NAPOLI

Laura Napoli was born and raised in northern Vermont and continues to make the area her home. When not spending her time on the warm clicky box (computer), she is the caregiver to four heating cats who provide her with heat, massage, acu-paw-ture, and purr-therapy in exchange for pets and catnip treaties. For more information, visit https://www.heatingcats.com

*Publications*

Book 1: The Tails of Little Flower

Book 2: The Pride of Little Flower

*Coming Soon*

Book 3: The Whiskers of Hope

Book 4: The Paws of Hope

HUMANS

- Alice O'Neil - Jessica's Mother *
- David O'Neil - Jessica's Father *
- Ben O'Neil - Jessica's Grandfather *
- Ms. Walters - Jessica's Spanish Teacher *
- Susie - Jessica's Best Friend *
- Joey - Jessica's Classmate *
- Mark - Jessica's Classmate *

BIPEDS

- Ambassador Jessica O'Neil (1A1)
- James O'Neil (3A41)
- Mitch (3A236)
- Nazari's Cub (2A84)
- Mother 1 (4A35)
- Mother 2 (1A102)

COUNCIL

- Senior Councilor Jennette Tabor: Saber
- Senior Councilor Clear Seas: Water World
- Senior Councilor Wind Rider: Flyer
- Senior Councilor Apakna: Ice World
- Senior Councilor Sammianna: Digger

- Councilor Marcus Surellis: South Plains District
- Councilor Jeran Frederick Chenzira: South District
  - *Mentor: Marcus Surellis*
- Councilor Paxton Parner: Jandolf Square District
- Councilor Ned Griffith: North Plains District
- Councilor Rip Current: Water World

## GUILD

- Senior Guild Master Elliana Reighly Khihar
- Guild Master Nardal
- Master Musician Thomas Chenzira
- Journeyman Marsee Bet Chenzira

## HEALERS GUILD

- Senior Guild Healer Nerissa Witherspoon
- Senior Healer Myra Bet Chenzira
  - *Mentor: Ammond Greyfoot*
  - *Mentor: Nazir Jabri*
- Master Healer Ammond Greyfoot
- Master Healer Kelly Goodwind
  - *Mentor Myra Chenzira*
- Master Animal Healer Nazari Jabri
- Journeyman Brice Morningstar
  - *Mentor Myra Chenzira*

## SHIPS GUILD

- Commander Oscar Rynhold
- Commander Nichola Sampson
- Ship Master Petra

## HONOR GUARD

- Senior Honor Guard Kendra Hunt
- Senior Guard Quinn Bluestone
- Honor Guard Avery Hunt

## OTHERS

- Theresa Greyfoot
- Maggie Chenzira

* Deceased

Note: All ranks and guild affiliations listed are those at the time they were first introduced in this book.

www.ingramcontent.com/pod-product-compliance
Lightning Source LLC
Chambersburg PA
CBHW062117290726
48975CB00001B/252